The Wild Swans

The Wild Swans

Peg Kerr

ASPECT®

WARNER BOOKS

A Time Warner Company

Grateful acknowledgment is given for permission to reprint from the following:
"The Swan" Copyright © 1950 by Ogden Nash. Reprinted by permission of Curtis Brown Ltd.

Aspect® name and logo are registered trademarks of Warner Books, Inc.

Warner Books, Inc., 1271 Avenue of the Americas, New York, NY 10020
Visit our Web site at www.warnerbooks.com

 A Time Warner Company

Printed in the United States of America
First Printing: May 1999
10 9 8 7 6 5 4 3 2 1

Library of Congress Cataloging-in-Publication Data

Kerr, Peg.
    The wild swans / Peg Kerr.
        p.   cm.
    ISBN 0-446-67366-8
    I. Title.
    PS3561.E645W55   1999
    813'.54—dc21   98-48530
                                                                        CIP

Book design by Giorgetta Bell McRee
Cover design by Don Puckey
Cover illustration by John Jude Palencar
Hand lettering by Ron Zinn

For Kij Johnson,
who teaches me grace

Prologue

Elias lay huddled in a ball under a dirty pink blanket in a corner of an abandoned warehouse, dreaming of swans.

In his dream, he flew swiftly through the early morning chill, the earth shrouded in curling mists beneath him. Other swans flew on either side of him, their necks stretched out full length, feathers fluttering at the tips as their wings pumped rhythmically, their feet tucked up neatly underneath. The rush of air made their pinions vibrate with a peculiar, throbbing hum. As the rising sun slowly turned the pale, pearly gray light to a warm yellow, the swan flying directly to his right caught and held his eye with an inscrutable, silent stare. Then, it banked, beginning a lazy spiral toward the earth below. The rest followed it, arrowing down to circle the roof of a lone cottage sticking up through the mist.

Elias wheeled to match their course, joining up with the flock again just as the cottage door opened and a figure darted out.

Elias shifted and muttered in his sleep. In the darkness of the warehouse, something knocked over a pile of cans with a metallic clatter and scuttled off into the darkness. A rat.

"Hey, Elias. You awake?"

Elias groggily raised his head, and as he blinked up at the dark silhouette stooping over him, the last swirling tendrils of the dream vanished. It took him a moment to identify the voice. "Gil?"

"Uh-huh."

"Time's it?"

"Little before midnight. I think."

"Mmm. Where's Andre and Tom?"

"Andre's out hustling with Luke. Don't know where Tom went." Striking a match, Gil stopped to light the end of a candle stuck in a tuna can beside Elias's head. Elias struggled up to a sitting position on his pallet of torn blankets and Gil sat down beside him. Rain spattered against the grimy, cracked window above their heads. "You got a fag?" Gil asked.

"No," Elias said. "I wish you wouldn't call them that," he added mildly as Gil rooted through Andre's small pile of possessions, pushing the dirty clothes and a syringe aside until he found a pack with four battered cigarettes in it. Gil tapped one out and leaned toward the candle to light it. Elias wondered how often Gil rifled through his things while he was away.

"Can't help it, guv," Gil said, taking a deep drag and smiling broadly. He was a wiry kid of seventeen, a year younger than Elias, dressed in black jeans with a belt buckle that read "Boy Toy" in rhinestones, a T-shirt ripped at the shoulder, and a black beret. "My dad got stationed overseas a lot. I was in England when I started smoking. Every bloke over there called 'em that." He raised an eyebrow and proffered the cigarette to Elias. His hand had a fine tremor.

Elias shook his head. "No, thanks." Something about Gil's words had snagged a memory of the dream. He saw again in his mind the thatched roof of the cottage, glimpses through the fog of sheep browsing in the nearby meadow, the low stone fences—"England," he murmured to himself.

"What?"

Elias shook his head. "Oh, just a dream I had." One last flash of memory welled up before the dream faded entirely: the swans were watching over someone, protecting him—or was it a her? As he looked around himself into the darkness of the warehouse, outside the trembling circle of light thrown by the candle, the feeling of comfort, of safety, ebbed away like dirty snow heaped up against a hot air grate. He shivered. He felt cold and hungry and, though he didn't like to admit it, even to himself, desperately scared. *There aren't any guardian angels here.*

"I gotta get some money," he said.

Gil tapped his cigarette ash into the tuna can. "You went to the plasma center, didn't you?"

"Yeah, but I didn't get much."

Gil nodded. "That's why I don't go no more. It doesn't help to be skinny when they pay by the pound."

"And they won't let me sell any more till Tuesday."

"You don't want to try sneaking into another center?"

Elias shook his head. "No, I think they're right. I'm about bled out for now."

"There's always Dumpster diving. Find something to pawn. Collecting cans."

"Uh-huh." He had been trying to do that the last day and a half, but other scroungers had picked over most of the Dumpsters he'd visited. He hadn't eaten since yesterday morning.

"You could grab an old lady's purse."

"No," Elias said firmly.

"It's easy."

"That's not the point. I'm not going to do it." He closed his eyes, trying desperately to find comfort in the fact that he'd rejected the idea so quickly, so automatically. Surely that meant he still had some standards left . . . didn't it?

But look how far he'd already fallen in just a couple of weeks. How long would it take before he'd be willing to seriously consider bashing in some old lady's face? Even with his eyes still closed, Elias could feel Gil's cool, steady gaze, and he imagined he knew exactly what it meant: *Don't think it'll be long before you change your mind.*

When he opened his eyes again, Gil was studying the glowing tip of his cigarette. "Or maybe . . . you could go out with Luke or me."

Elias opened his mouth and shut it again. Part of him wanted to answer, *Yeah, I suppose I could,* while another part screamed, *Jesus, no way. Not ever.* He felt cold dread gathering in the pit of his stomach. Maybe, he told himself grimly, this was what hitting bottom meant: trying to figure out which of two previously unimaginable alternatives was the least ugly. "What's it like?" he asked softly after a moment.

"Oh, it depends. Sometimes you just get fat guys from the burbs who want you to listen as they cry in their beer about how their wives just don't understand them."

"Really."

"Yeah. Don't count on it, though." He took another drag. "Most of the time you gotta earn it." He stubbed the cigarette out as Elias digested this. "It's an option. Let me know if you want to try. You've got other options, you know." He got up and stepped back toward his corner. Back into the darkness.

Elias looked down at his hands. His fingernails were bitten down to the quick. When had he done that? He couldn't even remember. He was losing all track of time. He leaned over and blew the candle out and settled himself again for sleep.

Other options—right. The only other option that would get me out of this is going home.

Only I don't have a home anymore.

Chapter One

Although I am a Country Lasse,
a lofty mind I beare a,
I think myself as good as those
That gay aparell weare a,
My coate is made of comely Gray,
Yet is my skin as soft a,
As those that with the chiefest Wines
do bathe their bodies oft a.

—17TH CENTURY BALLAD

On a certain clear May morning in 1689, in the first year of the reign of King William III and Queen Mary II, Eliza walked barefoot along a country lane in Somerset, carrying a basket heaped with freshly dug roots of the little flower the French call *dent-de-lion*. The basket weighed heavily on her arm, and she shifted it from one side to the other as she picked her way around patches of mud and puddles left from the previous night's rain. All around her, the newly baptized morning gleamed. Water droplets, transformed by sunlight into iridescent pearls, clung to the slender stems of violets and cowslips lining the pathway. In the fields ewes

called to their lambs, and the sound mingled with the shrill squab-
bles of sparrows in the hedgerows. The air, sweet with the scent of
wet meadow grasses, barely rippled the surface of the water pooling in the lane. Eliza sometimes lifted her gaze from the images of
birds flying in a cerulean sky reflected beneath her feet, to watch
the real birds passing overhead.

She was tall for a girl of fifteen and slender as a young linden
tree. Her reddish blond hair hung halfway to her waist, tightened
by the spring dampness into a mist of undisciplined tendrils. They
lifted from her shoulders with a feathery lightness as her steps
quickened to climb the hill. At the top, she turned down a track
passing through a gap in a stone fence, leading away from the lane.
She shifted her basket again as she rounded a copse of budding
apple trees—and then stopped dead in her tracks in surprise at her
first clear sight of the cottage beyond.

A carriage stood, incongruously, in the clearing in front of the
kitchen garden. Chickens warily stalked around its wheels, suspicious of this strange addition to their territory. Besides the four
horses hitched to the carriage itself, a saddle horse tied to one side
stood browsing through the garden's herb border; it raised its head,
ears pricked forward, and snorted at her.

Cautiously, Eliza took a few steps forward and opened her
mouth to call. The words died upon her lips, however, as her eyes
suddenly fell upon the coat of arms emblazoned on the carriage's
door. The blood drained from her cheeks at the shock, and she
dropped her basket, scattering dandelion roots in the grass underfoot. Her hands flew to the neck of her dress, and she drew forth a
narrow black ribbon tied around her throat. A small gold locket
strung on the ribbon fell into her muddy palm, glinting in the sun.

She did not need to look at it to know: the coat of arms on the
locket was the same, and that realization brought with it a heady
mixture of astonishment, excitement, and fear. She stood a moment cupping the locket in her hand, until she had composed herself again, and finally let out a long, tremulous breath. "Well, then."

Her fingers closed tightly over the trinket, and then she tucked it back into her dress.

Kneeling, she methodically gathered the roots back into the basket, her face serious and set. At the well, she drew up a dripping bucket of water and washed her hands carefully. Scrubbing away the last traces of the mud from her morning's work helped calm her nerves. Then she picked up the basket again and went to the door of the cottage. Steeling herself, she firmly lifted the latch and went inside.

Long ago, the cottage had been divided into two main rooms, with two fireplaces, one in each room, joined by a central chimney. The room she entered, the parlor, faced the front, and the other room, called the hall, where the cooking was done, overlooked the garden in the back. The open parlor shutters let in angled patches of sunlight that brightened the whitewashed plaster walls. Spring air wafted in with her through the doorway, mingling with the smell of fresh-baked bread from the hall and muting the faint undertang of damp wool, wood smoke, and lavender. A man and a woman, seated on three-legged stools squeezed between the loom and the bed, rose hastily at Eliza's entrance. A somewhat older man leaning against the wall drew in a sharp breath at the sight of her and straightened up more slowly. The four stood frozen in a tableau for a breathless space, and then Eliza stepped away from the threshold and closed the door. "Do you seek me?" she said politely, setting her basket down.

"My dearest Lady Eliza," the woman said impressively, stepping forward. She had a stout figure, laced so tightly into her fine dress of blue sarcenet that her color looked alarmingly high, despite a generous dusting of powder. With the *prétintailles appliqués* trimming her gown, the profusion of curls dressed with a scarf of striped Siamese stuff, à la Sultana, and the beauty spot patches applied to her forehead and cheeks, she looked the very figure of current French fashion; a more fantastic figure in an English country cottage could scarcely be imagined. She smiled with benevolent brilliance and took Eliza's hands. "My name is Mrs. Warren, and I serve as a companion to Lady James Grey, Countess of Exeter. These are my escorts, Robert Owen," she gestured toward the older man who had been leaning against the wall when Eliza came in, "and Edward Conway. We have been sent by your mother to bring you home."

"My mother is dead." Eliza gently withdrew her hands from the other's grasp. "This is my foster mother's home. Do you mean my father's wife?"

Mrs. Warren's smile slipped a little. She took a deep breath—or as deep as her stays would allow—and tried again. "Indeed, she is your father's wife, but that is hardly the term to use. In law, she is your mother."

She spoke evenly enough, but Eliza flushed at the suggestion of coldness that had crept into her voice. Painfully conscious that she had made a mistake, she stammered, "Forgive me, madam—I beg your pardon. I truly meant no offense."

"None is taken, my lady," replied Mrs. Warren, thawing once more.

"And," Eliza said, her heart beating quickly with shy eagerness, "my father wishes to see me, as well as my mother-in-law?"

"Aye," said another voice tightly at the doorway leading to the hall. It was Nell Barton, Eliza's foster mother, wiping red-rimmed eyes with an apron as she came into the room. "He finally calls thee to his side—like a poacher who starves and beats a faithful dog, yet still expects it to whistle to heel at his pleasure."

Mrs. Warren shot her a venomous look. "How durst you speak so of the Earl?"

"Prithee, how durst he use his own daughter so? Left her with me for ten years, for ten years an' it please you! With nary a visit, nary a letter to the poor girl!" Nell's gaze met Eliza's, lips trembling as her tears spilled over again. She turned scarlet, sensing she was making herself ridiculous, but despite Eliza's pleading eyes, the words kept tumbling out. "Well, I did my best, but how could I teach an earl's daughter to be a fine lady? An excellent, proper father, leaving her with the likes of me!"

Mrs. Warren opened her mouth to object, but Nell hurried on, "And yet never a moment's trouble did she give me, for she's as good-hearted, as fine a lass as . . . as . . ." Nell burst into sobs in earnest, throwing her apron over her face. "Little he knew or cared! But now, 'tis *enough with poor Nell Barton,* and *'tis time for the girl to come home.* Home! And where does the Earl think his daughter has been these last ten years?"

She sank onto a stool, overcome and acutely humiliated at having become unwoven before these fine people. And then she heard a footstep beside her, and a familiar voice saying softly into her ear, "Hush, Mother Nell . . . " and she leaned gratefully against Eliza's waist as the girl wound her arms comfortingly around her shoulders.

"Have you done yet?" said Mrs. Warren coldly.

"Mrs. Barton," Robert Owen interposed, directing a quelling glance at Mrs. Warren, " 'tis true, our coming here must be a shock. We are sorry you did not receive warning of our arrival. Belike you and the child would wish a quarter hour together alone before we go?"

"A quarter hour?" Eliza said in bewilderment. "Am I to leave so soon, then?" No one answered her. Mrs. Warren avoided her eyes, contenting herself instead with glaring at Nell. The young man, Edward Conway, looked at the floor. Robert Owen alone met her gaze, his expression softened by pity.

Numbly, Eliza looked about the small, crowded room. The familiar objects all around her stood out in a strange, sharp relief, as though to engrave themselves on her memory for one last private instant before vanishing forever. There was the loom her foster father, Tom Barton, had used, still set up with a length of half-woven perpetuana, untouched since Tom had left three years before. In the sudden silence, Eliza fancied she could almost hear the thump and clatter of the wooden shuttle, and Tom's merry whistle. There was the bed with the counterpane Nell had embroidered before her wedding, and there, Eliza's own first sampler, mounted upon the wall. Out the window she could see a delicate mist of new lettuce and herbs unfurling in the garden, and the first tendrils of beans just beginning to wind up the poles. She had spent countless mornings working there, hoeing and weeding, savoring the feeling of the damp earth crumbling between her toes. They had planted a cherry tree that spring; she would never taste its fruit now.

With an effort, she spoke. "I . . . I must fetch my tippet. And my other clothes—"

"You needn't trouble to pack much, my lady," said Mrs. Warren. "We will see to't you are more . . . suitably garbed ere you meet his lordship."

Nell stiffened, and Eliza saw and understood her indignation. She felt an answering flicker of fury begin to rise. "I needs must be alone with Nell to say my farewell," she said coldly. "And I will meet my father wearing my own clothes. He provided them, did he not? Surely he thought them suitable."

Robert Owen's eyes crinkled in amusement, and then his face became carefully bland again. He gave her a half bow. "We will leave you for a space, my lady. Mrs. Warren, Edward, would it please you to walk with me in the orchard?"

He shepherded them from their seats, soothing Mrs. Warren's gobbled protests and throwing an enigmatic look over his shoulder at Eliza as he led them out.

"I didn't know where thou had gone," Nell said. "When they came . . . and said thou must leave . . ." She pressed a hand to her mouth.

"I am very sorry. I . . . went for a walk." She had been out in the yard shortly after dawn, feeding the chickens, when a flock of wild swans had flown overhead through the dwindling morning mist, wheeling over the yard twice before flying away to the west. The sight had taken her breath away, and without understanding the impulse, she had left her chores to follow the path of the birds, until they had faded to distant specks in the brightening sky. She had felt a pang of guilt when she turned for home. Nell fretted whenever she roamed very far in neighboring fields and woods, worrying that without one of her friends from the village to accompany her, Eliza might be molested by a passing stranger. Neighbors might spread rumors, too, if they misconstrued herb-gathering expeditions as dabblings in witchcraft. "I . . . I found a goodly harvest of lion's tooth root on my way home, at least," Eliza continued at random, wanting to fill the sudden silence. "It should be enough to dye thy new petticoat."

But Nell's mind was not on Eliza's rambles now. "He did not provide the clothes, Eliza," she said dully.

"What, Mother Nell?"

"Thy father. Tom and I meant never to tell thee. Faith, I thought . . . But now thou must know, if thou art to return to them!"

"Know what?" Eliza asked, her brow wrinkling in confusion as she knelt at Nell's feet.

Her foster mother took her hand. "Thy father," she said slowly, "has not sent us aught for thy maintenance since two years after thou came to us—since thy seventh year."

Eliza gasped. "For . . . for eight years? *Eight years?*" Letting go of Nell's hand, she rocked back and gaped in consternation at the older woman.

Mutely, Nell nodded.

"But I . . . I am a fosterling!" Eliza stammered. " 'Twas his responsibility . . . he . . . Surely he—"

"Nay, child. Not one farthing."

Eight years! Eliza realized, quailing at the thought, what a terrible struggle it must have been when the money stopped coming. And yet her foster parents had continued caring for her, feeding her, clothing her, never even hinting the slightest thing was wrong.

Tom Barton had joined the Duke of Monmouth's rebellion against King James II four years before, only to see the hopes of reestablishing a Protestant upon the throne die in the bloody quagmire at Sedgemoor. They had waited many anxious days during the Bloody Assizes, fearing he would be executed, but instead, along with many others, he had been banished to the West Indies. Eliza had supposed the money her father sent was what had been supporting Nell since, and had comforted herself with that thought. But if he had truly sent nothing . . . if Nell, bereft of her husband and left with so pitifully little, had continued to faithfully provide for her . . . "Then it is to thy charity I have been beholden all these years?" she exclaimed.

All her anger and pain was for Nell, not herself, but Nell, misunderstanding, seized her hand again, saying fiercely, "Nay, child, do not speak so! Do not think 'twas cold charity only, but—"

"I don't understand, Mother," Eliza interrupted. "Why didst thou and Tom not write to my father and demand what was due thee?"

"Because we came to love thee, child," Nell said, tears trickling down her cheeks. The wet tracks glistened, reflecting light from the window as she bowed her head. "I have borne six wee babes, and God took them all from Tom and me. Would the Earl have taken thee from us, too, if we dared complain?" Her voice broke. "I could not have borne it, Eliza. I vow I could not."

"Oh, Mother—" Eliza leaned forward to press her hand to Nell's cheek.

"Hist, child, we have precious little time." She laid her fingers over Eliza's lips and sighed. "I remember when the Earl first sent thee to us, thou wert grieving so for thy mama. It made my heart ache to see thy hurt; thou would cry thyself to sleep every night, but so quietly! Dost thou remember?"

Yes, Eliza remembered, or at least partly. Her mother had died when Eliza was only four, and the image of her face was elusive, surfacing occasionally in dreams, like a leaf skittering over the face of a stream only to sink again. Eliza could conjure up bits and pieces: a dim echo of a voice singing in the garden, an impression of graceful movement as a hand reached to snip an embroidery thread, the curve of a smile directed at her father—but not a whole picture.

And yet if the memory of what she had lost had faded, somehow the pain of losing it had not. It had taken many months for Tom's warmth and Nell's patient kindness to melt her wall of reserve.

Nell pushed back a tendril of Eliza's hair. "Think now, and tell

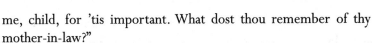
me, child, for 'tis important. What dost thou remember of thy mother-in-law?"

Eliza sighed. "We children met her for the first time the day she married Father. He introduced us and said she would be our new mama. We wished to please her, to make Father happy, but . . ." Her words trailed off, and she shivered, seeing again the strange lady at their father's side, with two chilly fingers extended for each to grasp in turn. The boys had all seemed so stiff and awkward and solemn as they made their bows. As Eliza bobbed to her shyly, the new Countess lifted an eyebrow and murmured in a low voice, "Prithee, is that your best curtsey?" before turning away.

"I cannot help but pity the lady, I think," observed Nell dryly, "marrying a man with twelve children."

Eliza shook her head. "I do not think she liked us, from the very beginning."

"Dost thou think so? Perhaps she was shy?"

"Perhaps. And yet . . ."

"Well?"

"My brothers and I were not permitted to attend the marriage feast. She gave us cups filled with sand and told us we must pretend instead."

"How strange!"

" 'Twas not a month later I was sent here. I sometimes thought, if I could have but stayed with my brothers . . ." Her words trailed off. "But then I would not have met thee."

Nell patted her hand. "We had best begin packing thy things." Stiffly, she got up and went to fetch clothes from the press in the corner.

Eliza went to get her cloak, hanging on a peg by the door. "Mother Nell," she said hesitantly, "why have I never heard from my father and brothers?"

Nell studied her face with a troubled expression. She knew that Eliza had wondered at her family's silence, just as she had, and grieved at it, too. Eventually, Eliza had come to accept her new home, and even thrive in it, for although naturally quiet, she had an open and affectionate heart. Yet Nell had long suspected that the roots had not gone down quite as deep as they might have. Eliza had many friends in the village, but she had always gently discouraged any warmer admiration from various local lads. For years a strange reticence had kept them from ever speaking of it aloud—until now.

There had been rumors, strange dark tales told of the Countess of Exeter, even whisperings that hinted at sorcery. Nell had shielded her foster daughter from the stories and taken care not to repeat them, and she was not eager to fill her ear with them now. And yet, she wondered: if the girl was to return to Kellbrooke Hall, should she not be given warning? "About thy father, I don't know; thou wilt have to ask him. As to thy brothers—I'm not sure, but I believe they may no longer be at Kellbrooke Hall."

"Truly?" Eliza looked thoughtful, and then brightened. "Perhaps they have been fostered out, too? Or they have been at school? And if Father is calling me home, perhaps he is calling us all home?"

"Perhaps," said Nell cautiously, smoothing wrinkles out of a kersey petticoat. Privately, she thought it a very strange thing for Lord Grey to send every one of his children from home, if that was indeed what he had done. "With the new Protestant king and queen, thy father's standing at Court has undoubtedly changed."

"That is why he sends for me now?"

"Aye," Nell said, adding reluctantly, "he may think it the best time to arrange some alliances to his advantage."

"What does thou mean?" Eliza's eyes widened. "Not . . . not marriage, surely?"

"I don't know, child." Nell felt an angry stab of pity as the girl paled. The sheer folly of it all seemed plain to Nell as never before. Surely, she thought, the Earl could not possibly expect a girl raised in a weaver's cottage to enter into a splendid marriage for political advantage. Eliza knew how to weave an ell of wool and hoe turnips, but that, Nell knew, was quite a different matter from knowing how to act as the mistress of a grand hall.

And it was her own fault, too, Nell realized with a sinking sense of shame. She had been so afraid of losing the girl that she had simply held her breath and let matters continue in the same way, trying not to think of the future. Now, too late, she berated herself bitterly for not having written to the Earl and brought him somehow to a sense of his own responsibility. If she had ruined Eliza's chances of reentering her rightful life by failing to do so, she would never forgive herself.

"Thou art a good girl," she said stoutly. "God knows thy father has no cause to feel aught but pride in thee." She hesitated. "Give thy mother-in-law thy respect, but watch her carefully before giving her thy trust. Make thy heart's faith in the good Lord thy anchor, and turn to Him in prayer whene'er thou art troubled."

"I will, Mother Nell. I promise. I only wish . . ." Eliza broke off, her lips trembling.

"What, child?" prompted Nell after a moment.

Eliza looked down at the cloak in her hands, and her fingers clenched tightly in the folds. When she spoke again, her voice sounded low and choked with tears. "I do not wish to go. I don't! How can I possibly leave?"

Nell took a deep breath and did her best to speak cheerfully around the lump in her own throat. "Now then, there is no need for such fond fears! Thou hast made dear friends here, true, but art thou not going home to thine own father and brothers?"

"I know," Eliza said, looking up with brimming eyes. "I know, and I do wish to see them. But my mother-in-law . . . And besides, how can I bear to leave thee all alone? Oh, Mother Nell," she added with a forlorn sob, "I shall miss thee so sorely."

Nell came over to the girl and hugged her fiercely, tears welling up in her eyes again, too. "I could not have loved thee more if thou had been my own flesh and blood. I know thou art returning to thine own people, but—if, perchance," she said humbly, "matters do not fall as they should—I will always have a place by my hearth for thee, if thou should ever need it."

There was pitifully little to pack. Scarcely a half an hour later, Robert Owen handed Eliza up into the carriage to sit across from

Mrs. Warren, and then climbed up onto the coach box. Eliza leaned out of the window to look back as Edward Conway clambered up on the saddle mount and the entourage circled around to leave the yard. Nell stood forlornly in the doorway, watching them go. She didn't wave, and neither did Eliza.

"That's done, then," Mrs. Warren said, in a tone of satisfaction. She settled back against the squabs with a sigh, as if dismissing from her mind a minor, unpleasant task, now successfully accomplished. Eliza, still caught up in her own numbed shock and grief, did not reply. Mrs. Warren eyed her surreptitiously and noted her remote stillness but mistook it for ladylike reserve. Lady Eliza had an air of quality, she reflected with cautious approval, even if the girl had been raised among simple folk. The possibility that Eliza might have qualms about going to Kellbrooke Hall or regrets about leaving her foster home simply did not occur to Mrs. Warren.

A rut made the carriage pitch violently as they turned onto the lane leading to Buckland St. Mary. "A pox upon these roads!" Mrs. Warren exclaimed, righting herself. " 'Tis a thousand pities the way to Taunton is washed out; 'tis more direct and has fewer stones. I should have liked to stay at the Harp and Ball tonight. They serve a very excellent ale." She sighed again, regretfully this time. "It must be the Black Boar, instead, at Ilminster."

"We shall not reach Kellbrooke Hall tonight, then?"

"Oh no, indeed, not until after supper tomorrow, I should think."

"Tomorrow," Eliza murmured. She pushed the window shutter open to a wider angle so she could look out over the fields. "Tomorrow I shall see my brothers again."

Mrs. Warren gave her a startled look. "Pardon, my lady?"

"My brothers. Or are they away at school?"

The silence stretched so long that Eliza turned to look at the other woman. "My lady," Mrs. Warren said finally in a perplexed voice, "I have served the Countess of Exeter for three years. I never till now heard that Lord Grey had any other children than your ladyship."

Now it was Eliza's turn to stare. "You have never *heard* of them?"

"Brothers, you say? More than one?"

"I have eleven brothers."

Mrs. Warren's eyes widened. "Eh, now! Eleven, my lady?"

Eliza nodded.

A silence fell, and stretched uncomfortably. "Eleven, you say," Mrs. Warren finally said helplessly. "Well, now. There must be an explanation, true enough. Eleven brothers—think of it! Bless me! Perhaps, as you say, they have been at school. Robert Owen might know," she added as an afterthought.

"Would he?"

"Aye, for he has served the Earl nigh on fourteen years."

"Why then, he was with the household when I first went to be fostered. I did not remember him." Eliza turned her head to look back as the carriage rounded a curve, her face troubled. "I will ask him. Tonight."

The carriage rattled on all afternoon, lurching. Mrs. Warren shuddered and moaned, fretting that they would break an axle and groping for her smelling salts, complaining of travel sickness. And then abruptly, she fell asleep, with her head tilted to one side and her mouth agape—except when the carriage would slam into another rut, and her teeth would snap shut with an audible clack. Otherwise, she remained quiet.

Eliza felt grateful for the silence. She spent the time absently gazing out the window at orchards and meadows, wondering uneasily about Mrs. Warren's odd ignorance concerning her brothers. The only explanation that made sense, that the Earl and Countess never spoke of any of his other children, seemed utterly unnatural to her.

She also brooded over her farewell to Nell. The irony of not learning until the very hour of parting how much she truly owed her foster parents did not escape her. She hugged to her heart the painfully bittersweet knowledge of the sacrifice they had made for her. It had been natural for her to mourn her own mother, and when the time for mourning had ended, it had been natural for her to learn to love Nell and Tom. But not until now did she truly understand how much they had loved her in return.

She would not forget, she vowed silently, and resolved to go back to Kellbrooke Hall willingly if only to make the Earl understand the debt of honor he owed to the people who had raised her so faithfully. Her thoughts faltered as she wondered secretly for a moment whether, in fact, her father *was* a man of honor—but surely he must be, she told herself hastily. Resolutely, she put all her doubts aside and instead concentrated on deciding how the Earl might best properly provide for Nell. Perhaps, she thought hopefully, he would pay to have someone from the village stay with Nell and help her, since she was alone. Or better still, he might arrange for a pardon for Tom, allowing him to come home now that a Protestant king and queen sat upon the throne.

Despite the comfort in these reflections, Eliza sighed to herself as the miles rolled by. "Ah, Mother Nell," she whispered, "why didn't you tell me?"

They drove into the courtyard of the Black Boar at dusk. Hostlers stepped from the shadows, seizing the lead horses' bridles as Edward Conway dismounted and Robert Owen climbed down stiffly from the coach box. Someone opened the carriage door, and Mrs. Warren darted out, muttering under her breath, "The beds will not even be aired, I doubt not. At least we may hope to sup decently. . . ."

Eliza, who had been dozing, climbed down more slowly and stood a few yards from the swarm of hostlers, blinking in the lantern light like an owl, too stupid with fatigue to follow the other woman inside immediately. Robert Owen finished giving his instructions about the horses to the head hostler and turned and saw her. The sight of her face gave him a jolt of painful surprise, just as it had when he first saw her that afternoon.

He knew Mrs. Warren to be a little privately disappointed in Eliza's looks. The Countess's companion had said as much that afternoon, as they had walked in the orchard while waiting for Eliza and Nell to finish their good-byes. The child had managed to keep her skin fair and unfreckled, Mrs. Warren conceded willingly enough, and her waist seemed narrow enough to suit the fashions. But she was overly tall, with a nose and chin too long and a mouth too wide and full lipped to suit Mrs. Warren's taste.

And yet, Robert Owen thought rather scornfully to himself, if Mrs. Warren had been somewhat more discerning she might have noted that while Lady Eliza's chin and nose were long and her mouth wide, the unusual length of her neck and high slope of her cheekbones balanced those features. The effect might be unconventional, but it was remarkably graceful. Or, perhaps, if Mrs. Warren, like Robert Owen, had faithfully served the first instead of the second Countess of Exeter, her eyes, like his, might have widened and then filled with sudden tears at the sight of Lady Eliza, so uncanny was the resemblance to her dead mother.

He flinched involuntarily as Eliza's clear, green eyes turned to meet his. She raised her eyebrows in inquiry as he walked over to her, and he gave her a wry half smile. "You remind me so of your mother, my lady," he said. " 'Tis truly wondrous, the resemblance."

Eliza smiled, and his heart skipped a beat. "Ah, of course, you knew her, then," she said.

"Yes, my lady," he said with a little bow. "A dear mistress she was to us all." He indicated the doorway with a gesture. "Hark you, now, will you not step inside? Mrs. Warren is no doubt bestirring every man and maid within for your comfort, and there's no need for you to stand out here in the muck."

"Do you remember my brothers, too?" she asked him as they crossed the threshold.

He stopped in his tracks as if he had just walked into a tree. "Your brothers, my lady?"

"Aye, Mr. Owen," she replied, annoyed and a little alarmed at his tone. "If you remember my mother, surely you know, even if Mrs. Warren does not, that she had eleven sons as well as a daughter."

He had grown strangely pale, even in the inn's dim lantern light. "My dear lady," he said in a strained voice, "will you be ruled by one who wishes you well with all his heart, and wants naught but to serve you?"

She stared at him, perplexed.

"Do not ask about your brothers, my lady, once you come to Kellbrooke Hall. Do not even mention them. If you do not wish to——" He checked himself and seemed to struggle internally for a moment. As Mrs. Warren bustled toward them with officious importance, he added in a hasty whisper, "Just mind you heed my warning, my lady. Please." He disappeared back out into the courtyard to take charge of the luggage, his face strained by a strange grief.

Eliza did not speak to him again that evening.

Chapter Two

It isn't easy being homeless in any city,
but my lord, New York is tough.

——HENRY CISNEROS,
FORMER SECRETARY OF HOUSING
AND URBAN DEVELOPMENT

The number one rule is, you don't ever get into a van."

Elias paused in the middle of threading his belt through the loops of his jeans and gave Gil a wary look. "No vans. Check. What else?"

Gil lounged on a pile of dirty sheets flung over a ripped sleeping bag, delicately paring an apple with a penknife. "If you come into a room, and find two guys waiting for you," he continued, tossing apple peels over his shoulder, "be real careful. If you find three waiting, and they're smiling, get the hell out of there as fast as you can. They'll probably want a heavier scene than you'd care to handle. Or else they don't want the scene at all. Just the queer bashing." He took a bite of the apple and gave Elias a critical once-over, his eyes narrowing. "Are you really sure you wanna wear that jacket?"

"What's wrong with it?" asked Elias, who had dug the jacket in question out from a Dumpster that very morning. "The rip under the arm doesn't show too much."

"It doesn't, but that's not the point. It's leather."

"Isn't that good?"

"Well, sure, just as long as you understand that some blokes might think you're trying to signal you're a top. Only I don't think you're exactly convincing as a top, if you know what I mean. You're kinda skinny."

"Uh-huh," Elias said cautiously. He had no idea what Gil was talking about and wondered whether he should be offended.

"You don't look menacing enough," Gil went on, and then paused as Elias stared at him blankly. "Do you even know what I'm talking about?"

"No," said Elias humbly.

"S/M. A top is the dominant. Sometimes that means a sadist, though not always. The bottom is the submissive." Gil took another bite.

"Oh."

"And if you can't pull off tricking as a top, maybe you want to avoid that stuff entirely. Especially your first time out. Having strangers take you for a bottom can be real dangerous."

"I'll take your word for it. What should I wear instead?"

Gil shrugged and pursed his lips. "You got a denim jacket, don't you?" He leaned to one side to snag something orange from under a heap of clothes and tossed it to Elias. "Wear it open, with this underneath."

Elias barely caught whatever it was in time to prevent it from smacking against his glasses. He held it up for inspection in the light knifing through a crack in the plywood window cover. A muscle shirt. Elias stared at it and suddenly, inexplicably, had to clamp down on a hysterical urge to giggle. *Don't you know that orange is definitely* not *my color, darling?* One glance at Gil's face, however, studying him with a kind of cold speculation through half-lidded eyes as he munched on his apple, made the urge fade away. The dread Elias had been struggling with since coming to Manhattan surged over him again nauseatingly, like an acrid taste of bile in his mouth. By sheer force of will, he forced it down. Again.

After a moment, Elias began unbuttoning his shirt. "So," he said deliberately, trying to keep his voice steady, "tell me how to do it. How do you pick up a trick for money?"

Gil rotated his apple and considered the other side. "You want to look like . . . like you know something they don't. Like you got a secret. That's what they want, what they're paying you for. Nervous customers are good. The ones that pay the best are the ones that are timid and polite, almost sort of apologetic. They've got the most to lose if they get caught."

"But how does it actually start?"

"You look. And he looks. And maybe you look away, and when you look back, he's still looking at you."

"Then what?"

"Okay, sometimes it's tricky. Some guys don't talk at all, they just look. That's all they do. You can be giving a guy bedroom eyes till he's practically coming in his pants, but he ain't gonna budge. Then you get the blokes who decide they don't like the way you're looking at them. Just break eye contact and move on if anyone you're scoping out is getting real pissed."

"But suppose he does like it? Then what?"

Gil shook his head. "You're really hopeless, you know that? So maybe he strolls up and asks you for a light."

"I don't smoke," Elias said without thinking.

Gil rolled his eyes. "Sure you do. You're smoking red-hot for him. Goddammit, it's a *line*."

"Okay," said Elias, feeling his face turn red. He dropped his own shirt on his pile of blankets, reached for the muscle shirt, and put it on.

"Or maybe he says something like, *Do you go out?*"

"Do you go out," Elias repeated.

Gil looked at him, amused. "What, do you think you're going to memorize all the possible pickup lines there are? It doesn't work that way. There ain't a fucking script, you bonehead. You just play the scene the way it happens."

"But I don't know what to say."

"That's just it. You don't say. The trick does."

"How do you make sure he's not a cop?"

"Get him to mention the money first. Don't you do it. And once you've agreed on the price, make sure you get the money up front."

Elias found his denim jacket and slipped it on. The familiar texture of the fabric felt comforting, although he wasn't accustomed to wearing it over bare arms. He sat down to pull on his boots. "So . . . after you've, er, hooked the customer, then what?"

Gil laughed. "What do you think? You find out what he wants you to do, and then you do it."

Elias sat still, looking at the boot in his hand. He tried constructing a picture of a faceless stranger, tried imagining the touches, and the quick breathing, and the release, but he found he couldn't do it. His mind refused to cooperate, sheering off instead into its own jittering panic and shame. *Try thinking about starving to death instead,* he told himself fiercely. *Maybe that will steady you.*

"What is it?" Gil asked.

Elias glanced at him questioningly, and then realized he had been silent too long. He gave a little half laugh. "I don't know, it's just that I've never . . . um . . ." He stopped, gave a rueful shrug, and bent down to pull on his second boot.

"Never?" said Gil after a moment, obviously startled. "Really?"

"Yeah, really," said Elias with a touch of defiance, wishing he'd kept his mouth shut.

"Oh," said Gil.

Elias stood, tossed his hair out of his eyes. "So. How do I look?"

"You look okay." Gil hesitated. "Do you want to try something with me, then? Just so you sort of know what to expect?"

Startled in his turn, Elias studied Gil suspiciously. Gil really meant it, he decided after an astonished moment. Had Gil always been hot for him and he just hadn't noticed? Or was the gesture simply meant as a kindness? He wasn't sure which idea unsettled him more.

"Would you pay me?" he said finally.

Gil's eyes widened, and then he laughed. "Hell, you're ready. Let's go."

The early September air rolling toward them from over the Hudson River was soft and damp, and smelled of salt and garbage. Gil and Elias poked their heads out around a plywood board, and then shifted it aside on screeching nails. The noise lifted the hairs on the back of Elias's neck. They slithered through the opening onto the first landing of the fire escape outside and, from there, lowered themselves over the railing and dropped to the ground. Gil took off his beret and stuffed it into his back pocket as Elias squinted into the setting sun.

"What now?" Elias asked.

"Now, m'friend, we walk. We look . . . interesting. And irresistible. And we see what happens."

"Where are we walking to?"

Gil shrugged amiably. "There are lots of places we can try."

"One of the parks?"

"I don't particularly feel like getting knifed tonight. I like to look for a place that's not too close to a bar, but not too far. If we don't get any action that way, we'll head toward the Port Authority bus station. That's a sure thing."

They headed north, up West Street, past crumbling warehouses lined with broken and boarded windows that seemed to stare at them like sad, empty eyes. Cars shot by them, leaving a twirling wake of skittering paper and dust that flew in their faces. Elias studied Gil out of the corner of his eye as they walked. How long had it taken Gil to develop that particular jaunty swagger? As they passed Clarkson Street, Elias tried to imitate it for a few steps, and Gil, who had been scanning the street around them, shot him a look with upraised eyebrows.

"Got a stone in your boot?"

"No," muttered Elias, abandoning the effort. He could feel his cheeks flush again. "So," he said after a pause, casting around for

something to say, "do you just turn up one of these streets or something?"

Gil started to answer, but stopped as a beat-up blue Chevy
pulled up a little ahead of them to their left. The driver adjusted the
rearview mirror and looked back toward them. Gil smiled. "Well,
lookee there."

"What?" Elias looked at the car, and back at Gil. "Is he . . . He
doesn't want directions or anything, does he?"

Gil smirked. "I think he's got some directions for me." He started
for the curb, but Elias, alarmed, grabbed his arm.

"Gil! You aren't getting in there, are you? You're not—"

"It's not a van, is it?" Gil shook off Elias's hand and strutted over
to the car to lean in the window and talk to the driver. The swift ne-
gotiations that followed apparently satisfied both parties, because
the driver opened the door and Gil hopped in without a backward
glance.

"Gil!" Elias yelled as the Chevy peeled away. "Gil! Where's the
bus station?"

No use. The car's taillights darted to one side as the driver pulled
around a van, and then dwindled until they disappeared in the distance. Elias stood, shifting uneasily from foot to foot as the twilight
deepened. Now what?

Although the air was warm, he shivered at the touch of the
breeze on his skin through the muscle shirt. Nerves, probably. That
somehow pushed him to the point of decision, and he pulled his
jacket close, squared his shoulders, and began walking again. There
was no point in heading back to the warehouse. He had resolved he
was going to do this, and in the end, he was going to have to do it
by himself, wasn't he? No, there wasn't any point in going back. If
he kept walking in the direction he and Gil had started in, eventually he should find a landmark that would help him figure out how
to find the Port Authority.

He crossed Barrow Street and paused to glance at a newspaper
in a corner machine. "September 3, 1981," read the date at the top;
he *had* lost track of time. The door to a bar opened just as he passed.

The blast of soul music pulsing through the open doorway startled him, and he glanced in that direction, catching the eye of the man who had just stepped outside. The man paused in the act of sliding his wallet into his inner coat pocket, and he gave Elias a half smile.

After a moment, Elias uncertainly returned the smile, and then ducked his head and continued in the direction he had been walking. The music died behind him in the distance, and gradually, he became aware of footsteps behind him. They didn't seem to be hurried, but they were close, and kept pace with him. Elias took a moment to steel his nerve, and then glanced back over his shoulder. It was the same man. He was black, and looked a couple inches shorter than Elias, and about ten years older. He stared intently at Elias and gave him another half smile, and a little nod.

Nervously, Elias stuffed his hands into his pockets, and then removed them again. He stopped at the next street, although there was no red light, and waited, staring straight ahead, until the man was beside him.

"Hey there, man," came a low voice to his right. The words were spoken gently, as if the speaker didn't want to scare him off. Elias felt his heartbeat speed up, and he swallowed.

"Hey there," he answered, his mouth dry. He forced himself to look at the man beside him and smile.

"So . . . you lookin' for a good time tonight, maybe?"

"Could be." The words were out of his mouth before he could bite them back. *Oh, boy. Here we go. I'm really going to do it.*

"That's fine. I'm lookin' for a good time, too." The man gestured with his chin across West Street, toward the piers, where the waves crashed against the crumbling seawalls. "I was thinking of heading down for the docks. Want to come along?"

The docks? "Uh . . . if I can find some fun there, sure." With one part of his mind, he realized dimly, he really meant it. He felt wary, but intensely curious, too, even aroused. *After all this time, I'm really going to find out what it's like. I wonder what he's going to want me to do? What will it feel like? Will it hurt?* A second part of his mind had definitely retreated into full panic mode: *What am I, nuts? This guy could*

*be a psycho. He could beat me up, even knife me. If he dumped my body into
the river, nobody would ever know what happened to me.*

"Some fun, huh?" the man replied, and he smiled. "Oh, I bet
something could be arranged." He gently put his hand on Elias's
shoulder and nodded, indicating they should cross West.

At the touch, Elias felt his breath freeze, suspended, in his
throat. And it was a third voice in the back of his mind that took
control at that instant, saying to him with the cold ring of truth: *I've
decided I have to do this, and I'm going to do it. No matter what.*

They walked in silence across the street, breaking into a run to
cross ahead of oncoming traffic. Elias managed to ease his breath
out slowly, and stuffed his hands back into his pockets. His fingers
were beginning to shake. He kept stealing glances at his companion, taking in bits and pieces: the shape of his hands, the slope of his
shoulders, the movement of thigh muscles in his jeans. The sight
made him feel as if a flock of sparrows were loose in his rib cage; a
warm itch began low in his groin. The man slowed to a walk as they
came to the other side. He had a spring in his step, a half smile still
playing over his face. At one point, he caught Elias looking at him
and laughed quietly. He changed direction in mid-stride, and Elias,
caught off-guard, almost collided with him.

"Sorry," Elias mumbled. He could feel his face heat up in embarrassment. The darkness probably masked it. He hoped.

"The trucks are down there," the man said, pointing.

The trucks? "Um . . . okay." They turned down a path and around
a corner to find a dark shape blotting out the first evening stars. A
truck trailer. The man led the way, squeezing between the trailer
and the wall. There was a recess in the wall three-quarters of the
way toward the water, and the man stepped into it and turned to
face Elias. His face, obscured by the shadow of the trailer, was featureless in the darkness. All Elias could see was the flash of his teeth
as he smiled again.

"Seems like a good spot, huh?" As Elias stepped into the recess to
join him, he felt hands reach for his belt.

Elias stiffened. "Wait," he said without thinking, his hands quickly covering the other man's.

"What?" The tone was surprised. "What is it, man?"

Elias stood silently for a long moment. *I really don't know if I can go through with this. And besides . . .* Frantically, he sorted through his memories of what Gil had told him. *God . . . I never even asked Gil what I should expect to get for money. And nothing's been said about price. How the hell am I supposed to get him to mention it first, anyway? If he's a cop . . .*

"What's happening?"

Elias listened to the breathing, warm by his ear, and made his decision. *So if he's a cop, maybe he'll put me in jail. At least I might get a meal.*

"I didn't . . . We didn't say anything about . . . money," he stammered, his voice sounding high and thin to his own ears.

The man's hands slipped out from beneath Elias's. "You want me to pay you?" His voice sounded surprised, Elias decided after an anxious moment, but not angry. Not yet, anyway. And he wasn't pulling out handcuffs or anything. Probably not a cop.

Torn between relief and embarrassment, Elias remained silent.

"At the *docks?* I ain't never had no one ask for money here before." He chuckled, a bass rumble. "You ain't never been to the docks before, have you, kid?"

"I . . . No."

"Here, follow me." He slipped out of the recess and squeezed his way between the wall and the trailer's side, moving toward the water. Elias followed him for only a few steps and then stopped, peering after him in the darkness.

"Kid, where are you?"

"Uh . . . here."

"Come on over."

Obediently, Elias slithered through the passageway around to the end of the trailer. The man was waiting for him there, a vague shape silhouetted against the dark, rolling water. He put his hand on Elias's shoulder again and pointed. "Look there. D'ya see?"

Elias turned and looked. The truck trailer bed was open. Inside, at the very end, he could barely make out a few hunched shapes, moving slowly in the darkness. He didn't understand at first, and then his ears caught the scrap of a whisper and a low moan. He felt his heart pounding again and an erection beginning to stir.

"There's only a few of 'em now," said the voice in his ear. "On a weekend night, late, after eleven, you might find close to a hundred men out here. Nobody pays for nothing. They're just doing each other. Making each other feel good. Understand?" He paused, as Elias strained to make out the dark, moving shapes, his skin crawling. He wanted desperately to be able to see the figures more clearly; he wanted just as desperately to turn around and bolt. "You want somebody to pay for it," the man continued after a moment, "you better try some blocks farther north. Unless . . . " Elias felt a hand touch the back of his jeans, slither around the side of his hip to grasp one of his belt loops. ". . . Unless you want to stay?"

His paralysis abruptly broken, Elias took a step forward. "No," he said quickly. "I mean—sorry, but no."

The hand let go of his belt loop. "Suit yourself, man," said the voice, still friendly, but a little disappointed, too.

Elias turned and went around the corner of the trailer. After a few steps, he slowed and looked back over his shoulder. In the shadow of the passageway between the trailer and the wall, he could see nothing. "Hey. Thanks," he called back softly.

"Anytime," the answer floated back. There was a scrape and rumble, as if someone had sat on the back edge of the trailer and hoisted himself up over the edge.

Elias walked swiftly back toward West Street, wishing he'd thought to ask about where to find the bus station.

Chapter Three

From all evil and mischief; from sin, from the crafts and assaults of the devil; from thy wrath, and from everlasting damnation,
Good Lord, deliver us.
From all blindness of heart; from pride, vain glory, and hypocrisy; from envy, hatred and malice, and from all uncharitableness,
Good Lord, deliver us.

—PRAYER BOOK, 1662

The party pulled away from the Black Boar's courtyard just after dawn. As they turned onto the road leading out of Ilminster, a fine mizzle began falling. Mrs. Warren sat in one corner of the carriage, wrapped up in a shawl against the damp, and kept up a running stream of commentary concerning the state of the roads, her difficulty digesting the morning's breakfast, various inns she had encountered during other journeys on the Countess's concerns, the spring planting, and the possible business of the folk they passed on the road. She proved a most inexacting companion, perfectly happy to continue her chatter for hours with very little encouragement from her audience. After a few failed attempts at diverting Mrs. Warren from monologue to conversation, Eliza contented herself with listening gravely and interpolating an occasional murmured "Just so," or "No, thank you most kindly, madam, I am quite comfortable," when offered, for the dozenth time, a pillow, a shawl, or a bottle of smelling salts. She found her companion's garrulousness amusing and, oddly enough, soothing. It allowed her to be silent, which suited her mood very well.

The day passed slowly as the carriage rolled, swaying, through shifting silver mists. The damp strengthened the carriage's odor of leather and wood. Trickles of water on the windowpanes made seeing out difficult. They halted twice at post houses to eat, providing Mrs. Warren with fresh fodder for comment on each occasion. Robert Owen and Edward Conway ate quickly and impassively, listening to Mrs. Warren's talk without response.

By the time they left the second post house and resumed their journey, the slow rain had stopped. A few rays from the setting sun pierced the thinning clouds to play over the newly planted fields. Robert Owen drove at a steady pace, keeping his eyes fixed straight ahead. As he guided the carriage expertly around ruts and holes in the road, he brooded over his exchange with Eliza in the innyard the previous night. He could not decide whether he should have risked saying more to her, to make her truly understand. Perhaps, he considered uneasily, he should try to speak with her once more before they reached the end of their journey. He did not feel at all confident that she would heed his warning otherwise.

The Countess had said she wished only what was right and proper for her husband's daughter—but, Robert Owen reflected gloomily, he knew the Countess. More than that, Robert Owen knew something else, something about the Earl's sons. The Countess did not know what he knew, but he felt quite sure that if she should ever find out what he suspected, his place would be worth a snap of his fingers.

Inside the carriage, Eliza leaned toward the window to watch the green meadows and orchards slowly rolling past. Mrs. Warren peered out over her shoulder. "We are drawing close, I see. That is Mr. Powell's farm, John Powell that is, my lady. Poor Mrs. Powell was carried off last winter by a fever, may God have mercy on her, but he has four fine young sons to help him. They sang a catch at the tenants' dinner last harvest, with most wonderfully pleasing voices. There is the lane leading up to Mr. Cotton's smithy, and to Mr. Dale's orchards. After we come around this curve, you will see— yes, do you see it now, my lady? That is the park, and the gardens. Yonder is Kellbrooke Hall."

Formal gardens flanked the house on both sides, and a wide green lawn stretched out before it. The house itself had been constructed of pale, golden stone in a double-pile, H-shaped plan. Large multipaned windows overlooked the lawn on the two main floors. The Earl's arms were carved in the tympanum on the pediment above the wide front steps.

Eliza drew in a sharp breath at the sight. She had wondered if her memories were true, if the place where she had been born would look familiar to her, or if she had somehow embroidered the picture in her mind to make Kellbrooke more than it was. The truth came as a curiously painful shock: the home of the sixth Earl of Exeter was even grander than she remembered.

The carriage turned up the long graveled avenue bisecting the lawn. "I remember that cupola," Eliza said suddenly, "with the golden ball on the top." She had turned to look back the day she left ten years before. The sun had struck the golden ball on the roof at an angle that made it blaze like a beacon. She had shut her eyes against the glare, or perhaps to stop her tears. When she opened her eyes and looked again, the carriage had already rounded a curve and Kellbrooke Hall had disappeared.

"I do not wonder that you remember it. 'Tis one of the best known landmarks of the county," Mrs. Warren observed with deep satisfaction.

"The house is so grand, much more so than I remembered."

"Aye, that it is," Mrs. Warren said, nodding, pleased.

"My father must have many servants, then?" Eliza ventured hesitantly.

"Oh, aye, my lady. Perhaps three score, or a few more."

Eliza's cheek suddenly felt hot; she pressed it against the window glass. "My father does not want for help, I see," she observed dryly. If the Earl could afford to keep three score servants, she wondered, how could he not pay Nell and Tom for caring for his own daughter?

"Indeed, there are many more who would be proud to do him any service."

"Such as tending his daughter, perhaps?" Eliza looked at the other woman, who blinked in surprise. "It does not seem that it was for lack of hands to help care for me that I was sent away."

Mrs. Warren was momentarily at a loss for a reply. "Perhaps," she stammered finally, "it was thought that . . . that your ladyship might thrive best in a more rustic . . . er, a more pastoral setting."

This attempt at explanation, once spoken, sounded most unsatisfactory to both the speaker and the listener. After a moment, Eliza took pity on her companion's confusion, gave her a small nod, and resumed staring out the window. Best to hold her peace, she decided, and wait to hear what the Earl himself had to say. Not entirely reassured, Mrs. Warren lapsed into an uneasy, uncharacteristic silence that lasted until the carriage rattled to a halt before the steps to the hall.

Someone shouted, the latch to the carriage door clattered, and the door opened, admitting a flood of sunset light. A groom stepped forward to let down the carriage step and then withdrew, bowing. Robert Owen climbed down from the coach box and handed Eliza out. "Welcome home, my lady," he said gravely, bowing. He hesitated for an instant, wondering once more whether he should seize the moment to speak to her again, but Mrs. Warren stood up to step down, too, and the fleeting opportunity was lost.

"Thank you, Mr. Owen," Eliza said. She thought she caught a flash of some expression of uncertainty or fear in his eyes. It was

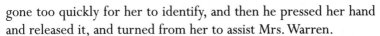

gone too quickly for her to identify, and then he pressed her hand and released it, and turned from her to assist Mrs. Warren.

"Willoughby, take Lady Eliza's bag inside. My lady, if you will follow me?"

Eliza took a deep breath and followed Mrs. Warren up the broad front stairs. Nervously, she counted the steps as she climbed; there were fifteen. The great front door swung open as they approached it, and a footman stepped aside to let them enter. Mrs. Warren paused to speak with him, as Eliza advanced a few steps into the room.

"Good evening, Pierce. Are my lord and lady at supper, then?"

"They are in the Great Dining Room now," the footman replied in an undertone as he shut the door, "and my lady asks that you wait with the Lady Eliza here in the Marble Hall."

"Here?" Mrs. Warren said in surprise, a frown making a crease between her brows. "That is—we have supped already on the road ourselves, but do they not wish for us to join them?"

"Refreshment may be brought to Lady Eliza's room tonight if necessary, her ladyship says."

"But that is—" Mrs. Warren checked herself and, after a moment, nodded. "Very well, then. Please inform my lady that my lord's daughter is safely arrived."

As the footman withdrew through a door to the right, Mrs. Warren turned to look for Eliza, who had stood a few yards from her. Rhombuses of golden light from the front windows angled across the black-and-white marble floor and dappled her shoulders and hair. "My lady?" said Mrs. Warren, coming to join her. "The Countess has said you are to retire to your own room tonight rather than join the rest of the household." This seemed cold, so she added uneasily, " 'Tis most thoughtful of her, indeed, for you must be very weary."

But Eliza, turning in a slow circle and looking around, did not hear. "I remember this room," she said pensively, "and a rainy afternoon, when we were all together here. We played leapfrog, and blindman's bluff. And James . . ." She stopped, and went over to gently finger a section of the paneling carved into a relief of leaves and flowers.

Curious, Mrs. Warren followed her. "What is it, my lady?"

Eliza's hand stopped and she beckoned Mrs. Warren closer. "James was tossing a ball to Charles, but Charles missed it. The ball hit the wall here and broke off the corner of this leaf. Do you see?" She laughed softly, immensely cheered by this simple proof of her brothers' existence.

"Eh, well, now," said Mrs. Warren, peering at the place where Eliza's finger pointed and nodding wisely. "That corner has been broken off, true enough. Strange, I never noticed it before."

Eliza suddenly remembered Robert Owen's advice that she should avoid mentioning her brothers. She gave herself a little shake and turned away—and drew in a sharp breath at the sight of a large portrait hanging on the opposite wall. "Mother."

"Eh? Oh—the first Countess." Mrs. Warren squinted at the portrait for a moment, and when she turned to look at Eliza again, her eyes widened. "Faith, you do resemble her most wonderfully."

Eliza stepped closer to study it. The artist had painted the first Countess standing, with one elbow on a column, the hand languidly raised to pull back a corner of drapery. The other hand held the folds of her gown. Her head was turned slightly, but the grave intensity in the heavy-lidded clear green eyes transfixed the viewer. Clearly, Eliza had inherited those eyes.

Seeing the portrait helped make her mother's face become clear in Eliza's memory again, too, and that realization brought with it a bittersweet surge of happiness. The expression in her mother's eyes warmed her, making her feel that her mother knew she had come home, and saw how she had grown, and approved of her. She found herself wishing wistfully that Nell and her mother could have met. They would have liked each other very much, she thought. "I do not remember that picture," Eliza said softly.

Neither Mrs. Warren nor Eliza noticed Lord Grey's wife, the second Countess, who at this point appeared in the doorway to the right. The Countess, who often found it useful to listen without being observed, did nothing to draw attention to herself.

"I think I remember hearing your lady mother had sat for it," said Mrs. Warren, "but it was completed after she died. Perhaps it had not been hung before you left Kellbrooke."

"I am pleased to see it." Eliza looked around and drew in another deep breath, consideringly. The air smelled faintly of beeswax. She smiled. "This is my mother's house," she said with quiet satisfaction. "My father built it for her."

Something in this remark made the Countess's face darken, and she finally moved into the room and spoke, saying dryly, "A pity Heaven did not grant her many years to enjoy as its mistress."

Mrs. Warren turned quickly and curtseyed deeply, her face turning pink. "My lady! Er, the Earl of Exeter's daughter, the Lady Eliza."

Eliza turned and curtseyed, too, shyly. "Madam."

The Countess did not nod or smile, but simply studied Eliza appraisingly. "Well. Let me have a look at you then." A silence stretched, as mother-in-law and daughter considered each other and Mrs. Warren waited uneasily.

On her part, Eliza felt a touch of surprise. Despite her erect posture and lifted chin, the Countess seemed so much shorter than she remembered. But then, of course, Eliza realized belatedly, the Countess would appear to be shorter to someone who had gone away as a child and returned years later as a young woman. More than this, however, the Countess was pregnant, in her fifth or sixth month at least. Eliza wondered at Mrs. Warren for not mentioning it. Pregnancy had not softened the Countess; instead, it seemed that the swelling of her belly had drawn the rest of her flesh to her more tightly. Neither the snowy ruffles on her Fontages cap nor the carefully curled *fripons* at her brow could disguise the hard lines ringing her mouth. Soft waves of expensive lace fell from her elbow sleeves, but her fingers, lightly tapping the clutch of keys on her chatelaine belt, were narrow, with bony knuckles.

The Countess, on the other hand, felt a surge of dismay at the sight of the girl calmly gazing back at her. She had ordered that the

Earl's daughter be left to wait in the Marble Hall, hoping to abash her with the magnificence of her surroundings, but the Countess had overheard enough to realize that the effect had not been as she intended. A quick glance at the portrait hanging above Eliza's shoulder made her tighten her lips, thinking, no, this would not do at all. The Countess had her coming child to consider; she did not want to awaken in the Earl memories that she had spent years lulling to sleep. She did not.

A moment's thought led her to a quick decision. "I am going to the stillroom," she said abruptly. "Will you please accompany me there before I take you to your room?"

"The stillroom?" said Mrs. Warren in bewilderment. "At this time of—er, is there something I might fetch for you from there, my lady?"

"No," said the Countess, keeping an edge from her tone only with an effort. "There are some particular herbs I need, and only I know where they are. You may help me by instructing the housemaids to bring a bath and fetch hot water to the West Rose Room." Her eyes raked Eliza impersonally from head to foot. "I should think it best for her to scrub away the stench of the stableyard before meeting the Earl." She indicated the doorway to the left with a sharp gesture of her chin.

Eliza reddened, and her lips parted to protest the Countess's insinuation, but Mrs. Warren spoke first, her words tumbling over themselves in her eagerness to agree: "Just so, exactly so, my lady. A bath will be most refreshing and proper, and exactly what Lady Eliza needs; my lady is exceedingly gracious to think of it."

The wary look of anxiety she darted in Eliza's direction as she spoke was so comic that Eliza's sense of the absurd could not help but respond. She relaxed and smiled at her traveling companion as the Countess turned away. "Thank you, Mrs. Warren," she said.

Mrs. Warren blushed gratefully and dropped another curtsey. "Bless you, my lady, it were no trouble at all. Welcome home, my lady."

The Countess did not second the welcome or even slow her

stride. Eliza had to hurry to catch up with her as she entered the smaller parlor adjoining the Marble Hall. Eliza glanced around, sorting through shifting wisps of memory as the two silently walked through the room and then turned a corner into the West Wing corridor. From there, a set of stairs led down to the lower kitchens.

A large pendulum clock on the staircase wall chimed the quarter hour as they descended, and Eliza paused at the landing, arrested by the mellow, reverberating sound. Here was another memory. The Countess noticed, and frowned. "This way," she said at the bottom of the staircase, gesturing toward the rear of the house.

They went through the low-ceilinged hall where the servants dined (two footmen and three housemaids, lingering at the table over tankards of porter, rose hastily to their feet as the two women came through) to a small wooden door beyond. The Countess opened it with one of the keys at her belt, and together they stepped inside.

One of the maids followed them in, hastily lighting several candles in wall sconces about the small room, and then, at a curt nod from the Countess, withdrew again, closing the door behind her. Eliza looked around, blinking as the light flickered and grew. She drew a deep breath; the air was redolent with the earthy smell of the fresh and dried herbs covering the trestle tables and hanging from hooks in the ceiling. Jars covered with waxed muslin and labeled pots stood in neatly ordered rows on shelves against the wall. Ignoring Eliza, the Countess picked up a mortar and pestle from a windowsill and moved to the shelves, breaking off a leaf here and a bit of dried root there, muttering to herself under her breath as she added each bit to the bowl of the mortar.

As the Countess ground her concoction to a fine powder with her pestle, curiosity drew Eliza over to one of the tables. Nell had taught Eliza as much about herbs and simples as any countrywoman might know, and she had also given Eliza a thorough grounding in the preparation of plants for dying woven cloth. Although the collection in Kellbrooke's stillroom was certainly larger and more varied than the humble gleanings in Nell's own larder, many of the plants looked and smelled familiar to Eliza. The cool and pungent scents made her wistful, homesick for her foster parents' cottage.

A bundle of fresh juniper branches lying on a bench to one side caught Eliza's eye. She reached out and broke off a sprig, and ran her fingers lightly over the springy needles. *The berries are most excellent good for all palsies, and a resister to all pestilences,* Nell used to say. *Admirable good for a cough, and for consumption and pains in the belly. And more, a sprig of juniper protects against all evil that would do thee harm.* She had insisted that Tom put a sprig into the band of his hat before leaving to join the Duke of Monmouth's ragtag army. Tom had laughed at her, but then, chucking her under the chin, he had affixed the sprig to his hatband, dropped a careless kiss on Eliza's cheek, and marched away with the men mustering from Buckland St. Mary's, Chard, Combe St. Nicholas, and Ilminster.

In the harrowing days that followed, they had received the news of the fall of the Duke's army at Sedgemoor and of Tom's capture. As they had awaited the judgment of the Assizes Court, Nell had put almost as much faith in that sprig of juniper as in her prayers for Tom's safety. Perhaps, as Nell insisted, the juniper had kept him alive. But even so, Eliza reflected ruefully, it had not prevented his transport to the West Indies. Some magics had strength, but still were not all-powerful.

Eliza crushed a few of the needles between her fingertips and held them to her nose to inhale the scent of the released spicy oil. Just as her hand dropped to her side again, the Countess abruptly turned and flung the contents of the mortar directly into Eliza's face. Astonished and caught in mid-breath, Eliza coughed and choked as she breathed in the fine dust. A strange lassitude swept over her, and then cold terror. "Wh-what . . . why . . . ?"

"Be silent," hissed the Countess, her eyes glinting in the shifting candlelight. A few last grains of dust released from the mortar drifted into the candle flame, snapping into violet sparks and then ashes. Eliza sneezed, and then simply stood blinking, struggling for breath. Tears ran down her cheeks, but she felt too weak even to raise her hand to wipe them away.

"Be silent," the Countess said again after a moment. Eliza had not spoken again, but it gave the Countess great pleasure to say the words anyway. She studied the girl with satisfaction, noting her pallor and how the alarm in her eyes gradually subsided to a dull stupor. She would see to it that the stupid wench would give herself no airs of importance now. "You will remain silent," she continued with relish. "You will do nothing but what I tell you to do, and you will not speak unless I give you permission to speak."

Wordlessly, Eliza nodded.

The Countess picked up a covered wicker basket, opened the door, and ushered Eliza out of the stillroom again. After locking the door behind them with the key, she prodded Eliza in the shoulder. "That way—back to the steps."

She did not notice the sprig of juniper still clutched between Eliza's fingers.

The Countess led the way up two flights of the West Wing steps and then south, toward the front of the house. She walked quickly, and without speaking, indicating changes of direction with sharp pokes of her forefinger to Eliza's arm. Eliza remembered little afterward of their progress through the passages of Kellbrooke. The angles of walls at the corners of corridors seemed strangely askew, and doorways and stairways gaped alarmingly. Eliza stumbled dizzily in her mother-in-law's wake, clutching balustrades and door frames for balance as she passed, her vision a shifting scrim of colors and shadows.

Finally, on the second floor, the Countess opened a door leading into a medium-sized apartment, hung with rose damask. Here, the scent of lavender pierced Eliza's haze, and her surroundings ceased to whirl around her. With a brazen clatter of curtain rings, a maid drew the last set of drapes over one of two tall multipaned windows, shutting out the twilit second-story view of the western gardens. Another maid emptied a last steaming pitcher of water into the footed tub drawn up before the fireplace, where a warm blaze hissed and crackled peaceably.

"You, there," the Countess said, gesturing to one of the servants. "Take off the girl's clothes. Come now, be quick about it."

There was no screen. Eliza stood passively, staring blankly into the fire as the attendant stripped her of her dress, her chemise, and underclothes. The other maid picked up a bottle of rose water from the table beside the bath and drew the stopper.

"No, do not add that," the Countess said, frowning. "Place the bottle back on the table, there, and leave us. Take the clothes with you, and burn them."

"Come here, girl," she said to Eliza as the servants withdrew. Eliza came over to the bath and stood quietly, naked, the silken tendrils of her hair stirring slightly in the eddies of warmth flowing from the fireplace. In her mind she felt neither shame nor anger— only the tactile impression of polished flooring under bare feet and the flow of air over her skin. The Countess stepped toward her, and Eliza met her gaze unflinchingly. The pupils of the girl's eyes were dilated enormously, like deep pools of water surrounded by thin rims of green moss.

The Countess's lip curled as she looked Eliza up and down deliberately, staring at her legs, her groin, her breasts. "Well, you look to be a healthy enough animal." Her eyes narrowed consideringly as she studied the locket nestled in the curve between Eliza's breasts. Just then, the basket in the Countess's hand lurched, distracting her, and she smiled. She lifted off the wicker lid.

Inside lay three enormous mottled toads, their sprawled legs intertwined. Carefully, the Countess shook back the lace dangling from her elbow sleeve and reached inside to pick one up. "When Eliza comes to her bath," she told it solemnly, "seat yourself on her head, that she may be as stupid as you are." She tossed it into the bath and picked up a second toad. "Place yourself on her forehead, that she may become as ugly as you are, and that her father may not know her." The second toad followed the first. Some of the drops from the resultant splash of water hit a log on the fire, making it hiss.

The third toad, more wary, tried to jump out of the basket, but the Countess snared it by its hind legs and held it firmly in her hand as it struggled to get away. "Rest on her heart," she whispered to it hoarsely, "that she will have evil intentions and suffer in consequence."

As the third toad fell into the tub, too, the surface of the water roiled fitfully for a moment. When the bubbles had died down again, the water was no longer clear, but a clouded green.

"Get into the water," the Countess ordered.

Eliza stepped up onto the pedestal and over the edge of the tub. Her foot parted the surface of the water and disappeared into the slimy murk. As her other foot came over and she lowered herself down, the sprig of juniper slipped from her hand at last and fell, like a benediction, onto the surface of the water.

Immediately, the water surged up in a churning column, rising above Eliza's head, and then slopped down into the tub again and over the edge to the floor, hissing. Eliza gasped and floundered on her knees, wiping streams of water from her eyes. The Countess gave a harsh cry.

And then abruptly, it was over. All was still; the water was clear again. Coughing, Eliza pulled wet hair from her eyes—and then saw the Countess, as if for the first time. Her eyes widened in astonishment. "Madam . . . ?"

Bobbing about Eliza's knees, three scarlet poppies floated on the surface of the water.

The Countess darted forward and seized one of the poppies, her face contorting with rage. "How did you do that?" She straightened up, crushed the flower in her fist, and opened her shaking fingers, letting the petals fall to bob on the water's surface again, like small, unseaworthy boats. "How did you do that?"

Frightened, Eliza recoiled against the side of the tub, almost oversetting it. The two faced each other, frozen for a breathless moment, and then the Countess stepped back, furious and afraid.

"You need not think," she spat venomously, her hand spasmodically clutching the folds of cloth over her belly, "that your father will spend *aught* for your marriage settlement. I will see to that." She hesitated, eyeing the locket around Eliza's neck again, torn between wrath and doubt, and then turned with a wordless exclamation and stalked out the door.

The slam made Eliza wince.

Chapter Four

A certain man went down from Jerusalem to Jericho, and fell among thieves, which stripped him of his raiment, and wounded him, and departed, leaving him half dead. And by chance there came down a certain priest that way: and when he saw him, he passed by on the other side. And likewise a Levite, when he was at the place, came and looked on him, and passed by on the other side. But a certain Samaritan, as he journeyed, came where he was: and when he saw him, he had compassion on him, and went to him and bound up his wounds, pouring in oil and wine, and set him on his own beast, and brought him to an inn, and took care of him.

——LUKE 10:30–34

At the corner of Christopher and Weehawken, a crowd of bike boys and muscle men spilled from the doorway of the Dugout, as if the throbbing rock music inside had built up enough pressure to begin oozing the party out into the street. Still jumpy, Elias walked by with his hands jammed in his pockets, keeping his eyes down and center. A small group lost in conversation wandered across his path, making him stop abruptly. He gave them a wary look, and one man caught his eye, smiled ruefully, and plucked the elbows of his companions until a path opened up. Elias threaded his way through carefully, trying not to brush against anyone. A sharp laugh behind him made him flinch, but he simply kept walking without looking back.

The experience at the docks hadn't turned out as badly as it might have, he had to admit. He hadn't been mugged or beaten up or anything. Maybe he hadn't gotten any money, but that simply meant he was no worse off than when he started. A shadowy picture welled up in his mind, unbidden, of the slowly moving shapes in the back of the truck bed. He shook his head, as if that would banish the memory, yet the image refused to disappear. He wasn't calming himself down; instead, his breathing quickened, and his heart raced even faster.

If nothing had happened, why had the whole thing unnerved him so?

A voice floated in his memory, at the back of his mind: *If you can't understand the whole picture, break it down into smaller pieces.* Mr. Stanley, one of his mathematics teachers, had said that once. Elias had spent a term mesmerized by the graceful way Mr. Stanley's hand moved the chalk across the blackboard until he realized he wasn't supposed to notice things like that.

He crossed Washington, frowning up at the redbrick building looming over him across the street. Well, the first piece was . . . relief. He hadn't gotten hurt, and he hadn't had to, well, go through with anything.

On the other hand, all he had done was put off the inevitable for just a little longer. And that meant he was going to have to muster up enough courage to pick up his first trick all over again.

Elias groaned at the thought. A commuter hurrying toward the PATH train entrance heard and swiveled his head to look back at him curiously. Elias ducked his head again, his face burning, and hurried to take advantage of a break in the traffic to cross Hudson Street.

Once the heat in his cheeks had faded, he turned his attention back to probing cautiously at his jumbled, half-formed thoughts, as if exploring a sore tooth with his tongue. Finally, he identified something else: chagrin. The acrid bitterness of the realization almost made him laugh. *Here I am, ready to . . .* He stopped, fishing for an appropriately crude expression. *Ready to sell my ass on the streets. Only I'm so inept at it, I can't even figure out how to find a buyer!*

Gil would have answered that someone ready to pay for a trick could always be found. *What a comfort,* Elias thought sourly.

The aroma of coffee and tea drifted over Elias from a shop he was approaching, mingled maddeningly with the heady smell of chocolate wafting from yet another shop across the street. Elias swallowed, closing his eyes in a combination of bliss and ravenous despair. When he opened them again, his gaze fell upon a mannequin in a store window, covered entirely in leather, from zippered face mask to stormtrooper boots. It brandished a large bullwhip. "The Leather Man" read the sign under the mannequin's feet. Elias's eyes widened.

"Excuse me, please," said a voice politely in his ear. Startled, Elias stepped aside from the doorway, and the two men behind him entered the store, walking hand in hand. Both wore leather vests and studded dog collars.

Elias looked up and down the sidewalk with new eyes. *What kind of street is this, anyway?* He started walking again, watching the store windows more carefully this time. "So Many Men, So Little Time" read a T-shirt in one. "Gay and Proud" read another. That one stopped Elias in his tracks again. *Gay and . . . Proud?*

A voice floated across his memory, so level with contempt it sounded almost expressionless. *You can go live with all the rest of the faggots. Live in a cesspool, if you want; I don't give a damn. I never want to see your face again.*

And when you die, you can burn in hell forever.

Two men sat on the stairs of a walk-up apartment, sharing a beer and laughing at some private joke. One rested his cheek momentarily on the shoulder of the other. In a window a story above, two other men exchanged a kiss, and then withdrew from view, closing the curtains behind them. The sight made Elias's eyes sting. *God . . . they make it look so simple. So . . . normal!* He blinked rapidly as he crossed Bleecker Street.

He let himself walk for another block without trying to think about anything. Past the grocery store, past the Lutheran church, a cowboy bar, a cigar shop. Now that he understood what section of town he was in, he felt almost afraid to look around. But when he did, there wasn't anything particularly alarming to see. Just knots of people, men and women both, dressed in T-shirts and leather pants, or tight shorts, or artfully ripped jeans, strolling past him, window shopping, enjoying the summer night air. *So what did you expect? Debauched orgies in the streets?*

As long as he could remember, he had heard whispers in the back of the classrooms, in the locker rooms, on the playground. *Faggot. Queer. Limp-wrist pansy-ass fairy.* He had known very early— everyone did—that there was no way you would ever want to be one of those. Faggots were the lowest scum of the earth. If you were a faggot, you might as well be dead.

Elias had always known that, deep in his bones—long before the whispers had begun swirling around him.

Slowly, a dull roar started in his ears, and he had to stop to lean against a store window. The glass was dirty, but cool, and he leaned his cheek against it gratefully. And then, because he knew he had to, he thought back to the docks again, and the last piece fell into place.

He had been so sure that tricking would mean having to do something degrading. Something painful and disgusting, like a punishment he deserved. And the trick would love the fact he was doling out money in exchange for humiliation. That was what all faggots wanted, wasn't it?

But instead, the man had been kind to him. That had seemed so strange. He had said that the men at the docks met without paying each other, just to give each other pleasure. And when Elias had decided to leave, the man had let him go, without threatening him, without hurting him. He had only seemed disappointed that Elias didn't want to join them.

Against the power of the rasping whispers, and the contemptuous voice coldly telling him why he no longer had a home, a single thought wavered, and slowly took shape: Maybe . . . it isn't true. Maybe it doesn't have to be true?

After a few moments, Elias's dizziness began to ebb a bit, and he realized that several people passing by were staring at him curiously, and so he turned his head and pretended to be studying the display in the store window.

Directly in front of him stood a full-length mirror. Carefully he pushed his glasses back and studied his own reflection, staring back at him. Perhaps it was his light-headedness that made his own face seem so strangely unfamiliar. His forehead, brushed by reddish blond bangs, was broad; the high slope of his cheekbones complemented the widest points of his jaw. His chin and ears were all well shaped. His nose might be a little long, but the width of his mouth balanced that.

The orange muscle shirt, though, looked ridiculous—strange and out of place. He stared at it, almost unable for a moment to remember where it had come from. *No. That isn't me.* Slowly, he buttoned the metal buttons on his denim jacket, covering the shirt entirely. The cut of the jacket made the set of his shoulders look good, and his build look slim and wiry. That was better: with the shirt out of sight, the rest of his features slid smoothly back into familiarity, as if a strange spell, a veil or a glamour placed over him, had been stripped away.

He hadn't been looking for another trick since he'd left the docks, he realized. He hadn't even thought of it. And he knew suddenly, as he stared into his own eyes staring back, that he was not going to. There had to be another solution.

Cautiously, he straightened up and pushed himself away from the window. Time to begin walking again. He didn't know what else to do.

An hour later, his strength gave out, and he collapsed on a bench in Union Square Park. It felt good to sit. He leaned back, feeling the slats of the bench press against his thighs and back, smelling the damp, earthy, urine-tinged smell floating up from the subway entrance nearby. Up Fifth Avenue in the distance, the Empire State Building gleamed. He stared at it for a long time and then, finally, closed his eyes. Here, in the park, the blare of taxi horns echoing against the buildings sounded strangely distant, like the muted call of crows in the tops of faraway trees. He sensed people hurrying by him, headed for the subway entrance, the rasping scuff and clack of their descending footsteps resounding hollowly from the stairway. A subway train passed beneath the street with a muffled roar, the sound mingling with the distant ringing in his ears.

After a moment or two, Elias heard another set of footsteps approaching from the left, but instead of continuing past him, they stopped a few feet short of the subway entrance. Next, he heard a scrape of something placed on the ground, and two gentle metallic thumps. The twang of strings being tuned startled him into opening his eyes again. A man stood a few feet away in front of an open instrument case, tightening the tuning pegs on a worn guitar. Plucking the D-string with a frown, the musician swiveled on one heel, caught Elias's eye, and gave him a crooked smile that made Elias's heart turn sideways.

Elias sat up a little straighter on his bench. The man had a soft mustache and carelessly cut dark hair that tumbled haphazardly around the collar of his shirt. The dim streetlight above the subway entrance fell across the planes of his face, throwing shadows under his cheekbones in a way that made Elias's breath catch in his throat. The man gave Elias a nod as he tuned the D-string slightly higher (to Elias's relief). Then, apparently satisfied, he swung into a lively jig, something at once sweet and merry and melancholy. Despite the sprightliness of the music, he kept his upper body still, except for strong hands moving swiftly across the strings, plucking and shaping the lilting measures of the tune with deft sureness. He played with the sleeves rolled back over his forearms, chin raised and eyes half-closed in concentration.

A businesswoman with a briefcase paused for a moment to listen, then dug out a dollar and dropped it into the guitar case. The musician nodded an acknowledgment in her direction as she disappeared down the subway entrance stairs. Ending the tune with a flourish, he turned and caught Elias's eye and smiled again. Elias wished for a dollar to give him, wished he could applaud, but could only sit speechlessly, paralyzed by the warmth of that smile.

The man turned his attention back to his strings. He plucked out another, slower measure, took a deep breath, and opened his mouth to sing.

His tenor voice was light and flexible, mellifluous with a rich burr, like sunlight caressing honeyed oak. Under the spell of that voice, Elias forgot everything: hunger and the rancid stink rising from the subway and the dull knife edge of despairing fear. Instead, he closed his eyes again and listened with all thought suspended as the musician sang with simple longing for home. A hush fell when the song had ended, and Elias sat perfectly still, hardly daring to breathe, until a sense of his own weakness crept back over him like an icy vapor, making tears brim over in the corners of his eyes.

The musician cleared his throat, as if to break the spell, and then the guitar introduced another melody, light and teasing. His voice changed, too. It sounded sly, full of laughter and mischief.

> If the beggin' be as good a trade
> as I have heard them say,
> it's time that I was out of here
> and jogging doon the brae.
>
> Tae the beggin' I will go, will go
> a beggin' I will go.
>
> I'll get me to the tailor man
> they call him Arnie Gray
> I'll gat him mak' a cloak tae me
> tae help me night and day.

Tae the beggin' I will go, will go
a beggin' I will go.

And all the time I am away
I'll let my hair grow long.
I will not pare my nails at all
for the beggars wear them long.

Tae the beggin' I will go, will go
a beggin' I will go.

And all the suitors of the town
I'll lead a merry chase
and coins of gold they'll throw tae me
all for my pretty face.

Tae the beggin' I will . . .

"Stop it!" Elias suddenly found himself on his feet, rigid and trembling with fury. "Stop it," he cried again, as the guitar faltered to a stop and the musician looked over at him in surprise. "What the hell do you know about it?" Elias said, his voice ragged. "You don't know the first thing about what it's like, you stupid asshole, you——" He choked himself off in horror.

A variety of expressions played over the musician's features: consternation, perplexity, and rueful chagrin. "Oh, Jesus . . . the music wasn't *that* bad, was it?"

Elias felt his face flaming up in blinding embarrassment. He swayed, looked around wildly, mumbling something—he hardly knew what—that came out incoherently, and suddenly his knees buckled. He found himself squatting, his hands flailing in front of himself. *I'm going to faint,* he thought with a sudden numb, surprised clarity. There was a sudden movement and he felt the other man's arm firmly across his upper chest, keeping him from pitching forward. "Here, now. Easy. Uh . . . can I get you to sit back on the bench? I can't hold you up and hold my guitar, too."

After a confused moment or two, Elias found himself back on

the bench, leaning forward with his head between his legs. He felt something pressing against a thigh to one side; that must be the guitar placed on the bench beside him. He could feel a pair of hands fixed firmly on his shoulders, holding him in place on his seat. Slowly, the pounding giddiness in his head receded. He made a slight shifting movement, and the hands immediately released him.

"You want to sit back up?"

Elias nodded, and the musician helped push him up.

Elias found himself eye to eye with the other man, who knelt on the ground before him. Self-consciously, Elias straightened up as best he could; he wished his damned hands would stop shaking. "I'm sorry. You must think I'm crazy. I don't know what came over me. I don't even know why I did that." He stole an embarrassed glance, but saw only friendly concern in the other man's face.

"You having a bad trip, or something?" the man said.

Elias gave a half laugh. "I don't do drugs."

The man hesitated, and then spoke again. "How long has it been since you ate, kid?"

Elias's gaze dropped. "I don't know." He looked at his hands and tried to think back—there'd been that banana he'd found that had fallen out of a crate behind the Korean corner grocery. "Sometime yesterday morning, I think."

He leaned forward with his elbows on his knees and his forehead on his fists. *What am I going to do? Dear god in heaven, what am I going to do?* The musician's knees disappeared from his field of vision, and the guitar was removed from the bench. He heard some steps, the scrape of the instrument case, and then felt a tap on his shoulder. He looked up in surprise.

The musician stood in front of him again, holding his guitar case. "C'mon, kid," he said, jerking his chin toward East Fourteenth Street. "I'll buy you a hamburger."

"Ah, no," Elias said faintly, even as his mouth flooded with saliva at the thought. "I couldn't."

"Course you can. You're too whipped to argue with me. I'm

hungry, anyway. There's a place on Second Avenue I'm thinking of, a little past Tenth. Think you can make it that far? They have great fries, too—but don't try the soup."

They walked slowly, with the musician unobtrusively offering Elias a steadying hand on his elbow when he swayed. Eventually they found the place the musician wanted, an underground restaurant called the Grotto, and sat down at a wobbly, scarred table set in a little backwater eddy by the kitchen. Clove cigarette smoke coiled low in the air, and the odor of hamburgers, pasta sauce, and frying onions made Elias's head swim.

The man got up to speak with the waitress for a moment and came back with a large glass of orange juice. "Here, drink up. This should stop the shakes." Elias took a sip, and then gasped and downed the rest. It really did work: he had barely put the tumbler down when he realized his tremors had eased. The tension flowed from his muscles like water, and he cautiously lifted one shoulder and then the other to stretch them.

"That's better, then," the man said mildly as Elias pushed the glass forward. "My name is Sean. Sean Donnelly."

"I'm Elias Latham."

Sean raised an eyebrow. "Elias? That's an unusual name. Can't say I've heard it before."

"It's a Puritan name," Elias said, offering, without thinking, his standard explanation. As soon as he said it, he felt like an idiot. *Some Puritan I've been today—out on the street trying to turn tricks.* He suddenly felt glad he'd closed his denim jacket over the muscle shirt.

"Really."

"Yeah," Elias said, and forced himself to smile. "It's an old family name."

"Old New England stock, I take it."

"Mm-hmm. My family came over early—some on the *Mayflower*, the whole bit. There's even a story about someone way back on the family tree who ended up condemned to death for witchcraft."

A bored-looking waitress slithered her way through the crowd and appeared, wraithlike, at their table. "Decided what you want yet, guys?"

Belatedly, Elias reached for one of the plastic-covered menus propped up between the napkin dispenser and the salt and pepper shakers. "Uh, I haven't even had a chance to look yet."

"I'll take the hamburger platter with Swiss and mushrooms," Sean said. "You got Guinness on tap, right?"

"Yeah."

"Fine, I'll have that. Thanks." Sean folded his menu back up and tucked it back next to the salt and pepper. "You?"

"I'll have the hamburger platter, too, with cheddar, please. And a Coke to drink."

The waitress nodded, rattling her earrings violently, slashed an underline on her pad, and slipped it back into her front pocket.

Elias smiled tentatively at Sean. "Thanks."

Sean smiled back encouragingly. The effect was dazzling. Elias groped around for something else to say. "I . . . really liked your music," he managed finally as the waitress came back and set their drinks in front of them.

Now the smile tugged at the corner of Sean's mouth. "That so? Well, my friend, you have a strange way of showing it." He took a sip of Guinness.

"Oh," Elias said, stricken, remembering. "That is—I'm sorry I interrupted. You didn't even have a chance to collect much money, did you? I . . . I . . . " He trailed off helplessly.

Sean waved a careless hand. "Forget it. It's not the money. I just busk for fun these days, anyway." He picked up his water glass, took a sip, and rattled the ice cubes. "So—you're a runaway, aren't you?"

"No."

"No?"

"Uh-uh." He looked down at his Coke. "I got kicked out."

"Huh. And it didn't have to do with drugs? Wait a minute," Sean added quickly, "you don't have to tell me, not if you don't want to. There aren't any strings attached to that hamburger."

Elias couldn't help but smile. He looked up again and studied Sean's face and decided, cautiously, that it seemed open, and willing to listen. He liked it. And Sean meant it, too, Elias realized: he really didn't have to say anything. Having a choice of whether to tell or not made it clear: he wanted to tell *somebody* the truth, and to choose to tell it of his own free will. The unspoken words had been weighing inside him for too long. He took a deep breath. "I was home for summer from school—"

"So you're in college?" Sean cocked his head, studying Elias with a quizzical expression. "I wouldn't have thought you were that old."

"No. Boarding school—prep school. I'd just graduated. I'm going to college next—" He caught himself. "That is, I was."

"A boarding prep school," Sean repeated with a neutral expression, but Elias understood what he meant and grimaced.

"Yeah, that's it. My family is the real East Coast Brahmin type, I guess." He hesitated. "The whole thing started about this girl."

"What, did you get her pregnant?"

Despite himself, Elias almost laughed. "No. *That* would have been forgivable, I think. Our fathers went to school together, and I've known her for years. As soon as I got home from school in May, my father started bugging me about her, and he kept it up all summer. You know, when was I going to go over to see her; didn't I want to take her to this clambake on Saturday."

"My god. You're not kidding about East Coast Brahmin types. What did they have in mind, some kind of arranged marriage?"

"No, nothing like that. But . . . well, yeah, I guess my parents always sort of hoped we'd end up together."

"So what happened when you dared refuse the hand of the fair Muffy?"

Elias did laugh this time. "Her name is Emma. And I like her; she's really nice. It's just that I've always thought of her more like a sister. I don't have one, you see." He glanced at Sean nervously. "More than that, I've just always known—I finally told my father it wasn't going to happen. Ever."

Comprehension began to dawn on Sean's face. "They kicked you out because you're gay?"

Elias sat silently, afraid.

A platter of hamburger and fries suddenly materialized in front of each of them, like a gift. The burgers were still sizzling, and melting cheese bubbled down the edges of the buns. Elias blinked; he hadn't even seen the waitress approaching.

"Eat," Sean said. Solemnly, he handed Elias a bottle of ketchup. Elias hesitated. *It's okay,* Sean's eyes told him. *I'm not going to beat you up or walk away. I'm not even going to send the hamburger back. It's okay.*

Slowly, Elias reached out and accepted the bottle.

For the next few minutes they both concentrated on their food. Elias chewed each bite carefully, afraid everything would come back up if he bolted the meal. The hamburger tasted greasy and salty and the fries burned his tongue. If he ever died and went to heaven, he decided, he'd want his first meal to taste exactly like this.

"It wasn't just the talk about Emma," Elias said finally, breaking the silence. He reached for his Coke and took a sip. "I think Father wondered then, but it wasn't until a few days later—someone sent him a letter. Anonymously. I think it was somebody from my school."

"What makes you think that?"

"Well," Elias said slowly, "there was another guy there I kind of liked. One night we were sort of messing around, just kind of wrestling, you know." He bit his lip, flashed another nervous look at his listener. "We ended up doing some things that we didn't quite expect we would . . . nothing too involved, exactly. Kind of . . . fondling. I mean, I didn't . . . We didn't . . . uh . . ."

"I got the picture," Sean interrupted, but without making it sound like an interruption. He didn't crack the slightest hint of a smile, for which Elias felt immensely grateful.

"Well. He panicked, blamed me for everything, and then clammed up totally. Wouldn't say another word to me for the rest of the term. So I figured it might have been because of what happened with him. Maybe he sent the letter because he freaked out, or he told somebody else."

"What'd the letter say?"

"Father wouldn't show it to me. But from what he said, I think it said it was sent because the writer felt it was his duty to inform him that his son was a pervert. A fudge-packing, candy-ass-fucking faggot."

"God. What a toadlike thing for somebody to do."

"Maybe I could have passed the whole thing off as a sick practical joke, if . . . if . . ."

"If you hadn't just talked with him about the girl?"

"Yeah." Elias stared at the grease left on his plate, slowly drew a french fry through a puddle of ketchup. "It's not like it was true—like I'd ever really even done anything! But I just knew there was something different about me, that I was different. I've known since I was five or six, I guess. And when Father came out of his library and demanded that I tell him, I just blurted it out."

Sean said nothing.

"My father's an elder in our church. And my mother—it about killed them both. They started yelling at me. I've never heard either of them yell before, ever! They said—" He broke off.

Sean gave him a moment. "They said what?" he finally prompted gently.

"I've got two nephews." Elias could hear his own voice getting ragged. "My brother's kids. I'd always baby-sit them in the summer. One of them is five, and the other is seven. I love them, you know? I suppose it's because I always figured I'd never have any kids of my own." He paused, took a breath, but his voice cracked again anyway. "My father said, he said he wanted to know—not even *if* but *how many times* I'd . . . with Josh and Kevin—" Helplessly, he looked up at the ceiling, but the tears spilled over anyway. "They've known me my entire life, but as soon as they found out, it's like I wasn't their son anymore. In their eyes, I'd turned into some kind of monster.

How could they, how could they *think* I'd ever do anything like that?"

Something nudged his hand. He looked down and accepted the paper napkin Sean handed him. "Thanks," he said in a muffled voice, wiping his eyes and blowing his nose.

"So they threw you out."

Elias nodded. "With the clothes on my back."

"Couldn't you go to your brother?"

"No. He's in med school and my parents are helping with tuition. He was there, visiting that weekend. Father told him if he ever had anything to do with me, he'd get cut off, too. He's just like my father, anyway. I'm sure he'd never leave me alone with his kids again."

Sean made a soft sound under his breath.

"I came to the city a couple of weeks ago. I didn't know what else to do. I had a little money at first, but somebody in the first flop I stayed at stole it while I slept." He gave an embarrassed shrug. "I guess I need to get more streetwise."

"That depends," Sean said slowly, "on whether you really want to stay on the streets. God knows they can be a real wilderness. Wouldn't you rather get off?"

Elias slowly doodled in his pool of ketchup with another french fry. "I guess . . . ever since my parents kicked me out, I've kind of been in shock. It's like I haven't been thinking clearly. But yeah, I want to get off. I don't know how I'm going to do it, though." He sighed and then tried to smile. "Anyway . . . thanks a lot for the hamburger." He started to stand.

"Wait." Sean laid his hand over Elias's. "Sit down."

Elias slowly sat down again. Sean studied him thoughtfully for a moment, and then said, "You said you're a high school graduate, right?"

Elias nodded.

"Do you have any skills or hobbies? Anything that could help you get a job?"

Elias chewed his lower lip for a moment. "I'm . . . not sure."

"Well, what did you do for extracurricular stuff at that school of yours?"

"I don't know—just things. You know . . . drama club. Photo club, chess club—"

"Wait. Photo club, you said? You do photography?"

Elias nodded. "Yeah. I took some courses, learned how to develop my own pictures."

A slow smile curved Sean's face. "I got a cousin who manages a photo shop."

Elias just stared at him.

"In fact," Sean continued, the smile growing wider, "maybe I could help you get a job there. I think I remember him saying something about being shorthanded."

"Are you kidding me?" Elias said uncertainly.

"No. You can come home with me. I'll call him for you tomorrow."

Elias looked down at his plate. The outline blurred, and the few remaining french fries seemed to drift and swim across his field of vision. "Why are you doing this?" he said, his voice a husky thread. "Why are you helping me?"

Sean hesitated for a moment before answering. "Because I'm gay, too."

"Oh," Elias said faintly. He looked at the man sitting across from him, one hand resting casually on his almost empty beer glass, the other on his knee, and he felt a sudden lurch in his chest, a warm glow of happiness. "But," he said cautiously, "that still doesn't explain why you should take in a kid from the streets. Why you should . . . trust me."

"No, it doesn't." Sean rolled the last jigger of his beer around in his glass. "I guess," he said, choosing his words with care, "it's just that . . . I don't believe in passing by on the other side of the road."

Elias frowned. Something about the choice of words sounded vaguely familiar. "Is that from a song or something?"

Sean grinned and swallowed the last of his beer. "You should finish off those french fries."

Elias did, and Sean pulled money from his wallet for the check. "It's okay. I'm happy to put you up tonight." He raised an eyebrow. "On the couch. Just so you understand."

Chapter Five

We enjoin thee,
As thou art liegeman to us, that thou carry
This female bastard hence; and that thou bear it
To some remote and desert place quite out
Of our dominions; and that there thou leave it,
Without more mercy, to its own protection,
And favor of the climate. As by strange fortune
It came to us, I do in justice charge thee,—
On thy soul's peril, and thy body's torture,—
That thou commend it strangely to some place,
Where chance may nurse, or end it.

—WILLIAM SHAKESPEARE, *THE WINTER'S TALE*

After storming from the West Rose Room and retreating to her own private rooms, the Countess had to struggle for a good quarter hour before managing to slow her breathing and school her features to her customary expression of calmness. Her loss of control shocked and rankled her, as much as her spell's failure. An unaccustomed fear added a chill to her racing thoughts as she paced the length of her chamber, wondering furiously what to do next.

She had underestimated the girl, badly, she realized, clenching her hands into fists at the thought. The Countess appreciated the value of timing, and she found it utterly galling to realize she had moved too quickly and been careless enough to show her cards prematurely. She despised mistakes, particularly her own—but this one, she hoped, would not be fatal. Further pondering offered one crumb of consolation: at least the Earl had not been there to witness her discomfiture.

If only, she thought in vexation for what seemed the hundredth time, the Earl had not been so insistent upon seeing the girl. For years he had been gratifyingly pliable, leaving almost all decisions to his wife. But he had suddenly taken it into his head that the time had come to put his affairs in order, including settling a marriage portion upon his daughter. The Countess had never dreamed that he would react to her long awaited and desired pregnancy in such a way. She had resisted him as much as she had dared, hoping it to be only a passing whim. But the Earl proved unexpectedly stubborn, and so she was forced to arrange to have Eliza brought back to her childhood home. The Countess hoped to use the opportunity to rid herself of the girl once and for all.

And now her first attempt had failed.

The child inside her lurched, and the Countess placed a calming hand over her belly, resolving silently not to make such a blunder again. Until she could be entirely sure of the Earl, she decided, her lips thinning, she would have to recover and repair the damage as best she could.

A knock at the Countess's door interrupted her thoughts. "Enter," she called absently, and a footman came in.

"Begging your pardon, my lady," he said, bowing, and gesturing apologetically with a serge-wrapped bundle, "but you were wanting to see the young lady's baggage before it was brought up to her?"

"Yes. Put it down on the floor over there. Thank you, Willoughby." She walked over to it as he left and looked down at it thoughtfully, the first tendrils of a new scheme beginning to coalesce in her mind.

The Countess suspected that even though the spell had failed, the girl wouldn't remember much of what had happened. And, she reflected, if she could win and hold the brat's trust just long enough—there might still be a chance to turn father against daughter irrevocably. She reached for a bell rope and rang for the maid.

For quite some time after the Countess left, Eliza remained kneeling in the bathtub, staring at the poppy petals bobbing on the water's surface. At first, she felt giddy and disoriented, as if awakening after several days of delirious fever, but slowly, the sensation of vertigo eased. In bewilderment, she looked around the room, wondering how she had come to be in this luxurious apartment. She remembered following the Countess into the Kellbrooke Hall stillroom. And then, suddenly, she was here, in the bath, and the Countess stood a few feet away, saying—Eliza frowned, trying to remember. The words hovered just out of reach of her memory, like a bubble skittering away from her touch on the surface of a brook. The Countess had been angry, though—decidedly so. That Eliza did remember, and she felt cold at the thought. She shivered violently. The bathwater was cooling down. She reached for a towel on the marquetry table beside the tub, wrapped it around herself hastily, and stepped carefully out of the tub.

One of the maids had left a dressing gown draped over a chair to warm by the fire. After drying herself, Eliza pulled it on and sat down to stare into the flames and wonder: what could she have said or done to offend her mother-in-law so?

As the blaze in the fireplace in the West Rose Room began dying down into softly glowing embers, the sound of the door behind her opening made her turn her head and then stand to face the door. Two maids came in, one carrying several linen-wrapped bundles, and another a portable dressing case; they put their burdens down on a small table set between two of the windows and bobbed their curtseys.

"May we fetch you aught else, my lady?" the first one said. "A bottle of rose lotion, perhaps?"

"Or do you desire some orange water, my lady?" asked the second.

Eliza barely restrained herself from curtseying in response. "Nay, indeed, thank you," she replied, turning faintly pink and feeling rather overwhelmed. "That is—if I might ask—where is my gown, please?"

"I have it here," the first maid replied. She unpinned and unwrapped the folds of linen from one of the bundles and shook out the folds of a gown dyed in bright shades of blue.

"But I mean my own dress. I do not see it here. Was it taken away, then?"

The two maids exchanged glances. "The Countess bade us do so," one replied uncertainly.

Eliza opened her mouth to protest and then checked herself, reflecting that her gown had been travel-stained, and that the Countess must have seen that and sent it to a laundress. Now that she had bathed, the idea of changing seemed quite agreeable. "But I have another gown," Eliza said. "It is in my bundle that I brought with me in the carriage." She looked around uncertainly. "Mrs. Warren directed it should be brought into the house, and yet I do not see it. What might have happened to it?"

The maids knew, and exchanged another look. They had seen the Countess rummage through Eliza's possessions with an expression of contempt and then order the entire bundle consigned to the fire. Neither servant, however, particularly wished to admit this awkward fact to the Earl's daughter. " 'Tis no matter, my lady," the second maid said smoothly. "We have here at hand everything my lady might need—a chemise with Flanders lace and a striped underskirt. And look, here is a stomacher, with the loveliest echelle ribbons."

"We have brought several pairs of shoes of different measures, so surely one will fit," added the other eagerly.

"They are all exquisite," Eliza replied with polite stubbornness, "but I do assure you, I would most prefer my own clothes."

"Of course, my lady," the second maid said, driven to the last ditch by necessity, "but the Countess has sent you this gown as a gift, and most *particularly* desires you to wear it."

"Oh," Eliza said blankly. "I see."

"She would understand, of course, if you refuse," the second maid added, managing to convey within her reassurance a note of doubt.

"Undoubtedly she would," agreed the first after a moment's hesitation, and her nod made the ribbons on her cap rustle.

"I would not wish to offend," Eliza said, her certainty ebbing away. She remembered the Countess's angry tone the last time she had seen her and wished again, vainly, that she could remember what the quarrel had been about. Yet if the Countess was sending such a fine gown now, she reflected, surely it meant that she regretted their disagreement as well, and wished to give her a peace offering. She did not wish to be seen as ill bred and churlish for refusing such a gesture of reconciliation.

"Very well, then. I shall put it on. Although," she added doubtfully, "I believe I shall need some help. Faith, I am not accustomed to such fastenings."

Accordingly, after Eliza had removed the dressing gown, the maids busied themselves around her, helping her draw the chemise over her head and fasten the gathers of the striped, quilted underskirt around her waist. One helped her put on the stomacher and laced the ties up the side as the other held the outer gown ready for Eliza to slip her arms through. "Pray, my lady, permit me. Now, pluck the sleeves of the chemise through—there, below the engagement ruffles. You see? A bit of frill from the chemise sleeve peeps out below the lace."

"Lovely!" exclaimed the other maid. "Here is a ribbon for the waist to match." They wrapped the outer gown over the edges of the stomacher, drew the edges together at the waist with the ribbon, and carefully folded and tied back the edges of the overskirt to show the brocaded lining. One of the maids kneaded the sweet bags sewn into the skirt split's edging with her fingers, perfuming the air with the cloying fragrance of jasmine.

"It is so heavy!" Eliza gasped and glanced behind herself as she pivoted. "Why—this gown has a train."

"Aye," said the first maid, smiling. " 'Tis the very latest mode."

"The cut of the corsage is wide," the other maid observed under her breath to her companion, "and the stomacher may be rather short."

"Why then, simply pull it down. We may adjust the lacing to suit."

"But then might the décolletage be a trifle . . ." Her words trailed off doubtfully as she frowned.

Eliza glanced down to where her locket rested upon bare skin and crossed her hands over it, exclaiming, "Oh! Surely I must have a whisk, or a pinner. I cannot be seen like this!"

Just then, a rap sounded against the door and the Countess walked in, a set smile on her lips. "Well then!" she said with brisk cheer. "What do you think of— Ah, I see you have put it on already."

"Madam, I give you my humblest thanks," Eliza said, curtseying. "It is far more grand than any gown I have ever been given. Your kindness—"

"Not at all, not at all, my dear," the Countess replied. One swift, searching look at Eliza's face convinced her that her hope had been correct: the girl remembered little, if anything. Relief made the Countess's smile grow even wider. "I own I felt uncertain about the color, but I must congratulate myself: that sapphire suits you admirably. Will you not turn around so I may see the whole?"

Obediently, Eliza did so. "It is truly lovely, madam," she ventured shyly as she faced the Countess again, "but . . . do you not think the neck should be more . . . more modest?" Her hand strayed up to cover her locket again.

"La, do you wish to let all the world think you the veriest bashful country miss?" the Countess replied with a laugh. "Nay, blush not, child. You must wear all your gowns like this—and most particularly when you meet your suitors."

"My suitors?" Eliza echoed, a little hollowly.

"Oh, indeed, my dear. Your father made shift bring you home, after all, because the gentlemen must see what it is they are considering buying, must they not?" Despite her resolve to speak lightly so the girl would suspect nothing, a tinge of venom crept into the Countess's voice. She could not help it. The mere thought that any part of the Earl's estate might be diverted to the girl's marriage portion rather than settled on her own babe made her throat tighten with anger. But she quickly spied the look of faltering dismay spring up in Eliza's eyes, and, cursing her own weakness, she hastened to inject some semblance of warmth back into her voice. "Why, see how the dress displays your charms! Lud, we shall have every lord in the land vying for your hand."

She gestured to one of the maids to open the dressing case and drew Eliza over to a chair. "And now let us see what we can do with a bit of ceruse. And perhaps a patch or two."

Eliza's eyes widened as the maid pulled out stoppered bottles of Venetian glass, pomatum and cream pots, colored crayons and rouge rags. She leaned forward with a quick intake of breath, a troubled line appearing between her eyebrows. "Are you . . . do you mean to *paint* me?"

The Countess gave her a sharp look. "If you wish to take your rightful place among the ladies who appear at Court," she replied, still smiling but with a warning edge to her words, "naturally you must paint."

"But—"

"It is *expected.*" She placed her hands firmly on Eliza's shoulders and held her breath at the tension she felt there. A heartbeat passed, and then another and another. No one moved. The maids stood at either side, watching surreptitiously out of the corners of their eyes.

Eliza felt the command in her mother-in-law's touch, and it puzzled her as much as it made her uneasy. She sensed an odd urgency underlying the Countess's friendly manner. Troubled, she ran a finger along the pleat of the gown's skirt.

The touch of the fabric made her think again of the Countess's generosity. She sighed and sat back again, and the Countess slowly released her own breath, too. "As you will, then, madam," Eliza said.

The Countess nodded, taking care to keep her face expressionless. "That jar, there, Fletcher. Let us begin with that."

The Countess worked quickly, dusting Eliza's face with white lead ceruse powder to bleach it to a ghostlike hue. Then, she rubbed the rouge rag into a pressed cake of cochineal-tinted paste and grimly spread it in thick, garish patches over the girl's cheeks. "The lip crayon now," she said as she stepped back to study the effect. The maid Fletcher proffered a crayon of rose pink, and the Countess shook her head and waved it away, pointing to another of a vibrant scarlet hue still nestled in the box. "No, that one."

Fletcher hesitated, glancing with a troubled expression at the swatches of bright rouge on Eliza's cheeks. "Madam . . . perhaps you might consider—"

But the Countess held up her hand and forestalled her with a freezing look. "And then you may go, Fletcher." After a pause, Fletcher placed the scarlet pencil in the Countess's hand, made her curtsey, and left the room, shutting the door quietly behind her.

The application of lip color was but the work of a moment. After affixing several gummed black taffeta patches to Eliza's temples and cheeks, the Countess declared herself satisfied. "And now," she said, wiping her fingers clean on a rag, "it is time for you to come pay your respects to Lord Grey."

"Now, madam?" Eliza said, startled.

"Why, naturally. Of course the Earl will wish to see you tonight."

Eliza sat silently, watching as the remaining maid placed the jars and bottles back into the dressing case and shut it again. She flinched at the snapping of the latches, like an animal starting at the slam of a cage door.

She fought down a panicked urge to flee. She had intended to be wearing her own clothes when she first met her father and asked that he compensate Nell and Tom for their sacrifices for her. But now . . . her cheeks suddenly felt hot, and she put her hands to them, wishing desperately for a mirror. The gritty touch of powder under her palms made her jerk them away again quickly. How, she wondered despairingly, could she have let this happen?

The maid brought over several pairs of shoes, and after several tries, Eliza found one that fit. "Come," said the Countess, holding her hand out imperatively, and Eliza helplessly rose to follow her, like a ghost compelled against its will.

The Right Honorable Lord James Grey, Earl of Exeter, sat nursing his port before a low fire in the marble withdrawing room next to the Great Parlor. Robert Owen and the steward, Thomas Griggs, were in attendance, with a sheaf of tenants' rolls and quarterly accounts spread out on the table before them. The Earl listened to them absently as they wrangled about the best methods for improving the drainage in the southwestern fields. On the whole, however, the port commanded a better portion of his attention.

Finally wearying of the discussion, he set his glass down on the table with a thump. The other two men looked at him in surprise, and the steward, who knew the exact price of the glass, winced slightly. "That will be all for tonight, Mr. Griggs," the Earl said. "Thank you."

As the steward gathered up his papers, a knock sounded on the chamber door. Opening the door, a footman stepped aside to let the steward pass through, and then entered and announced, "The Lady James Grey, the Lady Eliza."

"Stay, Mr. Owen," the Earl murmured, raising a hand as the other man bowed and stepped back as if to withdraw also. And then Lord Grey froze, his hand still in midair, as his eyes fell upon the slim figure in blue who entered the room a few steps behind his wife.

After a startled moment's silence, he heard a harsh, strained whisper say, "Anna?" His voice sounded strange and hollow to his own ears, echoing above the dull crashing thud of his own heartbeat. For an instant he thought he saw his first wife's ghost, with the locket he had given her around her neck, as pale as death—but no. He ran a shaking hand over his eyes, looked again, and saw that it was not. She had the same heavily lidded green eyes, the same curve of the mouth he remembered. But her cheeks and lips burned with red, a sign of blood, of life, and he knew *that* to be only mockery. His Anna was long dead, dead and buried and turned to dust these many years.

He felt an unreasoning surge of anger, and then remembered and drew in an unsteady breath. This was his daughter. He opened his mouth to speak, but his throat caught. He cleared it noisily and tried again. "Come closer, child."

Eliza came closer, stepping gingerly, as if picking a path over ice. A strange current of danger thrilled in the air about her. She did not see Robert Owen's eyes widen at her appearance, or his startled and accusing look at the Countess. Behind Eliza, the Countess remained where she was, her hands folded and her eyes hooded and silent.

Instead, Eliza had eyes only for the stooped figure in the chair before her. *Father,* she wanted to whisper, but for her, too, words caught in the throat. This gray and shrunken man, with the deep lines furrowing his brow and the palsied tremor shaking the lace of his sleeves, was not the tall and vibrant father she remembered. Her knees trembled, making her remember her curtsey. "Sir," she managed to say as she rose.

The Earl hesitated. "Er . . . you have had an easy journey?"

"Yes, sir. Mrs. Warren and Mr. Owen did everything they could for my comfort. And my mother-in-law has been most kind in welcoming me." She longed to say something more to him, but the distant formality in his manner checked her. It hurt her, for she remembered how she had kissed him and clung to him when she had left Kellbrooke Hall ten years before. For the first time, the thought struck her that the Earl had cheated himself as much as his children by sending them from home for so long. Perhaps he would not have aged so if he had kept his family around him.

"Ah," the Earl said vaguely, and his eyes met his wife's. Her gaze prodded him in a way he did not understand, and he said, "So what do you think of having a new half sister or brother, hey? Perhaps I shall have an heir at last."

Eliza would remember that moment long afterward, would spend many long nights lying awake trying to understand it. The strange half-apprehended tension coiling through the room heightened her senses, giving her knowledge, even as she drew breath to speak, that what she was about to say would be fatal. And yet, try as she might, she could not ever imagine stopping herself from saying what she said next, even for the sake of her soul's own salvation. Sometimes she wondered whether black magic had ensnared her, like the magic that had cursed Cassandra of Troy. Yet each time she rejected the thought, for she had only spoken the truth.

"An heir, my lord? But you have an heir. What of James? What of Henry, Edward, Stephen, and all the rest? You have as many heirs as any man might need."

Even as Robert Owen's jaw dropped open, even as he stepped back to be out of the Earl's sight and to give Eliza a frantic warning hiss, he knew with sinking certainty that all was lost.

The only sign of satisfaction the Countess allowed herself was a slight lifting of the chin, a quiver of one corner of the mouth indicating a smile sternly repressed. She remained silent.

"What?" said the Earl slowly.

"What of my brothers, my lord?"

The Earl's breath came in harsh, rasping sounds, and a vein in his temple throbbed. "James," he said, curtly. "Henry, Edward, Stephen, and all the rest. They are"—he swallowed and spoke with a sneer— "your *brothers?*"

"How mean you, my lord?" Eliza asked in bewilderment. "You are their father. Their blood is my own, for I am their sister."

The Earl's hand made a convulsive movement, and the glass of port teetered as if hesitating, and then fell and crashed to the floor. Spilled port spattered the Earl's stocking, soaking in like blood. "Those traitorous curs," he growled, his words rising to a roar as he stood, "those damned whelps?"

"Traitorous, sir?" Eliza gasped. "Who dares name them traitors?"

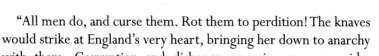

"All men do, and curse them. Rot them to perdition! The knaves would strike at England's very heart, bringing her down to anarchy with them. Corruption and dishonor, enemies on every side, demons thirsting for blood—but not me or my house, by God! We remain loyal to the Crown!" He broke off his rant and swayed on his feet for a moment, shutting his eyes tightly as if in pain.

Robert Owen, on his knees picking up the pieces of broken glass, entreated Eliza with his eyes, shaking his head desperately. She hesitated and then went on stubbornly, "I do not believe it! What evidence was there against them, sir? What proof?"

"Proof? Hah! Thou fool," the Earl sneered, opening his eyes again. "None was needed. Their guilt was black for all to see. It stank to the very heavens!"

"You refused to defend them when there was no proof?" Eliza exclaimed, horrified. "Abandoned your own sons?"

"Not my sons; I have disowned them."

Eliza's face went white. "And you accuse *them* of dishonor?"

"Eh? What?"

"Am *I* not part of your house, sir? As their sister, I entreat you, will you not reconsider and intercede for them?"

"If you are their sister," he snarled, "you are no daughter of mine!"

"Sir!" Eliza fell back a step, fear and alarm struggling in her face. "Please calm yourself, my lord!"

The Earl shook off Robert Owen's tentative hand at his wrist and glared at the girl. Through the veil of his rising blood-rage, and his astonishment that he could have thought her anything like Anna, she seemed to shrink, to twist, to coarsen. "Thou pert jade! Thou baggage, thou strumpet, thou painted whore! Thy brothers, sayest thou? If thou claims kinship with that filth *thou art no daughter of mine!*" But even as he saw her now for what she really was, he still saw Anna's eyes staring up at him, and the stricken expression in them drove him over the edge of madness. He raised a shaking fist and slammed it against her cheek, longing only to splinter that travesty, that horrible, twisted mask.

The blow drove Eliza to the floor, and horrified, Robert Owen stepped in between them and knelt over her. "My lord, no! Have pity!"

"Dare you defend her, sirrah? Do you align yourself with her, too? Have you grown so weary in my service?"

"I . . . I . . ." Robert Owen licked his lips, his eyes darting around the room. "I am your faithful servant, lord—but—I beg you—" His voice broke as Eliza stirred, raising her head groggily to stare up at the Earl in amazed disbelief. "There is no need to hurt her. She is but a child!"

"She is a pestilent harlot." The Earl reached a trembling hand behind himself for the back of his chair and all but fell back into the seat. "If she does not wish to be hurt, let her leave my sight forever. I charge you with it, Owen: see to it that she is expelled from the Hall."

His eyes met hers with fathomless coldness. "I care not if she lives or dies as long as she remains out of my sight, for I renounce all ties with her. I only pray that when she does die, she shall be consigned by Almighty God to burn in hellfire forever." He turned his head aside. "Go."

They all remained frozen in place for a moment, and then Robert Owen, sick with remorse and fear, turned to Eliza. "Come," he whispered, putting a hand under her elbow. "Up." Trembling all over, she seized his arm with a grip so tight that he winced. Together they rose, and he steadied her as she swayed. She buried her head in his shoulder as they turned toward the door. The Countess stepped quietly aside as they passed and then followed them out of the room.

"Child," Robert Owen murmured into Eliza's hair as they came out to the Great Parlor. "Child, hush. Hush, now. This will not aid you at all." She shook all over so violently with shock that for a moment he wondered whether he could hold her up if she fainted. She raised her face to his and saw the Countess over his shoulder.

"Madam," Eliza whispered. "Madam." Her knees buckled, and he shifted his grip to put an arm around her waist to support her. "Madam," she said again, holding out her hand imploringly to the other woman. "Will you not speak to him? Will you not defend me? I know he will listen to you. Oh, I pray you, have mercy!"

Robert Owen watched, fighting against his own urge to bolt as the Countess walked toward them. She came to a stop and slowly smiled—and then, as quickly as an adder striking, she seized the locket around Eliza's neck and tore it from her throat. Eliza cried out, and her hands flew to the welt left behind on her neck from the broken ribbon. Wide-eyed, she stared as the Countess looked down at the golden piece in her palm and then deliberately closed her fingers over it.

Her cold gaze turned to Robert Owen. "See that you do as the Earl bids you and oust her from the Hall immediately." Without another word, she turned her back on them both and strode quickly from the Great Parlor.

"No," Eliza moaned after the Countess had gone. "Not my mother's—no. She could not be so cruel." She swayed again, and he led her to one of the straight-back gilt chairs against the wall and helped her sit. Tendrils of her hair had fallen in her eyes and he brushed them away. Underneath, wide tracks streaked her face, where her tears had washed away powder and rouge. Still shivering, she wrapped her arms tightly around herself in numb misery.

"She could," he said. "She is."

"Why?" Eliza whispered.

"I am so sorry," he muttered. "If only I had—but I am a fool. Of course I should have known she would chouse you with such a scurvy trick as this, given the opportunity."

"What?"

"The paint." Angrily, he ran his thumb across her cheek and showed her the smudge on his skin. "You couldn't have known how the Earl felt about it."

"She told me—she told me I should wear it. That it was expected!"

"It might not have mattered, if you hadn't said aught about his sons. Why didn't you heed my warning?" And yet she could not be blamed, he knew. He should have explained more clearly when he had the chance, but he had been too afraid. His fist clenched and he thumped it against his thigh. "God forgive me for being such a fool!"

"But wherefore does she hate me so?" Eliza said in a small voice.

"Because——" He gestured helplessly. "Because she is like a cuckoo, pushing another bird's eggs out of the nest. She is greedy, and wants all that is his for herself."

"What has happened to my brothers? Why did my father——"

He gestured her to silence and leaned forward to speak in a low voice in her ear. "She accused them all of being part of the Popish plot. Do you remember, the Catholic conspirators who were discovered trying to kill King Charles?"

"*She* made the accusation?"

"Aye, my lady. Eight years ago."

"But," she said in bewilderment, "that was a Catholic plot to kill a Protestant king! And——" She broke off and did some calculations. "Why, eight years ago Benjamin would have been but nine years old! A traitor at nine years of age? How could my father have been so mad as to believe such a tale?"

"I can only guess what arts from the Devil she employed to convince him," Robert Owen said bitterly. "But yes, she made him believe they all converted to Rome and joined in the plot to kill the King."

"Eight years ago," she said, her eyes still glazed with shock. "That was just when the payments stopped coming for my foster parents. And he cast my brothers off? Just as he has disinherited me." She looked up at him again. "Were they imprisoned?"

He hesitated. "They disappeared, my lady."

"Where did they go? Surely you know where they went. Do you not?"

"You must leave here at once," he said, desperate to turn her attention. "It is not safe for you. If the Countess should discover you have lingered——"

"What could be worse than what she has already done to me?"

"Believe me, child," he answered grimly, "you do not wish to know."

She stared at him for a long moment. "She . . . she *made* them disappear? What did she do to them?" She gripped his hand until it hurt. "Tell me!"

"There is nothing to tell!" He checked himself and, lowering his voice, continued with forced calm. "I went out riding with two of your brothers one morning. At one point, they rode ahead of me, out of sight beyond a stand of trees. When I came around the bend in a road, all I saw was two riderless horses in a large, open field. Your brothers were nowhere in sight."

"But you must have searched for them!"

"Of course I did! But they were nowhere to be found. When I rode back to report their disappearance and rouse help, the household was in an uproar because the Countess had just leveled her accusations. All the Earl's sons were gone, and no one has ever seen them since that day."

She searched his face, trying to discover there some key to the mystery. "But . . . you do not really believe her, that they were traitors who fled. Do you?"

He hesitated, and then shook his head. "No. No, I do not."

"But surely you have some idea of what happened to them!" she exclaimed.

He opened his mouth, longing to tell her the rest. The horses had been terrified, had bolted from him, sweating, their eyes rolling; it had taken him the better part of an hour to subdue and catch them again. The field was so large, so empty and bare that there was simply nowhere the boys could have hidden themselves from his sight. It was uncanny, as if they had vanished into thin air. For a month before that morning, the Countess had barricaded herself for hours in the stillroom each morning. When he had ridden back to the Hall to raise the household for the search, she had already declared that all the brothers had fled. He could not understand how she could have known such a thing before he had even had a chance to report two of them missing.

The pieces did not add up to anything that made any sense. He almost managed to convince himself he had no choice but to believe the Countess's story. He had tried to mourn the boys as lost, to forget them and move on. Yet now, confronted with Eliza's searching eyes, he felt again the weight of the dreadful, lurking suspicions he had secretly carried within his heart for eight long years. But all the terror that had first pierced him on that fatal morning rose up again to choke off the words. "I cannot say what I truly believe, my lady," he whispered finally, closing his eyes. "I . . . I dare not."

"You must!"

"No!" Suddenly furious, he wrenched his hand from her icy grip and seized her shoulders. "You must think no more about them! Go back to your foster mother, where you will be safe!"

"And so you will obey the Earl and cast me out? You will obey *her?*"

"I can do nothing else," he said, his voice cracking. "I . . . I have two sons, my lady. I must think of them."

"Say you so? And yet you will not even speak to my father of the duty he owes me?" Her mouth shook. She could see the conflict struggling in his face, and so she pressed him again. "He called me a whore and a bastard, but you know it is a lie, don't you? Just as you know they lied about my brothers! How can you help expel me, even knowing I am my father's rightful daughter?"

He lowered his eyes in shame, and tears spilled down Eliza's cheeks again. "Oh, Mr. Owen. You said you wished me well with all your heart. You said you wanted naught but to serve me."

"I swear to you before God, my lady, that I can serve you best by convincing you to leave this accursed place behind you forever." He fumbled at his belt. "Here—wait. I have money."

She drew away from him then, her mouth frozen with contempt.

"Don't be a fool," he said sharply. "Take it to your foster mother."

He thought she would still refuse, but after a moment, she held out her hand, and he placed the pouch of coins within it and wrapped her cold fingers around it firmly. "Come." As he helped her tenderly to her feet and led the way to the marble staircase leading to the dark doorway outside, he thought that he had never done so much in his life as this single night's work to merit damnation on the last day of judgment.

Chapter Six

---

*I earn that I eat, get that I wear, owe no man hate,
envy no man's happiness, glad of other men's good,
content with my harm.*

—WILLIAM SHAKESPEARE, *AS YOU LIKE IT*

Light filtering through shifting leaves onto Elias's face woke him the next morning. He lifted his head from his pillow on the couch and raised himself on one elbow to look around, blinking sleepily, trying to remember where he was. The apartment's main-room window overlooked a quiet courtyard in the back. Opposite the couch and window was the kitchen, marked off as a separate area by a maple table. To Elias's left were the bedroom and bathroom. A shower was running behind the closed bathroom door; the water turned off and he heard a low, bouncy whistle, and memory came flooding back.

Last night, after ushering Elias into the apartment, Sean had played the gracious host, showing him the small bathroom and providing sheets and towels before disappearing quietly into the bedroom. The couch proved surprisingly comfortable, but Elias had not slept well. He lay awake for a long time, wondering if Sean really had in fact expected nothing sexual when he brought Elias home. Elias waited, muscles tense. The light under the bedroom door to his left went out, and he listened, straining to hear sounds in the next room above his own light breathing. When an hour had passed and no figure slipped out of the bedroom to join him on the couch, he finally closed his eyes and drifted off to sleep, unsure whether he was glad or sorry.

Now, as Elias reached for his jeans and slipped them on under the blanket, the bathroom door opened, and Sean came out in a cloud of steam, with a towel around his waist. He walked past the weight machine standing in the corner (evidently, he used it often), drying his hair briskly with another towel. Stray drops sprang everywhere, catching the sunlight as they trickled over his shoulders and disappeared into the down over his pectorals. One drop eluded the corner of the towel and slithered even farther. It left a glistening track as it nudged its way down through the dark brown hair curling around his navel, disappearing into the towel around his waist. . . .

"There's plenty of hot water," said Sean pleasantly. "Do you want a shower?"

Startled, Elias met his gaze, and when he read the wry amusement there, he realized he'd been staring. Elias looked away quickly, heat rising in his cheeks. "I'd . . . I'd like that. Thanks." Seizing the pile of towels, he retreated to the bathroom.

The hot water pulsing over his face and shoulders felt wonderful. Elias scrubbed hard, soaping and rinsing himself again and again to rid himself of every last trace of two weeks' worth of grime and stink from the warehouse and the streets. Then he heard the bathroom door click open and he froze, staring at the edge of the shower curtain like a startled animal.

"I was just going to start some laundry," Sean's voice said, reverberating hollowly across the tiles. "Would you like me to toss in your jeans and jacket, too? I have some clothes here I think would fit you."

After a moment, Elias found his voice and answered, trying to sound casually relaxed. "That would be great. Thanks." He heard

Sean moving around, saw a shadow on the curtain, and held his breath. Then, as the shadow moved away again, he thought of something else. "Oh, and you can . . . uh, just throw out the muscle shirt." He wasn't sure, but he thought he heard a chuckle before the door shut again.

Eventually, he reluctantly turned off the water and pushed the shower curtain aside with a rattle of rings. A pair of chinos and a blue polo shirt lay neatly folded beside the towels; underneath the pants he found a pair of underwear. He put the clothes on. The chinos fit a bit loosely around the waist, but wouldn't be too bad if he put on his belt, he decided. The shirt seemed just right.

The aroma of coffee wrapped around him warmly as he stepped out of the bathroom, making his mouth water. He went over to get his belt, draped across the back of the couch, and put it on. Several instrument cases lay crowded together in the corner. The stereo played Irish fiddle music, something bright and lively, turned down low. Curious, Elias tilted his head sideways like a parakeet, scanning the titles on the neat row of cassettes: Chieftains, Planxty, Silly Wizard, Alaisdar Fraser, Bothy Band, Horselips, The Dubliners, Battlefield Band . . . He picked up a cassette over to one side. The cover read "Clannad" and "Crann Ull." *Yeesh. Which is the album name and which is the band name?*

Sean glanced up from setting the table. "Sorry, I don't have any opera. Or Judy Garland."

Judy Garland? Rather alarmed, as if he had been caught red-handed shoplifting, Elias hastily put the cassette back in the row. "I don't particularly like Judy Garland," he blurted out. He felt as if he had missed some kind of joke. *Are gay men supposed to like her or something?*

The corners of Sean's lips twitched. "Neither do I. Well. Looks like I guessed about right on the clothes," he added, looking Elias over appraisingly. *Maybe even appreciatively?* Elias wondered, and hoped, suddenly, that Sean liked what he saw.

"They fit great. Thanks."

"It figures. I haven't been able to get into those pants for about three years."

Elias resisted the urge to observe that the jeans Sean wore suited him just fine.

"I've got coffee going." Sean went over to the cupboard and took out a couple of plates.

"Yeah, I can sure smell it."

"Cream or sugar?"

"Both. Please."

"Syrup okay for your waffles?"

"Yeah . . . but I don't want you to go to any trouble or anything."

"No trouble. They're frozen, out of a box."

They sat together at the table and passed the margarine and the orange juice pitcher back and forth. Sean spread peanut butter on his waffles.

Elias took his first bite and decided it had been too long since he'd had waffles for breakfast. What did gay men usually keep in their refrigerators, anyway? At least Sean hadn't served him quiche for breakfast. "So," he said, reaching for his orange juice. "What do you do for a living?"

Sean indicated the desk in the corner with a tip of his head. "I'm a writer."

"No kidding? What sort of stuff do you write?"

"I'm a freelance journalist."

Elias looked around the apartment with new respect. Sean's home was by no means lavish. Certainly the furnishings didn't resemble a photo spread out of *Architectural Digest*, although the room looked well appointed and comfortable. The stereo didn't look cheap, and a couple of limited edition prints hung on the wall. "I thought it was pretty tough to make it that way."

"It can be. It's more difficult if you're doing fiction."

"You seem to be doing okay."

"Well . . ." Sean's mouth quirked. "I'll admit I'm not doing it entirely on my own. My great granddaddy was a railroad robber baron, and my cousins and I got a trust set up for us. It doesn't mean I live in the lap of luxury, but it does keep me in beer and skittles." He got up and went over to the coffeemaker to retrieve the pot. "Oh, and speaking of family by the way, I gave Rick a call this morning."

"Uh . . . Rick?"

"Yeah, my cousin, the one who manages the photo shop. It's in Midtown, on Fifth Avenue. He's still looking for somebody." Sean filled both cups. "So I told him he might be getting a call from you later today. That is, if you want to follow up on the lead, of course?" He cocked his head, a mild challenge in the lift of his eyebrow.

The idea of landing a job, of being able to actually get off the streets, made Elias almost dizzy with relief. He raised his chin and met Sean's look squarely, aware he was being tested. "Can I call him now?"

Smiling, Sean looked over at the clock. "Mmm. Almost ten-thirty. He was a little grumpy when I called earlier, but by now he's undoubtedly had his first couple cups of coffee, so you should be safe. Yeah, go ahead. The number is on the pad by the phone."

Elias got up and dialed. The line rang twice, and then a voice answered curtly, "Van Hoosen Photography."

Elias took a deep breath. "May I speak with Rick, please?" he said firmly.

"Speaking."

"My name is Elias Latham, and I'm calling to ask about the job I heard about from your cousin Sean?"

"Yeah. Counter job, entry level. Got any retail experience?"

"Um . . . I worked for two summers in a department store in my hometown, in the electronics department. Selling mostly radios, TVs, calculators, that kind of thing. We didn't have too many cameras, but we sold some. I usually answered most of the questions about them, because I've been taking pictures since I was a kid. And I've had some photography courses at school, including darkroom experience."

"Yeah, well, this would involve working with commercial processing equipment, but that's okay, I'd train you in. And— 'Scuse me a minute."

The sound on the phone line became muffled for a moment, as if the speaker held the mouthpiece to his chest while speaking with someone else. Elias reached for his coffee cup and sipped at it to steady his nerves as he waited.

" . . . be with you in a second, ma'am. You still there?"

"Yes. Yes, I am," Elias replied, realizing after a confused moment he was being addressed. "Um . . . would you like me to send you a résumé or something?" He wondered fleetingly how he could work one up. Perhaps Sean might let him use his typewriter?

"What time can you get here?"

"Uh—excuse me?"

"Look, I need to hire somebody. I'm swamped with customers at the moment, but if you can get here in an hour, I'll give you an interview."

"An hour?" Elias glanced over at Sean and waggled his eyebrows. "Can I get there in an hour?" he whispered, covering the receiver.

Sean hesitated, and then nodded. "By subway," he whispered back.

"Yes, I can make it there by then."

"Fine. I'll be expecting you." Without any further ceremony, the line went dead.

Elias found he was grinning as he hung up the phone. He came and sat back down at the table. "If I can get there in an hour, I get an interview." His face abruptly fell in consternation. "Oh, god . . . all I have to wear are those jeans and that jacket. I don't even have a shirt!"

Sean picked up the plates and headed for the sink. "Just wear those clothes I gave you."

"Really? You'd let me?" Elias smiled, in gratitude and relief. "Thanks!"

"Sure. They'll do fine. And like I said, the pants don't even fit me anymore."

"Oh . . . what if he asks for my address? What should I tell him?"

Sean shrugged. "I can give you my phone number. You can say you've just gotten to the city, so you're crashing on my couch."

"I guess it's the truth, anyway." Abruptly, Elias remembered his manners and got up to help clear the table. As he put the orange juice back into the refrigerator, he glanced over at Sean, suddenly shy again. "Hey . . . uh, thanks. If I . . . if I really get the job, I won't ever make you sorry you recommended me."

Sean only smiled in reply. He had rolled his sleeves back to do the dishes, and Elias's attention was caught by the sight of his forearms. Strong, capable looking, with just the right amount of hair over the back of his hands. And those strong musician's fingers—Elias swallowed. His eyes met Sean's, and from the look there, he guessed that, again, Sean knew exactly what he was thinking.

"Here." Sean plucked a dish towel hanging from a cupboard doorknob and tossed it in Elias's direction. Elias was slow to catch it, and it smacked him in the face. "It's about a twenty-minute trip to Rick's shop, so we've got time to do the dishes. You can help dry. When we're done, I'll pull out the map to show you which subway to take."

Elias walked into Van Hoosen Photography an hour later. A chemical tang hung in the air. A man stood behind the camera counter, sipping a cup of coffee as he stocked a bin of film on the back wall. At the jangling of the bell hanging from the door, he turned around and saw Elias. "Yeah?" he said unsmilingly as he tucked the cup underneath the counter.

"I'm Elias Latham, and I have an appointment with Rick, the manager."

"Yeah, I'm Rick. Hi, Elias." Although a bit shorter than average, the manager had powerfully built shoulders and biceps. His intense blue eyes considered Elias appraisingly as he extended his hand across the counter. Elias came forward to shake it. The other man's grip felt firm and cool. He had a short beard and thinning, no-color hair gathered in a tail extending halfway down his back.

Rick leaned back to call over his shoulder through the open doorway behind him. "Hey, Tony, mind the counter."

"Yeah, just a second," responded a voice from the back.

Picking up his coffee cup again, Rick tilted his head toward the left. "This way." Elias followed him down the length of the counter and through a door at the back corner of the shop. Here, a narrow hallway led to a small office on the right, hung with black-and-white photographs and crowded with a desk, a table with two chairs, and a battered typewriter. Elias blinked and peered more closely at one of the photographs. Yes, it was a picture of Sean, grinning as he played his guitar for a crowd on a street corner, his hand lifted in a flourish over the strings. In the corner a small stereo system played a tape with the volume turned down low. Something by the band Yes.

"Sit down," Rick said, indicating one of the other chairs as he sat behind the desk. "You didn't bring a portfolio, I see."

"No," Elias said, with a stab of disappointment. Did that mean he didn't have a chance?

"Well, that's all right. This is an entry-level position, like I said. But I need someone with an artistic eye, who can talk with people who want help improving their pictures. Besides taking your turn in the back running the lab, you'd be selling cameras, film, accepting exposed film for processing, that sort of thing. We do a fair amount of custom work and some of our customers are pretty picky, but we run machine prints all day, every day. I've got a 5s and 8s printer and a Kreonite processor—do you know what any of that is?"

"No, I—"

"That's okay, you'll learn. That is, if you're interested."

"Sure, yeah—uh, do you do any actual photography? I mean, taking pictures?"

"Not the shop, but I do. Weekend weddings. Why?"

"Well . . ." Elias gave an embarrassed laugh. "Once, when I was working in that electronics department I told you about, a customer told me you can always tell a longtime professional photographer 'cause he'll always have one shoulder that's higher than the other, from toting all those heavy camera bags over the years."

Rick stared at him for a moment, expressionless, and then suddenly smiled for the first time. "Well, okay, so I guess you're ob-servant." He leaned back in his chair. "Tell me about how you started doing photography."

"My father gave me my first camera for Christmas when I was eight." He paused a moment, surprised by a small stab of pain at the memory. *Christ, my father bought me my first camera. He framed some of my pictures to hang them in the hallway. He used to sound so proud, point-ing them out to people who came over to visit:* My son took those. *Would he take them down now? Throw them away?* Elias cleared his throat, tried to recapture his train of thought. "It was a Honeywell Pentax, thirty-five millimeter. I must have used up about twenty rolls of film the first month, just playing with it."

Rick smiled again. "What did you photograph?"

"You name it, I took it. About a million shots of my family, the dog, the house. But you can only take so many pictures of your mother frying eggs or the dog sleeping, so after a while I switched to photographing stuff around town. I got interested in the effects of light on water and night photography. I played with different f-stops and shutter speeds, and weird camera angles. Within six months, I was begging for a telephoto lens. . . ."

As they continued talking about cameras, the portion of Elias's mind that was listening and evaluating himself was cautiously pleased. He was coming across okay, he thought. Intelligent, but not too cocky, eager to learn without being too ingratiating. Mr. Ideal Potential Employee. Hire this kid and put him to work. And then Rick asked a question that momentarily threw him into con-fusion.

"You're—what, about eighteen? High school grad?"

"That's right."

"Are you hoping for something part-time you can schedule col-lege courses around? I'm looking to hire full-time."

"I'm going to be—" Elias stopped himself. Of course he wasn't going to be starting the fall semester at Cornell. He'd been ac-cepted, but that was back when his parents were going to pay his tuition. Back before the path to his future ran into a brick wall.

Rick was still waiting. "That is . . ." Elias continued after a pause, "I'm looking for full-time work right now. I might look at starting night classes next term or something, at the university, maybe. But even then, I'd probably hope to be working full-time."

Maybe he could do that, he realized with a jolt as Rick nodded and moved on to the next question. Maybe he still could go to the university, putting himself through instead of having his parents pay. If he had a job, he could do it. Hell, maybe he could even call Cornell, explain that there'd been a change in his situation, and ask about financial aid. When he'd been kicked out, he'd been too stunned by the changes in his life to even think of doing that. Even if it was too late for him to start this fall, maybe something could be arranged so that he could go after saving up money for a year. Or perhaps Cornell could even put together a financial aid package that would allow him to start second semester.

He felt something shift inside himself at the thought, at the very idea that he might have the possibility of a decent future, something he might plan and work toward. *My god. I could have a real life.*

And landing this job is the first step, another part of his mind said firmly. Resolutely, he turned his full attention back to the interview.

They talked about the composition of some of the pictures hanging on the office wall, and more about the job duties and the hours required, and then Rick began wrapping up the interview. "So, do you have any questions for me, Elias?"

"Yes. Assuming I'm hired, would this job have any possibility of promotion eventually? If the company's pleased with my work, I mean?"

Rick scratched his beard. "Well now, theoretically if you learn everything about how the shop works, you eventually could be in line for the manager's position—but I guess you'd have to wait a long time." He gave a crooked smile. "I've been the manager for eleven years, and I don't have any plans to step aside for the up and coming."

"I see." A dead-end job, then, probably.

"And frankly, I'm afraid the salary isn't much over minimum wage." He raised an eyebrow at the change in Elias's expression. "You still interested?"

Elias hesitated. Not much above minimum wage. Could he live on that? *Better than earning nothing and living on the street, isn't it? If I can actually find a way to swing college, it wouldn't have to be forever. The important thing is, it's a start.*

He looked Rick in the eye. "Yes. I am."

After the interview he still felt keyed up and decided he wanted to sit and think for a while. Maybe that would help get rid of the jitters. Central Park was only a few blocks away. He jogged across Central Park South, past the statue of General Sherman, and crossed over to the path leading into the park. Here, under the trees, the light was green and peaceful. Pigeons foraged underfoot, skirmishing over crumbs from an abandoned croissant lying on the ground, barely hopping out of the way in time as mothers passed pushing strollers. A couple more minutes of walking brought him to the Pond. One of the benches was open, and he sank onto it gratefully.

For a while he just closed his eyes and sat, listening to his breathing and the distant cacophony of traffic sounds floating over the trees. His mind drifted back to the interview. It had gone well, he decided, mentally reviewing the questions and answers. Yes, it really had. How strange to realize, after those weeks of despair in the warehouse, that he really did have a skill that made him employable. If he hadn't talked to Sean, he might never have thought of it on his own.

Sean. It wasn't the interview, he suddenly realized, that had made him feel so edgy. It was Sean. Elias stretched his arms out along the back of the bench and opened his eyes again. A couple of swans floated serenely on the surface of the water a few feet away.

Elias had never been in a gay man's home before. Well, not knowingly, anyway. He had felt hypersensitive there, exposed, wary of anything suggesting any kind of sensuality. And yet it hadn't been scary, but . . . okay. Comfortable. He felt ashamed, almost absurd, having to face the bigotry underlying his surprise at how *normal* everything had seemed. What, no sequined dresses or feather boas bursting out of the closets? Sean worked for a living. He liked Irish music; he spread peanut butter on his waffles. And he was comfortable inside his own skin. Being gay wasn't the only thing about Sean that anybody ever had to know, the be-all and end-all, the only thing that defined him.

Even more than the bed for the night and the job lead, showing him that was the kindest gift Sean could have possibly given him.

He found a pay phone just inside the entrance of a deli down the block and called Sean. "He said he wanted the weekend to give us both a chance to think about it. But I think he's going to offer it to me."

"Really?" Sean sounded pleased.

"Yeah." Elias stuck a finger in his other ear to mute the sound of clattering dishes. "I got the feeling he made up his mind once he realized I knew what he meant by 'PhD's.' I guess he decided I was a good bet if I knew at least some of the weird jargon."

"PhD? What—Doctor of Philosophy? What's that got to do with photography?"

"No." Elias smiled. "It's what photographers call those new automatic cameras that've been coming out, the point-and-shoot type: 'Push here, Dummy.'"

Even through the tinny connection, Sean's laugh rang out richly.

"The question is," Elias went on, "if he offers it to me, should I take it?"

"Well, Rick's my cousin, so maybe I'm biased. But I think he'd be a good boss, as long as you always remember to keep the coffeepot full." Sean laughed again. "He does love a good argument. You'll probably learn more about Kant and Hegel and the causes of World War II than you ever thought you'd want to know. But he'll also teach you a lot about photography."

"The biggest problem might be the wage," Elias said slowly.

"Oh? Pretty low, huh? That's too bad."

"Yeah. I get the impression it won't be much above minimum. I'm not saying that taking a job with a starting wage is beneath me or anything," he added hastily. "But I started thinking that maybe I could take some night college classes eventually. I gotta be able to pay the rent, too."

"And groceries. Don't forget beer money."

"Yeah." Elias sighed. "Maybe a roommate. There are places that list people who're looking for roommates, aren't there?"

There was silence for a moment on the other end of the line. "Look," Sean said finally. "You don't have to make a decision on that right this minute. I've got an idea. Come on back to my apartment."

"Really? That'd be okay?" Elias felt light all over with relief and pleasure.

"Sure. And listen: I just got a call from a friend of mine who owns a time-share on a house on Fire Island. A couple of his friends who were going to be spending the weekend there just canceled, and so he invited me out instead. I think it'd be no problem for me to call him back and wangle an invitation for you, too. Would you like to go out to the Island for the weekend? It'll be pretty packed because of the Labor Day holiday, but it should be fun."

"Fire Island?"

"You've heard of it, haven't you?"

"Are you kidding? Of course I have." *Fire Island! My god—Father used to call it the Sodom and Gomorrah of the East Coast.* Elias took a deep breath and bounced up and down on his heels to nerve himself up to answer. "That'd be great. I'd love to come."

"I can introduce you to some people—who knows? You just might meet someone who's looking for a roommate."

Chapter Seven

For truth has such a face and such a mien
As to be lov'd needs only to be seen.

—JOHN DRYDEN, "THE HIND AND THE PANTHER"

Her face streaked with tears, Eliza stumbled down the broad marble steps of Kellbrooke Hall and out to the avenue. Just beyond the first gate lay a broad circle of crushed gravel for carriages to turn around; at the far end, the avenue resumed, leading away from the circle to the outer gates. Eliza began the long walk around the circle, her thin-soled shoes occasionally slipping on the shifting pebbles. Her tears made seeing her footing difficult, and she brushed them away, angry at her weakness, her breast throbbing with hurt and humiliation. Cold, watery light from the rising half-moon outlined with silver each blade of grass on the carefully tended lawn.

A breeze, perfumed with the scent from the flower gardens, made the skin on her arms prickle into gooseflesh. The only sound was the dreamy strumming of cricketsong. At the outer gate, she stopped and looked back. Kellbrooke Hall crouched in the moonlight, solid and indifferent, a faint silver gleam reflecting off the ball at the top of the cupola. A warm glow spilled from the windows, and she thought with sudden grief of her mother. Something inside of her wanted to wail to the heavens like a bewildered child, protesting that this was her mother's house, and her mother would never have allowed anyone to drive her away. But she remained silent, for the first Lady Grey was dead, and no one else would listen to her. The light shining from the front doorway cut off as Eliza watched; that was Robert Owen, closing the door. After a moment, Eliza resolutely turned her face away from her birthplace and continued down the avenue. She didn't look back.

She never saw Kellbrooke Hall again.

After almost a quarter hour, Eliza came to the juncture of the avenue with the common road, and she turned onto it. The stone fence by the side of the road made a dim line of white for her to follow in the moonlight. Except for Eliza the road remained deserted.

The night remained dry and warm at least, and the path was easy, but her dress weighed her limbs down heavily. Eventually she looped the train up over her arm. She walked at a steady pace, setting her feet mechanically one in front of the other, her mind numb of all thought, until she began stumbling from sheer exhaustion. Abruptly she stopped in her tracks and looked around, but could see neither cottage nor hamlet anywhere nearby. A small copse of trees grew to one side of the road. She had to rest, she realized wearily. She wondered whether she should try to walk farther and find a goodwife who might let her sleep on the floor of her cottage or even in a barn, for charity's sake. The thought of arriving on some farmer's doorstep long after sunset, dressed like a great lady and yet forced to beg for a night's shelter, made her shrink inwardly.

An inner instinct urged her to avoid other people, to hide herself like a wounded animal. After hesitating for another moment, Eliza turned off the road for the shelter of the trees. Her eyes took a few minutes to adjust to the greater gloom of the shadows here. She felt her way forward through the pathless undergrowth, keeping her hands in front of her face to brush low-lying branches away from her eyes as she went. Gradually, the brush plucking at her skirts thinned, and the growth underfoot changed to soft and springy moss. Overhead, stars shone through an opening in the trees, and she smelled the sweet, cool scent of bruised mint. She had come to the edge of a small woodland pool.

Her foot caught, painfully, on a stone, and she half fell to her knees. The hard knot inside her loosened again, and she wept for a time, leaning against a tree, her tears trickling slowly down her cheeks and soaking into the rough bark. When all her tears were finally done, she raised her head. "Lord, help me," she whispered. "Dearest Father, sweet Jesu, have pity upon me! Hold Thy daughter in the palm of Thy hand and watch over and protect her sleep."

The ground was a little higher on this side of the pond, and the moss quite dry. She raked an armful of leaves around herself, and then wearily lay down, tucking some underneath her head to cushion it from the tree roots. She lay quietly for a time, staring up at the stars. *Foxes have holes,* she thought to herself drowsily, remembering her scriptures, *and the birds of the air have nests, but the Son of man hath not where to lay his head.*

Oddly comforted, she cradled her head in the crook of her arm, and in a moment sank into a deep sleep. The breeze died away, leaving a gentle hush. Overhead, the stars wheeled slowly through the night, and no one came near to disturb her dreams.

Light filtering through shifting leaves onto Eliza's face woke her the next morning. She lifted her head from her pillow of leaves and raised herself on one elbow to look around, blinking sleepily, trying to remember where she was. Her gaze fell on the bright blue dress she still wore, dappled with patches of sunlight, and memory came flooding back.

Eliza pulled up her legs stiffly and rolled to her knees, twigs crunching underneath her. The dew had dampened her dress, and her ribs ached; she had been too tired even to loosen the strings on the stomacher before falling asleep. Brushing leaves from her hair, she staggered to her feet and painfully limped over to the pool. Tendrils of mist hovering over the surface shivered away as she dipped her hands into the water. Her touch broke the perfect stillness of the pool, making ripples eddy out from her hand in ever-widening circles. She drew a double handful to her mouth and drank, water drops trickling over her hands and soaking into the lace at her wrists. The cold made her gasp with pleasure, and greedily she drank some more. It tasted of moss, she thought to herself. Moss, and mist and secrets.

Finally satisfied, Eliza opened her hands to let the last of the water splash back into the pool. As the ripples stilled, the reflection that appeared on the water's surface jolted her with a dreadful shock, like the pain of an unexpected burn. With a smothered exclamation, she pushed her hair back and leaned forward to look more closely.

The face in the water leered up at her like a malevolent, decadent stranger. The lead ceruse made her skin not just pale but a dead white, the color of pallid grubs that hid from the sun under rotten logs. Her cheeks contrasted garishly, the rouge paste making her look as if she burned with a high fever, and the color only emphasized the red rims of her eyes. Her mouth, still smeared with scarlet, seemed to bleed like a wound, and the patches looked like nothing so much as flies clustering on the face of a corpse.

A painted whore, her father had called her. Eliza shuddered in revolted horror and shame, seeing now what he had seen and finally understanding how well Lady Grey had worked to ruin her. She wondered bitterly whether the Countess had mixed witchcraft with her paints, turning father against daughter with the aid of a magical glamour.

"It is a lie," Eliza whispered to the mocking mask in the pool. Angrily she thrust her hand into the water to shatter the reflection and jumped to her feet. "It is a lie! That is not me. I am no whore!"

The touch of the fabric of the dress her mother-in-law had given her suddenly seemed to burn her skin. She hastily stripped it all off: outergown, quilted underskirt, stomacher and chemise, shoes and stockings, and when she was naked, she jumped into the pool. The stinging cold made her yelp aloud and then laugh with a kind of giddy relief. She ducked her head underneath the surface and scrubbed her face vigorously with her hands. Then she rolled over and floated on her back. As she stared up at the blue arc of the sky above her, she felt as if something slimy clinging to her had melted away, dissolving into the quiet pool like a nightmare fleeing before the break of day.

Eliza swam for a long time, only climbing out reluctantly when her teeth began to chatter. A large rock stood at the pool's edge, warmed by the sun, and she sat there, running her fingers through her hair to comb out the tangles and spreading it out over her shoulders to dry in the warm air. When drips had ceased trickling down her waist and her bangs had begun to stir on her forehead from the breeze, she took the chemise and, gritting her teeth, tore the lace from the wrists. She drew it over her head and went back to the edge of the pool to look at herself again. There, she saw her own familiar face gazing back up at her, all traces of illusion banished. The sunlight caught glints of red in her hair, transforming them into threads of molten gold shining in a corona around her face. Eliza smiled in relief and went back to sit on the rock to think.

The growling of her stomach distracted her attention. She needed food and—she glanced at the dress heaped on the ground—new clothes. Where, she wondered, could she go, now that she had been driven from Kellbrooke Hall?

The answer to that, of course, became clear to Eliza immediately. *If, perchance,* Nell had told her, *matters do not fall as they should, I will always have a place by my hearth for thee, if thou should ever need it.* Nell's cottage was her home now, she understood with a thankful rush. She didn't need to be torn between two worlds anymore. Her father's world had cast her out, and she was truly Nell's daughter now.

Her mother-in-law had managed to cheat her of her true birthright. And yet it was better this way, Eliza told herself with fierce gladness. She had returned to Kellbrooke Hall not to assume the status of an earl's daughter but to win redress for her foster mother. But money wasn't what Nell wanted, Eliza realized, remembering the gnawing pain in Nell's eyes at their parting. Nell wanted a daughter, a child she could truly claim as her own. And after all, who had a greater claim to the love and duty Eliza owed a parent than Nell?

All that remained was for Eliza to go home and tell her so.

Eliza stopped at three farms before she found a woman approximately the same size as herself who had a dress that could be traded for the gown given to her by the Countess. Even then, persuading the farmwife to agree to the transaction took some time.

" 'Tis not filched, is it?" the woman said warily. She had set her butter churn aside at Eliza's appearance at her doorway and come out to look at the dress in the sunlight.

"No," Eliza replied. Under the circumstances Eliza could not blame her. Anyone lunatic enough to appear in a farmyard, barefoot and clad only in a fine lawn chemise, offering to exchange a rich gown slung over one arm for a plain one could not help but arouse suspicions. " 'Tis mine honestly. A gift, it was."

"And you want to rid yourself of it now?" The woman turned her attention from the gown to Eliza, puzzled. Something struck her as odd in the girl's expression. Whether it was sadness or weariness or something else, she couldn't quite tell, but it seemed strange in the eyes of one so young. Yet the woman couldn't quite bring herself to think the girl a thief. She must have powerful friends or relatives, or a rich patron if she could afford to all but give away something so valuable. But if so, what was she doing here, traveling alone and barefoot?

Eliza smoothed the line of one of the heavy sleeves, remembering the strange glint in her mother-in-law's eyes when Eliza had modeled the dress for her. "It . . . is not a gift I wish to keep," she said firmly.

That earned her another baffled look. Finally, the woman shrugged, wiped her work-roughened hands on her apron, and gingerly reached out to feel the texture of the brocaded outergown. "Why, 'tis much too fine for working use." She laughed raucously, revealing a gap in her teeth. "Fancy me slopping the pig wearing that! And I've naught but a few pence put by."

Eliza sighed. "I am wishful for only a simple gown in exchange, truly. And perhaps some food." She held the gown up by the shoulders and turned it so the woman could see the back. "I have a pair of shoes and stockings here, too, to go with it. If you cannot use the clothes themselves, could you not sell them? Or perhaps," she added, noting the young girl who had edged her way to her mother's elbow and was staring at the gown's rich blue like a moth drawn to the flame of a candle, "you could make the gown over for your daughter to use?"

The woman quickly glanced to one side and caught the look of naked longing in her daughter's eyes. "Aye," she said slowly, "perhaps." Not for a moment did she actually intend to let Susanna keep the dress; it would not do for *her* to wear while slopping pigs, either. But the woman had fond hopes of purchasing another cow before winter. A gown that aroused that kind of desire in Susanna might also be appealing to one or another of the more prosperous goodwives in the neighborhood—someone holding more coins in her purse than she had. And if this unknown girl was indeed simpleton enough to trade it away, why not profit from it?

Or perhaps, the farmwife thought, seized by a sudden flight of imagination, she was an honest girl who had been forced to become some rich man's mistress? Could she be now making her escape from her seducer and ridding herself of all her trappings of sin in order to hide from him? Well, if so, she would help her—not that it was really her business, after all. "Susanna, do you go to the chest in the front room and take out the gown of brown holland there." She eyed Eliza speculatively. "And what say you to some bread and a bit of mutton or so? I can give you cheese and a roasted egg to take along with you, too. Will that make the trade, then, if the brown holland fits?"

Eliza smiled in relief. "Aye, thank you. You are very good."

Susanna, brimming with hope, fetched the humble gown and was delighted when it proved to fit well enough. As Eliza shook out the gathers of the skirt and tugged at the sleeve seams to straighten them down the length of her arms, she felt comforted at the reassuring touch of the rough linen.

"You're sure, miss, you'll not be wishful to keep the shoes and stockings, too?" Susanna asked breathlessly.

Eliza glanced up at her and her lips twitched a little at the expression on Susanna's face, staring at the shoes. Since Eliza was accustomed to going barefoot all summer, the soles of her feet had hard calluses. Mud was easier to wash off bare feet than embroidered silk, anyway. "No. I do not want them," she said quietly. "Please take them away with the dress."

As Susanna bore away her booty in triumph, the farmwife brought out a trencher of bread and mutton. Eliza sat on a bench just outside the door of the cottage to eat it under the shade of an apple tree. As she chewed, she smiled at several children who had gathered around to stare, dirty fingers in their mouths, until their mother called to them sharply to go finish weeding the bean plants in the garden.

When Eliza had finished and brushed the last crumbs from her lap, she drew a dipper of water from the well to drink. The farmwife, who had been keeping a watchful eye on her as she finished her churning, now came out again to offer a napkin tied around the promised egg and hunk of cheese.

"The road at the end of this lane goes west to Wincanton, doesn't it?" Eliza asked.

"Aye," the woman said after due consideration. "West and a bit south. It's that muddy, but God willing, it will take you there."

Eliza tried to remember the names of some of the towns the carriage had passed on its journey to Kellbrooke Hall. "And is that the same road that passes Blackford and . . . and goes through Ilchester?"

"As to that, I don't know, mistress. You'll have to ask farther along the way."

"I see." Eliza swallowed her disappointment and picked up the napkin with the cheese and egg. "I will, then. Thank you, and fare you well." She set off down the lane to the road, leaving the farmwife behind her shaking her head at the strangeness of the whole business.

Returning home to Nell took Eliza a week.

She was reluctant to spend the money Robert Owen had given her, hoping to return as much of it as she could to Nell. She did use a few coins to buy bread and other food at farmhouses along the road. Carts passed her occasionally, headed for Wincanton or, farther west, to the great cheese market at Yeovil, but she simply stepped off the road to let them pass, wary of asking for rides from strangers. Inns stood at regular intervals on the road, beckoning her with the promise of warm meals cooked to order and a bed for the night, but she passed them all by, choosing instead to sleep under hedges and in barns, and once on the floor of the cottage of a friendly dairywoman. She earned her supper and breakfast the next morning there by spending several hours weeding in the garden.

The road had hills, never too steep, but the gradual rise and fall, rise and fall of the ground beneath her grew wearisome after hours of tramping every day. The third day of her journey brought rain and, with it, mud and floods. Eventually, the downpour grew so heavy and her way so difficult to see that she sought shelter in a byre. She spent the day huddled there, shivering, watching the rain drip from the roofline past the door as around her cows chewed their cuds and doves cooed in the eaves overhead.

A scrawny tabby cat came up to sniff delicately at her ankles in an inquisitive fashion and then settled down, purring, at her feet. She sat beside it in the straw and stroked its back for a long time, thinking. Now that she had decided upon her course, she felt increasingly eager to be back with Nell—back home, she corrected herself. Remembering what her father had said at their last meeting still gave her pain. But she was by nature a hopeful person, and as she brooded about it, she slowly came to understand that by disowning her, the Earl had in a way freed her, too. The constraints, the barriers she had always felt between herself and her friends in the village would be gone now. She might even be able to marry someone of her own choosing someday. Of course, she no longer had a dowry, but perhaps she might meet someone who would not expect that.

And yet, even as she tried to imagine what her life might be like now that her future was her own to shape, a troubling thought still gnawed in the back of her mind.

What could have possibly happened to her brothers?

Finally, on a cloudy afternoon an hour or two before sunset, she turned off the lane to the track leading to Nell's cottage. Her steps quickened eagerly as she rounded the copse of apple trees. The last time she had come around this curve, she reminded herself, the Earl's carriage had stood in the yard, waiting to take her away. There was no carriage there now, of course, only a few chickens scratching around in the dirt before the cottage. Eliza frowned, a small crease of worry appearing between her brows, wondering what they were still doing outside. At this point in the afternoon Nell ordinarily had them herded into the coop behind the cottage.

And then she saw the red rag tied to the door latch, swaying a little in the late afternoon breeze.

She gasped and began running to the cottage. "Mother Nell? Mother Nell!"

The cottage door opened just as she reached it. Old Mistress Pollard, a neighbor who lived in the next cottage down the lane, stood in the doorway, her mouth open in surprise. "Oddsfish, Eliza! Why are you here? Nell did say you were gone forever." She caught Eliza's arms as the girl tried to push past her. "Nay," she said quickly, "you mustn't go in there, child—"

"Where's Mother Nell?" Eliza said through her teeth, her heart hammering hard with fear.

"—unless you've already had the smallpox?"

Eliza stopped trying to pass and stared up at Mistress Pollard, the blood draining from her face. "What?"

"The smallpox. Eliza—"

"No. Oh, no!" Eliza slipped past Mistress Pollard before she could stop her. Nell's bed stood only a few steps within the cottage's entrance, and she fell to her knees beside it.

Red curtains had been hung from the parlor windows, and the lurid light made seeing difficult. A basin of water and a rag had been placed on the table beside the bed. The airless room smelled closed and sour. Every red object Nell owned had been placed around her bed where she could see it, to help her combat the fever. Her shorn head lay still upon the pillow, eyes closed, face ravaged by oozing pox.

Behind Eliza, Mistress Pollard hesitated, and then said it gently: "You're too late, child. She's dead."

Chapter Eight

Fairest Isle, all isles excelling
Seat of pleasures, and of loves;
Venus here will choose her dwelling,
And forsake her Cyprian groves.

——JOHN DRYDEN, *SONG OF VENUS*

The jeans and denim jacket were out of the dryer by the time Elias got back to the apartment. Sean loaned Elias a small duffel bag to take and more clothes to pack into it. He even had a spare bathing suit to offer—not, Elias was relieved to see, a Speedo, but a pair of innocuous blue drawstring trunks.

"And here's some cash for the weekend," Sean added.

"Look, I don't want to—"

"Of course you don't want to," Sean interrupted him firmly. "And of course, you're going to pay me back out of your first paycheck. Aren't you?"

Elias looked down at the bills in his hand. "Thanks," he said unsteadily and slipped them into his pocket. "I will. Pay you back, I mean." He smiled, pleased to be trusted and grateful that Sean had made that allowance for his pride.

They ate a couple of roast beef sandwiches and then left the apartment. Outside, the East Village basked in late summer splendor. Afternoon sunlight caught gold tinges at the edges of leaves, hinting at colder days to come. They started in the direction of First Avenue, passing walk-up apartments and the entrance to the Ukrainian baths. Men leaned impassively smoking cigarettes against iron railings lining stairs that led down to lower-floor apartments. One caught Sean's eye and waved a packet filled with white powder, but Sean simply shook his head with an affable "Sorry, not interested." A woman with a weather-beaten face went by on the other side of the street, pushing a baby carriage with three dogs in it.

At the corner store they went in to pick up supplies for the weekend. "You can get groceries on the Island, but they're expensive because they have to send everything over by ferry. Oh, and we should stop at the liquor store up the block, too. Jerry'd like it if we bring wine for dinner."

At this second stop, as Sean wandered up and down aisles comparing labels, Elias tagged after him, aware of a twinge of unease. Perhaps Jerry was Sean's old lover, or maybe even a current one? It could be that agreeing to come at all was a mistake. He didn't particularly want to spend the weekend as an awkward third to the party if Sean and his friend wanted to be left alone.

After Sean selected a couple of bottles of Merlot and paid for them, they headed toward the First Avenue subway station on Fourteenth Street. By the time they had boarded the subway and found seats, Elias had decided he'd rather know the truth than remain in suspense any longer. "So," he said with careful casualness, "tell me about this friend of yours, the one who owns the house—Jerry?"

"Yeah, Jerry Simms. I met him at NYU Law School."

"You went to law school?" Elias raised an eyebrow. "Wait, I thought you said you were a writer. A journalist, right?"

"Yeah, well, I've been a lot of things," Sean said rather ruefully. "I took classes in law school for a year after"—he hesitated, so briefly Elias wasn't sure he had— "some time after college."

"Where'd you get your undergrad degree?"

"Northeastern. I majored in journalism and political science." The subway train pulled away from the station; Sean had to raise his voice to be heard above the rumble. "Anyway, I met Jerry in my contracts class. We were in a study group together, and we used to go out for beers after the bull sessions, to bitch about the professor. Jerry barely passed that class, but he stuck it out, unlike me. Now he makes a great living doing environmental insurance defense. Except he says the travel sucks." Sean smiled. The subway screeched as it began braking for the Sixth Avenue stop, a sound that set Elias's teeth on edge. "Anyway, he's invited me out to the Island a few times. And I bet Rafe will be there, too—he's Jerry's lover. At the moment, that is. It's kind of a moment-to-moment thing with them."

Elias nodded at this, doing his best to hold on to his poker face.

They transferred to the C at Eighth Avenue and then got out at Penn Station to board the Long Island Rail Road.

"How long will it take us to get there?" Elias asked.

"It's about an hour and a half to Sayville," said Sean. "From there, we take a taxi to the ferry—they leave the dock about once every hour. We should be on the Island by sunset."

"Yeah?" Elias said with a touch of wariness.

Sean took a closer look at Elias's expression and grinned. "You look like a kid who doesn't know whether to expect Christmas morning or a trip to the dentist. Count on it, Elias, you'll have a wonderful time this weekend."

"Well, I can't help wondering—"

"Are you kidding? A great-looking guy like you?" Sean leaned back in his seat and stretched out his legs. "I bet you'll fill your dance card for the weekend within a half hour of stepping onto shore."

"That . . . isn't exactly what I was worried about." What he *was* worried about got a little lost for a moment as Elias turned his head toward the window in a jumble of surprise, alarm, and delight. *Great-looking. He thinks I'm great looking.*

"Well then," said Sean, "what do you— Oh." Elias turned back to see Sean looking at him hard for a moment, apparently making a mental readjustment. "Relax," Sean went on gently. "You don't need to let any of those wild stories you hear about the Meat Rack get to you."

"I don't?" Elias said weakly. *The . . . Meat Rack? Oh, my god. What stories?*

"If it'll make you feel better, just stick with me. I'll help you get settled in, introduce you around to some people who won't give you any pressure you don't want."

"That would be great."

"On the other hand," Sean continued, waggling his eyebrows, "if you hook up with a hot trick for the weekend, I'll have the tact to know when to bow out."

"Thanks. I think." Elias wondered if his smile looked as strained as it felt. He felt a pang at Sean's words that surprised him. Looking down at the bag of groceries at his side, he found himself wishing that maybe Sean wouldn't be in a hurry to leave him to anyone else's company.

They passed back and forth sections of the *New York Times* Sean had picked up at the station. "Do you think Flores will take the Raiders to the Super Bowl again this year?" started an animated argument, with Elias championing the New York Giants and Sean the New England Patriots ("although I'll admit to a sneaking admiration for the Steelers").

Eventually, the conversation lulled. Elias glanced over the editorial page and then put it aside restlessly. He wanted to say something to break the silence, which had stretched on long enough to make him feel uncomfortable. He sneaked a glance at Sean, who was looking out the window at the Long Island scenery, humming lightly under his breath. *After all the years I wanted to meet someone like me, I don't even know what to say. When did you know you were gay? When did you first do it with anybody? What did your parents say, or haven't you told them? Do you ever think about not being able to have kids?*

So what do you ask when you really want to get to know someone?

"Why do you like Irish music?" he asked at random.

Sean's face lit up. "Oh, not just Irish. Gaelic, Celtic, the old English ballad tradition . . . " He paused. "I was ten the first time I heard someone play on the pennywhistle. It was a guy busking in Central Park. My god, I've never forgotten it. I'd been taking piano lessons for about a year at that point, suffering through those damn finger exercises, do-re-mi, dry as dust. And there was this guy playing what looked like a cheap sliver of metal, and he made it seem as natural as breathing to play this music that just about tore my heart out. It wasn't just that he was technically good, either, although he was. When you listened to it, his music made you feel like you really were a spurned lover, or a dying soldier, or a wanderer leaving your home forever." He sighed. "I don't suppose," he added with a touch of wistfulness, "that you've ever read James Joyce, have you?"

Elias blinked at the sudden change of subject. "Uh, yeah. Some."

"You have!" Sean said, delighted.

"Well, not *Ulysses* or *Finnegan's Wake*, I mean. But I've read *Dubliners*. And *A Portrait of the Artist as a Young Man*, just last year."

"Did you ever run across his idea about how art revealed itself, kind of as an illumination, or a revelation?"

"Joyce called it . . . um, an epiphany, I think. Is that right?"

"Exactly," Sean said, obviously tickled to be understood. "A glimpse of insight into other lives."

Elias thought for a moment. "I had a lecture in English class on that once. Do you remember that description in *Portrait* of the girl wading by the shore who looks mystically like a bird? She just looks at the hero without saying anything, but something about her sets his soul on fire. I remember when we discussed that section in class I said I'd love to get a photograph of a face like that."

"Have you seen the trailer for that movie coming out soon, *The French Lieutenant's Woman*? It's like the look what's-'er-name gives Jeremy Irons. Streep."

"Yeah. Yeah, like that. I remember how astonished I was when another guy in the class said he'd never experienced anything like that feeling, and he didn't know what the hell Joyce was talking about."

"Do you?"

"Yeah, I do. I mean, I think I've experienced epiphanies." *In fact,* Elias thought, staring at Sean's face, looking so pleased to be understood, *maybe I'm having one right now.*

"So have I. In music. Sex, sometimes, too."

Elias decided to let the last remark slide by. He cleared his throat and raised an eyebrow. "So—journalism and political science, huh?"

"Oh, well." Sean looked abashed. "I suppose I flirted with the idea of being an English major for a while. I spend too much time plinking on a guitar, too."

"And you cook a mean frozen waffle." Elias smiled.

"And I cook a mean frozen waffle. Guess I'm just a Renaissance kind of guy."

At Sayville they got off the train and headed for the taxi stand, lugging their bags and groceries. As Sean signaled the driver at the head of the line, Elias heard a voice behind him say, "Are you gentlemen headed to the ferry terminal? Would you allow me to share the ride?"

Elias turned around to find an elderly man in a tweedy coat with elbow patches regarding them with upraised eyebrows. A leather weekend case and several shopping bags rested at his feet. "Um . . . Sean?" Elias said in an undertone.

"Hmm?" Sean said, turning around. "Oh, you want to cab it together? Sure. Hop in."

The cab screeched to a halt in front of them, and the driver got out and slung their bags into the trunk. "I would prefer to keep that one with me," the other man said as the driver reached to pick up one of the shopping bags. "I don't want the fruit to get crushed." They all climbed into the backseat. The cab's interior reeked of sweat, engine oil, and cigarette smoke.

"The ferry terminal," Sean said, and the cab tore away from the curb.

Their companion slowly reached into his coat breast pocket, extracted a handkerchief, and touched it to his nose. "A rather interesting smell, isn't it?" he observed dryly in a low voice. "Quite . . . evocative, one might say."

Sean shot him an amused glance. The driver gave them a flat, uninterested stare in the rearview mirror as he signaled a turn.

"These Egyptian cabdrivers are hardly ever conversational," the other rider remarked, sotto voce. Sean and Elias exchanged a look as he pulled a wicker basket out of the shopping bag at his feet. "Let's see if these survived the trip—ah yes." He drew out and opened a container of strawberries, and, after due consideration, extracted one from the pile and popped it into his mouth. At the taste his eyes closed in utter bliss. "Excellent." He opened his eyes again and proffered the basket. "Won't you try some? They're really exquisite, the last of the season."

Sean shook his head, but Elias, suddenly aware he was hungry, took a few. "Thanks," he said. The berries indeed tasted very good, with a flavor both sweet and tart. Elias rolled them on his tongue slowly, watching the man rearrange the contents of his shopping bag in order to place the basket back inside. Elias caught glimpses of a feather boa and something sewn with royal blue sequins.

After organizing the bag to his satisfaction, the other man settled back into his seat. "So, have you two been over to the Island much this summer?"

"Just once or twice," said Sean.

"This is my first visit," Elias said.

"Indeed!" The man raised an eyebrow. "You have only just come out, perhaps?"

Elias blinked, taken aback. "Uh, yeah, I guess so."

"Well, a special occasion, then! I've been going to the Island for over forty years now myself."

"Really?" Elias said. "Wow."

"I've made many dear friends there over the years. My family, really." The man thought for a minute and smiled faintly. "We actually used to call each other 'sister,' you know. Odd how the language changes, isn't it? You young people today speak of being in the 'gay community'; we never thought of it that way. We came to the Island because it was one place where we could be what we knew we really were."

"And what was that?" Elias asked, fascinated.

"Well, I've always known what *I* am," the man said simply. "I'm a fairy." He looked out the window. "Ah, good, there's the landing."

The cab jolted to a stop with a suddenness that made them all lurch in their seats. Sean opened the door and they all got out. The cabdriver had already hopped out and was opening the trunk. Soon they all had their bags and were walking toward the water.

"We want that one over to the right, Elias," Sean said, pointing. "It goes to the Pines. The other one's headed for Cherry Grove."

"That's mine," said their companion. "Good to meet you, gentlemen. Have a splendid weekend. And you, young man," he said to Elias, "I hope you find your family here." He gave a thin smile and strode off toward the other ferry, the tail of the feather boa bobbing like a beckoning finger over the edge of his shopping bag.

Elias stared after him until Sean finally recalled his attention with a touch to his elbow. "Hey, Elias. We need to go stand in line for our tickets." He glanced in the direction Elias was still looking. "What is it?"

"That guy . . ." Elias's voice trailed off.

"What about him?"

Elias decided to screw up his courage and ask. "Are most of the guys who go to the Island like that?"

"Like what?" Sean asked patiently.

"Uh, you know . . ."

"You mean, kind of swishy?"

"Well . . . yeah."

"Do queens bother you?"

"They make me sort of nervous," Elias admitted. "They just seem so . . . out there, like they don't give a damn what anybody thinks . . . and I always do. Give a damn, that is."

"I felt the same way for a long time," Sean said unexpectedly. "Finally, I figured out I was just resenting them for being braver than me, which is pretty stupid when you get right down to it." He shrugged. "As for the answer to your question"—he gestured toward the crowd—"what do you think?"

For the first time, Elias took a good look around. The crowd fairly pulsed with weekend party spirit. Men in denim cutoffs lounged on coolers, chatting, sliding their seats and bags forward as the line inched along. Heads turned, eyes inscrutable behind sunglasses, watching others watch them. Many had taken off their shirts, displaying the results of hours spent at the gym and on the beach catching the rays. To one side, a group of half a dozen men played Frisbee, cheered on by whoops and clapping and the barking of an overexcited golden retriever. The light of the setting sun glanced off shoulders, biceps, and rippling abdominals, turning sculpted flesh to warm glowing bronze. "Oh, my," Elias breathed.

"It's really something, isn't it?" Sean said, grinning.

Elias nodded. "You know, I think I could get used to this."

By the time the ferry chugged into the harbor at Fire Island Pines the sun was more than halfway below the horizon. It finally disappeared, extinguished like the last spark in a piece of burned paper, as they disembarked at the wooden-plank town square. The sounds of parties in full swing drifted over the water from the various expensive pleasure craft docked on both sides of the harbor; the reflections of swaying Chinese lanterns bobbed on the water like dancing fireflies.

"Jerry's place is on Driftwood Walk. Let's get a wagon for toting the groceries."

"A wagon?"

Sure enough, little red wagons were available for rent at dockside. "I can't believe it," Elias laughed. "I haven't pulled one of those things behind me since I was a kid."

"There aren't any cars or roads on Fire Island, you know, just wooden boardwalks. Come on, Jerry's expecting us. I'll bet the fatted calf should be just about ready to come off the spit by now."

*   *   *

Dinner was not, in fact, roast beef, but fresh tuna steaks with artichokes and mushrooms. When dinner was over, they all leaned back in the Adirondack chairs on the outside deck, finishing their last sips of wine and sighing with repletion.

"That tasted great, Jerry," Sean said. "Thanks."

"Too much Madeira in the sauce, though," said Rafe, putting his feet up on the cooler.

Jerry, a tall man with salt-and-pepper curls clustered around a bald spot, laughed as he got up to clear the table. "What? Oh, come on, Rafe, that dinner was a work of art!"

"Yeah, sure, sure," Rafe grumbled into his beer. "That's exactly what it was. Art. Jer, I'm telling you that when I come home from work after an intense day in the trenches of corporate America, I need to be able to sink my fangs into a big haunch of something that once had red blood in it." He took a swig of beer. "I sometimes have visions of inviting all my old tricks from my Harley days over for dinner, just to see the looks on their faces when Jerry brings out a big platter of Chicken Grand Marnier au Pêche."

"You did empty your plate, you hypocrite." Jerry elbowed the sliding door open and headed for the kitchen with a stack of plates.

"Why can't you cook us something more butch?" Rafe shouted after him. "Like . . . shark, say. That would be appropriate for a lawyer to serve."

"Jerry's not a lawyer," Sean said. "He's a teddy bear."

"Cooked in something calculated to sear the tongue off," Rafe went on without noticing the interruption. "Like chili, maybe."

"Chili! With shark?" Jerry, back from the kitchen, shuddered and then looked thoughtful. "Maybe some Cajun spices, now. I remember a restaurant I tried once in New Orleans. . . ."

"I thought dinner was good," said Elias uncertainly, not wanting to get into the middle of an argument between the pair but still feeling that it was only polite to stick up for his host's cooking.

"Good?" said Jerry. "It was superb. Elias, you have excellent taste. Who wants coffee?"

"I can get the cups, or the cream and sugar or something," Elias volunteered. He followed Jerry out to the kitchen.

"Cups are in that cupboard next to the sink," Jerry said, pointing. Elias opened the cupboard door and carefully pulled them out. They were a Danish pattern—the same one his sister-in-law used, he thought—and looked expensive, like everything else in Jerry's kitchen. He reached for the sugar bowl on the counter and saw Jerry eyeing him curiously as he scooped coffee into the filter basket.

"So . . . have you known Sean long?"

"He's . . . um, kind of a new acquaintance." Elias looked down at the blue-rimmed cup in his hand, suddenly struck by the truth of it. *My god. Two nights ago I was eating out of Dumpsters and sleeping on a warehouse floor, and tonight I'm at a dinner party.*

Jerry fit the filter basket into the coffee machine and went to the sink to fill the carafe with water. "Oh, by the way, I put your bag by the stairs. You and Sean can sleep wherever you like. There's the room at the top of the stairs, or the smaller one by the bathroom . . . ?"

His voice trailed off into a question mark, and it took Elias a moment to catch on. *He's fishing around to find out if we're sleeping together.* Anxious to clarify matters, Elias said hastily, "Well, I don't know what Sean wants to do, but uh, I guess I'd like to go to bed pretty soon. I suppose Sean can have whichever room he usually stays in and I'll take the other one, if that's all right." Feeling a blush coming on, he went toward the refrigerator to fetch the half-and-half.

"You want to go to bed right away?" Jerry said, sounding startled. "You're sure? I mean, Rafe and I were talking about heading out to the Ice Palace. And there'll be parties going on all over the Island."

Elias hesitated. It certainly did seem stupid to go to bed early just in order to stake out a separate bedroom for himself.

"Sean will certainly stay out late," Jerry added.

Elias looked down at the half-and-half in his hand. *Yeah, and maybe if he's out for a good time tonight he doesn't really want a kid like me tagging along.*

Just then, Sean came into the kitchen with more dishes. Jerry appealed to him. "Hey, talk him out of it, Sean."

"Talk him out of what?"

"Elias here is talking about turning in early."

Sean turned to Elias with a look of surprise as he put the salad plates on the counter. Was he disappointed, too? "No kidding? Why?"

"It's okay, really," Elias said nervously. "I'm just kind of tired. I had the job interview, after all, besides the trip here. I'll have all weekend to party."

"But—" Sean began, but then seemed to remember something and let it drop. Perversely, Elias felt a stab of disappointment at how easy he was to convince.

Jerry headed back out to the deck. When he was out of earshot, Sean said softly, "I'm sorry."

Elias looked at him in surprise.

"Don't let me push you too fast," Sean went on. "I know it's tough to get started."

"It's okay," Elias said as he turned away, his heart beating hard. "It's really okay."

Elias padded downstairs the next morning, following his nose toward the smell of coffee and bacon. Just before he reached the archway, he heard Rafe's voice in the kitchen say, "So, Sean . . . where'd you pick up that young blond god, anyway? Terrific tush, if you ask me."

Elias froze. What kind of a night *had* Sean had last night?

"Funny, Rafe," Sean said mildly. "I don't recall any young blond gods flitting across my path recently, and I'm sure I would have noticed. Although lately I've been specializing more in the Rudy Valentino type. You know, tall and dark, flaring nostrils, that sort of thing."

Rafe laughed. "I meant Elias, of course."

Elias felt as if he'd been gut-punched.

"Are you letting your eye rove, Rafe? Jerry'd be so disappointed."

"Isn't he a bit younger than the type you usually toy with?"

"Who says I'm toying with him?"

"Ohhh." There was a pause. "You never struck me as the marrying kind, honey."

"Elias is a kid who needs a friend, Rafe. That's all."

"So far, eh?" Rafe said with heavy insinuation.

The pause this time lasted even longer. "What you don't know about me would fill the New York Public Library, Rafe. Pass the cornflakes, would ya?"

Carefully, Elias backed away from the kitchen doorway. *Maybe a walk along the beach before breakfast would be a good idea.*

By the time he walked back a half hour later, Sean was in the shower, Rafe was deeply engrossed in a copy of Vito Russo's *The Celluloid Closet*, and Jerry was out on the deck, eating his breakfast. "Come on out here, Elias, and help me finish all these pancakes. I'm afraid I got carried away making them. There's a plate here for you."

Elias joined him at the table and shifted a stack of papers to one side. "Sorry, let me move those," Jerry said. "I thought I'd squeeze in some work over breakfast and then I could forget about it all weekend." He took the stack over to the briefcase by the railing.

"Here's something else," Elias said, twitching another page out from underneath a place mat.

"Thanks—oh, no," Jerry said. "That's not from my office. Someone put it under the door. They said down at the Ice Palace last night that someone stuck it on every doorstep on the Island."

Elias looked at the paper. It was a reprint of an article from the *New York Native* by a Dr. Larry Mass. He scanned the first few paragraphs. "Something about . . . sarcoma. That's cancer, isn't it? In . . . gay men?"

"Yeah. Apparently it's been going around."

"What—like the cancer's contagious?"

Jerry shrugged. "I don't know. All I know is that *I* don't have it. Here, put that over on the drink cart, there, by the hot tub. How many pancakes do you want?"

By the time Elias finished his third stack of pancakes, Sean was out of the shower. He came out to the deck, barefoot and dressed in cutoffs, to towel dry his hair. Elias wondered if he was doing it on purpose. He strolled around the table to look over Jerry's shoulder as Jerry wrote in his daybook.

"So, what's on Mr. Gerald Simms, Esquire's 'to do' list for the day?" Sean asked. He gave Elias a wink.

"Nothing in particular," Jerry said, closing the daybook firmly and pushing it forward. "Just relaxing."

"My plans are vague, but will undoubtedly involve plenty of beer," Rafe called out from the living room. "Lots of sun. Maybe peeled grapes."

"I'm going to start with the beach," Sean said. "Coming, Elias?"

"Sure."

The weekend passed in a golden haze that occasionally felt a little surreal to Elias. Sometimes, as he ran down the beach into the waves with Sean splashing right behind him, or strolled along the boardwalks toward the next party, or lounged in the hot tub, head back, sipping something cool and tropical out of a blender, he found it hard to believe that it wasn't all a dream, that he wouldn't wake up again any moment in a dark, rat-infested warehouse. Jerry threw a party on Sunday night, and Elias stood out on the deck late, eating stuffed mushroom caps and marinated shrimp and listening to complaints about the rise in prices of rental shares, the incursions of young straight toughs looking for gays to bash, the mediocre food and poor service at the Island restaurants. Someone turned to him and said, "Jerry said it's your first time out here, isn't that right? What do you think of the Island?"

For one moment, Elias forgot all about the need to act cool. "I think it's the most wonderful place in the world," he said fervently. The men standing around who heard him laughed.

Elias felt his face heat up. "What was that?" Rafe said loudly, rather drunk. "What was that he said? The most . . . wunnerful place in the world?" Rafe blinked and appeared to be attempting to concentrate. "Tha's it. Bingo. Put his finger right on it. You said it, 'lias. You said it. Get this man a beer." He held a popper up to his nose and took a long sniff.

"I'll get it," Elias said quickly. "Um . . . I think I'd like to go for a walk, anyway." He turned and edged away from the knot of men, snagging a soft drink from the cooler on his way to the steps leading down to the beach.

"Elias!" someone called out behind him. "Hey, Elias!"

Elias didn't stop to answer, but instead went down the deck stairs and started toward the nearest boardwalk. He heard footsteps rattling down the wooden stairs after him.

"Hey!"

Elias turned.

It was Sean. "You big goof," he said and laughed. "Did you leave just because Rafe embarrassed you? Rafe thinks it's his job to embarrass everybody."

Elias stared at him hard and then looked up at the sky and laughed. "No. I guess I embarrassed myself."

"Why? Because you said you like the Island? Nothing wrong with that." He took a step closer. "Where're you heading?"

"Nowhere in particular, really. Along the beach. Maybe up to the ferry dock."

"Do you mind if I come with you?"

"I'd like that," Elias said, averting his eyes. They fell into step together and walked for several moments in silence. "It's just that . . . I've never felt so safe as I do here," Elias said suddenly. "All my life, I had this big secret. And then when my father kicked me out, I felt as if . . ." he groped for words, "as if I'd been cut adrift at sea."

"At the mercy of the storm," Sean murmured. "And now?"

"Secure. Feeling . . . the ground under my feet." Elias looked up at the sky over his head and laughed. "In the middle of the sea, I've found an island." *And maybe,* he added mentally, thinking of what the man in the taxi had said, *I've found my family.*

They had been walking east along the main boulevard and now came to a wooden square adjoining the harbor where the ferry docked. A card table had been set up to one side, with a banner hung over it. "What's that about?" Elias said. Sean shrugged.

They walked closer. Several men sat behind the table, and others stood in front of it, talking to them. As they came closer, they could see the words on the banner: "Give to Gay Cancer."

" . . . what it's about. We're asking everyone to chip in to help the research," one of the men behind the table was saying.

The muscular bodybuilder listening to him shrugged and shook his head. "I ain't got money to spare."

He started to walk away, but the first man's voice called after him with some heat: "Look, think about what you spend to pay the cover charge at the Ice Palace, and for the time-share for the summer, and the goddamn water taxi rides. Can't you please give us just a few dollars to help?"

The second man froze in his tracks and looked back. "I ain't got any money to spare for dickheads like you." There was a frozen, angry pause, and then he strode away.

"Way to go, Paul," another man behind the table murmured. "That's why we brought you along. Wonderful people skills."

"I can't help it," the first man, Paul, snapped. He hunched over in his chair, glowering, kneading his fists over the small cash box. "We've been begging all weekend and what have we raised? Maybe a hundred lousy bucks."

"Are you the guys who put that article on everyone's doorstep?" Elias asked.

"Yeah," the second man behind the table said, giving him a wary look, as if he suspected that Elias, too, might shoot off some smart-ass remark. "More than a hundred men have become sick with this thing, and many of them are dead."

"My lover was one of them," the third man behind the table said somberly.

"I'm sorry. I don't have any money with me," Elias said.

"Here," Sean said. He pulled out his wallet and threw several bills on the table.

"Hey, thanks, man."

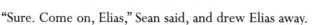

"Sure. Come on, Elias," Sean said, and drew Elias away.

Elias looked at him and laughed as they retraced their steps. "Do you always open your wallet for hard luck cases?"

"Maybe just the ones that deserve it."

"Oh," Elias said. His mouth felt dry. "Look," he said to change the subject. "The moon is rising."

"Let's head back along the beach."

They walked slowly, just at the edge of where the water had wet the sand, wrapped in a silence that felt both comfortable and yet somehow expectant.

"So you've enjoyed yourself this weekend?" Sean asked finally.

"Yes, I really have."

"I'm glad. I hoped you would."

"Thank you for inviting me." He hesitated. "I want . . ."

Sean waited for a moment. "What do you want, Elias?" he finally asked gently.

At the sight of him, standing there in the moonlight, Elias lost whatever it was he'd wanted to say next. *I want . . . I want . . . Oh, god, I don't know what I want. I want to see you standing there looking at me like that forever, and maybe do more than look.* He took a deep breath and stopped walking. "I want to learn from you."

Sean cocked his head. "You want to learn from me?" Elias could see the glitter of moonlight against his teeth as he smiled slightly. "You mean . . . like lessons?"

"You've given lessons before, haven't you?" said Elias, greatly daring.

"Music lessons," Sean said absently. He looked down at Elias's hand and then, as if it were the most natural thing in the world, took it in his own.

At the touch of Sean's hand, Elias felt his heart leap into his throat. He closed his eyes to concentrate on the sensation. *I want you to touch me.*

"You could play the piano, you know," Sean said in a low voice, lifting Elias's hand in his and gently running his fingers over it. "You have the hands for it."

"I do?" Elias said.

"Mmm-hmm." Sean took a step closer. "I've been admiring your hands."

Elias opened his eyes again and looked into Sean's. "Would you . . . show me what to do?"

"I'd like that." They headed away from the water then, and up the slope to one of the secret places hidden by the long beach grass from everything but the sky.

And there, in that secret place, Sean showed him.

Chapter Nine

The earth is all the home I have,
The heavens my wide roof-tree.

—W. E. AYTOUN, "THE WANDERING JEW"

Over the next two days, women from the village and surrounding neighborhood came to the cottage. Although Eliza gratefully accepted their gifts of bread, cheese, and ale, she politely but stubbornly resisted all offers to help her with the task of preparing Nell's body for burial. "Nay, 'tis only right I should do it," she said. "God forgive me, I was not here to ease her passing. 'Tis all I can do for her now."

When the more persistent ones pressed her, Eliza only shook her head and turned away, pressing her lips together tightly. Several took offense at this. Because no one saw Eliza openly weep for her foster mother, some muttered among themselves about her hardness of heart—until the village parson, Mr. Wood, saw the haunted, silent grief in her red-rimmed eyes. Being more perceptive than most, he firmly put an end to such talk. In general, however, most were secretly relieved to leave the task of readying Nell's body to Eliza. Smallpox was a dreadful thing, and Nell's death had come bitter and hard. None of Nell's neighbors had the least wish to share her fate.

And so Eliza alone draped the bed in black and then carefully washed Nell's smallpox-ravaged limbs and dressed her in her best dress. With infinite gentleness she combed and arranged Nell's hair and placed a red rose in her clasped hands, taken from the bush Tom had planted in the garden on their wedding day. Her heart hurt to think of Tom exiled so far away, not even knowing yet what had befallen his wife. Perhaps, she thought, when the news reached him, he might find a small crumb of comfort in knowing Nell had held his rose.

When she had finished with all the tucking and smoothing and arranging, Eliza lingered at Nell's side for a long time, studying the beloved face, once so animated and tender, now utterly still. Its emptiness smote Eliza to the core. "I was coming back, dear Mother Nell," she whispered. "Coming back home to bring my heart for thee to truly keep." She paused and tried to smile past the pain in her throat. "Home—'tis most strange, is it not? This was to be my true home, and all barriers between us had fallen at last, I had thought. But thou hast gone before to a place I cannot follow." Her fingers, trembling, brushed Nell's face. "Whom shall I give my heart's love to now?" Finally, reluctantly, Eliza spread the shroud over Nell's body. It would be raised over her face when the men came to bear her to the churchyard.

The last of Eliza's dresses were plunged into the black dye kettle that had been placed to simmer on the hearth. The harsh dye smell mingled with the scent of rosemary and yew sprigs and evergreen branches, cut and placed in the corner to be carried to the church.

Tom's younger brother, Richard, came from Combe St. Nicholas when he heard the news of his sister-in-law's death, and this was another trial for Eliza. A sour-faced bantam of a man, he lacked both his older brother's humor and openheartedness. In Tom's absence, he considered himself to be both the acting head of the family and chief mourner, and he found Eliza's presence puzzling and somewhat irritating. Since he had already had smallpox, there was no putting him off by pleading quarantine. On the morning of the funeral, when the pallbearers came to fetch Nell's body to the church, he stood at the foot of the bed, bouncing impatiently up and down on his heels. Occasionally, his gaze wandered around the room and his lips moved as he laboriously totaled up the inventory in his head. As the men lifted the body from the bed, he whispered harshly in Eliza's ear: " 'Tis not wool covering her corse?"

" 'Tis linen, Mr. Barton," Eliza said, staring at him.

"Nay, you must take it off her, then. I'll not be paying the fine for burying the dead in linen."

Eliza's eyes darkened, and a moment passed before she could trust herself to speak evenly. "I have money to pay it, if you do dislike it," she said, thinking of the bag of coins Robert Owen had given her. "The cloth is of your brother's own weaving. He would wish it for Nell, I think."

Despite her mildness, he caught the small flash of scorn in her eyes. He felt rather nettled at this impudence, and a note of belligerence crept into his voice. "All very well, do as you like, then. But I am only wishful to protect my brother's interests now. This place is his, and everything with it, and I will not have any squandering."

Eliza looked at him again quickly, startled and dismayed. She had not yet had time to wonder what might happen to Tom's property, now that Nell no longer lived. "Of course, sir," she said after a long pause. She bowed her head and turned away.

Because of the fear of smallpox, only a few followed Nell's bier to the church to see her properly buried. While they were en route, another mercenary consideration struck Richard Barton, and he sidled through the procession over to Eliza's side to demand whether she expected him to pay the fee to have Nell buried within the church itself.

Only the reflection that he was her foster father's brother and therefore due at least a modicum of respect kept Eliza from escaping eagerly from grief into anger. "I told the parson to have the diggers prepare the plot next to her babes, sir," she replied. "They were all buried together outside the church, and there Nell wished to lie, too."

"Ah." He nodded, pleased to have a face-saving reason to avoid spending money without actually appearing to be niggardly. Relief made him offer a compliment, for compliments, at least, were cheap. "She were a good wife to my brother, I suppose." Unfortunately, he ruined it by adding as an afterthought, "Barren though she were."

Eliza crushed the sprig of evergreen she held in her hand, feeling the pain in her fingertips from the sharp points of the needles. "She was a better mother than you could possibly ever know, sir. God knows she was better than I deserved."

He gave her a sharp glance and prudently fell back a pace behind her for the rest of the way to the church.

The small group of mourners gathered at the graveside and listened as the parson read the service: "Forasmuch as it hath pleased Almighty God of His great mercy to take unto Himself the soul of our dear sister here departed, we therefore commit her body to the ground; earth to earth, ashes to ashes, dust to dust; in sure and certain hope of the Resurrection to eternal life, through our Lord Jesus Christ; who shall change our vile body, that it may be like unto His glorious body, according to the mighty working, whereby He is able to subdue all things to Himself. . . ." After the final prayer, the pallbearers lowered Nell's body into the ground, and yew and rosemary sprigs were dropped over her shroud. Then the gravediggers set to work filling in the grave. Eliza winced inwardly at the sound of clumps of earth falling into the pit over Nell's body.

When they had finished, Eliza stepped forward and knelt to place more of Tom's roses on the mound. "Forgive me," she whispered, pressing her fingers into the cool, damp earth. The soil clung to her skin, clammy as guilt. "Forgive me, dear mother, for not being with thee at the end." Her heart eased a little, just a little, as she looked at the roses, for she had to admit to herself that surely Nell would not have wanted her to sicken with the smallpox and die, too.

She tried to hold to that thought, as friends and neighbors stepped forward to greet her afterward. Diana, a friend from the village, slipped her arms around Eliza's neck and gave her a kiss on the cheek. "Poor friend!" she exclaimed sympathetically. "Are you wishful for me to stay the night with you?" She lowered her voice, glancing sidelong at Richard Barton. "It might be more of a comfort than some others would."

"Faith, you speak the truth." Eliza smiled, warmed, but shook her head. "Your mother is very near her confinement, isn't she?"

Reluctantly, Diana nodded. "Aye. The midwife might be called at any time."

"Best you stay with her, then. You don't want to bring the danger of smallpox to her or the babe. But—thank you."

Diana sighed. "Very well." She squeezed Eliza's hand. "We shall all miss her."

Because of the smallpox, there was no funeral feast. By twilight, the few neighbors who had returned from the church with Eliza and Richard Barton had departed, except for Mr. Wood, the parson. Eliza went out to inspect the side kitchen garden and pull up a weed or two. The garden did not look as neglected as she'd feared it would be. In fact, Mistress Pollard and the other neighbor women who had helped tend Nell had cultivated it a bit, in between watches of nursing. The old work, the old familiar rhythms felt soothing. When she had cleared away the worst of the damage, she filled her basket full of radishes, lettuce, and other greens for a supper salad and brought them over to the well to wash.

At the front of the house, Richard Barton and Mr. Wood sat at the doorstep on stools, leaning back against the cottage wall, drinking ale. Talk drifted idly from the price of lambs and wool to rumors of new taxes that would come with the new king. Eliza heard their voices floating around the corner of the house, mingling with the smell of their tobacco.

"What will happen to this property," Mr. Wood asked after a lull in the conversation, "now that Mistress Barton is gone?"

Richard Barton leaned forward to refill his tankard with the ale jug at his feet. "I've been thinking—'twould be best for my oldest boy to come to live here. Aye, to keep its value up. The cottage would be big enough for him and his wife and their children."

Dismayed, Eliza stopped pulling up the bucket and turned her head to listen.

"In trust for your brother, of course, Mr. Barton?" the parson asked pointedly.

Richard Barton sucked in his cheeks meditatively. "Aye . . . in case he ever returns. 'Tis possible, what with the Protestant king now and all."

But if Tom didn't return, Eliza thought bitterly, it was probable that neither Richard nor his son would mind.

"Or," Richard Barton went on, "perhaps if it could be sold, enough could be raised to ransom Tom home again."

"Hmm," Mr. Wood said in a neutral tone.

Richard Barton shifted uncomfortably and cleared his throat. "I would not sell it if Tom did not wish it."

Mr. Wood drew on his pipe for a moment, troubled. "What about the girl?" he said abruptly.

"What girl?"

"Nell's Eliza."

"What is it makes her Nell's girl?" Richard Barton asked indifferently. "I know she's lived here for years. Just a hired neighborhood wench, isn't she?"

"I believe," Mr. Wood said slowly, "she is a fosterling. I do not know all the circumstances. I came to visit several times during Mistress Barton's illness. Before she died, she told me Eliza had gone to live with her own folk. I do not know why the girl came back; Mistress Pollard tells me she didn't know of Mistress Barton's death when she returned."

"Well, she'll just have to go back to her own folk, then," Richard Barton said, shaking his head.

Mr. Wood hesitated. He had to admit that the hard-faced man was within his rights. Mistress Barton was gone, and no children had lived to inherit. The law would clearly recognize Richard Barton as the proper person to act for his brother. Still . . . "I don't know if your brother would agree."

Richard Barton eyed the parson, wondering whether to say, *Tom's not here,* but he decided against it. "Look, you said the girl's not kin. Unless——is she a by-blow of Tom's?" Richard snorted. "If so, Nell had more patience than I knew."

"As I said, I do not know all the circumstances," the parson said stiffly, his lips thinning in disapproval.

"Well, if she's not Tom's, she's got no call on me or mine."

Mr. Wood noted that he was already speaking of Tom's property as his own. He sighed. "Well, if I am wrong, and there's no other home for her to go to . . ." He hesitated. "It seems a shame. She's always been a bright, polite-spoken lass, if a bit quiet. Perhaps she can hire herself out with someone in the neighborhood."

"Best for her to go to her kin. Aye, or go to the parish, if she has none." Richard Barton snorted again. "There always be places in the workhouse, I hear."

Eliza's knees felt weak, and she sat abruptly on the edge of the well. Never in her worst nightmares had she thought she might end up at the parish workhouse. She covered her face with her hands and tried furiously to think.

For one wild moment, she thought of going around the corner of the house and pouring out the whole tale to Mr. Wood. Yet common sense stopped her. Her father's refusal to pay the debt owed to Tom and Nell meant that any help Mr. Wood might give her would only be for charity's sake. That was true for anyone else in the village, too. As for Richard Barton, the cold variety of charity offered by the parish would probably be more than anything he would ever be prepared to offer her. But although it might be foolish, she did not want charity.

Therefore, she would not ask for it.

Mr. Wood did not yet know the Earl had disowned her. But once he began making inquiries, he would be sure to discover the degree of her destitution, and then his duty would be clear. If she wished to avoid being sent to the parish, perhaps forcibly, she would have to leave. Immediately.

Numbly, she thought of the Countess. No doubt she would be maliciously pleased if she ever learned that Eliza had been driven from her home—just as her brothers apparently had been.

Slowly, Eliza lifted her face from her hands and looked up at the rising moon. Her breath caught and then eased out slowly. Her brothers. Nell might be dead and Tom gone, but she did have family left. Eleven brothers, driven from their home, just like her. Eleven brothers—if only she could find them.

Where could they possibly be?

Without further thought, she pulled up the bucket and cleaned her hands. Leaving the basket beside the well, she quietly slipped through the side lean-to door that led into the hall. She tiptoed to the doorway leading into the parlor and listened. Mr. Wood and Mr. Barton still were talking outside the front door.

One stone flask had a stopper. Eliza filled it with water and slung the carry cord tied to its handle over her head. She picked up a loaf of bread and a wedge of cheese, hesitated, and reached for a knife. *Our Lord tells us to pray only for each day's daily bread, to teach us faith,* Nell always used to say. *The Almighty doesn't want us to fret about more than one day's portion of food at a time.* It must have been a comforting thought to her during the past several years, Eliza thought grimly, sawing the bread in half, whenever the larder became too empty.

The bread and cheese fit neatly into a folded square of lockram cloth. Knotting the corners together, she tied it onto the cord that held her flask. She took Nell's shawl from the peg by the lean-to door and slipped back outside. Off in the orchard a nightingale sang in liquid melody. Eliza tiptoed to the corner and listened. The parson was speaking now, telling a story about his boyhood in Devonshire. She eased back into the shadows and then picked her way across the yard to the outskirts of the orchard. Nell's black shawl pulled over her head covered the brightness of her hair; her black dress made it easy enough to slip into the shadows under the apple trees without being seen by the men. She struck out at a diagonal, heading for the road.

Once Eliza had reached it, she stopped and looked back over her shoulder. No one was in sight. She looked up at the moon again and blew out a sigh. "And now, dear Lord? Where must I go from this place?" Going over to the side of the road, she sat on a large rock to think.

She had no idea where her brothers might have gone since the day they had disappeared. Perhaps she might be able to find out more if she went back to the neighborhood of Kellbrooke Hall, but she did not want to go anywhere near the Countess. And after all, she thought ruefully, one direction might serve as well as another after so many years.

She felt alone and very frightened. At least her brothers had had each other.

But she was determined not to go back.

The words from one of Nell's favorite psalms came back to her: *In Thee, O Lord, do I put my trust; let me never be ashamed: deliver me in Thy righteousness.* Nell had read it aloud many times since Tom had been taken from them. Eliza looked down at her clenched hands in her lap and whispered the words aloud. "Bow down Thine ear to me, deliver me speedily: be Thou my strong rock of refuge, for an house of defense to save me. For Thou art my rock and my fortress; therefore for Thy name's sake lead me, and guide me. . . ."

The nightingale sang on undisturbed when she had finished. Eliza squared her shoulders and stood. She looked in both directions, up and down the lane, and then shrugged and spat into her out-stretched palm. A thump of her other fist into her palm made the spittle plop into the dirt at her feet to the left.

"That way then." She wiped her hands on the dewy grass, settled the flask more comfortably at her hip, and began walking.

Eliza walked for several hours before stopping to sleep in the lee of an old barn. A slice of bread and a hunk of cheese served as her breakfast; she ate it slowly and tried not to wonder what the next day's dinner might be. She combed her hair out with her fingers as best as she could, picking out bits of straw and leaves, and then shook out her skirts and began walking again.

The first day, she left the road to cut cross-country. She hopped over stone fences, striding across sheep meadows and along the borders of orchards and wheat and barley fields. Sometimes her path led her into cool woods rilled with brooks, where she bathed her feet and refilled her water bottle.

Her travel took her in a generally northern direction. Fortunately, the summer weather took a warm and pleasant turn. Overhead, high, puffy clouds sailed across the sky like tall ships across a sapphire sea, casting racing shadows over the meadows. Woodruff flowers bloomed everywhere underfoot, and the scent lifted Eliza's spirits, although it made her sigh, too, as she remembered St. Barnabas's day must be coming soon. She had made a Barnaby garland of woodruff and roses last year; Nell had helped her hang it from the ceiling to sweeten the air in the house. "Barnaby bright, Barnaby bright," she sang absently to herself, "light all day and light all night."

Eventually, Eliza came to the great road that curved north and east to Taunton and Bridgewater. A steady stream of people traveled along this route, in carts laden with fruit, vegetables, and bundles of newly sheared sheep fleeces, heading for the great town markets. At first, she followed the road's curve at a distance, wary of attracting unwelcome attention from local constables. When she had eaten the last of her bread, however, she drew closer, hoping to find someone traveling along the road who might sell her a bit of food for some of the last of Robert Owen's pennies. As she hesitated along the side of the road, wondering what to do, a man came walking toward her from the southwest, driving a flock of geese before him with a willow switch. He did not seem to be doing a very good job of keeping the geese together. As they came closer, Eliza could see why: he had to use one arm to support a young boy he carried on his back. As they came abreast of her, the man looked up and caught her eye. Several geese took advantage of his distraction

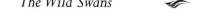
to dive toward a gap in the stone fence. The man lunged to flick the switch to stop them and swore as the boy lurched on his back.

"Good morrow, sir," Eliza said. "Oh, pray, may I help you?"

"Aye," the man replied in an exasperated voice, "if you might be willing—God's blood!" In the general flurry, one goose bounded off the path, gabbling excitedly and flapping up into his face. The man recoiled, batting it away. "Aye, if you would take the switch . . . my Jack has twisted his ankle, you see."

"Poor fellow!" Eliza rounded up the geese until they circled restlessly around the man's feet again. "Perhaps . . . I am wishful to go this way myself. Might I drive the geese for you so you may carry the lad?"

The man gladly accepted her offer of aid, and so Eliza gained a traveling companion for a short while. The boy, Jack, was shyly pleased with her, and he goaded his father into sharing a portion of their bread and bacon. When Eliza finally parted company with them at the Taunton market, the man drew a half dozen goose eggs from the carry bag slung from his waist and gave them to her.

After Taunton, she traded the eggs for ale and more cheese at one of the farms along the road and then struck out cross-country again. The land changed, becoming wilder the farther north she walked. Wheat fields and orchards gave way to moors in high summer flower. Her footing became more uneven and difficult, and clouds of gnats swirled above the fen grasses to fly in her face and hair. She wrapped her head and face with Nell's shawl and struggled on. Finally, just as she thought she would collapse in exhaustion, she came upon a low rise, with a flat area sheltered by a few large stones. There, she made a nest for herself with the shawl and lay back against a rock to watch the sunset through half-lidded eyes. As darkness fell, the vault of the sky above the restlessly shifting moor seemed enormous. Her feet ached, and her spirits sank to their lowest level ever.

This journey was quite different from the journey she had made from Kellbrooke Hall. Then, she had been traveling toward something, but this was simply wandering. As she stared at the crystalline stars wheeling above her, she felt light and weightless, as if dwindled down into nothingness. She breathed a prayer—she hardly knew what—and slept.

The calling of birds, shrill and sweet, woke her the next morning. Groaning, Eliza untangled herself from her shawl and sat up, stiff and sore. When she unknotted the cloth that held her bread, she discovered that she must have rolled onto it during the night, for the bread had been battered to crumbs. Sighing, she scooped them up and ate them as best she could, washing them down with sips from her bottle. Then she staggered to her feet and began walking again. Before long, her stiffness began ebbing away and her stride lengthened. She breathed in the summer perfume deeply and felt her sleepiness recede. Skylarks dipped and twittered above her, singing to the morning.

Eliza turned her face up to the sky to watch them as she walked—until a woman's voice abruptly drew her attention earthward again, saying mildly, "Good morning to you, child."

Eliza stopped suddenly in utter surprise. An old woman stood right in front of her, dressed as neatly and soberly as a Quaker, in a plain gray dress and apron, with a basket slung over her arm. Despite her wrinkles, her gray eyes were bright, and they met Eliza's with a hint of a smile.

"I . . . I beg your pardon, madam," Eliza stammered. "I did not expect to find anyone. . . . That is—" She remembered her manners and bobbed a curtsey. "Good morning to you, too, I should say."

"I came out this morning to gather some of these. Would you like a taste?" The woman folded back a cloth from the top of the basket and held it out for Eliza to see. There, nestled on the cloth, lay dozens of plump wild strawberries. The morning sunlight slanting across them made them glow with ruby-red light.

Eliza, suddenly aware of a sharp pang of hunger, took a few. "Thank you," she said. The berries indeed tasted very good, with a flavor both sweet and tart. Eliza rolled them on her tongue slowly, watching the woman rearrange the cloth over the basket.

"And why do you wander the moors, child?"

Eliza swallowed her last berry. "I am looking for my brothers." She smiled a little self-consciously. " 'Tis strange to confess I have managed to misplace eleven brothers, but I have. And I do not know where to look for them."

"Eleven, say you?" the woman said thoughtfully. "Yesterday I beheld eleven swans swimming, at the mouth of the river near here that leads to the sea. The sun shone on them, the light playing around their heads like crowns of gold."

Something in her words—a certain tone, a hint of a concealed meaning—reverberated oddly in Eliza's ears. She looked at the woman sharply, suddenly wondering . . . if God had indeed heard her prayer for guidance, what help would He send? And who would He choose to send it?

Another memory rose, unbidden, of the swans she had seen fly over the cottage on that fatal morning the Earl's people had come to take her to Kellbrooke Hall. The morning her life had changed forever. "Do you believe in . . . in omens?" Eliza asked a little breathlessly.

The woman said nothing, but only cocked her head, as if Eliza had not spoken and she still waited for a reply.

After a moment, Eliza sighed. "Could you show me where you saw them?" she asked.

"There, yonder," the woman said, pointing to the north. "Those taller shapes are the willows that grow along the river's banks. If you follow it downstream, you will come to the sea."

"Bless you for your kindness."

The corners of the woman's mouth twitched in a small smile. "I hope you find your family, child." And then she was gone, gliding away noiselessly, before Eliza could think to ask her anything else.

The river ran lazily, barely rippling at the base of the willow roots lining its banks, as if hypnotized by summer's warmth. Following the river downstream along its edge proved difficult, for the willow trees grew thickly, along with brambles and briars that plucked at Eliza's skirts. She persisted, however, spending the rest of the morning and most of the afternoon stepping over rocks and scrambling over the willow trunks that sloped toward the water. A small part of her mind wondered at the strangeness of her errand, even as she struggled along. Yet, something inside her drove her onward, stubbornly refusing to listen to common sense.

Long before she saw it, she smelled the sea, a wild, briny tang. The sun was beginning to dip toward the horizon when she stumbled, panting, around the last curve—and stopped, amazed by the sight, for she had never seen the ocean before. The wind had died down. Far out from shore the water's surface looked flat, like hammered silver, without a sail for as far as the eye could see. Waves lapped the sand gently at her feet, rising and falling like the breast of a sleeping child.

She walked into the water until the highest part of the wave covered her ankles. Sparkles reflected from the sunlight flashed in the sand underwater as the waves pulled back from the shore. The tug of the sand shifting under her feet as the water surged and receded made her laugh. She bent and dabbled her fingers in the water and then cautiously touched them to her lips. Her mouth puckered at the taste.

Bits of something white lay on the foam-covered seaweed just beyond the high tide mark. Eliza went over and knelt down to look. Feathers . . . she gathered them carefully and counted them, her heart beating quickly. Eleven large white feathers, perfectly shaped. She held them up in wonder to examine, and sunlight glinted off the water droplets hanging from their rippled edges.

As if in a dream, without knowing why, she pulled enough long hairs from the nape of her neck to braid into a golden red thread. A thorn from one of the bramble bushes along the river's edge had broken off in her skirt. She drew it out and used it to pierce the feathers' quills and tease the braided strand through each.

And then she simply sat for a long time without worry or thought, the feathers in her lap, watching the sea. The restless stubbornness that had driven her all day to this spot now seemed curiously peaceful, content to merely rest. And wait . . .

As the sun sank into a canopy of red and gold, she saw a line of swans like a long white ribbon flying over the water, one behind the other toward the shore. Her heart leaped up in her breast at the sight. She scrambled to her feet, clutching the feathers, and backed away until she felt bushes behind her. There, she crouched to hide herself.

With great thumps and splashes, the swans alighted right at the water's edge, quite close to her. A trick of the last sunset light warmed their flapping wings to a color like molten gold. As the edge of the sun finally slipped below the horizon, the swans all spread their wings and extended their necks, as if about to take flight—but instead they *elongated*. A tremendous light welled up, making Eliza gasp. When she could see again, she clutched the branches of the bush with a choking cry of astonishment.

For the feathers that had covered them had all fallen into the surf. They were no longer swans, but men clad in white. And although the years had changed them, she knew them immediately and sprang up with a glad cry, calling out their names as she ran.

Their heads turned as she ran toward them, and after the first heartbeat of surprise, they surrounded her and took her into their arms.

Eliza had found her brothers at last.

Chapter Ten

Come, you thankful people, come;
Raise the song of harvest home.
All is safely gathered in
Ere the winter storms begin.

——HENRY ALFORD,
"COME, YOU THANKFUL PEOPLE, COME"

Rick offered the job at the photo shop, and Elias accepted it. He started in the front, learning how to stock the shelves and write up orders accurately. "Make sure you fill everything out on the form," Rick told him. "If you don't mark whether a guy wants matte or glossy, count on it, he'll decide he wanted it the other way. And he'll lie through his teeth about it, trying to get the shop to eat the cost.

"Once you've got all this stuff down, and you know the cameras and types of film, then you start learning the procedures in the back. When I'm sure you can run the morning prints through the Kreonite without exploding it, I'm gonna hand the first shift over to you. As you may have noticed," Rick added, deadpan, "I'm not a morning person."

Elias spent his lunch hours on a bench in Central Park, basking in the sun by the Pond. As he ate his egg sandwich, he scanned apartment and roommate ads in the paper, circling the ones that looked interesting. Eventually, he would lay the paper aside and settle back to watch the brightly painted miniature boats tack across the Pond. Swans and ducks swam meanderingly over in his direction, eyeing him speculatively, and he went to the water's edge and tossed them his sandwich crusts. He didn't even realize how much he had come to depend upon this lunchtime routine until a day came when rain drove him inside, and he spent his lunch hour wandering forlornly around a drugstore instead.

At the end of each day, he took the subway back to Union Square and walked from there to Sean's apartment, smiling to himself. Everything felt different now, or maybe it was the training at the shop, making him see his surroundings with a newly awakened photographer's eye. Colors seemed to have more intensity, and surfaces—he groped to understand it—maybe it was that mellow September light, adding roundness and density to everything. *Or maybe things look different just because I'm eating more regularly.* He had a place to return to, a . . . He shied away from calling it a home. A base. The gritty memories of living on the streets faded as, day by day, he cautiously built for himself what he thought of as a normal life.

Or maybe it was the thought of Sean that made that stupid grin tug at the corner of his mouth as he jogged up the apartment steps. He never knew what Sean would be doing when he returned from work. Sean might be writing, surrounded by a blizzard of papers, a pencil gripped between his teeth at a jaunty angle like a tycoon's cigar. He might be at the stove cooking dinner, tasting something on a spoon, and his eyes would light up at the sight of Elias. The table would be set for two, the whole apartment redolent of garlic or curry. He might be sitting cross-legged on the couch, picking out a tune on his guitar, his face serious as he bent over the strings. Sometimes he'd be at the weight machine, his face glistening, bare arms flexing and straightening smoothly, a small towel around his neck. Once he was in the shower, and Elias had to wait outside for fifteen minutes before Sean got out, heard the buzzer, and let him in. "Well, that's stupid," he said. "Let me give you a key."

They always managed to touch within the first few minutes of Elias's coming in the door. Sean seemed to know how nervous he still was, like a wary animal just on the verge of spooking, and so he always made the first contact casual. He would tap Elias's elbow and ask him to put the water glasses on the table. Or he would place his hand nonchalantly on Elias's back as he stood in front of the refrigerator, so Elias would know to step aside to let Sean reach in to get the milk. And every night, when Elias had relaxed enough to stop tensing up every time Sean got close to him, Sean would reach over and knead the back of his neck or put an arm around his shoulder for a quick hug, saying, "I'm glad you're back."

As they ate, Sean would go over the possibilities in the paper with him, giving him advice about neighborhoods: "That's the Puerto Rican section; Loisaida, the people who live there call it. The yuppie developers trying to gentrify call it Alphabet City. It's still a tough neighborhood, lots of dealers and users. That one's in Chelsea. Lots of my friends live there, but you're gonna pay through the nose for rent. Lessee, this one's on . . . Ugh, no. Touristy. Great restaurants on the next block, though."

After doing the dishes, Elias would make some calls. He quickly decided he wouldn't be able to afford a decent apartment on his own and began concentrating on the roommate ads. The first several contacts he made proved to be fruitless. Two people who made appointments to meet with him failed to show up for the meetings. A third man sounded like he might work out, but was about to leave town for two and a half weeks before he could get together with Elias.

"Don't get worked up into a froth about it," Sean said. "You can take the time you need to find the right person."

"But—" Elias started and then stopped. *I don't want to impose on you anymore* was the polite thing to say, but the fact was, he *did* want to impose. He kept his tiny pile of possessions neatly folded and stacked in the corner of the main room at one end of the couch.

Except he didn't sleep on the couch anymore.

A day came that he didn't have to work. "Do you want to go out?" Sean asked absently that morning. "You could explore Little Italy, or some of those secondhand clothing stores on St. Mark's Place. Can't come with you, though; I'm up against a deadline for this article, and I gotta finish it today."

Elias hesitated. "Well, I thought I could run down to the corner store and pick up a few groceries for you. But then . . ." He looked out the window.

Sean did, too. A slow rain was starting to make the leaves on the courtyard trees tremble. "Oh, well, you could hang out around here if you like. I just won't be very good company."

Elias brightened. "You sure? That'd be okay?"

Sean gave him a measuring look. "Let's give it a try."

Not until afterward did Elias realize it had been a test. He brought the groceries back, put them away quietly, and then settled on the couch with the newspaper. Sean sat at the typewriter, engrossed in his work. At noon, Elias made a couple of sandwiches and put one on a plate at Sean's elbow, along with a glass of milk. He changed the tapes in the cassette player so Sean wouldn't have to get up to do it. After lunch, he chose a book off the shelf and settled down to read. A drowsy hush settled over the apartment, broken only by the cheerful racket of Sean's typewriter and the patter of the rain, sloughing slowly down the windowpane.

Sean gave him a curious look at dinner that night. "Where'd you learn to do that?" he asked.

"Do what?"

"The right way to act around a writer." Sean shook his head. "I haven't had too much luck writing when tri— when people are around. They usually get bored and start talking to me, distracting me. But you made it easier to work, instead."

The compliment made Elias duck his head, he was so absurdly pleased. Still . . . "What were you about to say? You haven't had much luck writing when . . . ?"

The pause stretched, and Sean smiled a little crookedly. "I was going to say *tricks,* when tricks are around."

"Oh." Elias looked down at his plate, toyed with his rice for a moment. "I get paid tomorrow. So I'll be able to pay you back the money you gave me."

Sean didn't seem to hear the slight distancing in his voice at all. "That's great, Elias. I knew you could do it. You're really making your own way now, you know?" He pushed back his plate. "Since I finished that article and you're getting your paycheck, why don't we go out tonight to celebrate? A friend of mine is having a music party."

They got back late, and stayed up even later, experimenting yet again with the ways their bodies fit together, feeling the texture of skin touching skin as they lay side by side. "All the lessons are sure paying off," Sean teased him. "You'll be ready for Carnegie Hall pretty soon."

Elias grinned. "You know what they say: practice, practice, practice."

Sean laughed and they rolled over again. When they finally fell asleep, sweaty and spent, their limbs were still entangled.

When Elias came back from work the next night, he discovered that the small pile of clothes he had kept folded by the couch was gone. Sean had put them away in a drawer in his room. Elias's toothbrush lay next to Sean's on the bathroom sink. When Elias pulled out the newspapers again over dinner, Sean no longer limited his comments to advice about the neighborhoods: "Nope, not that one. He picks his teeth and clips his toenails and nose hairs at the dinner table. And this guy eats in his room and stashes all the used plates under his bed. You won't know it for a week, until there's not a single dish in the cupboard, and his bedroom smells of garbage. Besides, his ass is flabby. Oh god, please, not that one! That one voted for Reagan!"

Elias laughed, and Sean grabbed the papers away and stuffed them into the kitchen garbage. Elias lunged for them and Sean wrestled him to the floor. Laughing, they scuffled until Sean rolled over on top.

"Oof—lemme up, you bastard!"

"What, and give up the home court advantage?" Sean dug his knuckles into Elias's side and Elias doubled over sideways on the floor, roaring with laughter.

Sean's face lit up with fiendish delight. "Elias—you're *ticklish!*"

"No!"

"Yes, you are! Wait, let's try here under the knee. . . ."

Elias writhed, trying to buck Sean off while still keeping a straight face. Finally, he collapsed into a state of total hysteria. What with one thing and another, he never got the newspaper back, either.

But the fact was, Elias never asked whether he could move in permanently. And Sean never asked if he would stay.

It just happened.

September passed, and with October the leaves began lazily drifting off the trees in Central Park, but Elias barely noticed the creeping foray of winter into the city. He felt something inside himself, like an ember slowly being fanned into life, making it impossible for him to feel the cold. Sean took him on the bus to Chinatown one Sunday morning. At a dim sum restaurant featuring headless roast ducks hanging in the windows, they stuffed themselves on steamed dumplings and noodles, piling up the small china plates in front of themselves like greasy poker chips. Afterward, they spent most of the afternoon browsing through the crowded shops. They wandered into one emporium that smelled pleasantly of ginger, dust, and oolong tea, where Sean bought an extravagant embroidered tablecloth and Elias a black cotton robe.

"Very fetching," Sean assured him. "I like how easily it can be unbelted, too. With one hand."

They got on the bus with their packages and settled in a seat for the ride back to Tenth Street. "I bought the tablecloth for Thanksgiving," Sean said as the bus lurched away from the curb. "It's my turn to host this year."

Elias felt an equivalent lurch in the pit of his stomach. "Your family, you mean?"

"Good god, no," Sean answered, surprised into laughter. "That is . . . I suppose I'd be willing to have Thanksgiving dinner with them, but they live in Boston. My dad and, um, his second wife. I guess I could take the train, but" —he frowned—"I just never have. Not since college."

"You have sisters?" Elias asked. "Brothers?"

"No." Sean lifted an eyebrow, and his voice took on an ironic tone. "Once I came along, my parents must have decided they didn't need any other brats like me. Anyway, I get together with this group each Thanksgiving; they're my family, really. You met Jerry and Rafe on the Island, and Nick and Amy at the music party. And there's Gordy and Ian, and Minta and Ruth. I think Leo and Philip'll make it, unless they decide to leave early for that gig Leo has in Chicago that weekend." After a pause, he said gently, "Did your family make a big deal out of Thanksgiving?"

"Yeah. We'd get together with my grandmother when she was alive. Turkey with all the trimmings, of course. Funny thing, though: what I always looked forward to the most was the pumpkin bread. That was the only time of the year Mother made it. I really love that stuff."

"Maybe you could bake some next week."

Elias turned his face away and watched his own reflection in the window. "Yeah, maybe. Except I don't have any idea what recipe she used." *And I can't call her to ask* hung unspoken in the air.

Sean cleared his throat. "Tell you what. If I can't find a recipe in one of my cookbooks, I'll give you Ruth's number and you can call her. She has more cookbooks than anybody I know. And she's a soft touch. If you're lucky and sound helpless enough, she might even offer to make it herself."

Preparing for the holiday turned out to be a lot of work. On Thanksgiving morning Elias chopped celery, apricots, and pecans for the stuffing as he eyed the decapitated turkey corpse lounging in the roasting pan. The wary apprehension his mother harbored toward Thanksgiving preparations every year seemed to make perfect sense.

But all went smoothly. Sean, Elias was relieved to discover, had done this before. The turkey meekly submitted to his ministrations, no doubt recognizing a master at work. Elias painstakingly spread out the new tablecloth and began setting out the silverware. "I sure hope no one spills gravy on this."

"That's what dry cleaners are for, if worse comes to worst."

Soon, the aroma of roasting turkey, mingled with sage and onions, began to fill the apartment, renewing itself with warm blasts whenever Sean opened the oven to baste the bird. "Is the Macy's parade still going on?" he asked as he banged the oven door shut again. "Turn it on, will ya? I always love seeing those dopey balloons."

The buzzer finally rang just as the potatoes went onto the stove to boil. Sean went downstairs to answer it.

Soon enough Elias heard voices coming up the stairs and then coming through the apartment door. ". . . wonder you're in such fabulous shape, Sean, with all these stairs to climb—oh, yum, yum, smell the turkey. Divine! Happy Thanksgiving by the way, darling, if I haven't said it yet."

"Happy Thanksgiving, Gordy," Sean said. "Come on in, Ian. Here, let me take your coats."

As Sean retreated to the bedroom with the coats, a man's head poked around the corner of the small entry hallway. He was short and rather plump, with a luxuriant white mustache under an unabashed beak of a nose. He radiated the sort of personality that could probably carry it off. "Hallo! Elias, right? Sean told us you'd be joining us."

Elias put down a pot and stripped off the oven mitt. "Yes, um . . ."

"Gordy White." The man beamed and came into the kitchen to shake Elias's hand. "Splendid to meet you. Yoo-hoo, Ian," he said over his shoulder. "Come and meet Elias."

Ian appeared and put a paper bag down on the counter. He had crooked teeth and a warm smile and smelled of pipe tobacco. "Elias? Ian Marshall." He stepped forward to shake Elias's hand. "Do you have room in the fridge for this salad?"

A knock sounded on the apartment door. "Let me, let me," Gordy exclaimed, and hurried to answer it. "Eewww! Who let you two in?" his voice said.

"Some bozo held the front door of the building open for us," a woman's voice answered. "Just like you're doing now, Gordy."

"Well, I can always slam it in your face, honey," Gordy's voice replied.

"If you do, you won't get any of this nice artichoke dip," a second woman's voice answered.

"Ooo, artichoke dip! Here, let me take that." Gordy came around the corner. "Elias, this is Minta and Ruth."

The two women smiled at Elias as they unwound scarves. Minta was the taller of the two, with a model's carriage, a mobile lip, and a glint in her eye that suggested an active sense of humor. As she took off her coat, Gordy exclaimed, "Where'd you get that skirt, Minta?"

"D'ye like it? A souvenir of my trip to Ecuador."

"It's utterly gorgeous; turn around and let me see."

Obligingly, Minta pirouetted, and the fabric flared out around her calves. The skirt certainly caught the eye: a riot of bright colors, it was sewn all over with little mirrors.

"Oh, splendid," Gordy caroled. "You simply must let me borrow it."

"You couldn't possibly wear it, Gordy," the other woman, Ruth, said, grinning. A button on her coat read "We Don't Care How They Do It in New York." She pulled off her hat, unleashing a wildly curly mass of prematurely white hair; she looked about forty. "It's too small for you."

Gordy pouted as he placed the covered hors d'oeuvres platter on the counter. "Couldn't you have gotten it with an elasticized waistband?"

"Ha," said Minta. "Finance your own wardrobe, cheapskate."

Ruth took a foil-wrapped package out of her capacious pocket as she relinquished her coat to Sean. She handed it to Elias. "Pumpkin bread."

Philip and Leo arrived next, cradling pecan and pumpkin pies in big, blunt hands, and then Nick and Amy, bringing wine. "We brought our instruments, too," Nick said, nodding toward a pile of black cases left by the door, "in case anybody wants some music later on. Unless—will the neighbors complain?"

Sean considered. "Well, I think Dick-the-dick's out of town, so it'll probably be okay."

"Who's Dick-the-dick?" Elias asked.

Sean gave him a look. "Our landlord. You haven't been here long enough to know why he's called that, but trust me, you'll find out."

Leo looked from Sean to Elias. "*Our* landlord?" he said archly.

The corner of Elias's mouth quirked, a nervous twitch. "Yeah. For the time being."

As he turned away to pull napkins from the drawer, he wondered suddenly for the first time whether Sean had ever slept with any of these people.

In short order, everyone had settled on the couch or the folding chairs Sean had scrounged out of the closet for the occasion. Sean poured drinks as the guests fell on the hors d'oeuvres like ravening locusts. Elias accepted a Coke and looked around warily. So . . . Leo maybe? Or Nick? How could he possibly tell? Sean placed his hand on Nick's shoulder, smiling at him as he leaned over to hand a drink to Philip. Elias watched, and wondered.

"So how did you all meet each other?" he asked the group at large.

"Oh, Leo and Sean hooked up playing music," said Philip. "It was at the Rathskeller, right, Sean?"

"Mmm. I think so—oh, no. It might have been one of Nick's parties."

"And we introduced Ruth and Minta to everybody," Philip went on. "Simple blatant self-interest. Ruth's been doing our taxes for years; we figure if we ply her with a good meal every once in a while, she'll refrain from blabbing all about our fabulous wealth to the IRS."

"You wish," Ruth said agreeably, tucking her feet underneath herself on the couch.

"Ruth and I are the tokens," Minta said, wrinkling her nose at Philip, and then flashing a smile at Elias.

"Token what?" Elias asked before he could stop himself.

"The token dykes," Ruth said, dabbing at a dribble of dip oozing from the corner of her mouth.

"The token lesbians," Ian added, lisping the words with relish, his eyes dancing as they met Minta's.

Minta groaned and threw a pillow at him.

Gordy laughed. "You mean the token *women*."

"Ahem," said Amy. "What am I, chopped liver?"

"It's different for you, Amy," Gordon told her cheerfully. "You're not here as a token woman; you and Nick are the token hets."

Elias let out a breath. Not Nick then, probably.

Amy rolled her eyes. "So how long have you and Ruth been eating turkey with these turkeys again?" she asked Minta.

"Mmm." Minta considered. "Four years? Maybe longer."

Elias nodded, and looked at Gordy and Ian. "How about you?"

"I met Minta when my company hired her to work on an ad campaign," said Gordy. "I do sales," he added as an afterthought. "Vitamins. Anyway, we were working together late one night on some ad copy. Somehow we got on the subject of how dreary the holidays can be if you're stuck celebrating them with the wrong people. We kept talking. Eventually I met Ruth and Minta met Ian. I guess she decided we were the right sort of people, because she arranged to have Leo invite Ian and me the next Thanksgiving."

"Yeah," Ian put in, "and Gordy cleverly brought his apricot mousse for dessert, to make sure we'd be invited back."

"That's right, you do photo ad layout, don't you?" Sean said to Minta. He jerked a thumb toward Elias. "Elias just got a job at a photo shop."

"Really?" said Minta, her face lighting up with interest.

"Well, yeah, but I'm only starting out."

"That's how I started out, too, in a photo shop." The conversation wended its way from there to commercial photography to art photography to gallery work, until the timer rang to remind Elias about the potatoes.

He took the pot off the stove, drained the potatoes at the sink, and dug around in the utensil drawer for the masher. "Isn't the turkey about done by now?" he asked.

"Oops, right," Sean said, hastily going over and opening the oven door.

"C'mon, Ian," Gordy said, shoving another cracker into his mouth. "Let's take care of getting drinks on the table. Everyone want wine?"

"You get the glasses, I'll pour," Ian replied. "Hand me the corkscrew."

"You forgot to say the magic word, honey," Gordy trilled in falsetto.

"Hand me the corkscrew . . . bitch," Ian mock-growled.

Elias gave them a startled look as Minta and Leo cracked up.

"Where're Jerry and Rafe?" Philip asked.

"Not sure," Sean said, as he levered the turkey out of the oven. "I know Jerry was coming in from out of town last night." He set the turkey down, went over to the phone, and dialed a number. After a moment he frowned and hung up. "No answer."

"They must be on their way. Or did Jerry get hung up on a connecting flight because of the holiday jam at the airport or something?" Philip asked.

"Well, if he did, I'm sure they'll call. We might as well start, I suppose. There's enough food here; they'll have plenty to eat when they decide to show up."

The talk ranged far and wide during dinner—over music, news, and politics. "My vote for turkey of the year is the city council. That vote last Monday, turning down *again* the ordinance prohibiting discrimination against gays . . ."

Ian snickered. "Don't act so surprised, Philip. It's not like they haven't had plenty of practice. What's that, the tenth time this decade they've kicked it downstairs?"

"It still makes me puke. They——"

"Philip's an optimist," Leo cut in. "He labors under the illusion that the city council is actually going to grow a spine one of these days." He pushed back his plate. "My vote for turkey of the year goes to what's-'is-name, Robert—no, Roger Jepsen. That Republican senator from Iowa, you know? The guy trying to pass the 'Family Protection Act.'"

"The what?" asked Amy.

"That's the one that says that if you're homosexual, in fact if you even suggest that homosexuality is acceptable, you'll be ineligible for veterans benefits, welfare, student assistance, or Social Security."

"My gawd. Hasn't the guy ever heard of the First Amendment?"

"Nope."

"Maybe he should come be senator of New York," Philip said savagely. "Between all the goddamn closet cases and the city council, he'd probably feel right at home here."

In the corner the phone trilled. Elias leaned back in his chair and picked it up. "Hello."

"Elias?" It was Jerry's voice.

"Hey, Jerry, happy Thanksgiving! We've been wondering where you are."

"May I speak to Sean, please?" said Jerry, sounding tense.

Elias signaled Sean with a chin lift and held out the phone to him. The conversation around the table hushed. Sean scooped up the phone. "Hey, there. You better get your butts over here if you still hope to get some dinner."

"What did Jerry say?" Gordy asked Elias in an undertone. "Did he say where he is?"

Elias, watching Sean, shook his head. Sean frowned as he listened.

The silence stretched and acquired an uneasy edge as Sean sat down slowly, his expression grave. "My god. Okay, thanks for letting us know. St. Vincent's? Do you want some of us to come, too?"

"What's going on?" Amy hissed.

Taking Rafe to the hospital, Sean mouthed at her. He listened a little longer, took a scrap of paper and pencil, and jotted something down. "You're sure you don't want somebody coming over tonight? Okay, then, I'll call tomorrow and see if he's up to having visitors." He hesitated, and then added, "He'll be okay, Jerry. I'll talk to you tomorrow."

He hung up the phone. "Jerry got back from Cleveland just this morning; he did get stuck at the airport overnight. When he got home, he found Rafe in bed, delirious, with a fever up over a hundred and six."

"Shit," Leo muttered, shocked.

"Yeah. It's pneumonia, Jerry thinks."

"My god. Was Rafe that sick when Jerry left town?"

Sean shrugged. "Jerry said he's been off his feed for a while, a month or so, but still, it must've been a surprise to find him like that. It's a good thing Jerry didn't take a cab directly here from the airport."

"No kidding."

The phone call had the effect of breaking up the group around the table. Leo and Philip got up and started clearing the table. "Feel free to wander over to the couch," Leo told Minta magnanimously. "Watch football and belch a lot and fall asleep."

"Gee, sounds like fun," Ruth said.

"We'll play you a lullaby," Nick said, as he and Amy brought their cases over and began unsnapping the catches. "But then I'm going to need to play something lively to wake myself up after that dinner. Leo, you brought a flute, right?"

"Mmm-hmm."

"Sean, do you want to play the harp?" Amy pulled out a fiddle and began rosining up her bow.

"Depends on how much tuning it needs."

"Why worry about tuning a harp?" Leo put in. "It's always out of tune, anyway, so why bother? That's why harpists always go off to fetch more beer while everyone *else* is tuning."

"I've been working on that slip jig," Nick said, cocking his head and smiling winningly as he pulled a concertina out of its case.

Sean laughed as he reached for the harp. "I can never resist a good rollicking slip jig."

"*If* you can keep up with me," Nick replied, lifting a challenging eyebrow. "And you'd better not miss the change this time."

"I *never* miss the change."

"Huh," Nick said, fitting his hands under his instrument's straps. "We'll see." He heaved a happy sigh. "Good food. Now I'm ready to play. Give me an A, somebody."

Elias stayed and listened as the musicians tuned their instruments, warmed up, and began playing. After the third piece, Gordy, who had been chewing absently on the ends of his mustache, abruptly stood. "I'm going to call Jerry and see if he wants me to come help him get Rafe to the hospital. Sean, can I use your phone in the bedroom?"

Sean looked up from the harp. "Jerry said they were leaving right away."

"Well, perhaps so, but I'd feel better knowing that at least I tried." He disappeared into the bedroom and shut the door after himself, but emerged a minute later shaking his head. "You were right," he said over the music. "They've already left." Sean, deep in the trickiest part of a chord progression, nodded his head absently.

A little lost in thought, Elias got up and threaded his way past Sean's chair. Minta glanced at him and smiled as he passed her on his way to the bedroom. *I'd feel better knowing that at least I tried.* The light was off in the bedroom; he didn't turn it on.

After closing the door, he sat on the edge of the bed and reached for the telephone on the nightstand. With a deep breath, he held the handset to his ear and dialed the number.

The phone rang tinnily in his ear once, twice, as his heart began thundering. *Maybe they're at Bob's?* He hardly knew if he felt relieved, or if, once having mustered the courage to call his parents, he could pick up the phone again to call his brother, too.

Abruptly, the ringing stopped. "Hello?" his mother's cultured voice said in his ear.

At the sheer surprise of it, his voice caught in his throat.

"Hello?" his mother repeated after a moment. "Who's there, please?"

He drew a ragged breath and dug his fingernails into his thighs. On the other end of the line, his mother made a small sound, too, an intake of breath in surprise. After a pause, he heard her whisper, a catch in her voice, "Elias?"

He squeezed his eyes shut, clenching his teeth over a sob. He wanted desperately to say something to her, anything, but his voice was wholly suspended now. His mother had always appeared to be coolly controlled to him, and that small note of pain echoing in his ear seemed more unguarded than any sound he had ever heard her make.

What was he calling to tell her, anyway? He could hear Sean's clear baritone singing in the living room, through the closed door. *I'm safe, Mother. I knew you'd want to hear that. I've found a new group of friends. And I'm with someone who's good to me, and I think . . . I think I'm beginning to fall in love with him. You'd like him, too, I know you would, if you'd only give him a chance. If you'd just give me a chance.*

Please. Please give me a chance.

"Elias?" his mother whispered again.

In the background, his father's voice said, "Who is it?"

Elias felt coldness wash over him.

"It's—nobody," his mother said, loudly, for his father's benefit. He could almost see her, batting the wetness away from her eyes, plastering her usual serene expression over her face. "No one. It's a wrong number."

The phone went dead.

Chapter Eleven

_____

Eternal Father, strong to save
Whose arm has bound the restless wave
Who bade the mighty ocean deep
Its own appointed limits keep
Oh, hear us when we cry to thee
For those in peril upon the sea.

——WILLIAM WHITING,
"ETERNAL FATHER, STRONG TO SAVE"

After the exclamations had died down and the first tears were wiped away, Eliza's brothers drew her away from the water to the edge marked by nodding beach grass, where a tangle of driftwood lay heaped upon the sand.

"Sit down, dear sister, sit down." Benjamin, the youngest, dusted sand off the end of a driftwood log for her as the others hastened to settle themselves around them. In wonder, Benjamin touched Eliza's face tenderly, tilting his head back to drink in the sight of her. "Faith," he laughed, his joy bubbling up, "who would have thought the pert lass who tormented us so at our play would grow so tall and beautiful!"

"I never did torment you!" Eliza laughed in turn. "Fie upon you, you belie me, brother!" She placed her hand over his, savoring his touch upon her cheek.

"She looks like Charles, think you?" Hugh said.

"Aye," said Benjamin, glancing at Charles and then tilting his head and studying Eliza critically. "A bit about the eyes, and the brow."

"Perhaps," James, the eldest, observed quietly, "but I think she looks most like our mother."

The brothers, at this observation, grew pensive. Eliza studied them all eagerly in turn, her eyes bright.

They were all tall, well-formed men, although quite thin and pale. Each possessed some feature of at least one of their parents: James and Henry had their father's black hair and gray eyes, and Edward, Stephen, and Robert had his large, square hands and broad shoulders. Charles and Frederick, with their high cheekbones and heavily lidded eyes, resembled their mother more closely. Geoffrey, Michael, Hugh, and Benjamin had a mixture of features from both mother and father.

Eliza heaved a sigh of pure happiness. " 'Tis a miracle we have found one another again." She blinked and looked around more closely. Their hair looked neatly barbered, and, even more fantastically, all were clad in extravagant matching suits of white velvet. "How in the name of wonder—what has happened to all of you? I saw you *change*—"

"Aye, you saw our curse," James replied, not liking the reminder. He picked up a stick and drove the point into the sand by his knee. "Every sunrise and sunset our shapes transform, as you have seen."

"Swans by day and men by night?"

"Aye. And ever since leaving Kellbrooke Hall, eight years ago, we have been homeless and wandering."

At the expression in their suddenly grave faces, Eliza shuddered. "But how did this happen to you? And why?"

"How?" James laughed bitterly. " 'Tis witchcraft, of course. And as to why . . . faith, who knows what worm of jealousy and spite has eaten away at our mother-in-law's heart, to turn her so against us."

"Did *she* do this, then?" Wide-eyed, she looked around the circle; they all solemnly nodded back at her.

" 'Tis a grave accusation to cry witchery upon anyone," Geoffrey said, "but—"

"I was there in the room when she did it," James interrupted flatly. "I *saw* her do it."

"I believe you," Eliza breathed. "I . . . Our father recently bid me return to Kellbrooke Hall. And from what I saw of the Countess there, I do believe she would do such a thing. I think . . ." She frowned. " 'Tis odd, I do not entirely remember, but I think she tried to ensorcell me, too."

"Did she, now?" James eyed his sister speculatively, a glimmer of hope kindling. "But you defeated her?"

"If she did try a spell against me," Eliza said doubtfully, "it must have been a failure. I do not know if aught I did made it so." She sighed. "She found another way, however, to undo me before my father."

"What was that?" Benjamin said warily.

"Do you know of . . . forgive me . . . of the Countess's accusations against you? Of . . . treason?"

The stick in James's hand snapped, and he leaped to his feet. "Aye, we have heard of them. They are a pack of filthy lies!" he burst out. "We are true subjects to the Crown!"

"I know! But our father believes her. You see, the Countess is . . ." She hesitated, and then forced herself to say the words. "The Countess is with child."

A heavy silence fell, broken only by the plaintive calls of gulls, dipping over the surface of the waves. The brothers exchanged looks as their hearts collectively sank.

"And our father said," Eliza continued after a moment, "that if her child is a boy, it will be his heir."

Now the brothers all looked to James. A spasm crossed his face. "The seventh Earl of Exeter, eh?" Abruptly, James turned and walked down to the water's edge. There, he picked up a stone and threw it savagely into the water.

Henry, the second oldest brother, got up and hurried after him. "Don't," he said into James's ear as he reached his side. "The Earldom is not any more lost to you than it was eight years ago."

"Is it not?" James replied bitterly.

"No." Henry squeezed his forearm with rough sympathy. "Our ties were cut long ago, as you know well, James."

James stared at the gulls for a while as Henry waited. "God's blood," James muttered finally. "After all these years it still sticks in my throat. Well, this news makes it even clearer that it is time and past for us to leave this land."

"There will be time and enough to talk of that," Henry replied. "But for now, take heart, man. We are all together again at last." He glanced up the beach to where Eliza sat, her face a pale oval in the twilight. "Look you, do not grieve her over a wound so old, and one she cannot help."

James sighed, cursing himself for a fool. "You are right, Henry. As always." The two men turned and trudged back up the slope of beach sand.

"Forgive me, James," Eliza said remorsefully as they drew near. "I little like bringing news that hurts you so."

"Nay," James said with an embarrassed wave. "It is only . . . I had hoped that someday, if the curse could only be lifted . . ."

"I understand, truly." Eliza's gaze fell to her lap, where she stroked the eleven feathers tied with the narrow braid of her hair. "You see . . . our father has cast me out, too. For when he told me he hoped for a new heir, I asked why he should need one, when he already had as many as a man could want." She grimaced. "He did not like that."

That drew a ripple of rueful laughter. "I'll warrant he did not," said Stephen.

"And for that he cast you out?" Robert said wonderingly.

Eliza nodded.

James drew a deep breath. "Your portion is the same as ours then, eh, little sister?" He stared down at the top of her bent head, and his heart stirred, both with pity for her and a little dismay.

"Well, then," he said with gruff heartiness, "we will bid you as welcome as we may."

"I say we must have a feast to celebrate our reunion!" said Benjamin, who was hungry.

"Aye!" exclaimed Michael, liking the idea. "Let us show you some of the canny tricks we've learned to provide for ourselves over the years."

"'Tis well thought," James said, setting his grievance aside and rubbing his hands together. "Now then, we must see what may be had. Michael—"

"I will see if there are fish," Michael said, getting to his feet and starting down the beach to the north.

"And I will hunt for crayfish," Frederick offered, rising to follow. Several others got up, too, and scattered to walk in several directions up and down the beach.

"And you, Charles," James said, "is it not your turn to sacrifice a sleeve to keep us warm tonight?"

Charles elbowed Geoffrey, sitting next to him. "If it is not Geoffrey's."

"Not mine!" Geoffrey said indignantly.

Shrugging good-naturedly, Charles took off his coat. Eliza started at the sound of ripping linen.

"What are you doing?" she exclaimed, horrified. "Your beautiful clothes—"

"Aye, they are very fine, are they not?" Charles said cheerfully, with an edge of sarcasm as he shredded the sleeve of his shirt into small bits. "Fear not, Eliza; we all shall have another suit just as elegant tomorrow night."

"It suits our mother-in-law's humor," Hugh added, "to dress us like princes in the wilderness." He was collecting dried beach grasses and small bits of driftwood into a heap. "Do not think we complain about her mockery, for we use our clothes as tools, you see. We bend nails from our shoe heels to make fishhooks . . ."

". . . knot garter strings into rabbit snares . . ."

". . . fashion coat sleeves into slingshots . . ."

". . . and start fires with shirt linen." Hugh accepted the small squares of cloth Charles offered him and delicately poked them into the pile of fuel he had gathered. He pulled the buckle off his shoe and struck a flinty pebble against it to make a spark. After several tries, the linen caught, firing the grass in turn as Hugh blew gently. He added more twigs as the fire spat and grew, and soon had a merry blaze going.

"Hugh starts and tends our fires," Charles said. "And a pretty job he usually makes of it, too."

"My red hair gives me the talent," Hugh said, winking at Eliza.

"Except when it rains, and we need it the most," Geoffrey grumbled.

Soon, Michael came trotting back up the beach, two large fish dangling in his hands. "Why, how did you catch them so quickly?" Eliza exclaimed.

Michael grinned proudly as he fetched a shell from its place under a large flat stone. The edge of the shell had been honed against a sandy rock to make it sharp; Michael used this crude knife to scale the fish and slit their bellies. "We took willow withies growing by that stream there," he gestured with the shell knife, "and wove them into basket traps, which we leave to float in the surf during the day. A length of kelp is tied to them, anchored under a rock."

Others followed with further offerings: pocketfuls of berries, crayfish, and mussels. "A thousand pities we have no pot for the making of a fish chowder," Michael remarked cheerfully. "But the fish will roast on sticks and the mussels and crayfish in the coals."

"Will there be enough for all?" Eliza asked anxiously.

"Aye, enough for all to have a taste at least. But you must have most of it, Eliza."

"But are you not hungry, too?"

"Do not worry. We do most of our eating during the day," he replied shortly and went to the mouth of the river to wash his hands, leaving Eliza to wonder.

With no knives or plates, the food was difficult to eat, and several suffered burned fingers. But all pronounced the meal excellent. Empty shells served as cups for the water poured from Eliza's stone bottle. Eliza went to the stream to refill it. When she came back, Hugh was building up the fire again, for the night had fallen fully. He smiled at her as she seated herself on the ground next to Benjamin.

James, Henry, and Edward sat a little to one side, their long legs stretched out before them on the sand, out of the immediate circle of firelight. "Hark you now, Henry," James said, recommencing an argument that had been going on for some days, "I tell you, the answer is not flying south. What will it serve us to go to France?"

"It will be warmer in the winter."

"Not much, and where could we hope to find safe shelter there? France has people still, with the same arrows and muskets that threaten us here. No, I thank you. The New World is our only hope."

Henry's only answer was to look skeptical.

Abruptly, James grinned. "You know I have the right of it, Henry. You simply cannot bear to give way to your older brother in the quarrel, eh?"

"I know you think we can travel that far——" Edward began doubtfully.

"Do not doubt it! The extra light will make it possible, if we follow the path of the islands north and west——"

"But what of Eliza?" Henry interrupted.

James stopped. "I . . . don't know."

Eliza's head turned at the sound of her own name. "What of Eliza?" she repeated, cocking her head at them.

James rose and came to kneel beside her. The other brothers exchanged significant looks and sat up. "We were considering our plans," James told her. "We have lingered in England to be near you, and our mother's grave. But we have come to wish to leave this land. It is dangerous for us here; Edward was shot in the wing several years ago. We dug the musket ball out of his arm after the sun sank, and nursed him in the woods as best we could, with what little art we had. 'Twas weeks before he could fly again. The winters are harsh and cold, and . . ." His words trailed off.

"And now there is the news I brought to you of the Countess," Eliza said.

James's eyes met hers levelly. "Aye."

"Where would you go?"

"To the New World," James replied. He gave Henry a sidelong glance, but Henry held his peace.

"Across the *ocean?* But surely it is too great a span to cross in one day! How . . . ?"

"We must go north; the farther in that direction we fly while midsummer is at its height, the more light we will have, for the sun stays in the sky later. Why, if we go far enough, there are places where the sun hangs for days in the sky without ever dipping below the horizon! Our path will then curve west, following a chain of great islands until we come to the New World."

"Alas, you would leave me behind?" she said, stricken.

He opened his mouth, but she said quickly, before he could speak, "No, you must go. Only—take me with you! I could not bear to be left alone again!"

"Take you with us?" he repeated, astonished.

"But Eliza," Stephen began tentatively, "you are not . . . you cannot fly with us."

"I know, but could you not . . . carry me somehow?"

An uneasy silence fell for a moment. Finally James said slowly, "Perhaps it could be done."

Henry turned to him, amazed. "How? What do you propose?"

James brooded for a moment. "We learned to shape the willow withies to make a fish trap. Perhaps . . . if we twined the withies with kelp to make the lengths flexible . . . could we not weave them into a kind of net to carry her?"

"But could we hold it and fly at the same time?" Frederick objected.

Benjamin laughed and jumped to his feet. "We can and we will. James, you are brilliant! Come, let us away to the river, to begin gathering them." He snatched up the shell knife and hastened away, with several of the others at his heels.

James waited until they were gone and then said to Eliza in a low voice, "Sweetheart, are you certain you have the courage to go? For I will not lie to you; you must understand the danger. Carrying you will force us to fly more slowly, and we will be flying over water. If the sun should set before we reach land . . ." His voice trailed off, but the picture conveyed by his words was clear to them both.

Sobered, but grateful for his frankness, she answered him just as honestly, "I can do no less than to risk myself, when you will all be endangering yourselves equally for me. But if you leave, I must come with you."

James smiled approvingly. "Brave heart! Whether we all live or perish, dear girl, we shall not be separated again."

"Then I will pray that God will watch over us all." She leaned forward to kiss him. "Thank you, James."

Benjamin, Michael, Robert, and Stephen eventually returned to the fire with lengths of willow withies and kelp draped like fantastical necklaces over their shoulders. They heaped them into a pile and the entire group gathered around to start the work. Making the net took several false starts. But Eliza had learned the principles of weaving from her foster father, and the brothers' experience in shaping the withies made the work go more easily. Soon enough, a large net, strong and firmly knotted, took shape under many busy fingers.

"But will it hold me?"

Henry grinned. "Climb upon it now, and see."

Eliza scrambled onto the net. The brothers picked it up, using loops they had set along the edges, at the ends of braided withies. "Together now—heave!" They tossed her into the air, like a child in a blanket toss at a fair. The withies and kelp creaked, but held. Laughing, she righted herself again in the net's center.

"It will serve," James announced with satisfaction as they set her down on the ground again. "We must rest now, look you, for we have a long journey ahead of us tomorrow."

They lay down and arranged themselves in a group for sleep, with Eliza in the center, still on the net. Benjamin spread his coat over her and settled himself to lie down beside her. She sidled over to make room for him, surreptitiously studying his face in the dying firelight. He was young, only two years older than she, but the shifting play of light and shadows made his features look drawn and sad. After a moment, she rolled toward him and asked timidly, in a low voice so the others would not hear, "What is it like, Benjamin, to become a swan?"

He lay silently, staring into the sky above for so long that she wondered if he had heard her. Just as she opened her mouth to speak again, he turned toward her, raising himself on one elbow, and said, "Have you asked any of the others about this?"

"Nay, I thought but to ask you."

Benjamin nodded. "That is well, I think. Robert might speak of it, if you asked, or Frederick, or perhaps Hugh. James, now . . . I would not ask James, were I you." He shifted his position, stretching his legs out, and gave her an appraising glance. "You are fifteen now?"

She nodded.

"I must be seventeen, then," Benjamin said reflectively. "It happened eight years ago." He sighed. "I was but nine years old."

Something in Benjamin's eyes made Eliza look away. She lay back and looked up into the sky. Someone tossed a last piece of wood onto the fire, making sparks rise and spiral toward the stars above until they winked out, spent.

"Henry and I were out riding that day," Benjamin said. "I should have been studying with a riding master by then; all of the others had started by age six. But she——" Benjamin paused, and said carefully, "Our father's wife told Father a riding master's wages would be wasted on us. We were stubborn, she told him, and lazy, and refused our lessons. It wasn't true, of course. But all the same, Father believed her and the riding master was sent away.

"Finally, Henry took pity on me and offered to teach me. We had been working together for most of the morning in the courtyard. I remember my despair at my own clumsy seat, for I was afraid of the horse at first, and it didn't come naturally to me at all. But Henry was very patient. He persuaded one of Father's men to ride outside the gate with us——"

"Was it Robert Owen?" Eliza interrupted.

"Aye," Benjamin answered, surprised. "Do you remember him?"

"Yes," said Eliza thoughtfully. "Yes. I do."

"We had reached the edge of a field——" Benjamin stopped, and then continued more slowly as the scene played out in his memory. "Henry had just pulled on his reins, and was turning to tell me something, when suddenly he gave a cry and doubled over in his saddle. I felt it, too, a moment later."

Even without seeing his expression, Eliza could hear in his voice the memory of mingled bewilderment and fear. "Felt it—paugh! It . . . exploded within me, like a ravaging fire. It seized my bones, wrenching my fingers and toes out to an impossible length, and compressing my skull until I felt my head begin to *shrink*. I heard all the bones in my neck and back popping, and my shoulders—and my feet—ah, sweet Jesu!" His voice cracked.

Eliza reached out blindly toward him and seized his hand, which clenched into a fist under her fingers. She could hear his harsh breathing over the murmur of the waves.

"I tried to cry out, too, but I couldn't," Benjamin continued, his voice trembling. "I could not see Henry, or aught else, only a blinding white light. My skin—the feathers were erupting over my entire body. I lost all sense of the horse beneath me, and I felt a confusion of sound and motion, as if a fierce wind had seized me and dragged me from a cliff. I was terrified——" He stopped himself abruptly and intertwined his fingers with hers. "Your pardon, sister—I little thought 'twould be so difficult a tale to tell after so long. But then, I've never told it to anyone before now." He lay back again and turned his face up to the sky. "There was no one to hear it."

A tear slipped down Eliza's cheek, trickling toward her ear, and she squeezed his hand.

"When I came to myself again, I was flying!" Benjamin laughed softly, with a note of remembered wonder. "Flying through the air, in an utterly strange body. But it was *my* body, and I knew how to use it. I *knew* how to fly—how to spread my feathers to search for updrafts, how to wheel and dive, and how to pound the winds with my wings to gain altitude. The field, the hall, the park and the pastures surrounding it—all the dear familiar landmarks I had known all my life dwindled away beneath me till they were but wee shapes and dappled colors." He paused, remembering that first incredible sight of the fields under his wings like a patched gypsy's coat spread out in the sun to dry, the river flashing through them like a curving seam of silver thread.

"A swan flew beside me, and I could see others, flying up from the grounds below. I couldn't *think,* the way I do when I am human, but somehow I knew that we belonged together, those other swans and I. We were simply a muddled group at first, flailing away at one another in panic. But we sorted ourselves out into a flock eventually and flew away into the west.

"I do not remember very much about that first day. None of us do. We must have traveled quite a distance from our home, and of course, we weren't accustomed to flying. Long before sunset, we had landed on a lake to rest and swim in the shallows. I thank God for that, for when the sun slipped below the horizon, we became men again." Unexpectedly, Benjamin laughed. "I suddenly came to myself flailing around in mucky water. Fortunately, I was near enough to the shore that I could stand up on the lake bottom. Stephen was next to me; I remember him staggering there with the water streaming down his face, picking water weeds out of his hair with a dazed look on his face. Geoffrey and Edward had to rescue Charles, who had been swimming in deeper water when he transformed back.

"Somehow we dragged one another out of the water. And once we had collapsed onto the shore, we whooped and pounded one another on the back, so relieved we were to be human again. We didn't understand at first, you see." Bitterness made his throat swell. "All we knew was that we had all been changed into swans at the same instant. Even if the spell was over, we were leagues from our home, utterly lost. We had no fire, and so we all huddled together, meaning to sleep as best we could and try to find our way back in the morning.

"The day might have been a blur, but that night I will never forget. The rocks chafed underneath us, and the insects bit. We were all cold and hungry and frightened. I finally slept a little, curled up between Henry and Stephen—but something caused us all to start awake again just before dawn. It was the magic beginning to steal over us again." A harsh edge crept into Benjamin's voice. "After eight years, we have become expertly attuned to the rising and setting of the sun, even when 'tis entirely hidden by clouds. We had an instant of realization before the spell took us and changed us again. The pain was not as great the second time. But in that moment, we began to understand what our fates would be."

Benjamin fished a pebble out from underneath his back and tossed it aside. "We are swans by day, and men by night. Yet to say it so simply does not even begin to convey the cunning, the . . . the *viciousness* of the Countess's malice. Every day, our minds are blunted and shadowed by magic, by our natures as mute animals. How far did I fly today? How many weeds and snails did I eat? Did I spend many hours preening myself?" In the darkness, he shrugged. "I could not tell you surely. Our days pass, one by one, year upon weary year, as if in a strange mist. Only at night can we think about what we have lost, forever estranged from our own kind.

"Think of it, Eliza. For eight years, I have not even been able to warm my hands in the sun. I have not looked upon my father's face, nor the faces of anyone else but my brothers. We have avoided all sight of men ever since Edward's injury. Bitterest of all, we cannot come to the Lord's table to receive His body and blood, or hear His word preached to the congregation."

"But what can bar you?" Eliza faltered. "There are evening services. I know you fear the treason charges, but surely after eight years few could recognize you—"

"No!" He sighed in frustration. "You do not understand."

"Then help me," she begged. "Help me understand, Benjamin."

A moment. Then, softly, "We are too ashamed."

"Ashamed?" She frowned, puzzled. "But why?"

Benjamin wavered, torn between the desire to unburden his heart and the habits of long silence. The sea waves rose and fell, rose and fell, hissing gently as they withdrew from the sand. Around them, the others had all fallen silent. One or two were asleep, but the rest were listening. The fire had burned low, and Benjamin could see only the dim outline of Eliza's profile in the friendly darkness. Somehow, the shadows obscuring her face gave him the courage to continue.

"We kept watch over you, you know. We didn't dare approach you as men, for fear we might somehow endanger you with the Countess. But we did fly past your foster home to see you."

"Truly?" she answered, touched.

"We never saw you with any young man, and we wondered. . . are you a maiden still, Eliza?"

She raised an eyebrow, surprised, and was grateful the darkness hid her blush. "I never was a lover yet."

"Is it wrong to ask?" he asked ingenuously. "I know little of the ways between men and women. I was so young, and there has never been opportunity. . . . I have spent almost as many years caught in this web of sorcery as I did as a human boy. Sometimes I think, if the spell were broken, I would not even know anymore what my true state should be, a swan or a man. I do not think I would know how to be a man. Simply a man."

He sighed. "Well," he continued, his voice low, aware of the ears of others, listening around them. "I spoke of shame. You see, when the magic comes to take us . . . I think it is what it must be like to be imprisoned in the grip of . . . of a merciless ravisher. Imagine it if you can, Eliza—being held captive, in the power of a faceless *thing* that creeps to you at every dawn to take you, to use you. Struggle hard as you will, you cannot resist it, and you cannot escape." At the sound of his ragged breathing in her ear, Eliza felt her flesh crawl. "When it releases you again at sunset, all you feel at first is relief at your freedom. Yet you know it will steal to you at dawn again. And you will suffer that humiliation, that" —his voice dropped to a growling croon— "that . . . *debasement* all over again.

"Imagine what it is to have everyone you have ever trusted turn his face from you. The only ones who understand, your only company, are your fellow prisoners, who suffer as you do. Search your heart as you might, you don't know why it happens, what you have ever done to deserve it. You don't know if your ravisher understands or even cares how your soul writhes as its touch invades you, defiles you. All you know for certain is that it will return to possess you again. And again, and again. Until you had liefer die, if only to end it!

"There are eleven of us; James is nearing forty. Most of us should have married and begun families of our own. James was already betrothed, you know, to Alice Rutland. He never speaks of her anymore, but I know he sometimes dared to fly to the home where she lived, until she married another. Losing her was the greatest part of his pain. Eleven of us. Think of how many grandchildren Father should have dandled on his knee by now! And yet, if the spell is never broken, our family line ends with us. No wives, no children, just eleven of us, living in the wilderness, growing older and older alone. One by one, we will perish—who knows? By accident, by musket ball, through cold or hunger in wintertime. We will go to our unmarked graves—if we even have graves—unwept for by anyone but one another."

She would weep for them, Eliza's heart cried. She was weeping now, but the tears ran too quickly even to allow her to speak.

"I think sometimes of what it will be like for the last one of us. I am the youngest. Very likely it may be me. Well. Now you know. Tell me then, sister," Benjamin said in the bleakest voice imaginable, "how can we come to God with this accursed taint upon our souls?"

The sound of her quiet weeping finally reached him. Some of the dark shapes around them stirred, lifting their heads in concern. "Oh, forgive me," Benjamin exclaimed, turning toward her, instantly contrite. "Forgive my wretched tongue, Eliza. What I said should have been left unspoken; 'tis not fit for you to hear."

"No!" she said, seizing his hands. "Only do not say God has turned His face from you, for did He not lead me to you? Believe it, Benjamin." She squeezed his hands, trying to will her conviction into him through the sheer force of her touch. "If there is any way to break this curse, I will find it. I swear it to you. And I will never rest until you are safe and wholly free again."

He bowed his head to kiss her hands, holding his. "You still wish to come with us, knowing all this?"

"With all my heart, I do."

The brothers awoke shortly before dawn, as usual. They gathered around the net where Eliza still slept, her hand tucked up under her cheek like a child's. Her other hand still held the feather bundle she had made. Benjamin twitched it from her slack grasp and gently tied the ends of the braided hair around her slender neck, smoothing it so that the feathers lay between her breasts.

"Shall we wake her, before . . . ?" Frederick said doubtfully, looking down at her.

James considered and shook his head. He knew it was cowardly, but deep down, he did not relish the idea of her watching during the morning change, and he suspected the others felt the same. "No. But there is more we can do to prepare. Is her water bottle full? Then bring those berry branches, and we will lash them to the net."

"Here are the rest of the willow withies," Robert offered. "Lash them on, too, and they can be used for repairs if the net should burst a hole."

They worked quickly as the pearly sky grew lighter and the horizon in the east brightened to gold. And then they simply stood, waiting, their breath quickening, faces turned toward the east like morning flowers opening.

As the first rays of the sun fell upon them, the magic transformed them with its familiar ruthless swiftness. Their clothes fell, empty, to the sand, and then melted away into nothingness like fairy gold. As the last flare of power died, the swans seized the loops at the edges of the net in their beaks and leaped skyward, beating their newly erupted wings against the damp touch of the dawn air.

Eliza came awake with a start, her heart hammering. The wind rushing in her face made her hair whip and billow out behind her, like a silk banner. She seized the webbing of the net with all her strength and gasped as she looked around—and down.

They flew swiftly through the early morning chill, the earth shrouded in curling mists beneath them. The swans flew on either side of her, their necks stretched out full length, feathers fluttering at the tips as their wings pumped rhythmically, their feet tucked up neatly underneath. The rush of air made their pinions vibrate with a peculiar, throbbing hum. As the rising sun slowly turned the pale, pearly gray light to a warm yellow, the swan flying directly to her right caught and held her eye with an inscrutable, silent stare. Eliza shut her eyes in terror and remained that way for many long minutes. But her brothers flew calmly and the net moved through the air steadily, without threatening to tumble her out of it. Eventually, her curiosity overcame her, and she ventured to open one eye a slit and look down.

The mists were beginning to lift, and she could see now that they were following the line of the coast. She stared in wonder at the delicate scalloped lines of waves, breaking against the shore. Farther in, to the east, she caught glimpses of tiny houses and towns nestled in among the trees, and rivers, winking at her in the ever-changing light. To her left, far, far below, she saw a ship. Its miniature white sails made it look like a distant seagull, skimming and dipping over the waves.

Something was tickling the back of her ear, and she turned her head to see several branches of blackberries lying beside her on the net. Her youngest brother flew directly above her, and she smiled up at him as she ate the berries, grateful for her breakfast.

The swans continued to rise until they were flying level with the clouds. One huge one, puffy and white, floated to one side, looking as vast as a mountain, and Eliza marveled to see her own shadow upon it, and those of the eleven swans, looking gigantic in size. She turned her head and gasped again to see a cloud hurrying toward them. Even as she braced herself, the swans entered it in a rush, and she laughed at her own fears, for the cloud was simply soft and damp and translucent, like fog upon a hilltop. She still could make out her brothers flying beside her, dimly, their outlines blurred into misty softness. When they shot out of the cloud into the sunlight again, infinitesimal beads of water trickled down the fringe of hair fluttering above her eyes, like dew upon a spiderweb.

Onward through the whole day they flew, like a winged arrow. The land dwindled behind them to a shadowy smudge and then dropped below the curve of the horizon, leaving nothing but the sea beneath them. As Benjamin flew above to shade her, Eliza drowsed, watching the dark green waves underneath her through hooded eyes. The caps of foam on them looked like millions of swans swimming on the water. Eventually, she turned her head to scan the sky again. A huge bank of clouds floated before them, and to her tired eyes' fancy, they seemed to form themselves into a range of snow-covered mountains. She wondered for a moment whether it was land she saw—one part in the center even looked like a castle, piled high with turrets and columns. She blinked, and the cloud was merely a cloud again. She frowned, wondering.

More hours passed, and Eliza began to grow anxious. The swans were laboring hard, and yet there was still no sign of land, and the sun was sinking lower and lower. As they flew back below the level of the clouds, the weather began to grow sullen and then threatening. Gusts of wind battered them, forcing the swans to fight to keep the net level. In the distance, Eliza could see a curtain of rain falling into the ocean. Lightning burst forth from a dark mass of clouds, flash after flash, like a darting needle in a clever seamstress's hand.

She searched the sea with all her might as the cold finger of fear grew, but still saw no sign of land. Nell's favorite psalm came to her again. "In Thee, O Lord, do I put my trust," she whispered, her hands clenching the webbing of the net spasmodically. "Let me never be ashamed: deliver me in Thy righteousness. Bow down Thine ear to me; deliver me speedily: be Thou my strong rock, for an house of defense to save me. For Thou art my rock and my fortress; therefore for Thy name's sake lead me, and guide me." She shut her eyes and prayed desperately, and then opened them again and cried out, for land was in sight.

But it was still much too far away.

The sun was touching the horizon. Eliza stared at it, sweating despite the cold, her eyes wide and dilated with fear. And then the swans darted down so swiftly that Eliza froze in terror, believing that they were falling. The next verse of the psalm flashed through her mind—*Into Thine hand I commit my spirit*—and then she saw the tiny speck in the foaming sea below. She sat bolt upright in the net. "My rock and my fortress!" she cried out above the storm. "Do you see it? There it is!"

Indeed the swans saw it, and were flying toward it with the end of their strength. The sun was more than halfway below the horizon as they plummeted toward the rock. At the moment they fell upon it, the last ray of light shone only like a star and then disappeared, extinguished like the last spark in a piece of burned paper. Eliza collapsed onto the cold, wet stone as her brothers turned back into their own forms with a flash of brilliant light.

A wave crashed against the rock just below their feet, and they all choked and sputtered in shock from the cold of the spray. "Hold the net fast," James shouted in a strangled voice over the roar of the thunder. "Don't let the waves carry it away!"

Geoffrey, Robert, and Hugh pounced on the net and sat upon it. Everyone scrambled to secure their hold, for the rock was barely large enough for them all to stand upon it. Laughing and crying, Eliza fell upon Benjamin's neck. "Ha! Are we all safe?"

"As safe as in God's own pocket, dear sister. As you knew we would be." She could feel him trembling with exhaustion in her arms. She pressed her cheek against his, overcome with thankfulness, and let the tears fall freely. In the rain, no one could see them, after all.

Chapter Twelve

I am not trying to romanticize that time into some cornucopia of sexual plenty. Its densities, its barenesses, its intensities both of guilt and of pleasure, of censure and of blindness, both for those who wanted a multiplicity of sexual options and for those who wanted clear restrictions placed on those options, were grounded on a nearly absolute sanctioned public silence. . . .

—SAMUEL R. DELANY, *THE MOTION OF LIGHT IN WATER*

February brought a thaw to the city. The blackened piles of snow melted just enough to uncover a jumble of cans, scraps of dirty paper, and cigarette butts. Then the weather froze again. Stripped of Christmas decorations, the streets looked even grimier than usual. Even the corner drug dealers seemed depressed.

Business started slacking off at the photo shop once the holiday rush was over. "And that means Rick has too much time on his hands," Tony groused to Elias one morning as they hung twinchecks on the film coming out of the processor. "He gets like this every February after doing the books. Money always comes in slow after Christmas, and the recession's making it worse. The month's short for bringing in cash to cover expenses, anyway. Just watch; he's gonna get a bug up his butt about how the bills ain't getting paid. Since he can't do anything about that, he's gonna start rearranging everything in the shop. And breathing down our necks."

Tony, on the other hand, handled February by turning up his country radio station in the darkroom and becoming even surlier than usual. Both symptoms were hard to take.

Nothing seemed to go right on one particular day. A large order came back from a custom framing house with the wrong color matting; Elias had written up the order incorrectly. "Of course we'll pay to have the mistake corrected," Rick assured the customer; Elias could see by the set of his shoulders how expensive correcting that mistake was going to be.

Then a batch of film came out of the processor inexplicably ruined: orange and contrastless. Rick groaned when Elias showed it to him. "Oh, no. That's the old Kodachrome X crap; it's supposed to be processed in the C-22 chemistry. Customer must have bought a whole bunch of it and bulk-loaded his own cassettes."

"I'm so sorry," Elias said, stricken.

Rick shook his head. "Not your fault. If he doesn't mark the cassettes right, how're you supposed to know? Kodak stopped making that stuff a few years ago when they switched to VPS and Kodacolor II, and everything runs in C-41 chemistry now." He sighed. "I hope the guy didn't want those pictures real bad."

"We can't do anything to fix them?"

"Well, *we* can't. Maybe a pricey custom house can save 'em. If he takes out a second mortgage."

Then an argument erupted when Rick discovered and confiscated a space heater Tony had snuck into the small darkroom.

"Aw, shit, Rick, I'm freezing my ass off in there."

"I don't care if it's as cold as your ex-wife's tits. The glow coming off that thing throws the color out of balance. You've wrecked every job you've printed in there this morning."

Rick turned his sights on Elias as Tony swore again under his breath and stomped off. "Did you change the stabilizer solution?" he growled.

"Um, yeah."

"Okay, then. You need to take your break now. Be back in an hour."

Glad to escape, Elias retrieved his bag lunch and left the shop. He took a few steps in the direction of Central Park and then hesitated. Sitting on a cold park bench, looking at a frozen pond, and feeling the wind send icy fingers down the back of his jacket didn't seem appealing. He felt restless, and so, after eating his sandwich, he decided to walk down Madison Avenue to get some exercise. The buildings lining the street looked flat and featureless, and sported the names of big corporations: General Motors, IBM, AT&T. The crowd was nattily dressed and in a hurry. Women strode by him, swinging their narrow briefcases, their heels ringing sharply on the concrete. Perfume drifted in their wake, mingling with the smell of auto exhaust.

The address on one building snagged a memory: Jerry Simms worked there, Sean had mentioned once. Impulsively, Elias ducked inside, scanned the lobby listing, and went to find an elevator.

When the elevator doors opened on the sixteenth floor, disgorging him into an oak-paneled lobby with deep leather chairs, he wondered with a faint twinge of alarm whether coming up here was really a good idea. Warily, he eyed the flower arrangement on the receptionist's desk. It had probably cost the equivalent of a week's worth of his salary. The receptionist looked like the same type of woman as those who wore evening makeup behind the cosmetic counters in department stores, the kind Sean called "well shellacked."

"May I help you?" she said in a discouraging sort of tone that suggested she rather doubted she could.

"I wondered if Jerry Simms might be in. Um, I'm Elias Latham, a friend of his. I'm afraid I don't have an appointment, but I was hoping he might be available."

"Please have a seat, Mr. Latham. I'll let Mr. Simms know you're here." She turned to her phone console, and Elias obediently went over to perch gingerly on the edge of a leather wing chair. It looked as though it should have had a sherry cart pulled up next to it.

In a few moments, Jerry came out into the lobby. "Elias," he said in a tone of surprise and came forward, hand outstretched.

"Hullo, Jerry," Elias replied, rising to shake it. "I just wanted to stop by and see how you've been doing, since the funeral and everything."

Jerry's face assumed a frozen blank look, and his eyes darted involuntarily to the receptionist. Elias, seeing this, uneasily followed his gaze. The receptionist was answering the phone.

"I'm sorry, Jerry," he said humbly. "Maybe I should have called first."

"No," Jerry said automatically. After a moment, he seemed to give himself a mental shake and realize he really meant it. He smiled. "No, I'm glad you stopped by. Are you on your lunch break?"

Elias nodded.

"Dorothea," Jerry said to the receptionist, "tell Kimberly I've stepped out of the office for lunch." He fetched a topcoat from a discreetly disguised closet in the corner, and they headed for the elevator together.

When they stepped inside and the door had closed behind them, Elias said, "What happened just now—I mean, did I say something wrong?"

Jerry hesitated and then smiled. It was a tight smile, more like a nervous tic. "It's okay. It's just that . . . I'm not out at work, you see."

"You're not—? God, I'm sorry, Jerry. You don't, uh, think what I said—"

"Dorothea was answering the phone; I don't think she heard anything, anyway."

They rode in silence until they arrived at the first floor. "Is Manny's okay with you?" Jerry said as the doors opened again.

"Um, sure. That is, I've never been there. Actually, I've already eaten—"

"Oh, but you'll join me, won't you? Or do you have to get back right away?"

Elias glanced at him, and the anxiously wistful look on Jerry's face startled him. "I've got time," he said. "I could use a cup of soup or something, I guess."

Manny's was apparently a place where ad executives and attorneys with lavish expense accounts met for business lunches. The walls were a cool jade, hung with botanical prints, and the dark green leather banquettes were large, with screens between them, keeping conversations private. A cup of soup there cost more than Elias had paid for a meal in a month. Elias selected the clam chowder. Jerry ordered a Caesar salad, picked out the anchovies, and spent the rest of the meal shoving the lettuce around the plate with his fork.

"So nobody at your office knows about Rafe?" Elias ventured.

Jerry shook his head. "No. I buried him, and that night I flew to Houston for a three-day deposition."

"My god. How——" Elias stopped, not certain what he wanted to ask. *How can you stand it?* Or *How can you be so callous?*

"I'm not saying I was worth a damn. Opposing counsel thought I had stomach flu 'cause I kept asking for breaks to go to the can. I'd shut the door to the stall and just . . ." Jerry's mouth quirked. "Well." He took a sip from his water glass. "But I kept our witness from blowing up the case, and nobody was the wiser."

There didn't seem to be any adequate answer to that. "How are you doing now?" Elias asked gently.

Jerry's hand clenched his fork, hard, and for a brief, horrible moment, Elias was afraid he was going to break down into tears. "Sometimes work's the only thing that keeps me going. It's kind of like a refuge, because no one knows there. I'm just the same guy to everyone in the office; I can almost pretend it didn't happen. But then I get mad at myself for even thinking that. I mean, I cared about Rafe." He lowered his voice. "I really loved him. How can I want to just wipe him out of my life? That would be like wiping out the part of me that he changed. And when I realize that, when I'm remembering him too much, I can hardly stand being at work."

"Do you really think you'd lose your job if the firm knew you're gay?"

Jerry shrugged. "I . . . don't know exactly what it was I was afraid of. I still don't. I just told Rafe I had to keep us a secret. He never liked it. We fought a lot about it before I accepted the job. But I told him it was a small price for us to pay for everything the job could give us—travel, a nice apartment, a house on the Island. And now guess what? I've got all those things, thanks to this great job. All I'm missing is Rafe."

Elias thought back to the morning in the photo shop. It had been a bad day; every job inevitably had days like that. What would it be like to have to deal with mistakes and annoyances and hassles while trying to keep secret the fact that your life was falling apart because the person you loved most in the world was dying?

"Did you have any idea he was so sick?" he asked.

Jerry spread his hands helplessly. "I don't know, I . . . What do you do? You look back on everything, and you second-guess yourself. What if I'd come home earlier? What if I'd paid attention to how run down he was the last couple of months? I don't know. Those last couple of weeks, there were times when I'd be at the office, working on some damn brief or something. And I'd be thinking of him, stuck on that respirator at the hospital, that damn machine breathing for him. I'd want so bad to tell the partners screw you, blow out of there, and cab over to the hospital. But like an *idiot* I'd stay at the office until seven o'clock, just like always. And do you know why? It was because I honestly never thought he could die. It just never crossed my mind he would."

Elias sat silently, unsure of what to say.

"There's something else." Jerry gave up all pretense of eating and put down his fork. He leaned over his plate and clasped his hands together, massaging them. "Something I didn't tell anybody at the funeral. See, Rafe's pneumonia was this weird, rare kind. They usually only see it in people who've had their immune system shot to hell. Like if they're taking drugs to keep a transplanted organ from being rejected. Or if they've got leukemia. Have you been following all that stuff in the *New York Native* about gay cancer?"

"Not really." Elias frowned. "Wait a minute—Rafe didn't have leukemia, did he?"

"No. He got pneumonia because his immune system shut down. It's the same thing: you get pneumonia, cancer, whatever, because your body can't fight anything off. The doctors are starting to call it GRID, for Gay-Related Immune Deficiency." Jerry licked his lips. "They're trying to decide whether it's infectious."

"What do they think causes it?" Elias asked, appalled.

"Nobody knows. Rafe's doctors asked all kinds of questions about diet, lifestyle, our sex lives. Said they were trying to coordinate information with the Centers for Disease Control." He paused. "They also said maybe it's poppers. Rafe used them a lot on the Island. I didn't so much."

Another silence fell, thick with unspoken fear and uncertainty, until Elias glanced at his watch and reluctantly reached for his wallet. "I have to get back."

Jerry batted at Elias's hand and reached for his own wallet. "Let me pick this up."

"Well . . ."

"Please." He forced a smile. "It helps some to talk."

"Um . . . only if you let Sean and me take you out to dinner next week. Deal?"

Jerry nodded. "Yeah, deal." He pulled out a credit card and placed it across the lunch bill. "Really, everyone's been great," he said, his voice husky. "I don't know what I'd do without my friends."

When Elias got home that night, he found Sean sitting on the couch in the dark, staring pensively out into the courtyard. His guitar lay on the floor at his feet.

"Hey there," Elias said softly, coming over and kissing the top of his head. He sat beside him on the couch arm.

"Hi," Sean said without looking at him. When Elias placed his hands on Sean's shoulders, he could feel tension coiled there.

"I stopped by Jerry's office today, went out to lunch with him."

Sean tilted his head to show he was listening, without looking up at Elias. "How's he doing?"

"It's been rocky. I told him we'd take him out to dinner next week."

"That'd be good." Together, they stared out at the blackened bones of trees, outlined against the city glow in the sky. Elias was just wondering whether he should offer to start dinner, when Sean said abruptly, "Gordy called. Ian's got cancer."

"What?"

"Just found out today."

Shocked, Elias wrapped his arms around Sean's shoulders, but instead of leaning into the embrace, Sean remained stiff and still. After a moment, puzzled, Elias pulled away.

"Let's go to the baths," Sean said.

Elias pulled his hands away. "What?"

"The baths—oh, look, I'm sorry. Forget I said anything." He got up off the couch like a spring uncoiling.

Elias sat up straight and blinked as Sean turned on the light. "Go? You mean, go now?" Elias felt a small bubble of panic welling up.

"We said something, once or twice, about going together sometime, but . . ."

"I've never been to the baths before," Elias said, his voice carefully neutral.

"I know that. Look, I shouldn't have brought it up." Sean went over to the refrigerator and began foraging inside. "I think there's some Chinese left over from last night. We can finish that up." He pulled out several white cartons, setting them on the counter, and then began digging in a drawer for spoons.

Are you tired of me? Elias wanted to ask. *Do you want me to move out?* But he couldn't say that, and so he looked at his feet and instead mumbled, "I just want to be with you."

"I want to be with you, too. But try to understand . . . I have to get out. I want . . . I need . . . I just want to forget about this for a while."

He sounded so forlorn, so wistful, that Elias said, surprising them both, "Well, let's give it a try, then."

"Really?" Sean turned around, brightening. "You'd come along with me?"

"Um . . ." *Oh, god. What have I gone and said?*

Sean must have seen some of his thoughts in his expression. "Does the idea scare you?"

"Well . . . yeah, it does," Elias said sheepishly. "A little."

Sean came over and sat down beside him. "Don't let it. It's like . . ." He groped for an explanation. "It's like the Island. Remember what it was like growing up, starting to figure out you were different and being afraid there was no one else like you in the world? That there was something wrong with you?"

After a moment, Elias nodded.

"And when I took you to the Island, remember how it felt? You said it was the first place you'd found where you felt safe, and you could really be yourself. Well, it's the same with the baths. There's a whole community out there, Elias, and you deserve the chance to explore it, experiment a little. I don't want you to think I'm the only fish in the sea. Do you understand?"

Elias didn't. But Sean was looking at him so earnestly that he nodded, reluctantly. He wanted to understand. Wasn't that enough for now?

"So you'll try it? You'll come along with me?"

He really wants to go, Elias realized with a touch of coldness. *I'm not the only fish in the sea, either.*

"Yeah."

A line of men inched their way forward toward the booth window. Elias felt as though they were in line for a movie. As Sean shoved a twenty under the thick glass, into the attendant's hand, Elias had a sudden wild urge to ask whether there were any seats left for *The Empire Strikes Back*. He bit back a hysterical giggle as the attendant licked a thumb and counted out Sean's change from a crumpled wad of bills.

Sean scribbled his name with a flourish on the clipboard and shoved it toward Elias. When Elias had signed, too, the attendant buzzed them in. "I paid for a couple lockers," Sean said. "Downstairs."

White double lockers lined the narrow changing room. The air smelled of sweat and Pine Sol. Sean handed him a towel and sarong wrap with the bath emblem on it and began unbuttoning his own shirt. Two lockers down, a mustached man stripping off his pants eyed them covertly.

Elias turned his back, took off his shoes and socks, his shirt, and then with an inward gulp, dropped his jeans and shorts. Quickly, he wrapped the sarong around his waist and knotted it as securely as he could. When he turned around again, Sean was dressed only in a sarong, too. He looked perfectly at ease.

"Kind of quiet in here tonight," Sean said cheerfully as they closed their lockers and put their key straps on their wrists. "But I'll bet the back rooms are busy. And you should see it on a Saturday night."

Now Mustache was staring at Sean's crotch.

Community. Right.

"Come on," Sean said.

They went past the showers and mosaic pool. The first door led into a brightly lit TV room. Several men lounged here, sipping Cokes and watching *Hill Street Blues*. Another attendant perched on a tall bar stool, arms crossed across his chest, watching the scene impassively. No one seemed to be having a wild orgy on the floor or anything. Elias paused to look around nervously, but Sean continued walking toward a second door across the room.

"Um, should we just hang around here for a while?" Elias asked.

Sean winked at him over his shoulder. "The lights are lower in the next room."

Elias followed him, with the sensation that he was deliberately stepping over a cliff.

Sean was right; the lights *were* lower here. Elias's toes sank into thick carpeting. He froze and blinked, reluctant to begin walking until his eyes had adjusted to the gloom—and then he jumped as he felt a hand snake under the fold of the wrap around his waist. He almost yelled, but by the time he had spun around to see who was goosing him, whoever it was had already brushed past him and wafted around a corner, presumably in search of other prey. Two doorways stood in front of him; which one had he just stepped out of? Sean chuckled, low, in his ear.

"This is the Maze," he whispered. "You never know what you might find around the corner here."

"Don't leave me," Elias whispered back, disoriented and suddenly terrified. He closed his eyes, ashamed of how lost he sounded. Sean's hand, warm and strong, reached out to knead his shoulder. Elias barely restrained himself from clutching at it. He could feel his own heartbeat thundering in his ears.

"Relax, Elias. It's supposed to be fun."

He gently pushed Elias's shoulder, and they began walking into the gloom, following the twists and turns of the Maze. Sensations came in bits and pieces. Here and there a dim spotlight illuminated a shoulder, a flash of curling hair, a ghostly face, upturned, with eyes closed, breathing heavily. Without even meaning to, Elias kept pressing up against flesh: an arm, slippery with sweat, a hairy pot-belly, somebody's rump, muscles rhythmically tensing and relaxing. He shrank back, not wanting to discover what might be found on the other side of that rump, and held onto Sean's elbow for dear life. Someone moaned softly not far from him, a low, urgent sound of impending climax, with slurping sounds as a counterpoint. It made the hairs stir on the back of his neck. Hands reached out from all directions to grope at him: dry and warm, sweaty, thick-fingered, calloused, demanding, tentative. One patted his cheek just below his eye, lightly, as if it approved of him.

A change in the flow of air on his skin made him sense they were moving through a doorway into a larger room. Faint light glimmered up ahead; he could see a press of shifting bodies silhouetted against it. Then, blocked by the crowd, they stopped. "Sean?" Elias whispered tentatively after a moment, but there was no reply, only a low, breathless chuckle and a whispered, "Yeah, yeah, do it. . . ." Sean? Someone else?

Then the crowd parted in front of them, and Elias gasped in heart-thudding astonishment. They had reached the heart of the Maze, the orgy room. A small spotlight trained on the enormous central bed dimly illuminated a mass of undulating bodies, surrounded by watching, silent men. How many watchers? Seventy-five? A hundred? The heap of bodies on the bed heaved, re-formed, reconfigured. Nipples, cocks, mouths, hands, buttocks moved and grasped and thrust and engulfed. The only noises were a few soft moans, some sucking sounds, heavy breathing. How could so many men be so utterly silent?

Someone stepped up behind Elias, like a dancer taking a position on the mark. A pair of hands slid around his ribs from behind, and the touch of fingers against his nipples made him start violently. He felt a mouth press hungrily against his neck and begin working its way down his back toward the sarong at his waist. Staring at the figures on the bed, he felt at once paralyzed and horrified and incredibly aroused. What was that mouth going to *do?*

And then Sean was moving again, and Elias wrenched himself free of the hands and mouth to follow. He could still feel their tracks on his skin, tingling almost painfully at the touch of the air. "Sean? Sean!" he hissed.

"What?"

"Get me out of here."

"What is it?" Sean asked, instantly concerned.

"Just get me out," he insisted, trying to control the shaking radiating from his gut.

"This way." They pushed through the hypnotized men watching the bed, and stumbled out of the orgy room into another corridor. There was a bit more light here. Elias leaned against the wall, dizzy with relief.

"You all right, Elias?" Sean asked, sounding concerned. "What is it—claustrophobia or something?"

Elias didn't answer for a moment. He wrapped his arms around his chest, still shivering. "Or something," he replied finally.

"It was crowded in there." Sean hugged him, and Elias felt tears sting the corners of his eyes in relief at the familiar touch of Sean's arms around him.

After a moment, Sean pulled away and brushed a strand of hair out of Elias's eyes. "This section has smaller rooms—more private. We can look and see what kinds of tricks are waiting there."

Elias stared at Sean, and seeing the anticipation, the exhilaration in Sean's expression, he felt something crack and shrivel inside himself. *Why are we doing this? I don't want this.* He closed his eyes and shivered, thinking of the orgy room. *Okay, be honest. It makes me scared and sick, but dammit, it makes me incredibly hot, too.*

But that wasn't enough. He didn't want a bunch of anonymous partners. He wanted Sean. But if Sean needed to trick with others, and if he wanted to do it without feeling guilty about Elias . . .

"Look at that guy," Sean whispered. "He's checking you out."

Elias looked. It was true. Tall, washboard abdominals, leonine eyes . . . the man jerked his head toward the doorway of one of the cubicles lining the corridor and lifted an eyebrow in inquiry. At Sean's nod, he ducked inside.

"He's in great shape." Sean pushed Elias forward to the doorway.

"And here's someone for you," Elias replied, his mouth dry. He stepped back against the cubicle door frame as a shadow moved toward Sean, bent, and murmured something into his ear.

Sean laughed. "Sounds good," he said. He cocked his head at Elias as the other man draped an arm familiarly over his shoulder. "So . . . have fun, okay?"

"Sure." Elias watched the two of them walk down the corridor to another open room. Sean's sarong was off before they went inside.

From the darkness inside the cubicle behind Elias, a voice spoke softly: "So. What do ya want? Anything your heart desires . . ."

Chapter Thirteen

Begin to weave and God will give the thread.

——GERMAN PROVERB

After leaving their rock the following morning, Eliza and the swans continued their journey in stages, flying from Iceland to the southern tip of Greenland, and from there to the northern wilds of the New World. Finally, shortly before sunset several days after leaving England, they touched down on a shallow bay protected by a lushly wooded promontory. A small chattering stream spilled into the bay, giving them a source of fresh water. Eliza splashed her way to shore, plunged her hands into the rivulet, and drank gratefully. The coldness of the water shocked her, making her throat ache as it went down. She sat on a pile of stones heaped at the water's edge, wringing out her skirt as she watched the swans swimming quietly in the shallows. They stretched their wings, shaking out the feathers, and then folded them wearily on their backs. Several plunged their heads below the water, dredging up water weeds to eat.

One swan, Benjamin, clambered up on shore and stood for a moment on the narrow sandy spit. He extended each black foot, one after the other, out behind himself, fastidiously flicking off water drops. And then he came to her, hopping up onto the rock where she sat. "Hello," she murmured, edging back to give him room, a little taken aback. He stared at her with eyes like obsidian chips and then abruptly settled himself down next to her. Cautiously, she reached out to gently stroke the soft feathers at the base of his neck. "Are you Benjamin?" she whispered.

He arched his neck, twining his head around her hand.

They remained together so until sunset, when the other swans came up on shore. Benjamin hopped down again to join them, and as the sun sank below the horizon, they regained their rightful forms. As they gathered around Eliza to offer her their evening greetings, she caught the remnants of a strained, grave expression in their eyes.

But they spoke to her cheerfully enough. " 'Tis a promising-looking place, is it not?" James said.

"Aye, it is very beautiful."

"We are all growing weary of travel. Rest yourself here, Eliza, and we will look about to see if it might suit us to bide here awhile."

The memory of that look in their eyes made her thoughtful as she watched them drink from the stream and then turn away to clamber over rocks and plunge into the fringe of the woods to scout. Several nights in their company had made much about their temperament clear to her. They were tender and teasing with her, and sometimes merry, sometimes quarrelsome with one another, like any other group of brothers. She admired the dignity they displayed despite their ordeal, a certain serenity and steadiness of spirit. Since the first night she had joined them and talked with Benjamin, none of them had spoken to her about the spell again. But underneath all she sensed a sadness, almost a despondency, painful as a raw wound.

Shortly, a shout floated toward her from above the beach. "Come and see, Eliza," Geoffrey said excitedly, reappearing upon the beach. "We have found a fine bedchamber for you."

Eliza followed him through the deepening twilight, edging her way through the thick forest undergrowth and up a slope to a site overlooking the bay. Here, a large rock dominated a clearing before the mouth of a cave. Creepers overhung the mouth of the grotto, like a fine veil. Inside, dry sand covered the cave floor. "Why, this is wonderful, Geoffrey!" she exclaimed. "We may all sleep comfortably here."

In the midst of everyone's praise of Geoffrey's find, Benjamin interrupted with sharp concern: "Look you, Eliza is shivering."

"Oh! It is nothing, only that my skirt is wet."

"We must gather wood so Hugh may start a fire."

They did so, and soon Hugh had a crackling blaze going on the rock before the cave. "You must sup on mussels again tonight," James told Eliza apologetically, offering her some he had gathered as they all came to sit around the fire. "I fear they will pall upon you soon."

"I am thankful to have them," Eliza said honestly, while thinking to herself that she was even more thankful that she did not need to make water weeds her dinner.

"We must set out some rabbit snares tonight," Stephen said.

"I do not know how familiar the plants will be here," Eliza said, "but I can forage tomorrow and try to find some berries or salad herbs or perhaps tubers we might eat."

"And our task it will be to scout," James declared. He frowned at the darkness around them. "I hope few people live near this place, since this land is thinly settled, yet we must be sure."

Eliza sighed, thinking wistfully that she would not mind having other people near.

"I fear it may be lonely for you, Eliza," Benjamin said tentatively, echoing her thoughts. "Particularly during the days. I hope . . . I hope you will not regret that you have come with us."

Eliza blinked and smiled at him. "Why, I may look forward to your company in the evenings." She drew a deep breath. "And it need not be for long, if only I can find a way to break the spell—"

"Do not tease yourself thinking of that," Frederick said, a bit more sharply than he intended. He paused, and then continued in a tone of flat finality. "The spell cannot be broken."

Eliza stared at him. "Know you this for a certainty?"

Frederick hesitated. "Aye! Nay . . . it has been so long. Everything we tried failed."

"What did you try?"

"We did not try anything," Charles said with a reproving glance at Frederick. "How could we hope to brew a simple or make a charm to defeat this? What do we know of magical arts, compared to the Countess?"

"I fear I must be as ignorant as you," Eliza admitted.

"We did try prayer," Frederick snapped, clenching a fist. "The last hope of the desperate. It failed us. God failed us. And we have been left with no hope at all."

Shocked, Eliza looked around the circle, but although the other brothers shifted uneasily, none spoke up to contradict Frederick. And in that silence, she felt the burden of all the years of despair, of desperation and hopelessness, her brothers had endured, like a weight threatening to crack her heart. "I do not know how to answer you," she said finally when she could trust herself to speak calmly. "Except to say that if there is no hope, I must persevere to find a way to break the spell without it. And I shall, Frederick, believe me, for have I not sworn never to rest until you are free?"

"You have more faith than I do, sister," Frederick said soberly, a little ashamed of his outburst.

"Then let it give you strength as it does me," she replied and rose. "I will go to bed now." She swallowed past the lump in her throat. "Heaven grant that I may dream how to save you."

As she lay down in the cave in preparation for sleep, she thought again of the woman she had seen on the moors, who had guided her to her brothers. Surely that had been an answer to her prayer, she thought hopefully. "Merciful Father," she whispered, "Thou hast sent me help before, now in Your mercy, send it again! It cannot be Thy will that they should suffer so. Please, dear Father, send me a messenger again; show me the way to free them." In the midst of these meditations she fell asleep. For a time she slept without stirring, and then a vivid dream came to her.

She seemed to be flying weightlessly, high through misty air toward the cloudy palace she had seen on their journey over the ocean. The radiant figure of a fairy came forth through the cloud portals to meet her. Eliza shrank back in awe and a little fear, for the fairy's face shone like a star, and the gaze of her gray eyes seemed to delve to the innermost secret places of Eliza's soul—and yet those eyes looked familiar, too. Eliza had seen them in the face of the old woman on the moor, who had given her berries and told her of the eleven swans swimming nearby.

"Your brothers can be released," the fairy told her. "But only if you have courage and perseverance. Water is softer than your own hand, and yet it polishes stones into shapes; it feels no pain as your fingers would feel. It has no soul, and cannot suffer such agony and torment as you will have to endure.

"Do you see this?" The fairy held up something like a green wand. "It is a stinging nettle. You will find quantities of the same sort growing around the cave where you sleep. No others will be of any use to you unless they grow upon graves in the churchyard. These you must gather, even though they burn your hands with blisters. Break them into pieces with your bare hands and feet, and they will become flax, which you must spin and fashion into eleven coats with long sleeves. If these are then thrown over the eleven swans, the spell will be broken."

The fairy held up a finger in warning, even as Eliza clasped her hands together in joy. "But you must remember this," the fairy continued, her glowing face grave. "From the moment you begin your task until it is finished, even if it should occupy years of your life, you must not speak. The first word you utter will pierce through the hearts of your brothers like a dagger. Their lives hang upon your tongue. Remember all I have told you." And as her voice faded away to a whisper, she reached out to touch Eliza's hand lightly with the nettle.

A searing sensation flared, enveloping Eliza in a nimbus of pain. She awoke with a gasp and lifted her head in confusion, her heart pounding. Sunlight filtered through the curtain of creepers over the mouth of the cave. Her brothers had already left for the day, leaving her alone. Eliza turned her head—and saw, lying next to her on the floor of the cave, a nettle like the one she had seen in her dream. With a cry, she sat up and hugged herself with delight. She offered up a heartfelt prayer of thanks, scrambled to her feet, and left the cave.

Eagerly, she paced the circumference of the clearing at the cave's mouth, and within a few moments found a thick stand of tall nettle plants, just as the fairy had promised her. Without hesitation, Eliza plunged her hand into their midst and seized a nettle stalk. At the first touch of the bristly hairs covering it against her skin, she sucked in a breath, biting her lip to choke back a cry, and hot tears rushed to her eyes at the sting. But she grasped it firmly and pulled, breaking off the stalk in her hand, and reached for another. Soon, a great heap of nettles lay at her feet. Ignoring the blisters beginning to rise on her skin, she stripped off the serrated leaves and trod the stems underfoot on the rock before the cave. The stalks twisted and split under her feet, coating them with green juice. The nettle sting hurt her feet, too, although walking barefoot had toughened her soles. But she fixed her thoughts firmly on her brothers to give herself courage, and began pulling out the tough fibers from the core of the nettle stems.

She had a good quantity of flax broken by the time her brothers returned that evening. Henry, Charles, and Michael came in sight first, climbing up the hill from the water's edge, and they hailed her as soon as they saw her.

"Eliza!"

"Good evening to you, sister."

"Have you enjoyed this day's fair weather?"

Eliza turned a smiling face toward them and set her work aside. She longed to speak, to tell them what her dream had revealed to her, but mindful of the fairy's warning, she remained silent.

"You certainly have been busy foraging," Charles said, smiling down at her as he walked up. "What is this—ouch!" Snatching back a hand that had reached out to touch a nettle, he put his finger in his mouth to soothe the hurt and stared at her, wide-eyed. "What are those things *for*? They can't be good to eat!"

"Look at her hands!" Michael exclaimed, appalled. "Eliza—what are you doing?"

Eliza hesitated and then placed one of her swollen hands over her mouth and shook her head.

Henry knelt beside her and took one of her hands in his own to examine it. "God's blood, Eliza," he muttered, and then placed a hand on her cheek and looked deeply into her eyes. "Can you not speak, my dear?"

She shook her head again, and winced as he squeezed her fingers in agitation.

"I'm sorry," he said, stricken.

"James!" Michael shouted, his voice rising in alarm. "Edward, Stephen, everyone, make haste! Come quickly!"

Soon, all the brothers were gathered around. Henry explained the situation in a few words, and they all stared at Eliza in fearful perplexity.

"Is it—" Stephen stopped and swallowed. "Could it be some new sorcery done by the Countess?"

"Surely her magic cannot reach across the ocean!" Geoffrey began in horror, but Eliza was shaking her head again. She held up for them to see some of the fibers she had pulled from one of the stalks that afternoon. With gestures, she tried to make them understand her purpose, but they simply shook their heads, as puzzled and alarmed as ever. She blew out a breath in frustrated chagrin, reflecting ruefully that if she had only taken a moment to think before seizing her first nettle, it might have occurred to her to wait to inform her brothers that night of what she intended to do, *before* beginning her task.

"Oh, your poor fingers, Eliza!" Benjamin exclaimed, falling to his knees before her. With infinite gentleness, he took her hands in his own. "Are you . . . Have you found some way . . . Are you doing this for us?"

Her face lit up in a radiant smile, and she nodded at him, beaming. The brothers stared at one another, and then back at her.

"All this pain . . . is for us?" Benjamin said in a choked voice. He brought her hands up and gently pressed them against his lips. His tears fell upon her skin, and it seemed to Eliza that where his tears fell, the pain in her hands ceased.

The next day, Eliza took some of the broken nettle stalks she had soaked overnight and began picking some of the fibers out of the inner pulp experimentally. The fibers pulled free much more easily than she had expected. She stared down in wonderment at them, curling suggestively around her fingers. Although she had never worked with nettles before, Eliza was very familiar with the steps necessary to harvest and prepare linen flax, and she knew it to be a long, wearisome process. Linen flax had to be dried in the sun and then left to rot in running water for several days. After more drying, the stalks had to be beaten with the flax brake and scutched with a swingling knife, to separate out the plant material from the fibers. Next came the hackling, or combing of the fibers, and then spreading and drawing, when the fibers were sorted according to fineness—in all, twenty operations were necessary to prepare linen flax for the spinning wheel.

She would have expected nettle flax to require similar preparation. But now, when she twisted the fibers she had culled, the nettle sap seared her skin, making her hands burn and throb, but the strength of the crude thread held when she tested it with a hard tug.

It was impossible, she realized, sitting back and staring at the tow thread in her hand. Impossible, and yet it was happening. . . . It occurred to her that perhaps this was why the fairy had said the only nettles to be used were those growing by the cave and in the graveyard. They were the only ones that would allow her to prepare the thread so quickly.

Trying to work with the fibers still full of sap would make the job all the more painful, but after all, Eliza reflected, she did not have time to wait for the work not to hurt. If the coats could be prepared all the more quickly, so much the better for her brothers.

Looking around, she spied an apple tree at one side of the clearing, which suddenly gave her an idea.

With mounting excitement, she notched a stick at one end with a sharp stone and then picked an apple from the tree and jammed the stick through the core. Now she had a crude drop spindle. She started the thread by twisting some of the fiber with her hands and tying it to the part of the stick that emerged at the apple's bottom. Then she drew the twisted fibers up over the apple's side and fixed them around the notch at the top of the stick with a loop. She set the apple spinning. As she let the spindle drop, she added more fibers to the end of the thread just above the stick's notch. The apple's rotation twisted the fibers into a continuous thread. When the spindle touched the ground, she drew it up, undid the loop from the notch, and wound the thread around the stick just above the apple. Refastening the thread's end to the notch, she reached for another handful of fiber and began again.

In this way, she worked all morning and well into the afternoon, preparing and spinning a coarse tow thread. As she spun, she considered how the coats might be fashioned. After some thought, she got up and found two young saplings growing closely together. She tied an end of thread to one of the saplings, then wound it tautly around both trees, setting each loop of thread just above the previous one, up the length of the trunks. When the loops set on the trees were half the length of a man's body, she broke the thread and tied it off. Taking a second length of thread, Eliza wove it up and down through the loops in the opposite direction to fashion a tube of flax. It would work, she thought in satisfaction as she pulled the thread tightly. She could make sleeves the same way, using sticks set at a narrower distance apart, and then baste them to the body of the coat.

When her brothers returned that night, they were grieved to find her still silent, but she showed them a smiling face, cheered by the thought that she might soon be able to free them.

On the following morning, after transforming back into swans, the brothers rose in flight from the small, secluded bay where they had taken shelter with Eliza and circled away toward the west. Their course took them over the roofs of a town lying only a few miles inland. One of the houses they flew over belonged to the Reverend William Avery, who was just sitting down at his writing desk that morning, with an inward sigh, to craft his Sabbath-day sermon. He found concentration difficult, for the day had dawned fine and clear, and an eddy of air, laden with the luxurious scents of summer, crept underneath the window sash to slyly tickle his long nose. In comparison, he reflected ruefully, the apostle Paul had never before seemed quite so dry and dusty. As he reached for one of his precious sheets of paper and a pen, a man appeared on horseback in the lane below. William Avery paused in the act of setting pen to paper and leaned forward with interest, for the man was his neighbor Jonathan Latham.

Jonathan was a handsome man in his early twenties, with carelessly cut dark hair that tumbled haphazardly around the collar of his shirt. He certainly had managed to rivet the fascinated attention of almost every maiden in the town. Although he was one of the youngest county magistrates in the history of the colony, no one could say that he did not deserve the honor. He had a keen intellect, and an unpretentious self-confidence and ease of manner with his fellow men that the minister uneasily suspected he lacked in comparison.

"Good morrow, my good Reverend," Jonathan greeted him cordially. "Have you time enough to bear me company today?"

"Good morrow, Mr. Latham. Alas, no, for I must prepare my sermon—"

"Ah, your sermon, of course. What is your text?"

"It is taken from the seventh chapter of Romans, on the nature of sin and the law. The subject is a difficult one, but I have preached upon the text before, to my previous congregation."

"Hmm." Jonathan's quick eye noted the minister's rather wistful air. He cocked his head with an irrepressible twinkle in his eyes. "You might save paper by simply using your former notes rather than rewriting afresh what is no doubt an already admirable homily."

The idea, the Reverend reflected, seemed alarmingly tempting. "Did I not know you better, Mr. Latham," he replied sternly, although in fact he was secretly amused, "I would think you an irreligious man."

"Well then, it is my great fortune that you do know me better!"

The Reverend smiled. "What is your errand that requires my company?"

"Why, to go hunting with me, and Goodman Hubbard and Goodman North. You have been as busy as myself with the council of safety; your larder must be as bare as mine."

William Avery was very gratified by this invitation. He sometimes privately thought it a little odd that he should so treasure any sign of warmth of regard on the part of the younger man. One would think the natural order of things should have dictated instead that Jonathan Latham seek favor from him, a clergyman and community leader. But Jonathan, it seemed to William, did not want his approbation, but instead, even more flatteringly, his friendship. And William Avery, who had left his previous congregation in a cloud of recriminations and rancor, and knew without a doubt that *he* had never captured any maiden's fancy, was grateful for that friendship. He felt comfortable with Jonathan Latham as he did with few others.

"You tempt me," William admitted. "And yet . . ." He sighed with real regret. "I fear I must wrestle with the angels today and concentrate on my duty at hand."

Jonathan lifted an eyebrow roguishly. "If you ride with us into the wood, you may then lift up your eyes to the hills, from whence cometh your help—even to write your sermon, perhaps."

"Even the Devil may quote scripture, they say," William replied dryly before he could stop himself, and then winced inwardly at his own words. He had not meant to be so rude.

But Jonathan simply sat back in his saddle with an infectious shout of laughter that made his horse prick up its ears. "Oh, come along with us, man! Goodman North is vexed to the blood over another jangle with his wife and needs some cheer."

"I little consider myself as competent to offer counsel upon the affairs of the heart," William said with a small, wintery smile.

"Oh, indeed, I do not ask you to! Simply getting him out of the reach of Goody North's tongue for a day will effect the cure."

William's mouth twitched. "I see. An act of Christian charity. How then can I refuse?" He rose. "Very well, I will join you. Give me but the opportunity to saddle my horse and pack a saddlebag."

Within the hour, the four men rode out into the woods, with flint-locks loaded, primed, and at half-cock. Three of Goodman Ethan Hubbard's dogs ranged alongside, noses eagerly pressed to the damp earth. Although the men kept a sharp look out for signs of small game and deer, not to mention Indians, their talk, as usual, chiefly concerned not affairs of the heart, but politics. "Of course Andros must be sent to England for trial," Goodman Hubbard insisted as they rode. "Andros, Dudley, Randolph, and the rest of the villains."

"Randolph," Goodman Timothy North sniffed in a tone of deep contempt, and spat into a clump of ferns.

"Upon what charge?" Jonathan asked, just to be perverse.

The two younger men stared at him. "Why, he is a bloody traitor, that's what!"

"It will be interesting to see how the committee of trade will treat the case," Jonathan replied, a glint of amusement in his eye at the thought. "They can hardly censure the colony for casting out its governor, when they have just done the same with King James." He ducked his head to avoid a branch as his horse stepped over a log.

"I do not dispute we have chafed under Andros's rule," William said. "Yet consider the difficulty of his position, coming in directly after the colony's restructuring. 'Tis not his fault the charter was withdrawn."

"I wonder that you were voted to the council of safety at all," Hubbard muttered.

"Unfair, Ethan," Jonathan protested. "Reverend Avery wishes to see the charter restored as much as any of us."

"But how can he defend someone who tried to sell us out to the French and the savages?"

"I simply say you must consider the evidence carefully before joining in the general contempt," William said stiffly. "I have read the depositions concerning Andros's so-called betrayal to the French, and I find the evidence flimsy at best. Hate his policies if you will. I do not defend his overturning of long-standing land titles, for example. But beware false judgment based upon heated passions and wild rumor. That, my friends, works only to satisfy the Devil." He stopped himself abruptly, suddenly aware of his own hectoring tone and the sullen look on Hubbard and North's faces.

Goodman Hubbard opened his mouth to reply heatedly, but North gestured sharply to interrupt him and pointed toward one of the dogs, which was nosing about in excitement at the foot of a small rise. "Look. Blackear has caught some scent."

The men drew rein to watch. A second dog caught the trail, too, and bayed, springing away with its nose to the ground.

"A deer, think you?" Jonathan said, reaching for his flintlock and checking his brace of pistols.

North grinned. "Let us go see."

Eliza had just eased the completed body of the first coat off the saplings when she heard the dogs, and the sound made her look wildly around in alarm. As the sound of barking and growls neared, she seized the coat and her bundle of broken flax and fled with them back into the cave. Trembling, she wrapped the coat around the flax and sat on it, against the wall. Through the veil of creepers, she could see an enormous dog bound up onto the rock, disappear back down into the ravine still barking, and then reappear with two other dogs. They clustered in front of the cave and raged at her, stiff-legged, and she flinched back, covering her ears at the noise.

Soon, the hunters had clambered up the rise and stood, panting, at the entrance to the cave, pistols ready in their hands. "A bear?" Goodman Hubbard said uneasily.

Cautiously, Jonathan lifted a swath of creepers and peered

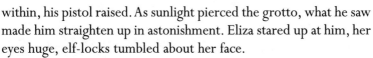

within, his pistol raised. As sunlight pierced the grotto, what he saw made him straighten up in astonishment. Eliza stared up at him, her eyes huge, elf-locks tumbled about her face.

"Not a bear?" William called.

" 'Tis a girl."

"A *girl?*" William repeated, dumbfounded.

Jonathan put his pistol away and took a step toward Eliza, and she started violently. He could see she was trembling. "Call back the dogs," he said over his shoulder. "They frighten her."

Goodman Hubbard and Goodman North pulled the dogs away and made them lie down on the other side of the clearing. Jonathan cautiously stepped forward again, spreading his hands open as William peered in over his shoulder. "Do not be afraid, child," Jonathan said softly, as if fearing to startle a doe about to take flight. "We are not savages; we will not hurt you." He studied the cluster of feathers tied about her neck and dangling between her breasts, and then turned his attention to her face for a long moment, noting with admiration its clean planes and curves. When she leaned a little away from him cautiously, something made him catch his breath in enchantment at the grace in that small movement. "She is beautiful," he whispered, half in wonder. He knelt down slowly at her side. "How came you here?"

Eliza, mindful of the fairy's warning, shook her head, for she dared not speak.

"Who is she?"

Jonathan waited for her to answer, but she remained silent. "Can you not answer?" he asked gently. She watched him warily, but he smiled at her so kindly that the last of her fear disappeared.

"Perhaps she is French and cannot understand us?" Goodman Hubbard suggested doubtfully, craning his neck to see into the cave.

"But what would a French girl be doing in the woods all alone?" William asked, puzzled.

Goodman North snorted. "I don't know. What would any girl be doing in the woods all alone?"

"Has she fled an attack by savages?"

Jonathan, never taking his eyes from Eliza's face, shook his head. "I do not know." He tentatively extended a hand and touched the feather charm, and then reached out for her hand. "She understands us, I think, but she seems to be mute."

At his touch upon her fingers, she opened her mouth soundlessly in pain, and he looked down in surprise. "What——?" The sight of the swollen blisters on her hands twisted his gut. He drew his breath in a hiss through his teeth in sympathy. "Come out into the light, child. Reverend, come look at this."

He drew her gently but inexorably out of the cave and held her hands up in the light. William came closer to peer at them. "I don't know . . . some kind of inflammation, but not a putrid infection, I think."

"Goodwife Carter would know," Goodman Hubbard offered.

Goodwife Carter was the town's midwife and herbwoman. "Aye, that she would," Jonathan replied thoughtfully.

"What's in here?" William said, his eye caught by the bundle of flax, wrapped in the nettle coat, on the floor of the cave. He stooped under the veil of creepers and went in to pick it up. A nettle leaf still clung to the end of one length of the flax, and his fingers brushed against the stinging bristles. He yelped and jerked his hand back.

"What is it, Reverend?"

Eliza, seeing what he was doing, suddenly lunged toward him, terrified that these men might destroy the coat without understanding what they were doing. By reflex, Jonathan's arms seized her up short by the waist, and she strained and flailed in his grasp. "Hey, lass, hey, peace, bide a bit!" he exclaimed in surprise.

William backed up a step, alarmed by the desperate look in her face. "Give it to her," Jonathan told him hastily. William put the bundle and coat into her arms, and she immediately stopped struggling. After a moment, Jonathan cautiously released her. She did not move, but simply stood, hugging her work to her breast desperately, her eyes wild and wary again.

"May I see what it is you hold?" Jonathan asked her gently. "Fear not, I will not try to hurt it." After a moment, reluctantly, she relaxed her grip and allowed him to unfold the coat enough to see its shape. "By all that's holy, what is *that?*"

"This is what stung me," William offered, pointing cautiously to the nettle leaf without touching it. Gingerly, he put his offended finger into his mouth, wincing.

"Let me see that," Goodman North said, reaching for the coat and bundle. At Jonathan's reassuring nod to her, Eliza reluctantly released the coat and bundled nettle flax to Goodman North for his inspection and watched him anxiously as he turned it over in his hands, perplexed. "I recognize this," Goodman North said, a crease appearing between his brows. "A nettle leaf. I have been burning those accursed things off my fields for five years."

"Weaving raw nettles?" Goodman Hubbard's jaw dropped. "Is the girl mad?"

A pause fell and stretched, as the men stared at Eliza uneasily. Jonathan broke it finally, saying, "We must take her back to the town with us."

"You can't mean it!" William exclaimed.

Panic flared up in Eliza anew at the thought of abandoning her brothers. She tried to snatch the coat and flax back again, but once more Jonathan seized her about the waist, capturing her arms. "Ho, there, child, stay!" Goodman North stepped back, hastily, still holding the completed coat. Pinioned in Jonathan's arms, she sagged in his grip and began to weep in despair.

"Don't cry," he murmured into her hair, distressed at her anguish. "Do not cry! I will not hurt you; I would cut off my hand before I would frighten you . . . but you cannot remain here all alone. We will take you somewhere where you can be cared for; you will be safe there." Carefully, he pulled away from her, keeping a firm hold on her shoulders, and tried to lead her toward the edge of the clearing, but as she strained to escape his grip, she stumbled, limping. He glanced down at her feet and exclaimed in horror at the sight of the raw, oozing patches covering them. "Look! Oh, she cannot walk. Goodman North, do you and Goodman Hubbard go down and lead the horses up as close as you can. I will carry her the rest of the way to set her on my horse's back."

The two men headed down the hill, Goodman North slinging the coat and nettle flax over his shoulder as the dogs loped after them. Jonathan gently forced Eliza to sit on the rock. She continued to weep and wring her hands, longing to be able to tell him why she wanted to stay.

William shook himself out of a kind of paralysis and stepped forward. "You cannot take this girl back," he said forcefully.

"Why ever not, Reverend Avery?" Jonathan asked absently as he brushed a tendril of Eliza's hair away from her tearstained cheek.

William glowered down at the two of them, hardly able to articulate why a weeping girl filled him with such alarm. It was not that she wept, he decided. It was the way Jonathan was looking at her. "I think she is mad," he growled finally.

"Mad? Oh, surely not. But even if she were, do not even the mad deserve pity?"

"Or perhaps . . . she is bewitched." *Or else she is bewitching you,* he added mentally, his flesh crawling at the fascinated light in Jonathan's eyes as he stared at the girl.

"Don't speak nonsense."

William clenched his fists. "We believe," he said desperately, "that God has ordered the world that all the elect might live under the law of relatives. *Quorum unum uni tantum opponitur.* All must be in some relationship, opposing in paired contraries, one subordinate to the other, and all subordinate to God: parent and child, master and servant, ministers and the elders over the congregation, rulers over the subjects of the state."

"Indeed?" Jonathan threw him an ironic glance. "Tell that to the former Governor Andros."

William gnawed his lip with frustration, feeling helpless at making his meaning plain. "A governor who abandoned his duty—well, but you stray from the point."

"What is your point?" Jonathan said sharply.

"Damnation, man," William exclaimed through his teeth, "you

studied Ramist logic! I know you have read the *Dialectica*; I gave you Richardson's commentary myself! This girl," he pointed at Eliza accusingly, "stands in no covenant relationship to *us!* She is no sister, no child of ours, no member of our church, and has no claim upon us! And if we take her into our fold" —he sniffed and swept Eliza with a withering look— "who knows what wrath of God she might call down upon our community? What if it be the Devil that guides these strange actions?"

Jonathan stood up fast, an unpleasant look in his eyes. But he checked himself and blew out a breath. "For shame, William," he said quietly. "You, who preached a sermon just this Sabbath past on the lesson of the Good Samaritan."

Slowly, William's face turned a dull red, and his eyes dropped. His soul thrashed in pain to be reflected in Jonathan's eyes and dismissed as small and mean. He felt as if he had been slapped.

"The girl goes with us," Jonathan continued, softly but firmly. "Have no fear; she will have a proper place in the community. Goody Carter can look to her hurt . . . and now that I think upon it, the neighbor girl helping Goody Carter has recently left to go to housekeeping with Nathan Miller. Perhaps this girl—"

"She will be useless to Goody Carter," William said spitefully, still smarting at Jonathan's reproof. "She is touched in the head, if she be not bewitched."

"Let Goody Carter be the one to decide that." He bent down and picked up Eliza in his arms. She shook her head desperately, tears continuing to flow down her face. "There now, be comforted," he said to her soothingly as he carried her down the rise and set her on the back of his horse as Goodman North held the reins. "You will thank me for this someday." He swung up on his horse behind her as William mounted, too, and they turned the horses' heads toward the town. Eliza turned her head to look back over his shoulder, until the rise with the cave at the top was long out of sight. Then she turned her face to the west, where the sun was beginning its slow descent to the horizon. Her tears continued to flow, unchecked.

Chapter Fourteen

[The swan] looks in the mirror over and over
And claims to have never heard of Pavlova.

—OGDEN NASH, "THE SWAN"

Elias and Sean didn't go back to the baths together. They didn't talk about the experience, either. Sean continued to go, sometimes at Elias's suggestion. But whenever Sean asked Elias whether he'd like to come along, too, Elias would smile brilliantly and offer some excuse: "I just came from there," or "Nah, hard day at work today. Thought I'd just sack out tonight." When he finally resorted to "Sorry, I have to wash my hair," Sean got the hint and didn't ask again. Sean continued to trick with others, but, by unspoken agreement, he never brought other men home.

There were several subjects they avoided discussing, Elias realized when he thought about it. It wasn't that they didn't have plenty of animated conversations. They could sit for hours in the garden of Yaffa Cafe, eating noodles and talking about Sean's next article, or the books they'd picked up in an afternoon's browsing at the Strand. They went to the Gray Art Gallery and analyzed composition and lighting in the photographic displays. They mapped out an itinerary for the world tour Sean always said he would take someday. ("Do you realize no one's ever really bothered to take Irish music to the people of Java? Or Morocco, or Papua New Guinea? Not to mention the penguins of Antarctica. I think this is a terrible oversight.")

But they didn't talk about what had happened at the baths, or about how Sean sometimes went out at night and came back four or five hours later, without any explanation. Elias wondered if he went other places for sex besides the baths. Movie theaters? The parks? Back rooms in the bars? He didn't know, and he couldn't ask.

He thought a lot about it, as the icy grip of winter receded and spring began stealing over the city. The grass turned green in Central Park, and a fine green mist appeared on the trees. Elias sat on his favorite bench, watching the swans swimming and the endless motley parade of people passing by. He pondered the way silences could stake themselves out between two people, even two people who loved each other. His mother and father, for example, had let the silences grow so large and malignant that surely they were more bound together by the walls between them than by anything else. The silences became dead places, no-man's-land where nothing grew. The thought that he and Sean might end up imitating his parents' marriage frightened him.

A picture could be worth a thousand words, he remembered. Sean had given him a Pentax K1000 camera as a gift over the winter holiday. A solstice gift, Sean said; Sean didn't celebrate Christmas. Elias had been experimenting with the camera ever since, taking pictures of Sean, the street in front of the apartment, the swans in the park. As spring turned into summer, he began playing with the prints of Sean in the darkroom after work, studying the moments without words between the two of them.

Sean understood immediately when Elias brought the pictures home to show him. "Interstices," he said. "The cracks in between things, the intervals. Anticipation before something happens."

"Exactly."

Sean sat at the table, supper plate pushed aside, with the prints spread out before him. He stroked his mustache as he studied them.

"I rather admire this." He picked up one showing a close-up of Sean's arm reaching out from behind the shower curtain to seize the towel on the bar. Just *about* to reach it, the muscles flexed, fingers clawed and tense. That was why Elias had taken it; he found Sean's hands fascinating. Light coming from the frosted glass window in the shower stall outlined Sean's silhouette, translucent through the shower curtain.

"I do, too," Elias replied, attempting a leer. "I'd jump his bones in a minute."

Sean laughed that rich laugh Elias was always angling to hear. The conversation got off track for a while—most pleasantly—but when they came up for air, Elias reached for another picture and showed it to Sean. "This one's my favorite."

"Wow."

The camera had caught Sean, leaning against the counter in the kitchen reading a newspaper, his face a study in intense concentration. At his elbow, a cup of coffee had been caught by the camera in mid-plunge toward the kitchen floor (Sean's arm had knocked it off the counter a split second before). The coffee cascading out of the cup looked like a strange, molten plastic form.

"Hey, I remember that. That was when my favorite cup broke." Sean glanced up at Elias, approval warm in his eyes. "You're good at this, you know?"

Elias nodded, pleased. "Yes," he said simply. "I am."

"You should do something with it. Take some courses, maybe?"

"Well . . ." Elias thought wistfully of his deferred college plans. *Maybe . . .*

"There are so many galleries around here, too. What if you tried to put together a portfolio? Or maybe we could collaborate on something."

"What do you mean, collaborate?" Elias asked, startled.

"Lots of the articles I do could use pictures. We could find a project we could work on together, sell it as a package deal." Sean hesitated. "That is, if you're interested, of course."

"I'd love to," Elias said quickly. "And thank you." He looked down at his pictures, a smile hovering on his lips, touched and grateful. "It means a lot to me to have you ask."

"Okay, then. Let's keep our eyes out for the right project."

Sean wandered back to sit at his typewriter for the rest of the afternoon, leaving Elias to mull over his pictures. His father had written him off as a pervert, he reflected wryly. Weird to think that, comparatively, to his and Sean's group of friends Elias might really be considered more of a prude. Look at the tough time he had getting over the idea that Sean needed to trick with others, for example. And since everyone considered it so *normal,* he couldn't bring himself to ask Sean, *Am I part of your life the way you're part of mine? Do I mean something more to you than all these other guys? Or am I just somebody you keep around to warm the bed, listen to your music, and help pay the rent?* He sighed and put the pictures away.

Still, a collaboration—that seemed hopeful. There were other little things, too, signs of . . . something. He usually bought a book with every paycheck, keeping them piled by his side of the bed. He tripped over the stack one morning and ripped the dust jacket on Mary Renault's *Funeral Games.* When he came home that night, the stack was missing.

"Where'd my books get put?" he asked.

"Your books?" Sean said. "Oh, they seemed to be getting beat up where you were leaving them, so I shelved them."

Elias looked at the bookshelf. "In with yours, you mean?"

Sean raised an eyebrow. "You don't mind, do you? I didn't think you would."

"No. No, of course I don't," he said, thinking of his parents, who had kept their books separate in all their years of marriage. "They're a lot better off there. Thanks."

Jerry stopped by the apartment one night and gave Sean and Elias his key, inviting them to make free use of the house on the Island during the Fourth of July weekend.

"But you'll be there, too, won't you?" asked Elias.

Jerry hesitated and then shook his head. "No, too many depositions coming up."

Sean frowned. "Fourth of July falls on a Sunday. They don't hold depositions on Sundays."

"Well, no." Jerry shrugged. "But I've been traveling a lot lately. I just don't want to spend my holiday weekend getting on a train and hauling my ass out and back on the Long Island Rail Road. It seems too much like work."

Elias and Sean exchanged a look. "Have you been out to the Island at all this year, Jerry?" Sean asked quietly.

"Not very much." Jerry took a deep breath. "It's still hard. I miss him too much out there."

Sean nodded. "Sleeping okay?"

"Not really," Jerry mumbled. "But that's partly because . . . well, I went to see a doctor about it today. I just got this attack of shingles."

"Shingles? No kidding."

"Yeah. They hurt like hell. And they make my back look leprous; I'd hardly look any good in a bathing suit. So I just plan to stay home and take it easy this weekend. Staying up all night partying is about the last thing I want to do." He looked depressed. More than that, he looked gray-faced with exhaustion. He swayed in the doorway. "Look, I gotta go. Take the key, will ya? The house has basic canned groceries on hand; you'll have to buy the fresh stuff." He forced a smile. "Have a randy time out there this weekend. Okay?"

"Okay. Catch up on your sleep." Shutting the door after him, Sean looked thoughtful.

"He's lost weight," Elias ventured uneasily.

"Yeah." Sean looked down at the key he was holding, bounced it a few times in his palm. "Well, we can go, check on the house for him. At least that'll be one worry off his mind."

Party goers packed the Island that weekend. They strutted along the beach, danced at the Ice Palace, and jammed the water taxis that cruised endlessly like sharks between the Pines and Cherry Grove.

Since Jerry wasn't there to host a party, Sean and Elias didn't see as many of the usual crowd that they knew. Sean ran into someone on the beach he'd met before playing at an Irish bar, who invited them to a party on Saturday night. Some of the other people there were musicians, too, and Sean borrowed someone else's guitar to join the music circle for a couple of hours.

Elias listened for a while, and then wandered out to the deck to talk with other people. An hour later, when he came back in to use the bathroom, Sean was nowhere in sight. That puzzled him. Had Sean gone to fetch a beer from the kitchen cooler? He started toward the other end of the house to look, but stopped when the sound of Sean's voice made him glance into one of the darkened bedrooms.

There, moonlight pouring through the window etched a knife-thin line on Sean's profile, and the silver glints shot through his hair and beard made Elias wish for his camera. Sean had his head turned away, looking at someone else. In the reflection of a closet-door mirror, Elias could see another man's hand creeping across Sean's waist like a spider, trying to insinuate its way into his jeans, as the other hand reached for Sean's zipper.

But as Elias stepped back hastily, not particularly wanting to watch Sean with a trick, Sean's voice said, pleasantly but firmly, "No, I don't think so."

"You thought I was good enough for you last time." The other man sounded surprised and a little irritated, as if being turned down was an unusual experience. "So why not?"

Elias paused in mid-turn, suddenly curious. He'd heard that voice on the phone before, calling Sean about some freelance writing assignment or something. *Yeah, Sean. Why not?*

"You know I'm keeping company with Elias now."

"That kid?" Elias could hear the sneer in the other man's voice.

"He's not a kid," Sean said mildly.

"I didn't think his dick was big enough for you. I've seen you at the baths often enough."

"The baths are different. But I know *you*."

"Oh. I see." God's-gift-to-men sniffed. "You won't trick with friends. Your relationship has progressed to the point where you only fuck around behind his back with *strangers*."

There was a pause, and then Sean's voice said with a dangerous purr, "You know, I've changed my mind."

"Oh?"

"Yeah. I'm not turning you down because I know you. I'm turning you down 'cause you're an asshole."

At the rustling sound of movement, Elias turned and fled back up the hallway. His sudden appearance made several heads turn; he gulped and quickly stole to a corner to sit down.

After a minute or two, Sean came back to the living room, too, a small frown between his eyebrows. His eyes fell on Elias and they exchanged a quick smile as Sean took a vacated seat by the door. Elias pretended to turn his attention back to the musicians as he thought over what he had heard.

It seemed odd that he found the conversation comforting somehow—Sean was clearly still tricking around, after all. But there was a part of himself he was saving for just Elias. A small part, but it was Elias's alone. He hugged that thought to himself as the fiddle sang and moaned in counterpoint to the waves out on the beach.

For now, maybe, it was enough.

Elias started a night class in photography in the fall. And Sean came up with an idea for a joint project: they would collaborate on an article about Gordy's annual wine-making party.

It was a mild September day and the weather was gorgeous when they arrived to join the crowd of fifteen or twenty people gathering in the courtyard behind Gordy's brownstone on the Upper East Side. Philip and Ruth set out opened wine bottles and an impressive array of appetizers on the tables as several other people pushed ladders up against the wall.

"My family's been doing this for over thirty years," Gordy said. They all tilted their heads up to admire the vine trained against the wall, with bunches of purple frosted globes nodding between the

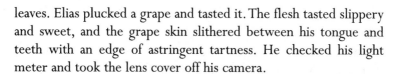

leaves. Elias plucked a grape and tasted it. The flesh tasted slippery and sweet, and the grape skin slithered between his tongue and teeth with an edge of astringent tartness. He checked his light meter and took the lens cover off his camera.

"What kind of vine is it, Gordy?" Leo asked. "Is it a Concord?"

Gordy shook his head. "I doubt it, but nobody knows, it's so old. All I know is, it makes good wine." He handed out cutting knives and gestured vaguely toward the buckets waiting against the side of the house. "Have at it, everybody."

Soon people began handing down buckets piled high with grapes. The starter crew washed them and stripped them off the stems. Then they tossed the grapes into the hopper of the crusher (which looked, as Sean remarked cheerfully, like an old-fashioned washing-machine wringer on steroids, with a really bad attitude). A progression of grinning volunteers turned the wheel—Elias got some great biceps shots—and the juice, pulp, and skins oozed sloppily into the tub below.

Gordy wandered over, wineglass in hand, to peer at the level in the tub, and then straightened up to watch the pickers. "Eighteen pounds of grapes to a gallon," he muttered absently to himself and glanced at Elias. "We made a hundred and twenty bottles last year; I was hoping to beat that record." Abruptly, he went over to the corner of the patio to sit heavily in a wrought iron chair.

Elias grabbed a cracker and cheese from the hors d'oeuvres table and went to squat beside Gordy's chair to take some long shots. They would look good, he thought. The light was striking, and the composition had human interest. Minta stood with her head thrown back, laughing up at the pickers. One guy leaned from the ladder above her, pelting the crusher crew with grapes. Sean was reaching with his knife to one side of his ladder to slice a thick stem; with infinite care, he placed the bunch in his bucket. He wore a sleeveless tank top of electric blue that showed off a great tan. Elias had a sudden fantasy of him working barefoot in an Italian vineyard, stripped to the waist in the sun. If he hoisted a wicker basket full of grapes to his shoulder, the movement would make his pecs swell so delightfully . . . He shivered, grinned, and took another shot. He'd have to tell Sean about that one.

Of course, Sean looked great in Irish sweaters, too. Too bad there weren't many vineyards in Ireland.

A trio of barefoot revelers in one corner of the courtyard were stomping more grapes into the bricks in a wild parody of a flamenco dance. Apparently some of the guests had been sampling the pleasures of the fruit of the vine for a while.

"Keith, I'd appreciate it if you'd cease and desist," Gordy called. "You'll raise dust that'll get into the tub. And save the grapes for the wine."

"Awww . . ."

Gordy chuckled and settled back in his chair as Elias took another shot. "Everybody's sure having fun," Elias commented, pulling out a fresh roll of film and reloading.

"Yeah. They always do." A pause, and then: "I wish Ian could be here," Gordy said softly. "He really wanted to be."

Elias glanced up from his camera and caught the wistful look in Gordy's eye. After casting about for a moment for something to say, he offered lamely, "At least Jerry's with him."

Gordy brightened. "That's true. Even if he's on a different floor. They can compare notes on all the hunky nurses." He sighed and fidgeted in his chair, wearily, as if he found sitting uncomfortable. "You know, Elias . . ." He paused, as if trying to decide what to say.

"What, Gordy?" Elias prompted after a moment.

Gordy sighed again. "I'm planning to set about twenty bottles aside. For Ian's funeral. I don't think it'll be long now. And"—he glanced sideways at Elias—"I'm setting aside another twenty bottles for me. I don't know if I'll have a chance to do another harvest. I just wanted you to know . . . you don't have to worry about drinking it."

"What are you talking about?" Elias forced out, although he was dreadfully afraid he knew exactly what Gordy meant. He could feel his hands growing cold.

"I had the fermentation barrel sterilized with sulfur." He

shrugged, as if embarrassed. "I always do anyway, of course, but the point is, I didn't touch it, or any of the other equipment. And I had Minta and Ruth do all the food. I mean, since nobody really knows what causes it—"

"Gordy—" Elias sat back heavily. "Gordy . . . are you . . . ? Have you . . . ?"

Gordy held his gaze for a long moment, and then slowly leaned down and rolled up his pant leg. A purple blotch mottled the calf there, like a wine stain.

Oh, Jesus. The smear wavered, and blurred, and Elias wiped his eyes angrily with the back of his hand. "Who else knows?" he said hoarsely.

"A few people. Ruth and Minta. They've been utterly lovely. I haven't told Ian, though. Maybe it won't be necessary." *Maybe there won't be time before he dies,* he clearly meant.

"How long have you known?"

Gordy grimaced as he let the pant leg fall. "Officially? About three weeks. But I've suspected a lot longer than that, really, because of that cold I couldn't shake, and those absolutely miserable night sweats." He snorted. "When I think of all those vitamins I took, all the money I pissed away, literally—I probably had the most expensive urine in Manhattan. As if vitamins had any kind of chance against this."

"You're . . . you're not giving up!"

"Oh, no." Deliberately, Gordy took a sip of wine. "I like living. I'll put up a good fight. But you forget," he added, lowering his voice. "I've seen what Ian's gone through. I know what I'm up against. I don't know if anyone has beaten this, or if everyone who gets it is going to die."

"Everyone is going to die, someday," Elias said quickly.

Gordy considered. "True. But this . . ." His face grew grave. "I honestly think it's a curse. From the devil himself." He put down his wineglass and got up. "C'mon. It's time to start the wine-press."

* * *

That night, Elias asked, "Sean, did Gordy tell you—"

"He told me."

A depressed silence hung over them for a moment.

"Do you think you'll use it in the article?"

"What, that he has AIDS?"

"He talked about how it might be his last harvest. It could, I don't know, make the article more poignant, don't you think?"

"Elias, we can't say anything in print about him having something like that."

"Well, not without getting his permission, of course—"

"No." Sean's tone sounded like the slam of a security gate coming down. "Leave the writing to me."

After a pause, Elias said, "Yeah. Sure."

The article Sean wrote, about a group of friends reconnecting each year at an annual wine-making party, balanced the upbeat human story nicely with interesting bits about home wine-making. The photograph of Gordy did look rather melancholy, perhaps, but maybe his expression was just an effect of the angle of the light. They made a tidy sum when they sold the article and photos to *Food and Wine*.

If a picture was worth a thousand words, Elias wondered, what kind of story might he tell? He started keeping a photo album that autumn. Often, when he came home from work, he would find Sean paging through it meditatively. There were the pictures from the bash they'd thrown for Halloween—Sean and Elias had dressed as the Captain and Tennille. Thanksgiving at Nick and Amy's—the dogs got into a roaring fight under the kitchen table in the middle of the reel, but even though the audience screamed with laughter, none of the musicians lost a single beat. Jerry had been too sick to come; Ian was already dead. New Year's Eve at Times Square. They'd gone with Leo and the new guy he was seeing, Kiyoshi. Leo had told them he was still friends with Philip; they ate lunch together once a week in fact. Philip was doing fine, Leo reported—well, except for this staph infection that he was having trouble shaking. . . .

It was all there in the background, Elias realized while looking through the album later, like the distant cacophony of traffic on the other side of a closed window. You think you can ignore it, but it keeps getting a little louder, a little closer, irritating at first, and then more and more ominous. There was a kind of anxiety among their friends, even the ones who seemed entirely healthy. No one liked to talk about it much, although Elias was sure it was on the mind of almost everyone in their circle. There'd be some passing reference—Philip had written an angry rebuttal to that *New York Native* essay that suggested that the bathhouses be closed, for example. Then everyone would drop it again. A couple of times that winter, he'd see a man massaging his own neck with an abstracted air at a party when he thought no one was particularly looking. Checking the lymph nodes.

It took him longer to see the story in the pictures of the interstices. The first thing was the dust on the weight machine.

He'd gone to put a book back on the shelf next to it. He placed his hand on the bench while leaning over it to replace the book, and when he stood up again, he saw the outline of his hand in the dust on the black vinyl.

Sean had always teased him about being a neat freak. *It's not that I'm a slob,* he'd say, *but I've never been in a relationship with anybody who actually* dusted *before.* And that was the strange thing. Elias had never needed to dust the weight-machine bench, because Sean used it every day.

Didn't he?

Elias looked more closely. Sean always followed the same routine when lifting weights. Why was the pin holding the weights set *there?* It was less than half where Sean usually placed it for the last set of reps.

Why?

Such a small thing. Hardly worth noticing, let alone mentioning. And yet . . . slowly, Elias reached down and removed the pin. He hid it behind a book on the top shelf.

He waited a week. Sean didn't say anything about it.

After two weeks, he decided Sean hadn't noticed because he'd stopped lifting weights. So what? Why not *ask* him about it?

Sean did most of the laundry since he was around the apartment for much of the day. The next detail Elias picked up on was that the sheets were being changed almost every day. The two of them didn't particularly cuddle in bed, but sometimes in the middle of the night, the hot, oily-slick touch of Sean's skin startled Elias into wakefulness. Sean would say nothing about it in the morning—but a new set of sheets would be on the bed when Elias got home from work that night.

Around the solstice, Elias realized that Sean, the original night owl, didn't want to stay out at music parties as late as he usually did. Sometimes when Elias called from the shop in the middle of the day, Sean still sounded groggy.

"What are you still doing in bed this time of day?"

"Who says I was in bed?"

"You sound so tired, Sean. Are you okay?"

"Just haven't had my coffee yet."

Nothing, it's nothing, Elias told himself. *He's been putting in a lot of hours on that latest series of articles. Just get some extra-strength coffee to keep around the apartment, and don't worry about it.*

Although he kept taking pictures and developing them at the shop, looking for a pattern, a part of him wordlessly dreaded what he might discover.

January segued into February, and at the shop, Rick descended into his usual midwinter grouchiness. Sean bought an Irish harp from Nick and started working on some Turlough O'Carolan tunes. The city council sent another gay rights proposal down in flames in March. Elias sent for some college catalogues and financial aid applications. "I'll Tumble 4 Ya" was on jukeboxes *everywhere.* Jerry came down with *Pneumocystis carinii* and went on the respirator at St. Vincent's and then, to everybody's surprise, was taken off of it three weeks later and allowed to return home. The trees in Central Park leafed out, and the knife-edged shadow lines on the sidewalks softened to blurred curves, edged with buttery yellow light.

And then, one night in June, Elias stayed at the shop after his shift to experiment with the new enlarger. He took a test roll he had just developed and set the enlarger to print some five-by-sevens and eight-by-tens. When he heard the dryer switch off inside the print processor, he went to pick up the prints from the hopper outside the darkroom.

He rifled through the stack quickly and stopped at the second to last picture, a mirror shot of Sean's face, taken from the bedroom. The color wasn't quite adjusted correctly, he noted. Probably he had to remove the cyan to the filter pack in the enlarger—Sean's face seemed slightly yellow. The tilt of his head cast angular shadows under his cheekbones and the reflection of his eyes, staring back at the camera . . . Elias went over to the window to examine the expression more closely in the sunlight coming into the shop. What was it about those eyes? After a moment, he went into the office to compare the picture in his hand to the one of Sean that Rick had mounted up on the wall.

When had Sean's eyes gotten so sunken?

The sudden jangle of the phone startled him so badly he almost dropped the picture. He knocked over the paper-clip holder while picking the phone up, before he remembered Rick was supposed to be answering it up front. "Van Hoosen Photography."

"That you, Elias? It's Sean."

"Yeah, it's me. Sean—"

"Hey, I got a surprise for your birthday. Kind of last-minute—I didn't want to mention it because I wasn't sure if Gordy would come through for us. But he managed to snag these tickets—"

"Tickets to what?" Elias asked, still eyeing the picture in his hand.

"Want to go to the ballet tonight?" Elias thought he detected a certain smug note in Sean's voice.

Elias felt his eyebrows go up. "The *ballet?* Are you serious?"

"I'm serious. Gordy got us tickets to the Trocks—Les Ballets Trockadero de Monte Carlo. They're performing at City Center Dance Theater. Ever heard of them?"

Elias vaguely remembered seeing an advertisement somewhere. Maybe the *Village Voice*? "Um . . . a male dance troupe or something, right?"

"A male drag dance troupe. Gordy's coming, too."

"Does he feel up to it?"

"Guess so. And he's got two other tickets he's trying to find someone to take. Maybe Leo and Kiyoshi, if Minta and Ruth can't make it. Come on, Elias. You'll love the show. Trust me."

"Ladies and gentlemen," the announcer's voice began, and the rustle of people taking their seats died down. "In accordance with the greatest traditions of Russian ballet, there will be changes in tonight's program."

The audience tittered.

"In this evening's performance of the second act of *Swan Lake*, the role of Odette will be danced by Mademoiselle Fifi Chang. The Marche Slav will be performed by Yurika Sakitumi, and the Dying Swan will be danced this evening by Ludmila Beaulemova. We wish to remind you that the use of flashbulbs in this theater is strictly prohibited. Sudden bursts of light tend to remind some of our more fragile ballerinas of terrible Bolshevik gunfire."

Elias and Sean exchanged grins as the audience cracked up. "And finally," the announcer concluded cheerfully, "we are pleased to announce that Mademoiselle Fifi Chang is in a very, *very* good mood this evening."

To applause, the curtains went up as the familiar strains of Tchaikovsky began. Von Rothbart stormed onto the stage, waving his cape around grandly. With a smirk, he adjusted his cuffs and gesticulated broadly into the orchestra pit, presumably to show everyone who hadn't read their program book yet that he was an evil sorcerer. He then exited stage left, dragging a rope attached to a papier-mâché swan on a wheeled trolley. The spotlight dutifully tracked it off the stage.

Next, Beonno came onstage, a cheerful youth with a fetching feathered hat and a crossbow. The tights looked sensational on him.

He was soon joined by Prince Siegfried—an amiable young man, apparently, who appeared to consider Beonno a good friend even if Beonno did almost put a crossbow bolt through his gut at his sudden appearance. A flurry of pantomime established that Prince Siegfried hunted a swan. Beonno exited, presumably to continue the chase elsewhere, and as the Prince turned, the object of his pursuit fluttered onto the stage.

"Oh, my *god*," Elias heard someone mutter in the row behind him. "Didja ever see a swan princess before with such hairy armpits?"

It was incredible, Elias decided. The costume, the wig, the big arched feet, dancing *en pointe*, the delicately graceful arm movements—Odette really did look and move like a ballerina. And then something would puncture the illusion—a foot placed in an exaggerated position, an expressive look directed at the audience, a deliberate stumble. Once, as she spun on one toe, supported by her devoted lover, she apparently ran out of momentum and, with a comical grimace, resorted to hauling herself hand over hand on her partner's shoulder to complete the turn.

The Prince and Odette quickly established, through a combination of dance and pantomime, that Odette was under an enchantment that turned her into a swan by day, but that the Prince's devoted love could break the spell. Other enchanted swans joined them in a group dance, with much simpering and fluttering (and occasional missteps and pratfalls). The Prince informed Beonno emphatically, upon his return, that he had now entered a no-swan-hunting zone (one of the swans emphasized the point with a delicate kick that knocked Beonno right off his pins). As the time drew near for Odette to turn back into a swan, Von Rothbart, like a true spoilsport, interrupted a passionate pas de deux to tear Odette from the Prince's embrace. The sorcerer dragged her offstage, and the agonized Prince fell to the ground, senseless, as the curtain fell.

The company trooped onstage en masse to accept, with many flourishing bows and preening curtsies, the audience's applause. Mademoiselle Fifi Chang graciously accepted a bouquet of roses, and as the company stepped back, the curtain fell again and the lights went up for the intermission.

"You were right, Gordy," Kiyoshi said as they all stood up. "I'm glad you had Leo nag me into coming; they're hilarious."

"They're even funnier if you know much about ballet," Gordy replied. "I've never been able to look at *Swan Lake* quite the same way since seeing the Trocks perform it."

Elias eyed Sean as they made their way out to the lobby. Sean looked fine—well, maybe a bit tired, his expression drawn and pre-occupied. Elias studied him surreptitiously, remembering the picture he had developed that afternoon. Well, okay, so Sean's legs didn't look quite as good as Kiyoshi's, but then Kiyoshi made his living as a bicycle messenger. Still, Sean looked fit, his hands strong and capable. Were those same jagged lines and harsh shadows still there in his face? Or had it been just an effect of the weird color balance when he'd printed the photograph?

"Enjoying the show?" Sean asked, his eyebrow raised.

"Yeah. My parents took me to the ballet once or twice, but I've never seen anything quite like this." He hesitated, wondering whether to say something about the picture, but just then Leo, Kiyoshi, and Gordy walked up to join them, and the moment was lost.

Yurika Sakitumi opened the second act with "Marche Slav." ("I doubt," Gordy was heard to remark, sotto voce, "that the relation-ship between an abstract concept like freedom and the symbolic use of draperies has ever been so clear."

"Was that supposed to be Marxist or something?" Elias heard Kiyoshi whisper back.)

Next, the central curtain came down and a spotlight illuminated stage right. Nothing happened at first, and then as the music began, the spot fled over to stage left to shine on a sylphlike figure wafting from the wings, her back to the audience. Elias felt a faint shock of recognition and checked his program book—yes, "The Dying Swan," music by Camille Saint-Saëns. He remembered a public television show he'd seen once with some old archive footage of the ballerina Anna Pavlova performing her signature piece. Ludmila

Beaulemova was dancing it exactly the same way—well, except he doubted Anna Pavlova had left feathers from her costume drifting onto the stage in her wake.

The cello music swelled; the swan's life force grew fainter. More flapping, more feathers falling, and a preliminary onset of rigor mortis made the swan stagger for a moment. An expression like languid alarm crossed her features as the audience laughed. She fluttered, wobbled, and collapsed ever so gracefully, one leg tastefully extended before herself. A few exquisite, plaintive death throes and, finally, she expired, lying on the stage with one wing sticking straight up in the air.

The lights went out and then the spotlight reappeared to show Ludmila Beaulemova on her feet again, making a deep, heartfelt obeisance to the audience, arms elegantly extended behind her back. She slipped offstage and then came mincing back for another bow. As the applause strengthened, she looked up to the balcony and broke into tears, touchingly overwhelmed by the audience's tribute. She knelt and indicated in pantomime placing her heart at her feet.

Elias, grinning as he clapped, glanced over at Sean.

Sean was crying.

The sight didn't make sense at first. Was it just that he'd been laughing so hard? No, he wasn't even smiling . . . Sean noticed Elias looking at him and hastily wiped away the moisture on his cheeks with the edge of his hand. He began clapping, too.

"Are you okay?" Elias asked in a low voice.

Sean shrugged, obviously unhappy at Elias's observation. "It's nothing."

Elias forced his attention back to the stage as the applause died down and the lights went up. As the audience began to stand, Ludmila Beaulemova came out again, arms lifted, blowing kisses to the audience.

Gordy was too tired to go out after the show, so the group broke up and Elias and Sean took the subway home. "That piece about Carrie Nation, now," Sean said as they found their seats. "That was really something." He grinned. "Choreography by what's-'er-name; axes by Ace Hardware. I tell you, I was moved. I will dedicate the next bottle of Guinness I drink to her. The amazon of the temperance movement!"

"I'm sure she'd be touched."

"So which was your favorite part?"

Elias considered. "I guess I liked *Swan Lake* the best." His foot idly toyed with a scrap of paper on the floor. "It reminds me of a book I saw when I was a kid . . ."

"What book?" Sean asked after a moment's pause.

"Funny, I haven't thought about it in years. It was a collection of fairy tales I kept checking out of the library. My mother tried to keep me from taking it out once, I remember. I mean, why was her son so fascinated with this *fairy tale* book?" He paused. "I never made that connection before. Guess she was worried about my masculinity even back then.

"Anyway, one tale told the story of a girl whose brothers had all been enchanted by their stepmother, so they were swans by day and men by night. She had to weave shirts out of nettles to save them and break the curse over them. And she had to remain silent while she did it or the brothers would all die." He felt as if he were babbling. Why couldn't he talk about what was really on his mind? *Why were you crying, Sean? Why can't you tell me?*

Sean nodded. "I see the connection to *Swan Lake*. That's a common folktale motif, the mortal turned into a bird." He had to raise his voice to be heard over the subway's roar. "There's an Irish version of the tale, you know, called 'The Children of Lir.' I sometimes sing from parts of the longer ballad form. In that version, the sister is enchanted by the stepmother, as well as her brothers."

"Does she manage to save them?" Elias asked lightly.

"She breaks the curse. But it hardly matters. Once the spell is broken, they all die at the end of the story."

Elias shivered. The lights flickered on and off as the subway plunged onward.

Chapter Fifteen

Hail, wedded love! mysterious law! true source
Of human offspring, sole propriety
In paradise, of all things common else.
By thee adult'rous lust was driven from men
Among the bestial herds to range; by thee,
Founded in reason, loyal, just and pure,
Relations dear, and all the charities
Of father, son, and brother, first were known.
Perpetual fountain of domestic sweets,
Whose bed is undefil'd and chaste pronounc'd
Present or past, as saints or patriarchs us'd.
Here Love his golden shafts employs; here lights
His constant lamp, and waves his purple wings:
Reigns here, and revels not in the bought smile
Of harlots, loveless, joyless, unendear'd,
Casual fruition; nor in court amours,
Mix'd dance, or wanton mask, or midnight ball,
Or serenade, which the starv'd lover sings
To his proud fair, best quitted with disdain.

—JOHN MILTON, *PARADISE LOST*

The widow Goody Patience Carter lived beside the salt marsh on the east side of town. Her plot of land was neither large nor rich, for her husband, Josiah, had chosen it, and it was widely agreed that whenever given any opportunity, Josiah Carter had always had an unerring knack for making the wrong choice.

There were those who joked that Goody Carter should have been named Silence rather than Patience, for she was a great talker. Some even said that her husband had died as much from a wish for some peace and quiet as from the effects of too much drink. Those who smiled at her volubility, however, had to admit that she was no mere empty-headed chatterbox. She had, in fact, both a shrewdly observant eye and a boundlessly generous heart.

Moreover, she possessed a skill essential to a superior midwife: she knew how to keep her neighbors' secrets. After her husband's death she pieced together a spare but respectable living for herself and her two children from her garden and animals, supplemented by trading her herbal remedies and nursing for goods with her neighbors.

The hunting party, with Eliza, came out of the woods to the north of Goody Carter's small property. After the men divided among themselves the wild hares and woodcocks they had shot, Goodman North transferred the rough bundle made of the nettle flax to the Reverend's horse. Then he and Goodman Hubbard left to follow the road back to their farms.

"Is Goody Carter in sight?" Jonathan asked.

William shifted uneasily in his saddle. "Perhaps she has been called to Goodman Parker's home? I spoke with their girl yesterday; she said Goody Parker was very near her time."

"I see Katherine," Jonathan replied, nodding toward the door of the house where a girl of thirteen or so had just emerged to feed the chickens foraging around the doorstep. "Let us go speak to her."

They hailed Katherine and sent her to fetch her mother. Goody Carter soon appeared, wiping her plump hands on her apron. "Why, good afternoon to you, Reverend, Mr. Latham," she said in surprise. She was a big woman, with strong fleshy arms and a ruddy, good-humored face with a sprinkling of moles over the corner of one lip. A fringe of black curls spilled out of her cap and over her forehead. "Is Dorcas low again, good Reverend? I had thought the gargle I brought her would make her comfortable."

"Nay, Dorcas is better," William replied. He felt taken aback at her assumption that he had come personally to fetch medicine for his servant, but then smothered his irritation with a stern warning to himself to cultivate the humility proper to a minister of God.

"We have come to you for help for this girl, Goody Carter," Jonathan said, dismounting. Carefully, he pulled Eliza off the horse's back. "We found her alone, in the wood. I will carry her—do you have a bench or stool inside where I may set her down? For, see, her feet are inflamed and raw, and her hands, too."

Patience stepped forward, squinting a little, to look at Eliza's hands. "Poor girl!" she exclaimed. "Aye, make haste and come inside, Mr. Latham. Mind the doorstep, for I fear me the board is loose. I have asked Daniel to nail it down any time this last fortnight but he— Reverend Avery, have a care, the doorstep. Katherine! Pray you bring the washbasin and the pitcher I just filled from the well."

She lifted the wooden latch and led the small party inside to the parlor, where the aroma of bean and turnip soup drifting in from the hall filled the air. Eliza looked around warily. Although the walls were whitewashed, the floor had not been swept, and several meals' worth of dishes covered the table. The bed, with a pile of washing dumped upon it, had been left unmade. Patience Carter had many virtues, but a firm command of the housewifely arts was not among them.

If she felt embarrassed to have two of the most important men in the town see her home in such a state, Patience gave no sign. Hastily, she removed a couple of bread pans from a bench and dragged it away from the wall. Jonathan set Eliza down there gently. When Katherine brought the basin, Patience laboriously knelt down, grunting, to place it on the floor. "What is your name, child?"

she asked as she guided Eliza's feet to rest in the basin. "How came you to be so hurt?"

"We don't know her name," Jonathan said.

Patience looked up at Eliza in surprise as she picked up the water pitcher. "Can she not tell you?"

"We think she can hear and understand us, but she is mute."

"Yet she can hear? Perhaps her wit is diseased, or she has suffered some kind of attack. Did she have any other hurt?"

"We don't—" Jonathan began, but stopped as Eliza shook her head.

"Ah, you can understand me, can you?" Patience said kindly.

Eliza nodded.

"Well, then, I must ask you my questions, instead of speaking to those around you, as if you were deaf or witless, eh?" Patience set the pitcher down and leaned forward, frowning, to look closely in Eliza's eyes. Gently, she took Eliza's chin between her thumb and forefinger, turning her head so that the sunlight from the window shone in her face. She leaned in, so closely that for a startled moment William thought she was going to kiss the girl, but she was only comparing one eye to the other. "The apples of your eyes are the same size, and respond well to light. No blow to the head, then, I think."

"She was making—where is it?" Jonathan began.

"Here." William, who had come into the house behind the others, had the bundle of nettle flax and woven cloth under his arm. He put it on the table for Patience to see. "This leaf here, you see— Goodman North said it was a nettle."

Patience's eyebrows rose in surprise, and she looked at Eliza's feet and hands again. "She has been breaking nettles with bare hands and feet? Why would she— Here now, don't touch that, child," she said quickly as Eliza stepped out of the basin and rose to limp eagerly over to the table. "Some leaves are still clinging; you will burn yourself again."

Eliza reached for the bundle anyway—until Jonathan seized her hands and gently pulled them back. Eliza wrenched one free, but

William twitched the bundle out of her reach. She slammed a fist against the table in frustration.

"This happened in the woods, too," Jonathan said tensely, trying to recapture Eliza's other hand.

"Take that outside, out of her sight, Reverend Avery," Patience said quickly, and William did so. "Let her go, Mr. Latham, you will only vex her more. Child, harken to me. Child!" She took Eliza by the shoulders and gave her a shake. Once Eliza looked at her, Patience immediately released her. "Your work will be kept safe for you," Patience said reassuringly in answer to Eliza's stricken look. "But look you, we must now tend to your hurt. Please, come sit down again."

For a long moment Eliza hovered indecisively on the edge of flight. But Patience smiled at her, gesturing in the friendliest possible manner toward the bench. Eliza looked over at Jonathan, who nodded encouragingly. "Goody Carter will help ease your hurt," he said. "Will you not sit and tarry with us?"

Reluctantly, Eliza came and sat down again. Patience helped ease her feet back into the washbasin and then emptied the pitcher into it. Eliza hissed at the touch of the water against the raw, oozing patches. Patience shook her head, clucking her tongue. She beckoned her daughter over and hoisted herself to her feet. "Here, Katherine, bathe her hands and feet. Carefully now, wipe the dirt out of the wounds with this." She handed Katherine a rag and went over to the sideboard to fetch a candle.

"Can you help her?" Jonathan asked her in a low voice as she lit it at the fireplace.

"Aye, if it be only nettle burns. I have no dock leaves in my house now, but I do have dock root in my stores; a decoction of that will give her ease. It will take but a shake of a cat's whisker to prepare. I can gather the leaves tomorrow."

Patience went down to the cellar with a candle and soon came back, drawing long slender dock roots from her waist pocket. As she busied herself at the hearth, raking up coals and setting up a kettle on the trammel hook to boil the root in cider vinegar,

Jonathan went to sit on the bench beside Eliza. The afternoon light pouring through the western window onto her unruly hair caught glints like curves of molten copper wire, so bright they almost hurt the eye if he stared too long. Rarely had he ever seen a maiden with uncovered hair. He wished he could know what she was thinking, as she looked quietly around the room. He thought her gaze seemed interested and observant, if still wary and watchful. She certainly did not look to him to have the vacant gaze of a half-wit. She became aware of his regard and her eyes met his for a moment. The intensity of silent thought in them intrigued him. He wondered whether she was curious to know what manner of man he was. He smiled at her, hoping to coax a warmer expression from her in return. Although she held his gaze for a long moment, she did not smile back, but merely turned her attention back to the basin. William, coming back in from outside, noticed the silent exchange and frowned.

"A word privately in your ear, Mr. Latham," he said, placing a hand on Jonathan's shoulder. "And you, Goody Carter." Jonathan rose from the bench and followed him, and when Patience had covered the kettle and stepped over to join them, William said, his voice lowered, "We must decide what is to be done with her. She is an alien. And as an alien, she may not, by law, linger here in the community without any business for longer than three weeks."

"Unless examined and approved by the local authority," Jonathan amended, a small gleam in his eyes. "As magistrate, I believe I am that authority."

After a moment of dismay, William recovered himself, saying, with a small bow of his head, "Indeed. Yet how can you discover her business and the moral fitness of her character if she cannot speak? Or will not," he added darkly.

A baffled silence fell for a moment.

"Can she write?" Jonathan said suddenly, a new hope springing to life.

" 'Tis a good thought. Well, let us see." Patience went over and gently dried Eliza's hands with a lockram towel and then fetched a slate and slate pencil. "Do you know how to use these, child?"

Clumsily, because of the blisters on her hands, Eliza took the slate. She raised the pencil to write upon it . . . and then hesitated. *The first word you utter will pierce through the hearts of your brothers like a dagger. Their lives hang upon your tongue.* Eliza did not think that writing and speech were the same, yet she wondered now whether the fairy would agree. The fairy had clearly warned her, above all, to keep the nature of her task to herself. Perhaps the constraint was truly about whether or not she told another at all, rather than about whether the telling was in speech or writing. If that were true, then the first touch of a pencil upon a slate might be just as fatal to her brothers.

She couldn't know for certain, she realized with a rush of despair. She looked up at the intent faces watching her. Jonathan and Patience, at least, showed nothing but sympathetic interest, and she longed to unburden her soul to them in response. And yet . . . reluctantly, she put down the pencil. Risking her brothers' lives for her own comfort was simply unthinkable.

Jonathan sighed in disappointment as Eliza placed the slate on the bench at her side.

"A great pity," William said slowly, and he sighed, too. "How can we ever learn aught about her?"

Patience laughed and shrugged. "Dear me, child," she said, giving Eliza a conspiratorial wink, "if our good Reverend should ever have babes of his own, we must hope they never will be left in his care if they fall sick, eh?"

Jonathan threw William a speaking look. "She baits you, my friend."

William sniffed, knowing it, too, but was unable to resist saying, "I do not dispute I may lack a woman's touch as a nurse, Goody Carter, but I do not see—"

"Faith, sir, exactly so! And if you do not see, 'tis because you do not look. Why, if I only cared for people who speak or write, how could I help a young babe with worms, or a man fallen into insensible fever from unbalanced humors? A poor nurse I would be, indeed! No, any healer who wishes to earn the fee must watch for other, harder signs. This girl," she gestured toward Eliza, "has much to reveal about herself, even if she can neither speak nor write. We only need take the time and trouble to study, to learn it."

"I do confess I had thought," Jonathan began, throwing William a glance, "that she might stay with you, Goody Carter. If you could do as you suggest, watch her, and find out about her . . ."

"Hmm," Patience said consideringly.

"Yet there may be a danger," William said doggedly.

"From *her?*" said Jonathan, incredulous astonishment at the very idea plain in his voice.

Patience laughed her characteristic merry laugh. "Why, I think my arm is stout enough not to fear any danger from a girl with wounded hands and feet."

"Then you will take her?" Jonathan said eagerly. "If you give her some simple tasks, perhaps you can learn about her, as you say."

She went back over to the bench, took the rag from Katherine, and lifted Eliza's feet and then her hands carefully to inspect them. "With those hands, she may not be able to work much at first," Patience said. She went to take the dock root kettle from the hearth.

"Come now, Goody Carter, what can persuade you?" He thought for a moment, and an idea occurred to him. "I heard Goodman Noah Fish saying something to you after meeting this last Sabbath. About a debt—"

"Aye," Patience replied a little shortly, not liking the reminder. "I bought some boards last winter from his sawmill, to repair my still-room lean-to. I had planned to pay with the new calf I expected this spring, but the cow miscarried." She set a piece of cheesecloth over a bowl and poured the kettle contents through to strain it.

"I will pay to redeem the debt," Jonathan promised. "If you will provide her with bed and board, at least until I have to examine her in three weeks and"—he stopped, trying to think of an excuse to call before then—"and if you, er, will mend a half a dozen shirts for me."

Patience blinked in surprise, but after a moment's thought, she nodded. "A fair bargain, I think, Mr. Latham."

"Then we are agreed?" he said eagerly, extending his hand.

"Ah, but you forget one thing."

He looked puzzled. "And that is?"

She shook her head in disbelief and indicated Eliza with a small jerk of her chin. "Her. Does she *wish* to stay?"

She went over to the bench, motioned her daughter aside, and added part of the decocted dock root solution to the basin. "Nettle in, dock," she half sang under her breath. "Dock in, nettle out, dock rub nettle out." She poured the rest of the solution into another basin and set it on the table. "Here is another bowl for your hands, too. Dabble your fingers in it. There." She smiled when, after a few moments, Eliza lifted her hands out of the water and looked at them in blank surprise. "Eh, they do feel better, do they not?"

Eliza nodded. In fact, the relief from the nettle sting was great, although her hands and feet still felt swollen.

"Put them back in to soak more," Patience told her, and Eliza did so. "I'll make a salve of flax seed and slippery elm bark for you," Patience continued, "and then wrap your hands and feet. We don't want the wound closing with proud flesh. I will find some dock leaves tomorrow and rub your skin with the juice and then dress them again. I would like you to stay here with me for several days so that I may be at hand to watch how they heal."

A frown line appeared between Eliza's brows. She was not certain of the way back to the cave. Worse, her nettles had been taken away, and the fairy had admonished her that not just any nettles could be used. She was not sure how or even if she could get them back, but perhaps if she waited a few days, something might happen to restore them to her.

And yet, her brothers would be so frightened and worried for her when they returned and found her gone. She wondered whether they would be able to find her, if she was not free to look for them.

As she wavered, torn, Patience gave her a keen look. "You're sharp set, ain't ye?"

Eliza consulted her stomach, and nodded.

"I have bean soup, and bread and cheese to fill your belly. And an apple tart, too. . . ." She raised an eyebrow as her words trailed off invitingly.

Jonathan bent down so his face was almost level with Eliza's. "Please stay," he said simply. "Goody Carter will be good to you, and it would please her to have you as her guest. It . . ." He hesitated. "It would please me if you would allow us to make you comfortable. And you can give her help in exchange, if you are willing. Will you not remain with her for a while?"

He looked at her so earnestly, so wistfully, that to her own faint surprise, as her eyes met that look, something about it made her nod once in agreement, almost without meaning to do so.

"Good!" Jonathan said, his smile warm with gratitude.

"Reverend, Mr. Latham, will you sup with us?" Patience offered. "Or stay at least to drink a mug of cider?"

William managed not to look at the dishes on the table as he declined. "Nay, you are very kind, but work on my sermon awaits, and Dorcas has no doubt dressed my dinner already. Mr. Latham," he added pointedly, "you will accompany me back to town, I hope?"

"Aye," Jonathan said reluctantly, standing. "I should go, too, I suppose." A happy thought struck him. "But . . . perhaps I might accept your kind invitation later this week, when I bring the shirts?"

To William's dismay, this plan was rapidly agreed to. Recognizing the inevitable, William merely bit his lip and smiled, fearful of arousing Jonathan's stubbornness by arguing the point.

Patience accompanied the men outside as they readied themselves to take their leave. As Jonathan mounted his horse and gathered up the reins, he said to Patience with a touch of anxiety, "You will take good care of her. Won't you?"

She managed to reply soberly that, aye, of course she would, with only a quiver at the corner of her mouth betraying her. Satis-

fied, Jonathan turned his horse's head and touched its sides with his heels. "Coming, Reverend?" he said back over his shoulder.

"In a moment," William said, climbing up into his own saddle. Once Jonathan had ridden out of earshot, he said in an undertone to Patience: "See that she is given a coif, so her hair may be decently covered." Without waiting for a reply, he turned his horse and flicked the reins, urging it to a trot to follow Jonathan.

Goody Carter had excellent skills as a nurse, and Eliza's hands and feet were very soon on their way to healing completely. For the first day or two, she merely sat quietly in the kitchen yard on the bench outside the doorway, looking up at the sky hour after hour. But then, one day, Goodman Danvers arrived to call Patience to his house to apply a roasted sorrel poultice to his son's lame foot. When Patience returned, she found Eliza hobbling around the parlor slowly, pulling a broom across the floor. Eliza had taken care to sweep in the corners and under the legs of the dresser that held the pewter plates, something Patience had not bothered to do for over a year. She had used sand to scrub away the sticky spot on the floor where Patience had spilled a dose of Solomon's seal syrup. And, as Katherine reported, she had tended the fire, unasked. Although secretly very satisfied, Patience made no more outward notice of this initiative than to thank Eliza politely. She privately instructed her daughter and son, however, to watch and let her know whatever else the strange girl took it into her head to do about the house and yard.

The next night, Jonathan arrived for supper bearing his talisman of admittance—a half dozen shirts bundled under his arm. Patience served a simple pottage, made of leftover broiled fish and greens from the midday dinner, and Jonathan ate his helping without noticing much about the taste. He talked with Patience about the arrival of the new blacksmith, Goodman Norcross, into the community, the rumors of troubles with the Indians to the north, and the difficulty caused by the rivalry of the two local brewers for the town's business. And all the while, he covertly and openly watched Eliza.

He exerted himself to interest and even amuse her, and tried to make her feel included in the conversation by stopping to explain to her who the people were they were discussing. Although she did not laugh or even smile at his stories, she listened carefully to all that was said, he was sure.

He recounted a tale for Daniel about a trapping trip he had taken the previous winter, and as his face grew animated with the telling, Eliza found herself studying him in turn. She had always liked to study people. She sensed his interest in her, and it made her realize that he watched people carefully, just as she did. That perceptiveness, in fact, was what made his stories so interesting. She liked him, she decided. He had an open frankness in his manner that appealed to her, and a generosity of spirit that tried to see the best in people.

As the sun sank lower toward the horizon, Eliza gradually grew restless, and her attention wandered outside the window. Patience noticed, and threw Jonathan a significant look. "Do you wish to step outside for a breath before bed, then, child?"

Eliza rose from her bench, and like a ghost, glided out the door.

"What was that about, then, Goody Carter?" Jonathan asked, puzzled, as the door closed behind her.

Patience sighed. "Every evening she wishes to be outside to watch as the sun sets. Something about the time of day seems to grieve her heart, I think; I do not know why." She and Katherine cleared the plates from the table, and then Daniel went outside to saw wood at the woodpile behind the house, and Patience went to the cellar to skim the barm from the ale to mix with flour and water to make the next day's bread sponge.

Quietly, Jonathan went outside. Eliza stood in the yard, motionless, watching the sky as the sun slipped below the horizon. Jonathan sat on the bench and waited. As the last rays of the sun disappeared and the golden brilliance of the clouds in the west faded to rose and gray, she turned to face him. Her cheeks were wet.

"Will you come and sit with me, then?" he said gently, wanting

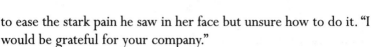

to ease the stark pain he saw in her face but unsure how to do it. "I would be grateful for your company."

Slowly, she came over to join him on the bench. For a time, they simply sat together companionably. A few stars came out, and the sound of crickets and frogs from the marsh filled the purpling twilight with peaceful song.

He began to speak, almost at random, telling her about his work as magistrate. "It is always interesting and varied, which suits me, for I fear doing the same work day after day would be a trial for me." He gave a deprecating half smile. "God gave me a temper too easily restless. I license innkeepers and sellers of fish, clear the highways of obstructions, oversee military commissions and the town's provision for the poor. I act to protect church doctrines and prevent against profanation of the Sabbath. And I mediate disputes, both locally and for the county court." He hesitated. "The trick of it, you see, is having a heart always open to God's guidance. And willingness to learn and listen."

The stars overhead grew bright and clear, twinkling with hard-edged brilliance. He could not see her face anymore in the deepening shadows, although he could hear her quiet, steady breathing. He listened to that breathing for a long time before he dared to add: "I would wish to . . . always listen to you.

"Even if you ever speak to me only with your eyes."

The Sabbath-day meetings were the only opportunities William had for several weeks to observe Eliza. He noted with approval that Goody Carter had dressed her modestly, and accepted with a satisfied nod the midwife's assurances that the girl's hands and feet were healing properly. He had the opportunity to observe her narrowly while the deacon lined the psalms, reading the verses so the congregation could sing the responses. She did not sing, of course, but instead sat quietly with all apparent attention, only moving to munch the fennel seeds offered her from Goody Carter's handkerchief. During the nooning break, she did not exchange covert glances with the young men in the congregation, but stayed near

Katherine and Daniel Carter, eating the brown bread luncheon from Goody Carter's hamper, her eyes modestly downcast. Satisfied, William turned his attention to preparing mentally for the afternoon sermon and prayers, and he gave her little more thought.

He would have been shocked to learn that Jonathan had ridden out thrice in that fortnight to sup at Goody Carter's house. But Jonathan did not tell him.

When three weeks had passed, the two did go together, at William's insistence, to the midwife's home to formally fulfill the requirements of the Alien Act, with Jonathan as the appointed examiner and William as a witness. "Although," Jonathan pointed out, "it may be argued I do not have the authority to expel her, even for cause, because I think there may be honest doubt about whether the law can even *be* applied. Since the question of application of all laws is entirely open until the colony hears the Crown's decision about the restoration of the charter."

"We do not know," William said lightly, "and therefore, surely the best, most conservative course is to follow the established custom until matters may be clarified."

"Very well," Jonathan said. "I *am* curious to know what Goody Carter has discovered about her."

To Jonathan's private disappointment, Eliza was not there when the men arrived. "I sent her with Katherine to Goody Porter's," Patience explained. "They were going to wind quills, for Goody Porter is setting up her loom to warp a piece."

"That was undoubtedly wise," William agreed. "If the girl cannot speak with us, we can make our judgment by listening to your frank opinion of her."

"What have you learned about her?" Jonathan asked as they sat down at Patience's table.

Patience brought some tankards of cider. "To begin," she said, offering one to each man, "she knows how to make cheese."

Jonathan sat up straight. "Indeed?" he said, intrigued.

William took a draw from his mug and raised an eyebrow. "To make cheese? Of what import is that?"

Patience smiled. "Do *you* know how to make cheese, Reverend?"

"Why, er . . ." His words trailed off.

"You make it with rennet. Would you even recognize rennet if you saw it? It must be heated with several gallons of milk—do you know how long it takes until the curd forms?"

"No."

"Oh, an hour or two. And do you know what you must mix into it after breaking the curd and draining off the whey? A little of your fresh butter. And after you have packed it into your press, what must you do to it while turning it as the whey drips out?"

"I confess I have no idea," he admitted. Jonathan, he noted with some irritation, was grinning behind a hand at his discomfiture.

"You must change and wash the cheesecloth covering it, several times. And after you repack the cheese in dry cloth, how long do you leave it in the press, my good Reverend, before taking it out to powder and put in the dairy house to age?"

"I do not know, I tell you," he replied, more sharply than he intended.

"Thirty or forty hours or so."

"No one has ever taught me how to make cheese," he snapped, feeling obscurely criticized.

"That, good sir, is my point. Someone *has* taught her. A careful housewife, I deem, who taught her the importance of thorough pressing, and the virtues of cleanliness." She waited a moment for that to sink in. "She knows herbs. Not so much the native ones, though. And she does not know their healing properties, but instead how they may be used as dyes."

"Hmm."

"She can dress a fowl, tend a fire, and bake. She knows which plants are weeds to pull up in the garden, and she is very deedy with her needle—she mended one of your shirts, in fact, Mr. Latham, and did a pretty job of it." She went to fetch it from a work basket in the corner.

"And so she has had a proper maiden's instruction," Jonathan said, taking the shirt from her and turning it in his lap to examine it.

"Indeed she has. She is used to hard work and labors diligently and willingly. I do not even have to ask her; she finds things to do."

The men glanced about the room. The pewter on the sideboard had been wiped, and the usual covering of crumbs was gone from the table. Someone had made the bed that morning. All the blankets, shirts, and dresses that had been spread out on the benches and floor during the last visit had been put back into the storage chests. The floor and hearth were swept clean and the andirons scrubbed. Jonathan and William exchanged a look, the meaning of which was plain: the house looked cleaner than either had ever seen it.

"And one thing more." Patience smiled. "She can read."

"What?"

"Can she indeed?"

"I came in one afternoon to find her head bent over my Bible. She had been reading the Psalms."

"But why then will she not write?" William demanded.

Patience shook her head. "I do not know." She hesitated. "And another matter: whenever she stops her work, she does it to watch the sky. She is looking for something." She sighed. "What it is she looks for, I do not know. And every sunrise and sunset, some grief steals over her. It goes away quickly, and she will go back to work. But it always comes again."

Thoughtfully, Jonathan turned the shirt over in his lap. The rent in the sleeve had been neatly darned. He turned it inside out to look at the stitches more closely. His fingers brushed against something, a patch of thread where he did not expect it, and he looked more closely.

On the inside of the shirt, right at the spot that would rest over his heart, a tiny white work design had been embroidered, a small cluster of forget-me-nots. He rubbed his finger absently over the smooth, neat stitches, and then, carefully, so that no one would see, turned the shirt back.

"She is a good worker, then?" he said briskly. "As good as the last girl you had?"

"Oh, aye, much better than Joan." Patience snorted. "Thank Providence Nathan Miller proposed and took that lazy lie-abed off my hands."

"And the girl reads scripture," Jonathan said softly to himself, his fingers suspended over the hidden white work. He glanced at Patience. "And her carriage, it is as it should be?"

"She has always been the veriest modest, proper maiden."

"Is she attentive during your evening devotions?"

"Aye, and during Sabbath-day meeting, too."

Jonathan nodded. "She has shown herself to be diligent, obedient, and open to God's word. Are you content to continue boarding her, Goody Carter?"

"Aye," Patience said slowly. "I confess I do wish I knew what troubles her so. But she is a hard worker, and a good-hearted girl."

"Jonathan," William said faintly, but he sensed that his moment to argue was perhaps already past.

He was right. "I have made my decision," Jonathan said firmly. "The girl stays."

Jonathan and William rode back to town together. When they parted company at the tavern, Jonathan immediately turned his horse's head toward Goody Porter's farm. He met the two girls on the path walking back.

"Good afternoon," Jonathan said, drawing rein.

"Mr. Latham," Katherine Carter said, bobbing a curtsey and grinning.

In surprise, Eliza raised her eyes to meet his and dipped a polite curtsey, too. She felt real pleasure at the sight of him. Few in the town, she had discovered, could speak so easily to her without seeming to be bothered by the awkwardness of her silence. Patience was one, but that was different: Eliza's silence did not trouble her simply because of the inexhaustible flow of Patience's chatter. The magistrate, on the other hand, possessed the knack of speaking with her without making the conversation seem truly one-sided. He would ask her questions, and wait for her to nod or shake her head, truly interested in her opinion. He read her expressions, and at the tilt of her head, the wrinkling of her nose, or a shrug, he would say in response, "Do you know, I have never been sure of that myself," or exclaim, "I knew you would agree!" His eyes turned toward Eliza now, and she could see her pleasure reflected in him.

"Good afternoon to you," he said gently. As he looked down at her, he had a sudden flash of memory, of her warm hair, unkempt and tangled, tumbled about her shoulders. Now it was covered, all bundled modestly out of his sight, making her neck look even longer, more slender. He had never noticed before how the weight of a woman's hair could make a swelling curve in her cap, just above her neck.

Jonathan dismounted. "Would you please tell your mother," he said, addressing himself to Katherine, "that I have taken your friend to . . . to see something. I will escort her home when we are finished."

Startlement contended with curiosity on Katherine's face, but she ducked another curtsey and nodded. "I will tell her," she replied shyly. There was an awkward pause, and then Katherine shrugged and resumed walking down the path.

Jonathan waited until she was out of sight, and then turned to Eliza. "I would like to invite you to come see my home. Will you?"

Surprised again, Eliza nodded.

And so it was that Magistrate Latham's servants were exceedingly disconcerted by the unexpected arrival of their master at home in the middle of the day, with the strange girl who had been staying at the midwife's home. If Jonathan noticed their consternation and curiosity, he gave no sign of it, but simply dismissed them to their tasks, leaving him and Eliza to walk through the house alone.

It was an exceedingly fine house, built of clapboards, with an overhanging second story, and gable windows set with casement sashes. "My grandfather was one of those come to these shores with

John Winthrop," Jonathan told her. "My father built this house, but he and my mother were carried off by a fever the following winter. My younger brother died of diphtheria in his second year, and my sisters have married and moved away. The house has been mine alone since my twenty-first year."

As he walked her through it, he carefully pointed out all the comforts, from the fireplaces in each room to the wide staircase and closets and the airy windows. Everything had its proper place, and the air smelled of lavender, and the currants Jonathan's housekeeper had cooked that morning for jelly.

The meaning of the unspoken question behind this trip to Jonathan's house, the reason for his earnestly hopeful manner, slowly began to dawn on Eliza. This was no idle tour; he was showing her his home to find out if she could imagine herself as its mistress. Her heart began to beat more quickly at the very thought, and she stole a glance shyly at his face as they mounted the stairs together. She liked him, esteemed him, certainly—did she feel any more for him than that?

Could she learn to love him?

The memory of her responsibility to her brothers smote her again, a whiplash of dismay. Eliza still had not seen the swans at all since the day Jonathan had taken her from the cave. She had struggled against the growing fear that they had abandoned her, flying on without her. But perhaps she was wrong, and they still searched for her. If so, then making a home with Jonathan would be like abandoning them all over again, just when they needed her most.

On the other hand, if she could not find a way to complete her task, she wondered how she could possibly marry Jonathan at all. She would have to remain mute for the rest of her life, never speaking a word to her husband or perhaps, someday, her own children. Eliza shivered, despite the warmth of the sunlight coming through the windowpanes.

On the second story at the end of the house, Jonathan showed her another room, smaller than the rest, but carefully and comfortably furnished. Green paragon hangings decked the walls.

"I thought that . . . with the green hangings," he said a little uncertainly, "this room might remind you of your former home. And see . . ." He went to a chest in the corner, opened it, and beckoned her closer. "It might please you to have these with you, to think of that time."

She came to look, and what she saw inside made her gasp and brought the blood rushing to her cheeks. She reached into the chest and touched the thick bundle of stripped nettle stems that had been taken from her. Underneath these lay the partially completed coat and the rest of the nettle flax she had prepared. The thought that now she could work again for her brothers' release made her face light up in the first smile Jonathan had ever seen her make. She reached out and took Jonathan's hand and kissed it.

"It makes you happy?" he said, his uncertainty melting away in dazzled delight with that smile. She nodded, her face aglow.

Overjoyed, Jonathan pressed her to his breast. "And . . . can I make you happy?" He held her out at arm's length again, and tenderly touched her face. "Would it content you to come make your home with me, as my bride?"

The look in her eyes gave him all the answer he needed.

Chapter Sixteen

The water is wide. I cannot cross o'er
Neither have I the wings to fly
Give me a boat that can carry two
And both shall row, my love and I.

—"WALY, WALY," TRADITIONAL

Elias switched his schedule to take the next day off since it was his birthday. At Sean's suggestion, they walked down to Avenue A, to Leshko's for breakfast, where the smell of coffee and frying sausage curled around them tantalizingly as soon as they stepped through the door. "One of the booths in the back is open," Elias suggested, pointing.

Sean shook his head and nodded toward another booth at a front window, where a man and a woman were just standing to leave. "I want to see the park." The man put on a pair of red-rimmed heart-shaped sunglasses as he threw some money on the table, and the two sidled past Sean and Elias to squeeze out through the awkward entryway. The waitress, a doe-eyed woman of twenty or so, appeared as if conjured to clear and wipe the table. Sean and Elias then claimed their spot, sliding across the cracked burgundy vinyl seats as she poured them coffee. Elias wrapped his hands around the thick, white china cup and took a slug of the hot liquid gratefully. It was strong; he made a face and reached for the cream and sugar.

"Know what you want?" the waitress asked with a heavy Ukrainian accent.

Sean peered at the specials written on poster board and tacked over the counter. "Um . . . well, I'll have eggs, sunny-side up, and sausage."

"And I'll take the buttermilk pancakes, with a side of bacon."

The waitress hurried off, tucking her pad into her apron pocket with a practiced gesture.

Sean half turned in his seat and stared moodily out over Tompkins Square Park. Elias studied Sean's face surreptitiously while stirring sugar into his coffee, trying to see the first, faint signs of thinness, of wasting, that he thought he'd detected in that photograph yesterday. He thought of the tears he'd seen on Sean's face during the Trocks last night. "Gordy says he's still planning on marching in the Gay Pride parade," he said finally. "I hope he's up to it."

Sean stirred, and seemed to recall his attention from far away. He took a sip of coffee and made a noncommittal "mm."

"How did he seem to you last night?"

"Well, *I* can't tell," Sean said a little irritably. "Whether he's sicker than usual or not, he's always Mr. Positive Attitude, like he can cure himself through pure force of will." He hesitated a moment. "Ruth told me that if you ask him how he's doing, he'll always tell you his . . . whaddaya call it, that blood count measurement . . ."

"His, um, CD4 count," Elias said.

"Right, the CD4 count. Unless it's fallen under five hundred. Then he won't mention it." Sean sighed.

"I heard him telling Leo about those meditation tapes he's been trying. And the vitamin therapy."

"Right. But not a word about his CD4 count."

Their breakfast arrived; Elias spread a golden veil of butter on his pancakes and poured syrup over them as Sean cut away the crispy, delicate frill around the edges of his eggs. They ate for a while in silence. Two-thirds of the way through his pancakes, Elias tried again. "The *Times* finally did a page one story on AIDS last Thursday. Did you see it?"

"No," Sean said.

Elias chewed his bacon, wondering how far he could push. He shifted, and a broken spring in the banquette seat jabbed him in the thigh. "I really think you should read it," he ventured finally.

Sean looked up sharply at Elias. "Look—I'm probably too moody to be very good company this morning. But this is a damn depressing conversation you're trying to start. It's your *birthday,* Elias."

Spit it out. "I . . . was developing a roll at the shop yesterday, and when I looked at some pictures of you, I thought you . . . you didn't look . . . right somehow."

"What, like I'm sick? I'm not sick. I'm just run down. Haven't been sleeping well. You know I had that cold—"

"You've been losing weight, haven't you?"

"A little."

"Just like Jerry did. And Ian. And Gordy."

Sean's face looked expressionless, but his hand tightened around the handle of the knife he was holding. "What are you saying." Said flatly, not like a question.

You know what I'm saying. "Don't you ever think about the future, Sean?" Elias said, exasperated. *Stupid, stupid. As if there was anything he could do now to keep from getting infected. He is infected.*

And that probably means I am, too.

"You want to find out about the future?" said Sean. A flurry of expressions crossed his face, too rapidly for Elias to make them out, and then he threw his silverware down on his plate with a metallic clatter. He had eaten only about half of his breakfast. "I can arrange that." He wiped his mouth with his napkin and caught the waitress's eye. "Could we get our check now?" Rising, he began to fish through his pockets for cash for the tip.

"Sean?" Elias said, with the desperate feeling that he had lost control of the conversation. "What—"

"I'm going to take you somewhere. Think of it as . . . another birthday present."

"Where?" Elias asked warily.

Sean's smile quirked ironically, but Elias could sense tension simmering underneath. "It's a surprise."

Sean ignored all further requests for information, and Elias finally gave up trying to engage him in conversation and simply followed in his wake. A bus dropped them off at the edge of the East Village, on a street Elias had never explored before. "Here," Sean said, indicating with a flourish a narrow black storefront; the shop's name, "The Silver Penny," was painted above the door in blue and silver script, surrounded by silver stars. "This is where I wanted to take you."

A bell tinkled sweetly as they entered, and the aroma of myrrh, sandalwood, and burning candle wax drifted toward them, tickling Elias's nose. The walls were painted a light muted blue, subtly sponged with silver. A series of rosemary wreaths, set with votive candles in glass holders, hung suspended by ribbons from the ceiling, like medieval chandeliers. More candles burned on shelves throughout the shop, despite the bright June sunlight outside. No other customers were in sight.

"Lizzie?" Sean said, looking around and raising his voice. "You here?" He started forward, past the rack of art cards on display, and Elias followed, eyeing pots of sculpted ivy, books on tarot, incense and incense burners, and jars full of dried herbs. He ran his hand over a glass case displaying wands, knives with ornate handles, cups, miniature cauldrons, crystal balls . . . It seemed to be a sort of magic shop. Overstuffed chairs with antimacassars invited customers to sit while leafing through the books.

They heard a step in the rear of the shop, where silk scarves in a riot of colors hung over a doorway. A hand pushed the fabric aside, and a woman stepped into the space behind the back counter.

Something about her quietly arrested attention. Not her clothing: she wore a simple black dress, and a narrow black scarf tied back the reddish blond hair that hung in undisciplined curling tendrils halfway to her waist. The only spot of color came from tiny gold feather charms woven into a miniature braid hanging at one side of her face. She was overly tall, with a nose and chin too long and a mouth too wide and full lipped, but the unusual length of her neck and high slope of her cheekbones balanced those features. The effect might be unconventional, but it was remarkably graceful.

Sean smiled and went to take her hands. "Did you light a bonfire for Midsummer's Eve?" He leaned forward to kiss her cheek and said something else to her in an undertone.

Elias waited, but the conference continued for a few moments. He did not hear the woman, Lizzie, speak, although he saw her nod her head once. He didn't want to seem to be eavesdropping, so he meandered back to the front of the store, wondering why Sean had brought him.

He had just started to get absorbed in an almanac of English folklore, when Sean reappeared unexpectedly at his side and said in his ear, "Lizzie will answer a question for you."

Elias looked up from the book, startled and a little confused. "Excuse me?"

Sean pointed toward the doorway at the back of the shop. "It's the birthday present I was talking about. You just have to ask her a question, and she'll answer it."

Elias stared at Sean and hastily put the book down. *And what question do you want me to ask?* He looked around the shop, and the pieces fell into place. "You mean she's like . . . like a fortune-teller? What does she do, look into a crystal ball?"

"Well, yeah. Or sometimes she uses tea leaves or the tarot. Or she just, well, *knows.*" Misreading the look on Elias's face, he added impatiently, "It's not a put-on. She has the gift, and she doesn't do this for everybody. C'mon."

He started toward the back, but Elias impulsively grabbed his arm to stop him. "Wait, Sean. I——" He glanced at Lizzie and then uneasily looked away. "Look," he said, lowering his voice, "no offense, but I don't really want to do this."

"What? Why not?"

"If what she does is real . . . if you're telling me she's some kind of a witch or something—"

Sean's eyes narrowed. "You got a problem with that?"

Elias laughed uncertainly. "I hardly know. I was raised Methodist."

"What's that supposed to mean?" Sean's voice now had a dangerously icy edge.

"Well, in my church . . . we were always warned to stay away from the occult." He shrugged, unnerved by the stony look in Sean's eye, but feeling unequal to explaining himself better.

"She's a Wiccan, Elias. Not a devil worshipper, if that's what's bothering you. It's just another religion."

"Yeah, well, I don't know what a Wiccan is, but *my* religion says a witch shouldn't be permitted to live. If I—" Elias stopped, arrested by the change on Sean's face. "For god's sake," he went on hurriedly, "I meant—that's just a figure of speech. I'm not suggesting she should be dragged out in a tumbril and killed or anything—"

Sean's stony control suddenly cracked and boiled over, terrifyingly, into molten fury. "You sanctimonious prick! Do you have any idea what the fuck you're saying? Don't you know why they call us faggots? Huh?"

Elias took a step backward, wide-eyed in astonishment. "Sean—"

"They used to burn people like us alive as fuel to burn witches!" Sean all but screamed in Elias's face. "Why the fuck should cocksuckers like you and me listen to whatever shit the church shovels out about witches?"

"I . . . I . . . Sean—" Elias held up his hands, aghast and terrified. He had never seen Sean in a rage like this before.

Brick-red, Sean wavered and flexed his hands—he seemed almost about to hit Elias. "Aw, fuck you!" He made a sound in his throat almost like a sob and then turned and rushed from the shop, slamming the door behind him hard enough to make the windows rattle.

As the door bell's jangle died away, Elias staggered back against the display counter, a numb shock spreading over him in waves. His breath came in gasps, like a runner's. Then he remembered Lizzie and straightened up to face her. "Ah . . ." he began shakily, feeling the heat rising in his face, "I'm sorry . . . so sorry. . . ."

He stopped, for she simply looked at him, face serene, with no hint of revulsion or dismay at the scene he and Sean had just enacted. Utterly impassive, in fact. Her green eyes met his, at once unguarded and impenetrable, cool like the shade of leaves during the heat of midsummer. His breath eased out without his noticing. *Ask her a question.*

He blinked, wondering suddenly, absurdly, whether he should buy an art postcard as a sort of apology. Instead, he gave her an awkward nod and stumbled out of the shop.

When Sean didn't come home that night, Elias started calling friends at 9 P.M.

"A fight?" said Frankie, surprised. "You two never fight."

"There's a first time for everything."

"What was it about? Oops. Sorry, darling. Not my business."

"I don't even know what it was about, to tell you the truth. Have you heard from him?"

"No, not since that little bash of Harry's on Memorial Day."

"Look, if he calls or comes over, tell him . . ." Elias hesitated.

"I'll tell him I'm expecting you at my door any moment," Frankie offered. "With a magnum of imported champagne, a case of poppers, and six gorgeous and *extremely* well hung Asian sailors. Fresh off the boat."

"Thanks, Frankie," Elias said, grimacing. "That'll really help."

"And then I'll tell him that if he promises to get his ass back over there to beg your forgiveness immediately, I'll send you home right away. Mostly unravished."

"You're all heart."

"Anytime, handsome. But honestly, don't worry, Elias. He probably just needs to go off and be bitchy for a while."

* * *

"What's that again?" Nick said, raising his voice over the noise in the background—another music party, apparently.

"Is Sean there? Have you seen him?"

"No, not tonight. But I didn't expect him. Daegen's here playing harp, and he and Sean don't get along at all. Not surprising, actually: Sean says Daegen's playing sucks."

"Gone?" said Minta, startled. "Since when?"

"Well, I don't know if he's *gone* exactly. He just hasn't come home."

"I haven't heard from him, Elias, sorry. Did you call Gordy?"

"I called a bunch of people. Gordy hasn't heard from him, either. Or Leo, or Stan, or Chris, or—or anybody!" He sighed. "Maybe I should call Jerry."

"Elias—Jerry's back in the hospital."

"What? When?"

"Checked in today. They think—" Her voice cracked. "They're afraid it's toxoplasmosis."

Elias squeezed his eyes tightly and leaned his head against the wall. "That's not good," he managed after a long pause.

"No." After a pause, she said hesitantly, "I don't know but . . . do you think he could have gone to the baths?"

Elias's head snapped back up. "I'm an idiot. And Minta, you're a doll. Thanks."

"Well sure, honey." She laughed ruefully. "Just add it onto my tab. I should have enough to buy my Mercedes any day now."

He headed down First Avenue toward the Club Baths at a jog. At the corner of Second Street and First Avenue, he could see the line of men snaking along the sidewalk. He saw something else, too: a scarecrow-thin figure bouncing jerkily up and down in a sort of weird tap dance of rage, ranting at the men lining up to get into the baths. Wild-eyed and gaunt, with hair in matted dreadlocks, he wore a collection of rags too small for him, and his knobby ankles and wrists stuck out, making him look like a grotesque marionette forced to dance madly by a hyperactive puppeteer. Another man tried to catch his wildly gesturing arms, pleading, "No, Ramon, honey, leave 'em be, baby. Leave 'em be and come home with TJ."

The dancing man ignored him. "Ain't nobody going in there coming out alive, hear me?" he yelled in a high, raspy voice. "Huh? Hear me, muthafuckers? Go in there—you think you getting sweet meat, but it's a lie! Devil done told you a lie!"

"Ramon!" the other man wailed. "For god's sake, leave 'em be!"

"Christ," one man said in an undertone to the man ahead of him just as Elias came up to the end of the line, "what a wacko!"

But the rest of the men said nothing, just shuffled along as the line moved slowly forward. Eyes front, refusing to notice.

"Nothing in there but ghosts, muthafuckers," Ramon jeered. "Men walking around dead, like me! Looka me, faggots! Looka meeeee! I'm dead!" He cackled and capered, arms flying, as a squad car pulled up. A cop got out and walked around the car warily to assess the situation. A couple of the men in the line looked over with interest now.

"He sick," the other man, TJ, said anxiously to the cop. "Don't hurt him, man. He be real bad sick, he gets off his head. But he ain't gonna hurt no one."

"I'm not going to hurt him," the cop said in a flat voice, "long as he calms down and comes along with me. What's his name?"

"Ramon."

"Okay, Ramon, come on now. Why don't you come sit in the back of my car, and we'll talk."

But when the cop slowly approached and tried to take Ramon's elbow, the man went wild, flailing out with his fists. In twenty seconds, the cop had him down, face mashed against the sidewalk, and was snapping cuffs on him, as TJ hopped up and down in agitation, wringing his hands. "Oh, sweet Jesus, don't hurt him, don't hurt him. He start bleeding, you never be able to stop it—Ramon, baby, don't, oh, don't—"

The cop wrestled Ramon up and started dragging him to the car, just as Elias reached the front of the line and was pulling out his wallet to pay. "Ghosts!" Ramon wailed like a lost soul. "Ghosts!

Don't go in there! You go in there, you already dead! Hear me, muthafuckers? You already dead!"

Elias hesitated at the lockers, looking down at the towel and the terry-cloth-lined sarong the attendant had thrust into his hands. The hell with it, he decided, throwing them down on the bench. He'd go in fully clothed. He didn't need a shower, and he certainly wasn't here to get laid. He was here to find Sean.

He checked the TV room only long enough to confirm that Sean wasn't there, and then headed out the door leading toward the Maze. He waited in the darkness, impatiently, for his eyes to adjust, and then began edging forward cautiously. What if he passed Sean in the dark without even seeing him? Or if he did find him, maybe in the middle of doing something involving a lot of sweating and heavy breathing, what could he do? What should he do? Drag him off, like the sorcerer tearing Odette from her lover's arms? He had a sudden vision of the agonized Prince left behind, falling to the floor of the orgy room, overcome by grief and sexual frustration. Maybe several princes, come to think of it. Oh well, he thought sourly, someone would be nearby to console them, no doubt.

He felt the first touch on his shoulder, soft and tentative. The hand slid down, heading for his waist. He wrenched away and hurried forward, feeling his way along.

Around a dim corner, one figure crouched in front of another. The man standing moaned and his lips drew back in a rictus of a smile; the ultraviolet spotlight made his teeth look purple, with black gaps. Dentures, Elias realized.

The touch of hands continued, gentle, reaching out to grope him from all directions with insistent desire. The sensation made him shiver, and he brushed them all away like insubstantial wisps of fog, dispersed with the flick of a hand. Warm flesh pressed up against him, and bodies swirled around him like wraiths, whispering coarse, dimly heard suggestions in his ear with hoarse chuckles, only to disappear behind him as he pushed on.

Sean—he scrutinized faces as all the eyes around him scrutinized

his crotch in turn—*where are you?* Something inside him throbbed with
hurt. He stayed in the orgy room just long enough to be sure that
none of the silent watchers or the figures writhing on the bed was
Sean, and then passed through quickly to head to the rooms upstairs.

At the door to the first cubicle, he paused. What to do—look inside each one? He leaned against the wall, listening to the assorted
muffled moans, slaps, and squeals floating out into the hallway, and
an unutterable weariness came over him, as if he had spent the
night pursuing a will-o'-the-wisp. *I can't.* He closed his eyes and
tried desperately to remember why he had come.

"Ya waiting for a room?" a voice beside him said.

Elias's eyes snapped open; he turned. A man stood beside him,
potbelly sticking out over his sarong. He had thinning hair and
crooked teeth, and when he smiled at Elias, so wistfully, so hopefully, it almost broke Elias's heart. "No," Elias said.

A puzzled expression drifted across the other man's face.
"Say . . . what're you doing with your clothes on?"

Elias pushed himself away from the wall. "I'm . . . going home."

The sound of the guitar coming from the living room woke him,
soft and peaceful, like a caress. Groggily, he turned to look at the
clock. 4:18 A.M. He lay for a while looking up at the shuddering shadows on the ceiling, sketched by moonlight shining through the courtyard trees. A scramble through his memories finally came up with the
name of that melody: "Tiny Sparrow." Sean had played it before.

He drew on his robe and padded out to the living room. Sean sat
on the couch, silhouetted against the window, his face in shadow. He
did not look up or stop playing as Elias came in, which somehow
seemed comforting. Elias sat at his feet on the floor, leaned back
against the base of the couch, and let the music wash over him. The
melody flowed out surely from under Sean's fingers, a peace offering, liquid consolation, and the knot in Elias's gut eased in response.

The song concluded; fingers on the strings hesitated, hovering
on the brink of another melody, and then stopped. Sean drew a
deep breath. "I'm sorry," he said.

Elias nodded in acceptance. He didn't reply *It's all right,* for it wasn't, and they both knew it. But he was glad Sean had said it, just the same. It helped.

They sat together in silence for a long time, as Elias thought back over what had been said in the store. What *had* happened there, anyway? "Sean," he asked softly, and hesitated, trying to find the right question. "Do you believe in God?" he ventured finally.

Sean took awhile to answer. "Five years ago I would have answered, 'Absolutely.' Three years ago, I would have said, 'No way.' Now . . ." He sighed. "Now, I'm not sure." He cleared his throat. "I was in seminary, studying to be a priest, you see."

"What?" Elias straightened and looked up at him in astonishment. "A Roman Catholic priest, you mean?"

"Yes." As Elias digested this, Sean added, with a trace of sarcasm, "Thank you for not laughing."

Images collided in Elias's mind: Sean straightening up from the harp, face alight from the music as he reached for a bottle of Guinness. Lolling in bed, blinking sleepily as a lizard in the morning light. Typing ferociously at the typewriter, pencil clenched firmly between his teeth. Cruising the baths. "It's . . . not a way I've ever pictured you before, I suppose." He thought of Sean taking him off the street and feeding him a hamburger. Giving him a home. "But I don't see any reason to laugh. Not at all."

"Hmm. Thank you. I think."

"So . . . what happened?" Elias asked cautiously.

Sean sighed again. "I fell for another seminarian."

"Did you know then you were gay?"

"Well, yeah, I knew, but I hadn't admitted it to myself. My family were staunch Catholics, and I thought . . . I *tried* to make myself believe that the fact I'd never been attracted to women meant I had a vocation. You know, a calling to be a priest. It felt like a place, a role, where I could fit in. And when you grow up feeling different all your life, you want a place to fit in so badly." His voice sounded wistful.

"I know."

"But then I met Bill."

"Was he . . . uh . . ."

"Yeah, but it was his first time, too. We kind of came out for each other. And once we did, that somehow changed everything. For both of us." His voice became dry. "Once we woke up to what was going on and tried to figure out what to do . . . it became clear we had a major difference of opinion on our hands. He wanted to stay with the church, try to change it from the inside. I told him he was crazy. The church has been around for two thousand years. How could one man, or two, change something as hidebound as that?

"In the end, I decided to quit. I hadn't taken my final vows yet, but I had been ordained as a deacon already. I broke with everything I'd believed in up to that point, by walking out." He rubbed the side of the guitar with a thumb. "My word had really meant something to me up until then."

Unbelievable. Of all our friends I would have sworn Sean was the one who'd really come to terms with himself the most. "Maybe it shows your word *did* mean something to you. You knew you couldn't take final vows if you didn't mean them honestly."

Sean shifted restlessly on the couch. "I don't know. Maybe that's why I've never been able to stick with anything since then. I tried law school, tried being a professional musician, a writer. I thought I had worked it all out in my mind. But now I find myself . . . doubting.

"So, do I believe in God? I can't say. Except I wonder if—" He stopped.

"You wonder if . . . what?"

He thought he saw Sean's lips tighten in the dim light. "Never mind."

Elias looked at him and suddenly knew: *Punished. He thinks he's being punished. Because he knows he's sick, maybe dying—he rejected God and now thinks God's rejecting him.*

He took a deep breath. "Sean . . . what I said yesterday, at Leshko's about . . . about the way you've been looking lately—"

"Wait," Sean said, holding up his hand. "Elias, please. Not now. It's . . . your birthday, or it was. And I've done enough to ruin it already. We'll talk about it, though."

"When?" asked Elias, quaking a little inside.

"Soon." The corner of his mouth quirked up in an ironic curve. "I promise."

Sean called him the next morning at work. "I have to see you," he said tensely.

"Well, sure," answered Elias, his heart skipping a beat. "We'll see each other tonight—"

"No. Before that. When do you go on break?"

"Half an hour from now."

"You go to the Pond on your lunch hours, right?"

"Yes. Sean—"

"Right. I'll see you there." He hung up.

When Elias walked to the Pond a half an hour later, he saw Sean from a distance, sitting on a bench looking at the swans. The day was warm, but Sean wore a light jacket. His fists were jammed into the pockets; his face looked strained and unhappy.

Elias came up to stand beside him, but Sean didn't look up. "I'm here," Elias said finally.

"I . . . went to see a doctor this morning." He stopped.

Elias waited. Sean still didn't look up. "What did he tell you?" Elias asked finally.

Sean's jaw worked silently as he stared out over the Pond.

"You have to say it out loud, Sean."

"Saying it out loud . . . means I'm going to die," Sean said hoarsely.

"No," Elias said, moved by a strange and terrible pity. "No. Not until you say it aloud do you begin the fight, and until you start fighting, you don't have a chance." He felt light, weightless, as if something or someone immeasurably wise had seized possession of his body to speak to his lover through him. A curious sort of grace.

"I've got AIDS." Suddenly, shockingly, Sean burst into tears. A swan on the water wheeled in a half circle, startled by the noise.

Elias hurried to sit next to him, to put his arms around him, and Sean buried his head in Elias's shoulder and cried great racking sobs. Elias wrapped his arms around him and rocked him gently for a long, long time, throat tight, oblivious to the reactions of passersby. *Now. Now we know. Now it all begins.* He had the sensation, as he pressed his forehead against Sean's cheek, that he couldn't even tell where Sean's skin stopped and his began. If he could just close his eyes and hold Sean tightly enough, then perhaps not only their limbs, but the very molecules of their bodies would intertwine, so they would never have to fear being separated by anything. Or perhaps the city around them would slow or even disappear, leaving just the two of them, alone in a protective bubble where they would be safe.

Gradually, Sean's crying stopped. He scrubbed at his eyes with the back of his hand. Elias pushed the damp curls back from Sean's forehead, and Sean straightened up stiffly.

"I should have told you earlier," he said, his voice thick, strained. "I've suspected it. But I wouldn't go in and get seen, because I didn't want to hear it." He looked down at his thigh, wiped his hand on it.

"It's not a surprise to me, Sean."

Sean looked at him quickly, eyebrows upraised, and upon meeting Elias's look, he nodded thoughtfully. "No. I suppose it wouldn't be." He fidgeted uncomfortably on the bench. "The doctor said . . . I mean, you should tell your partners, I suppose. Like I'm telling you. So they can, um . . ."

"There isn't anyone I need to tell."

Sean frowned. "I know you can't do anything about tricks at the baths, but—"

"Sean . . ." Elias spread his hands and gave a little half laugh. "I've never been with anyone but you."

Sean stared at him uncomprehendingly for a moment, and then a look of horror dawned. "What? But I saw you with . . . when we went to the baths together . . . you went into the room, I *saw* you—"

"Nothing happened!" Elias sighed and shrugged. "I told him I'd changed my mind, that I didn't want . . . Sean, I knew you'd think I was crazy, and you don't understand it, and that's why I let you think otherwise. But I've never wanted anybody else but you."

"No. No!" Sean's denial sounded like a wail of pain.

"It's true!" Elias shook his head in bafflement as tears started down Sean's face again. "Why does that bother you?"

"If I'm the only partner you've ever had," Sean said fiercely, his voice trembling, "and what they're saying about how it spreads is true, then . . . then I'm going to be the one who kills you. Me!" He caught his breath. "I love you, Elias."

Elias closed his eyes as if absorbing a blow. He thought he had steeled himself against anything, and he had—except for the pain of hearing those words, so long awaited, and now said under these circumstances. "We don't know if I'm going to get it, too," he replied when he could trust himself to speak steadily. "But if I do, well . . . you picked me up, took me off the streets, after all, Sean. You've already saved me. I suppose I owe you my life anyway."

He opened his eyes and put his hand on Sean's shoulder, giving it a little shake as Sean bowed his head in despair. "Look," Elias said bracingly. "I'm not sick. Not yet, anyway. We have to think about you. We're going to fight this thing. And we're going to find a way to beat it. I'm going to be with you."

"I'm glad," Sean said, his voice a thread of a whisper. "I'll need you." The swans swam closer, thrusting out their necks and arching them, spreading their wings in the sun. They looked unbearably beautiful. "So what do we do now?" Sean said. His voice tried to sound normal, but Elias heard the current of dread underneath.

"We call GMHC. And . . . well, Gordy, I suppose. And your doctor. They'll tell us how to get started."

Then they just sat, side by side on the bench, silently watching the swans.

Like an old married couple.

Chapter Seventeen

She went her way homeward
With one star awake
As the swans in the evening
Move over the lake.
The people were saying
No two e'er were wed
But one has a sorrow
That never was said.

—"SHE MOVED THROUGH THE FAIR,"
  TRADITIONAL

Together, Jonathan and Eliza came to William's study, where Jonathan asked William's assistance in performing the covenant of marriage.

"Marriage?" William exclaimed, his eyes widening, "My dear Jonathan—surely you must be jesting!"

"Why, Reverend," Jonathan replied, frowning, wondering at William's tone, "I do most heartily protest I was never more serious in my life."

Utterly taken aback, William stared with narrowed eyes at the couple standing before his desk. Eliza's hand rested lightly on

Jonathan's arm, and at the disapproval in the minister's voice, her gaze rose steadily to meet his.

She watched how he strove to regain command of his face. William quickly schooled his expression to a blank neutrality, but this did not mislead her. That instant's struggle made plain to her that he could not like her, that he was appalled by the proposed match. The minister's attitude did not surprise Eliza, but she felt a pang of disappointment, for she knew Jonathan valued his opinion.

While growing up with Tom and Nell, she had always sensed a difference between herself and other people, which had often made her lonely. The silence she had kept since committing to breaking the spell over her brothers made her feel even more isolated. Jonathan's willingness to reach out to her, to love her, despite that silence, had come almost as a shock, a revelation both strange and sweet. The realization that she wanted him in return warmed her heart like an inner glowing ember. But now, in the face of William's disapproval, doubt crept in again, bringing a chill like a cloud slowly drifting over the sun. She glanced up uncertainly at Jonathan.

The quick, reassuring smile he returned to her, the tender press of his hand over hers, aroused such a wash of surprised horror, dismay, and rage in William's breast that he all but choked. After a frozen moment, he deliberately unclenched his hands and forced a thin smile. His quick protest had been a mistake, he realized, for it had made Jonathan bristle. He must proceed more softly.

"Forgive me—I do confess myself to be surprised. Nay, astonished. Please——" He indicated a bench. "Sit you both down, so we may confer."

Jonathan drew the bench out from the wall for Eliza and gestured to her to seat herself first, a courtesy that somehow set William's teeth on edge. "The decision is sudden, I warrant you," Jonathan said easily, sitting beside her.

"Such swiftness argues that the decision may have been made— forgive me—too lightly," William said cautiously.

"Perhaps," Jonathan said, unoffended. "But it might also mean we have found in each other the person God intended for us." He smiled down at Eliza. "And then the proper thing to do," he said to her directly, "is to act to fulfill God's plan as swiftly as possible." She smiled in return.

William thoughtfully rubbed his chin, trying to understand his own unease. Jonathan's desire to marry was only right and proper, he had to admit to himself. God had formed Adam and Eve to be companions to one another, and marriage was plainly the state the Almighty desired for His human creation. William did not believe love had much to do with the decision to wed. Proper marriages, in his opinion, were formed when one decided that the time had come to marry and then set about finding a suitable person.

What he simply could not understand was what had made Jonathan choose this girl.

"It would please us greatly," Jonathan said, scattering William's thoughts again, "if would join our hands together. Do not tell the committee of safety," he added with a boyish grin, "that I ever had aught good to say about the revocation of the colony's charter. But I confess I am glad the change of laws permits you to perform marriages as a minister. I had liefer you bless my union, my friend, than to have to ride to another town to find some strange magistrate or justice of the peace to marry us."

This was too much for William. "I would be most heartily glad to do it, if . . . *if* I were confident you have indeed found in each other the person God intended for you." He did not look at Eliza as he said this. He found it easier not to look at her.

"I tell you I have," Jonathan said, stiffening a little in annoyance.

"Come, man! The happiness of married life requires that a man and a woman must be suitably fitted to draw together in this most holy yoke, matched equally in birth, education, and religion. You are a magistrate, of considerable importance to the community, well born and highly educated. But this girl . . . you know nothing of her. You do not know . . ." He paused, wondering how far he could press.

"Well?" Jonathan challenged.

"She can hear, yet she will not speak. She can read, yet she will not write. It is uncanny."

"I cannot tell you why she cannot speak or write, Reverend," Jonathan said slowly.

"Or why she refuses to do so," William said darkly.

"As you will," Jonathan conceded. "But I have faith that God's reasons for this shall be revealed in time. Meanwhile, I know that her place is at my side, and mine is at hers."

"What is it you desire in a wife, Jonathan?" William said desperately. "Are you not wishful for a woman who offers you wise and faithful counsel, who hears the secrets of your heart and shares her own? A woman who joins you in prayers each evening and teaches God's word to your children? Or could it be you would choose to take this girl to wife because her silence means you never can truly know her, and therefore you are free to imagine her to be aught but what she really is? She may be vicious, she may be a witch—"

"Fie, Reverend Avery!" Jonathan exclaimed, shocked.

Eliza sat up stiffly, eyes widening, and felt a cold touch of fear.

"The fact she is mute," William said doggedly, "tempts you to ignore any truth you do not wish to see."

Jonathan looked at Eliza for a moment, his face thoughtful and still, and she held her breath. Finally, he turned back to the minister with a crooked smile. "I must, in good faith, weigh your words carefully, of course, Reverend. I am beholden to you, for you have always spoken what you deem to be truth to me. I see the danger of falling into such an error, and so I own your warning is justly made."

William nodded, his eyes intent on Jonathan's face.

Jonathan took a deep breath, wanting to choose the right words carefully to calm his friend's fears. "But I am a magistrate; I must also weigh evidence. You allow your fears to overrun the facts. We have no reason to believe she is a witch." He took Eliza's hand. "I will remember your words. And yet, upon searching my heart, I cannot find fault with my intent to wed her. I am still resolved, Reverend, to join my life with hers."

Eliza let her breath out slowly and felt the prickle of tears in the corner of her eyes.

"I—"William stopped, and then blinked as a realization came to him, bringing with it a sharp flare of hope. "I am sorry I must refuse your request," he said evenly, "yet I fear performing the ceremony cannot be legal."

"What? Why?"

William shrugged and with an effort kept himself from smiling. "Since we do not know her name, we cannot formally announce the banns to ensure there is no impediment to the marriage. And of course, without the banns . . ." He let the words trail off.

Eliza felt her heart sink.

Jonathan opened his mouth—and closed it again, turning very red. A flash of anger, underpinned with uncertainty, made him draw his brows together. He gave Eliza's hand a squeeze, and when she turned to him, he asked urgently, "Is there an impediment? Are you already married or betrothed?"

Eliza shook her head.

"Have you ever been married?"

Again, Eliza indicated no.

"May I see your Bible, Reverend?" Jonathan said abruptly.

William frowned, perplexed, and then carefully lifted his Holy Book from its place at the corner of his desk and shoved it forward. "Why, if I may ask?" he ventured, as Jonathan opened it.

"*I* am going to name her," Jonathan said with a dangerous edge to his voice as he began turning pages. "With the first woman's name I find in this book, and you may use it to announce the banns."

"You cannot do that!"

"I most certainly can. Be it Deborah, or Miriam—"

Or Jezebel, William thought acidly.

"—that shall be her name, and if—" He broke off and looked up in surprise as Eliza reached over and gently took possession of the Bible.

Silence fell as she took the book into her own lap and began turning pages with a whisper of paper, searching for something. She found it quickly and handed the book back to Jonathan, her forefinger tapping on the page.

Jonathan read where she indicated with dawning delight until William could contain his curiosity no longer. "What?" he asked. "What did she show you?"

Jonathan looked up, grinning with a wolfish satisfaction, and placed the Bible back on the desk, swiveling it around so William could see. "She has turned to the first chapter of the Gospel of Luke. It tells the story of Zechariah and Elizabeth, the parents of John the Baptist, and how Zechariah was rendered mute by the angel of God."

Eliza pointed to the page again and tapped her other hand to her chest. Jonathan looked where her finger pointed. "Elizabeth?" he said.

Eliza nodded.

"Your name is Elizabeth, truly?"

She smiled and nodded again, relieved and pleased.

"Elizabeth," Jonathan said again, tasting the syllables, his face softening. "It is beautiful. I am pleased to have your own name to call you . . . Elizabeth."

"Look at the Gospel lesson again, Jonathan," William said urgently. "Zechariah's lips were stopped by the angel because he displeased God with his lack of faith, his . . . his unwillingness to hear God's message."

"And as a sign of God's presence," Jonathan replied stubbornly, "when Elizabeth had fulfilled God's promise by giving birth to John, Zechariah's speech was restored. The name Elizabeth means 'consecrated to God.' What further sign," he added with a kind of triumph, "do you require, Reverend?" He closed the Bible with a thump. "Now: will you marry us, yea or nay?"

As William looked at him, he realized with a sinking feeling that he had lost the argument. Nothing would change Jonathan's mind now, not even if William were to point out that his own name, William, meant "resolute protector," that he opposed the match only because he had Jonathan's interests at heart. If he remained adamant in his refusal,

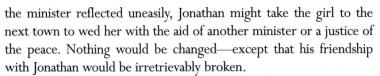

the minister reflected uneasily, Jonathan might take the girl to the next town to wed her with the aid of another minister or a justice of the peace. Nothing would be changed—except that his friendship with Jonathan would be irretrievably broken.

Or worse yet, William feared, continuing to refuse might tempt Jonathan into committing the damnable sin of fornication. Better to marry than to burn, he reminded himself glumly.

He heaved a sigh. "Very well," he said, very unwillingly. "The first announcement of the banns will take place this coming Sabbath, declaring the betrothal of Jonathan Latham and Elizabeth . . . Elizabeth, er—"

"Call her Elizabeth Wood," Jonathan said firmly. "For there I found her, in the wood." A smile hovered about his lips. "And thank you, Reverend Avery. You shall not regret this."

And so it was that Jonathan and Eliza stood before the congregation on the following Sunday for the formal announcement of betrothal, to the astonishment of many. More than one maiden wept some private tears of grief or vexation, as suited her temper, although in truth, none had cause to say that Jonathan had ever treated her unkindly or broken faith in any way. And all agreed that no one had ever seen him look at any girl in the village the way he looked at the strange, dowerless newcomer. Patience Carter was perhaps the person most delighted with the match.

The reading of the banns was repeated at the two Sabbath meetings following, and on a golden morning in September, Jonathan and Eliza joined hands before William to be married. Jonathan spoke his part of the ceremony in a firm, clear voice, pitched so all within the meetinghouse could hear. Eliza made her covenant vows by nodding in response to the questions William put to her, and by placing an X under the record of the marriage in the register, opposite the name Jonathan had chosen for her. William blew on the page to dry the ink and then carefully closed the book again, his face rigid and impassive.

Then everyone in the congregation trooped to Jonathan's house, where his servants had set trestle tables under the trees, spread with breads and sweet butter, roast meat, pies, cake, sackposset, and rum. William took only a small cup of rum, speaking to no one, and he left early. Jonathan and Eliza walked together, arm in arm, to greet their guests. As they accepted congratulations and toasts, and Jonathan laughed and Eliza smiled at the various jokes, they never really took their eyes from each other.

Only a few guests still lingered until the sun sank low in the west, for there were chores to be done, and a full day's worth of work waited for all upon the morrow. Patience was one of the last to leave, her broad face beaming with smiles and flushed from the rum. "Bless you, my dear," she exclaimed, leaning forward to kiss Eliza on the cheek. She patted Eliza's hand and said warmly in a lower voice, "If it be a sorrow to you, my pretty one, that you have no mother here today, remember you may always turn to me instead in the same way."

Eliza pressed her hand and kissed her gratefully in return, thinking that her presence did much to fill the hole in her heart left by Nell's absence on this, her wedding day.

"You have done a good day's work here," Patience continued, winking at Jonathan. "And do you a good night's work tonight, Magistrate Latham, so I may collect the midwife's fee from you nine months hence." She laughed her rich, ribald laugh and clouted him familiarly on the shoulder as he blushed. Then she strode off arm in arm with her daughter, weaving a bit unsteadily, and her voice drifted back to them, singing a hymn so beautifully it could have made the angels weep.

Eliza's smile slipped a little as she turned her face toward the west, where the last curve of the sun was dropping below the horizon. The clouds just above that point dazzled the eye like molten gold, and the waning light made everything else look amber, as though viewed through a glass filled with honey. She closed her eyes and her heart flew toward her brothers, like the point of a compass turned unerringly toward the north. She wondered sadly if they were well, if they had any inkling what had happened to her that day. The memory of the partially finished coat and the nettle flax waiting for her in the chest upstairs rose up to comfort her.

She heard a step next to her and opened her eyes to find Jonathan watching her. She brushed the moisture from her eyes and held out her hand to him, smiling, touched by his anxious look of concern. His face lit up in response, and he drew her hand up to rest in the crook of his elbow.

"My dear wife," he whispered to her, savoring the words, "shall we go inside?" They smiled privately at each other, and Jonathan led Eliza over the threshold of their home.

The servants had already gathered before the hall's fireplace, and there Jonathan read the evening's scripture and led the prayers to end the day. He performed his religious duties as the master of the house with his usual careful devotion, and she knelt beside him, listening with full attention, head bowed. Each felt something else, too, a wordless joy from the presence of the other that added a sweet poignancy to their worship.

After the last amen, he drew her to her feet, took a candle as he bid the servants good night, and led her up the stairs to the bedroom. Her fingers trembled in his as they entered the room, and he felt his heartbeat quicken.

She stood before the bed, looking about herself as he lit another candle. The quilt Patience had given them as a wedding gift had already been spread on the bed. When he set the candleholder on the table and held out his hands to her, she came to him without hesitation to clasp them lightly. His hands felt warm and strong to her, and she wondered at the coldness of her own fingers. She did not want him to think her cold to him, and she searched his face anxiously, hoping to find there again a longing for her to match her own. He thought her face looked a little grave, her eyes dilated. It cut him to the heart to think she might in any way be afraid of him. He remembered what the midwife had said, that she had not had her mother with her today, and he suddenly wondered what she understood about what happened between a man and his wife. The thought made him feel even more nervous, but protective of her, too.

"I . . ." He hesitated, and his eyes wandered over to the pitcher and basin. "I see Sarah did not leave water; I will go fetch some. Goody Carter left your nightclothes for you in the chest under the window."

She nodded, understanding he had found a way to give her a private moment to herself, in case she felt shy to undress before him. She did feel shy, and his perceptiveness pleased and touched her.

When he returned five minutes later, she stood before the window barefoot in her nightgown, her fingers untying the strings of her cap. "Let me," he said gently, his mouth dry. She tilted her face up to his as he put down the pitcher and then, with infinite care, eased her cap back from her brow and placed it on the table.

A sigh escaped him as he tenderly lifted the coil of her hair from the nape of her neck and unwound it, so that the silken rope fell over her shoulders and tumbled down her back. The brushing touch of his fingertips on her neck made her shiver with pleasure. He could see, in the shadowed hollow of her throat, the rapid movement of her pulse. His fingers slowly traced her high cheekbones, the delicate curve of her ears, and then luxuriously buried themselves in the soft ruddiness of her hair, lifting it and loosening it to float freely over her shoulders. From there, his fingers drifted down to explore the matched planes of her shoulder blades, and, then, greatly daring, glided forward to find the soft curve of the underside of her breasts. He smiled at her ragged intake of breath.

"I . . . do not know what you know, Elizabeth," he breathed. "Will it content you to let me . . . discover it? And to teach you what you do not know?"

She stepped forward, eyes shining, to place her hands gently on his chest like a benediction, and lifted her lips to meet his.

In the quiet hours of the deep night, she awoke, still cradled in his arms. Jonathan stirred in his sleep and murmured something into her hair. She nestled her cheek against him to soothe him with her touch and smiled to hear the sound of his heartbeat, calm and steady. Sleeping in a bed with another felt strange, but she felt sure she could grow to like it very much. The slow rise and fall of his chest began lulling her to contented drowsiness again.

And then, at the very edge of sleep, she heard again the call that had awoken her: *Eliza*. Her brothers' voices, calling her name faintly as if from very far away: *Eliza. Eliza.*

She raised her head to listen. Jonathan, disturbed by her movement, turned over, and she brushed a hand over his shoulder apologetically and sat up.

Ten minutes of concentrated listening convinced her the voices had indeed been a dream. But now she was thoroughly awake. She looked down wistfully at Jonathan and then rose soundlessly and padded to the chest to fetch a shawl. Throwing it over her shoulders, she stole her way out of the room without waking her husband.

The room he had shown her was two doors down. She eased the door open and found her way to the chest along the wall by the moonlight spilling through the window. Inside lay the stripped and broken nettle stems, her first partially finished coat, and the small quantity of coarsely spun thread left over. She held up the coat and frowned, wondering how she could add the sleeves to finish it. Using the saplings as a framework for weaving the spun nettle flax had worked well, but that would not be possible now that she had left the woods. Her foster father had shown her how to weave pieces on a frame loom he had created from lashed sticks—perhaps she might fashion something similar to make the body of the next coat. As for the sleeves, the frame loom would work for those, too, or perhaps they could be knit. She would also have to replace her apple-and-stick drop spindle in order to ready more thread.

As she ran the finished thread through her fingers thoughtfully, she could still feel the burning but not as sharply, because the juices had dried. Still, she knew the blisters would come back as soon as she began breaking fresh nettle stems again to extract fibers to spin into more thread. She wondered if she could at least slather goose grease on her fingers to shield her hands. "Break the nettles into pieces with your bare hands and feet," the fairy had told her. Eliza frowned. The admonishment to use *bare* hands presumably meant unprotected. Using grease might spare her from pain, but it might also undo all her efforts to break the spell. She sighed. At least she could keep a jug of the dock decoction in the chest, to slather on her hands afterward.

Her fingers tightened on the coat and then, reluctantly, she put everything back into the chest. More work would have to wait until she had a spindle and some way to do the weaving.

She tiptoed back to her own room. Jonathan had not changed position since she had left him, and stealthily, she slid under the bedclothes next to his side. He turned and put an arm over her in his sleep, drawing her close. Very soon, she was warm again.

Eliza and Jonathan quickly settled into their life together. Jonathan's work continued much as it always had. Sometimes he remained at home, engrossed in meetings in his office with the town's clerk of the writs, interviews with freemen to find a new bailiff for the town gaol, or interrogations of witnesses concerning various disputes about wages. On other days he met with the committee of safety in the taproom of the public tavern, or rode out to mediate the squabble between Goodman Corwin and Goodman Gibbs over a pair of sheep shears, or to sternly warn Goody Clarke that her absence from the next Sabbath-day meeting would not be tolerated. When Jonathan rode home again, tired from a long day of soothing ruffled tempers and repeating patient explanations to the obstinate, he found it pleasant to find his wife waiting for him, surrounded by the warm lamplight spilling from the doorway.

Eliza's days, too, were busy. She rose early to stoke the fire and to prepare for the household and eat a hasty breakfast of toasted bread and cheese, turnips, or oat porridge. Then there was the garden to hoe and weed, small beer to brew, linen to wash and mend, geese to pick, bread to bake, and a host of other tasks and occupations to fill her time until well after sunset.

Her muteness necessarily made directing the servants' work a challenge, but she soon worked out with them a crude system of hand signals, which served them for most of the day-to-day activities. On the whole she liked them rather well. Goody Grafton, the widow who had served as Jonathan's housekeeper since his parents' deaths, at first proved inclined to be prickly, rather resentful of her demotion in status now that Eliza had joined the household. Being an honest woman, however, she soon had to acknowledge that the magistrate's new wife was neither lazy nor a fool. There was something to be said for working for a mistress who never scolded when the fire went out. Sarah, Goody Grafton's assistant, and Jonas, who chopped wood and did the stable chores, were even more easily inclined to adore a mistress who gently recalled attention to the task at hand with a touch on the shoulder rather than a clout on the ear.

Patience Carter stopped by frequently to visit. Often, she invited Eliza to accompany her to a new mother's lying in, a quilting party, or a neighbor's house for an afternoon spent spinning, or coiling and fitting a new rag carpet. "For the neighbors should know the new bride isn't too proud to barter changework, if you want them to come to help you at hog-butchering and soap-making time."

It did not take long for the midwife's sharp eyes to note that while Eliza looked cheerful and healthy enough, she often seemed to be almost nodding off from fatigue. Worried, Patience took it upon herself to consult privately with Goody Grafton. "How is it that your mistress is so often weary? Is she retiring very late after sunset? Does she stint herself on her meat or beer?"

"Nay, I think not," Goody Grafton replied and frowned, thinking. "But 'tis true as you speak, now that I think upon it . . . she often does droop in the afternoons and early evenings."

"Perhaps the magistrate keeps her from her rest. *He* seems refreshed enough each morning, I trow."

Mrs. Grafton's mouth pursed up in disapproval at this bluntness. "I could not say, Goody Carter," she observed primly. "And even if I could, it would not be my place to do so."

Patience brightened. "Or perhaps she may be breeding already. I will provide a tonic for her; will you see she drinks it each night?"

Mrs. Grafton softened a bit. "If it will help her, you may trust me to do it."

Eliza remained oblivious to Patience and Mrs. Grafton's concern for her. Except for the sorrow weighing on her heart whenever she thought of her brothers, she would have been blissfully content. Jonathan did everything he could to make her happy, and her answering love for him grew stronger every day. In the evenings after supper, they established a pleasant custom of sharing a companionable hour sitting before the fire. Eliza busied herself with her mending as Jonathan wrote letters concerning the county's business. Sometimes, when the sound of the quill scratching across the paper ceased, she looked up from her work basket to see him studying the soft lines of her face in the firelight, and he would say, smiling, "Have I told you yet today, Elizabeth, how dear you are to me?" Words hovered at her lips then; she longed to tell her love in return and to confide her task to him.

But each time, the memory of the warning in her dream kept her silent.

Every night, when Jonathan fell asleep, she crept away from their bed to her little chamber to work on the coats. Using a drop spindle she had secreted in the chest, she soon spun enough thread to set up a stick loom. She wove rectangular pieces to make the sleeves first, rolling them into cylinders once they were off the loom and then hastily basting them closed and attaching them to the body to complete her first coat. Then she quickly set up the loom again and started the next coat.

In this way, as the autumn deepened, she wove coat after coat, staying each night until her hands began fumbling from weariness and she could no longer keep her eyes open. Then she would wipe her hands with the extract of dock, put everything away, and steal back to snatch a precious few hours of sleep lying next to Jonathan.

But when the time came to begin the seventh coat, she found she had broken and spun all the nettles she had, and there was no more nettle flax. She had to go get more.

Use the nettles that grow near the cave. No others will be of any use to you unless they grow upon graves in the churchyard. Eliza gathered the six coats she had finished and clutched them to her breast for a long time, thinking. She had to pluck the nettles herself, but she could not be sure of her way back to the cave. The churchyard, then, was her only hope. The thought of venturing forth to wander among the graves in the darkness made her quail—she squeezed her eyes shut tightly and prayed desperately for courage.

As if in reminder, Benjamin's voice came back to her in whispered memory: *We will go to our unmarked graves—if we even have graves—unwept for by anyone but one another.* Her brothers. Eliza lifted her head. She was doing this for her brothers, she told herself firmly, and if she failed them now, after all her work and pain, what hope could they have? Resolutely, she opened her eyes and stood.

As she reached for her shawl, her eyes fell upon a glimmer of white inside the chest. She hesitated and then pulled out the bundle she had placed there, of eleven feathers strung on a narrow braid of her hair. As she lifted the loop over her head and settled the feathers on her heart, she felt a calm spread over her, whispering to her, *You will not walk alone. Heaven will watch over you.*

She stopped at her room to dress hastily and then crept down the stairs and lifted the latch to step outside, her heart beating quickly. The waning moon hung low in the sky, a thin arc veiled over with wisps of clouds. Her breath puffed out in a cloud of frost as she pulled up the hood of her cloak. The darkness made her think momentarily of going back for a lantern, but she decided against it. The faint glimmer of starlight was enough to show her the way, barely, and besides, she would need both her hands to carry the nettles back.

Eliza began walking, staying a little to the side of the ruts in the road to avoid the mud and keep the wooden pattens on her feet from clattering against the occasional stone. The air smelled moist and cold, with a tang of cider, cut hay, and manure. A stick snapped underfoot as she turned at the fork of the road, and the crack sang in the frosty air like a reverberating shot, making her start in nervous surprise. Anxiously, she looked behind her, but no one stepped out of the shadows to demand her business, and no dog barked at her passing. After a breathless moment, she touched the feathers she wore around her neck for reassurance and started forward again, feeling very small under the slowly wheeling stars. The back of her neck itched, as if aware of eyes, watching her in the darkness.

In fact, her passage did not go unobserved. William had passed a restless night, and after an hour or so of lying awake, he had decided to sit at his desk to look over his sermon notes again. As he reached for a candle on his desk to light at the carefully banked embers of his fire, a movement in the darkness outside made him stop and peer through the window. There, he saw Eliza's hooded figure, staring back over her shoulder down the road. After a moment, she furtively began moving forward again. Puzzled, William craned his neck to follow her, and he frowned as she stopped at the fork in the path leading to the churchyard. When she looked back over her shoulder again, William saw her face for the first time and straightened up in shock. "Mistress Latham?" he muttered aloud. "What does she out here at this hour?"

After a perplexed moment, William went to fetch his cloak and slipped out of his house to follow her, his puzzlement rapidly congealing unpleasantly into something else, grim and cold. He looked up at the moon and then stared into the darkness down the fork she had taken. He caught a glimpse of her figure gliding along the fence, and with a shiver of dread, he started after her, moving carefully to keep his steps silent. After twenty paces or so, she paused again at the gate to the churchyard, and he slipped behind an oak tree to watch and see what she would do next.

Taking a deep breath, Eliza lifted the gate latch and entered the churchyard. The grass grew long here, and her pattens sank into it; she had to move carefully to avoid tripping. The darkness seemed even deeper than along the lane, for the shadowy bulk of the meetinghouse effectively blocked out the little light available from the moon. She froze and blinked, reluctant to begin walking until her eyes had adjusted to the gloom—and then jumped as something rustled against her petticoat. She barely kept herself from screaming, but by the time she had spun around in a full circle, whatever it was had already brushed past her and disappeared. All she could see was tombstones, pale rectangles shining against the darker grass in the faint starlight, some upright, some leaning at a slant. The land dipped slightly here, and so mist gathered in the hollow to curl around the graves, languidly caressing the monuments to the dead. She could feel her own heartbeat thundering in her ears; she felt disoriented and suddenly terrified.

Drawing her cloak tightly around herself, she began walking into the gloom, threading her way through the graves. The faint stirring of air in her wake drew up from the earth something cold, something that smelled warmth, human blood, life—and reached after them yearningly. William, watching from the distance, gasped and strained to see: here and there dim patches of starlight made their way through the trees, illuminating fragments of mist that seemed to coalesce into momentary shapes: a shoulder, a flash of curling hair, a ghostly face, upturned, with eyes closed.

Thunderstruck, William staggered back, shuddering. He had certainly suspected something; he had been unable to comprehend how such a strange young woman could capture Jonathan's heart so completely without uttering a single word. But even in his worst imaginings, he had never dreamed of a horror such as this.

"Oh, Jonathan," he breathed, full of fear for himself and terror and grief-stricken pity for the soul of his friend, surely now in mortal danger.

He knew it now with utter certainty: Eliza was a witch, damned by Almighty God for all eternity. She had proven it by coming here tonight and using her power to conjure the dead.

A wraith moaned softly not far from Eliza, a low, urgent sound, making the hairs stir on the back of her neck. She froze as ghostly hands made of mist reached out from all directions to grope at her: clammy and cold, demanding, tentative. One patted her cheek just below her eye, lightly, as if it approved of her, and she shrank back, both in pity and skin-crawling revulsion, lips moving in silent prayer.

And then the scraps of mist seemed to part in front of her, fleeing in all directions, and Eliza gasped in heart-thudding astonishment. An open grave gaped before her, like a new wound in the earth, dug by the sexton just that afternoon. Ghostly shapes writhed inside it, heaved, reconfigured, like translucent bodies pressed against one another trying to crawl out; other ghosts hovered about the grave, as if watching.

Something moved behind her. A pair of skeletal hands slid around her ribs from behind, reaching blindly to embrace her human warmth, and the icy touch of bone against her nipples, even through the cloth of her cloak, made her start violently. She wrenched herself away, clamping down a scream with all her might, and the tracks of that touch burned against her skin like cold fire as she fled to the side of the graveyard abutted by the meetinghouse.

The patch of nettles appeared so suddenly out of the mist as she stumbled forward that she almost blundered right into it. With a sob of thankfulness, she threw herself to her knees and began wrenching the roots of the plants out of the earth, not even noticing the burning in her hands in her desperation to get what she needed and escape again. Soon, a thick bundle of stalks lay heaped on the ground. Panting, she scrambled to her feet, threw a corner of her cloak over the bundle, and lifted it, staggering. She looked around wildly for the ghosts, but although they seemed more solid, hanging motionlessly in the air over the open grave and staring at her with burning eyes, they did not approach her again.

Shivering, she picked her way as quickly as she could along the side of the meetinghouse until she arrived back at the gate. As she fumbled for the latch, struggling not to drop the nettles, William shrank back farther into the shadows of the thicket. He did not emerge again until she had passed him and was well on her way down the road again.

He glanced at the meetinghouse longingly but did not dare to linger so near the churchyard, even in that holy place. The Devil's allies must be out in force tonight, since a witch prowled the roads and ghosts roamed abroad. Safer to go home, he decided, to pray with all his might for God's holy armor to protect him as he faced the trials he knew would come.

William clutched his cloak tightly and headed for home. Yes, he would pray first.

And then he would go to see Jonathan.

Chapter Eighteen

There is no fear in love, but perfect love casteth out fear.

—1 JOHN 4:18

The first few months after Sean's diagnosis passed in a blur for Elias. He rarely thought to pick up his camera, and so had few images to help anchor his memories. Jerry died in August, and they heard more bad news in early September: Gordy was going blind from CMV retinitis and Philip had to be hospitalized for treatment of cryptococcal meningitis.

But gradually Elias's shock subsided in the face of a determination, a promise to himself that grew stronger with each passing day: whatever it took, whatever sacrifices had to be made, Elias would make sure that Sean defied the odds. If he helped Sean hang on to his health as long as possible, then maybe, just maybe, if they kept their ears to the ground, they could get in on some of the experimental treatments. Surely, he thought hopefully, in a country with the best medical system in the world, the cure for AIDS would be found soon.

As Elias's resolve crystallized, Sean began running a fever that continued day in and day out, without any discernible cause. He got dizzy when he tried to work at his typewriter, and so he spent more and more time in bed instead of writing. "And even if I could stand to sit there very long," he complained one night as he picked listlessly at the beef stroganoff Elias had cooked for supper, "I couldn't write anything. My brain is mush."

"Don't worry about it." Elias tried to soothe him. "Just concentrate on getting over this bug so you can gain your weight back. That's the important thing." He gestured with the pot hopefully. "Do you want more? I used a really good burgundy in the gravy—can you taste it?"

Sean shook his head fretfully and shoved his plate aside. "Maybe I'd do a better job of shaking this thing if I only knew what it *was*." He sighed. "Thank god for the trust fund. At least we don't have to worry about the rent payment or the health insurance premium if I can't finish an article soon."

Elias agreed, but privately he couldn't help but worry. Sean had Blue Cross through a writer's union, an 80/20 plan. That twenty percent was really going to hurt if Sean had to be hospitalized for any length of time.

Gay Men's Health Crisis had set them up with a crisis counselor who had stayed with them a couple of days when they'd first gotten the news. Elias read their newsletter faithfully, hoping to keep abreast of the latest research. GMHC also matched them with a buddy named Patty, who came to visit Sean and help with chores and errands once or twice a week, while Elias was at work. At first, Sean seemed quite dubious about the choice, voicing some of his misgivings one afternoon in the bedroom after Elias had gotten home from work.

"It's not that he dresses in drag—"

"Um, I think he wants to be called *she,*" Elias ventured. "You have to admit she makes a convincing woman." He'd been taken aback at his own first sight of Patty.

"—or the fact that you clean the dishes better than he—than she does. It's her singing that gets to me."

Elias cocked his head and listened to the voice crooning above the sound of running water in the other room. "She sounds pretty good, if you ask me. Better than a lot of singers who show up at Nick's music parties."

"But she's singing Patsy Cline." Sean broke into a hacking cough that continued for some time. *"Patsy Cline,"* he said in disgust when he had gotten his breath back. "In *my* living room."

"An opportunity to broaden your musical horizons, Sean."

"I like my musical horizons just fine where they are, thank you very much." Sean slumped back against his pillow. "Patsy Cline. Now I know I'm dying."

Elias ignored this grousing, certain that Patty would bring Sean around, and eventually she did. Elias suspected that the change in Sean's attitude had something to do with the obscure Irish beers she tracked down and brought along whenever she visited.

"Ya gotta keep their interest up in eating and drinking," she observed cheerfully to Elias one afternoon while Sean slept. "Not that I'm trying to knock him on his can, you understand, but maybe if he has a good beer to guzzle he'll be more interested in eating a nice, fatty pizza to go with it. Something that'll help keep his weight up. Not if I made it, though—I'd burn it. I'm about as lousy a cook as I am a housekeeper." She laughed her trademark ribald laugh, belly shaking, as she dumped a pile of clean clothes from the laundry basket onto the couch and briskly began sorting. "That's the key, Elias. You've got to fight the wasting. If he doesn't up his food intake or if he starts having trouble with diarrhea, he's gonna really lose some serious weight."

"He doesn't have much appetite, with these fevers."

"Well, find ways to sneak extra calories into him, then. Stir an instant breakfast powder into a milk shake, for instance. If he gets diarrhea for more than a few days, start him on Gatorade and get him in to see the doctor for a stool culture."

Elias reached for a pile of T-shirts to fold. "That's a good tip about the breakfast drink powder. Thanks."

"Experience. I've picked up a thing or two."

"So you've been doing this for a while?"

"Since almost the very beginning. A couple years now. Sean's my fourth buddy match."

"How do you find the time to help four AIDS patients?" Elias asked without thinking.

After a short pause, Patty smiled thinly as she reached for another pair of jeans. "My fourth match in a row, I should have said. The other three have died."

The simplicity of the statement slipped under Elias's guard, giving him a jolt. He smoothed the T-shirt he had been folding until the colors began to swim and shift, and then he stared out the window at the trees in the back courtyard, trying to keep the tears at bay. The lowering sun filtered at an oblique angle through the yellowing leaves. Some were already beginning to fall, fluttering down to the ground in leisurely spirals like confetti. "I'm not going to lose Sean. Somehow . . . somehow we're going to beat it." His words sounded hollow to his own ears.

Patty stopped sorting clothes and looked at him for a moment in silence. "What if you fail?" she said finally.

"I . . . I can't. I *can't* fail."

"Why?"

"Because I love him too much."

"And the families and the friends and lovers of all the people who've died so far—you think they didn't love the ones they lost?"

"I didn't mean . . . I don't know what I mean." The corners of his mouth trembled. "How can you stand to do this? Be an AIDS buddy, I mean?"

"Ah." Patty began piling the folded clothes into the laundry basket. "Back when I had a bartending job, there was this guy at the place I worked. A waiter. Totally gorgeous." Patty's face lit up in memory. "Oh honey, I had such a crush on him! Well. He started getting sick—no one knew what it was back then. He went down fast. Quit work, and no one heard anything about him for a month. I went to visit him, and he was already dead. *Pneumocystis.* His landlady said he'd died in his apartment, alone. Refrigerator empty, lying in his own shit—he must have been too sick to get help, maybe too far out of it to realize how much trouble he was in until it was too late. I always felt terrible he hadn't turned to me." She sighed. "GMHC started up soon afterwards. Soon as I heard about it, I signed up."

Elias thought about the past year, the slow undercurrent of fear he had sensed growing among all of their friends as the news about AIDS had spread. Lately, he'd noticed he was feeling tired, just a little low on energy. Was it just that he'd been trying to do too much because Sean was sick? Or could it be something more sinister? What were his own chances? Surely Patty, too, must be aware as she took care of sick people that she might be looking at her own future. "Are you ever afraid?"

Patty pursed her lips and absently rubbed the mole at the corner of her mouth with one finger. "This may sound strange, but I believe in reincarnation, you see," she said slowly. "I believe that sometime, in a previous life, someone turned to me for help . . . and I didn't give it. I was afraid to help then, I think. Something about Mikel's death made me remember that. And I decided I just couldn't be afraid this time. I couldn't make the same mistake again. You have to return to your mistakes and correct them. Even if it's several lifetimes later."

"If I knew . . ." Elias paused and then sighed. "If I only knew why this is happening to us."

Patty gave him another one of those unsettlingly penetrating looks. "Why do you think?"

Elias hesitated, remembering the conversation he'd had with Sean the night before Sean had told him of his diagnosis. "A friend of mine, Gordy, says . . . it's a curse," he said slowly.

"Interesting theory." Patty smiled crookedly. "Sounds like something out of a fairy tale."

Elias shrugged and began sorting and pairing socks.

"Hmph. Goodness and virtue always win out in the end in fairy tales, don't they? A very simple idea, really: the powerful AIDS witch, going around, zapping the wicked." She assumed an evil leer, flourishing an imaginary magic wand. "Whap! Take that, naughty boy! An appealing idea to those who prefer their morality . . . uncomplicated.

"Too bad for them real life ain't so black and white."

The following afternoon Rick appeared at Elias's elbow as Elias clocked out. "Got a minute?" He jerked with his chin toward his tiny office.

"Sure," Elias said, surprised, and followed him in. "What's up?" he asked, sitting down as Rick closed the door.

Rick picked up his coffee cup, fingered it absently for a moment, and then seemed to realize it was empty and put it down again. "The shop's been sold. To a chain. They have their own manager they want to bring in and . . . well, Friday's my last day."

Elias felt cold delicately creeping in the pit of his stomach, like the first sheet of ice spreading over the Pond in early winter. "Oh, shit. *Rick.*" He stopped, tried to collect his thoughts. "Are you . . . ? Do you . . . ?"

"S'okay." Rick shook his head and gave him a little wave of the fingers. "It was my decision to go, really. I could have stayed on for a bit in sales if I'd wanted to."

"After managing the shop for thirteen years? Oh, c'mon, Rick!"

"Exactly." Rick's smile looked more like a grimace. He looked around at the walls of his office, as if noticing them for the first time in a long time. "It's probably a good idea for me to get off my goddamn butt and do something different. Jenny's job's going okay, so we'll be all right until I find something." He hesitated. "Elias, look . . . if I find another job in management and I've got an opening on staff, I'll let you know about it. In case you ever get into a jam. I mean, I hope things'll work out for you with these new people—"

"But . . . ?" Elias raised an eyebrow.

Rick sighed. "I don't want to poison the well. I've tried to smooth the way for you—told them you were my best on staff. But when chains buy independents, they like to clean house, so your chance of hanging on to this job may be slim to none, anyway. And

I think you should know that the guy who's going to be the manager, Carl—well, he strikes me as kind of a bigot." Rick shifted uncomfortably, avoiding Elias's eyes. "I heard him make a couple of fag jokes."

"Oh."

"So you're gonna have to do some thinking about how badly you want to try to hang on to this job. If you do, you might need to play your cards close to the vest. For your own protection."

"Stay in the closet, you mean. Keep my mouth shut."

"Not with me." Now Rick met his angry stare steadily. "Never with me. But I'm not the manager anymore."

"I see." Elias sighed. "I understand. Thanks for telling me. And I'm sorry, Rick. About your job, I mean."

"Yeah." A gloomy silence fell. Rick broke it after a moment, his gaze going to the picture on the wall of Sean, playing his guitar. "How's Sean doing?" he asked gruffly.

Elias looked down. "Not good."

Rick nodded, the drawn lines around his mouth making him look strangely older. "I'm sorry, too."

The conversation with Rick was the first in a whole series of incidents that began soon after Sean fell ill.

"What's wrong with your roommate?" Elias heard a voice say behind him one morning as he went out into the hall to run out the garbage.

Elias looked around and saw their landlord staring at him, the little sour-faced man Sean called Dick-the-dick. "Uh . . . what makes you ask?" he stammered, startled out of his private thoughts.

"He looks damn sick."

"I . . . He's just kind of run down," Elias said lamely. He stuffed the bag of rubbish down the incinerator chute, feeling his face heating up. He hadn't meant to lie, hadn't even thought about what he would say if asked about Sean by someone who didn't have any business to know.

"Huh." The other man bounced up and down on his heels, his

stare uncomfortably measuring. "That better be all there is to it. Don't want people to have any reason to be afraid to come into the building."

"What?" Elias said stupidly, unable to understand the implication at first. Once he did, he felt trapped, furious, afraid. What did the man think, that he'd lose all his tenants if it became known that someone who had AIDS lived in the building? He just stood there, unable to think of any retort stinging enough.

Finally, the landlord shrugged. "There better not be any trouble about the rent getting paid on time." He walked away to his own apartment, slamming the door behind him.

Then there was the time he came home to find Sean just hanging up the phone, his face red and grim. "That was Leo," Sean said, "passing along a message from Nick."

"What, is the music party canceled tonight?"

"It is," Sean said bitterly, "for me. Leo says Nick doesn't want me to come. Amy's afraid to have me there."

It took a moment before Elias could bring himself to speak, for the blow seemed so unexpected, not to mention cruel. He knew how Sean loved the music parties and husbanded his scant strength for each one; sometimes the contact with other musicians seemed to be the only thing that kept him going. "I . . . can't believe . . . can't believe that Nick——"

"Amy's pregnant," Sean broke in, his voice trying to sound matter-of-fact, although the bleakness in his eyes showed what it cost him. "I . . . can understand it. She's scared." He looked over at his guitar case in the corner. "But the bloody bastard didn't even have the guts to tell me himself."

Something vital seemed to go out of Sean after that. The guitar and harp cases began to gather dust, too, like the weight machine, and he stayed in bed more and more. The fungal infection in his mouth that had bothered him since August worsened, and the fever he ran every day crept up higher. Then he began to complain of pain when he swallowed, and to Elias's alarm, his weight loss started accelerating. Prompted by Patty and at Elias's insistence, Sean reluctantly went back to the doctor, who recommended hospitalization to start him on an antibiotic IV. After almost a week of arguments, Sean finally consented to be admitted.

But despite the antibiotics, Sean's difficulty eating continued, even with a range of drugs prescribed by a gastroenterologist. So the next step was an endoscopic biopsy, in which a flexible fiber-optic tube was inserted down Sean's throat to examine his esophagus. The doctor looked serious when he gave them the diagnosis: the thrush had developed into severe esophageal candidiasis.

"I recommend," he said carefully, "that you have a catheter inserted into your chest. The surgery to install the catheter is relatively minor; we can use a local anesthetic. It will give us better access to your blood system to continue the antibiotics to fight your fever, and we'd need it, too, for the antifungal drug I have in mind that I'd like to try."

"How long will I need to keep the catheter in?"

There was a short pause. "Perhaps indefinitely. We have to get those ulcers in your esophagus under control or you'll keep losing weight. You'll need to be in the hospital, on the drug for at least six to eight weeks to start."

"Six to eight weeks!" Sean exclaimed, exchanging a stunned look with Elias. "And then what?"

The doctor hesitated. "You do understand that since your immune system is suppressed, if we stop giving you the drug . . ." His words trailed off and Sean winced.

"So there's no guarantee I'll ever get off it again?"

The doctor shook his head.

Sean looked at his feet, stony-faced, for a long moment. "Okay, okay," he said finally. "Do whatever you have to do."

The doctor nodded and stood. "I'm going to go speak with my P.A. to start the process of setting up the surgery."

After he left the room, Sean said, "Well, there goes the world tour. The penguins are going to be so disappointed."

"Not necessarily," Elias managed. "It's . . . a temporary setback. Maybe . . . maybe, if you get the drug, soon you'll get better enough that they can discharge you. Or we could learn to give you the medicines at home."

"Huh. I'm no expert, but it doesn't sound from what he said like I'm going home anytime soon."

Elias swallowed, not sure where to find the line between reassurance and meaningless lies. "We're in this together, Sean."

"Sure," Sean replied. His face had the expression of a man overtaken by disaster, like a mountain climber who steps in a place he thinks is solid that instead turns out to be a thin snow crust over a bottomless crevasse.

Two days later, when Sean had the catheter installed, Elias took the day off work to be with him.

During the surgery, Elias sat in the small adjoining waiting room, staring out the window at rain-drenched gray and barren rooftops. It was depressing. The air stank of hospital disinfectant and stale cigarette smoke. The drone from the wall-mounted television in the corner mingled with the murmur from the nurses' station and the thumps and mechanical groans from the ancient elevator down the hall.

The view from the window didn't change, however, and so after a while he turned his attention to the people passing in the hall. Orderlies trundled oxygen equipment by, followed by housekeepers pushing linen carts. Patients shuffled up and down the corridor in their bathrobes, their slippers making flapping sounds against the scarred linoleum. A resident stepped outside a room across the hall, made a notation on a chart, and dropped the clipboard back into the rack with a clatter. A man and woman got off the elevator and went to speak with someone at the nurses' station. Visitors, maybe. Other workers walked by briskly on other mysterious errands, badges clipped to their hospital uniforms. Were they doctors, nurses, medical students, dieticians, social workers? Or something else? It occurred to Elias that he would probably be learning more about hospitals in the next several months than he could possibly ever want to know.

"You're waiting to hear about Mr. Donnelly, aren't you?"

Elias turned and saw the woman in surgical scrubs standing in the doorway, eyebrows raised in inquiry. She looked tired.

"Yes. He's out of surgery?"

"Uh-huh. Everything went fine. They'll be wheeling him down to room 408 in a few minutes, if you'd care to wait for him there."

He went to the assigned room, where he lingered impatiently in the doorway, looking up and down the hall, watching for Sean's arrival. Finally, two orderlies came around the corner, pushing a litter carrying Sean.

"Look—there he is."

"John!"

The man and woman he'd seen at the nurses' station suddenly broke into a half run, following the litter. The woman seized Sean's hand and held on to it tightly. Her eyes eagerly searched Sean's face with such avid attention that she almost tripped over her own feet as she hurried alongside. Elias stared. He had never seen them before.

Sean turned his head woozily to squint up at her. "'lias?" he rasped.

Elias cleared his throat and stepped aside from the doorway. "I'm here, Sean," he said.

The woman stopped abruptly, brought up short by Elias's voice. She allowed Sean's hand to slip out of hers and stared at Elias with an expression of unreadable intensity as the orderlies turned the litter to push it into the room. The man came up beside her and stared at Elias, too, his hand creeping up to touch the woman's shoulder.

"Wha' you two doing here?" Sean said, managing to sound at once accusatory and rather groggy.

The man cleared his throat. "Rick called us."

"I'll have his hide." Sean coughed, a long hacking spasm, as the orderlies lowered the bed rail and transferred him to the bed. "No reason f'you to come from Boston for this." One orderly transferred the IV bag to the pole by Sean's bed and then both orderlies left, taking the litter with them.

"John. Please. Of course we wanted to come." The woman appeared to be on the edge of tears.

"I told you. I go by Sean now." Sean lay back wearily and pulled the sheet up, hiding the place where the new tube emerged from his chest.

"I'm . . . I'm sorry," she stammered. "Of course . . . I'll try to remember." She bit her lip.

These people must be Sean's parents, Elias realized, thunderstruck. Well, his father and stepmother, anyway. He felt suddenly, deeply ashamed: he hadn't even thought of contacting them to let them know Sean was in the hospital, nor had it occurred to him to ask Sean if he had.

The woman looked at Elias. "May we come in?" she asked him humbly, with a tone that suggested she rather expected him to refuse.

Entirely alarmed at being asked to make this decision, Elias stammered, "Well, of course . . . but you understand Sean hasn't been feeling . . . uh . . ."

"Oh, don't be ridiculous," Sean said pettishly. "You didn't make the trip down here to stand outside in the hall. Come on in."

After a moment's hesitation, they all filed into the room and found places around Sean's bed. The woman took the only chair, and Elias and Sean's father found places to lean against the wall. The other bed was empty. An awkward silence fell.

Elias broke it finally, holding out his hand to Sean's stepmother. "I'm Elias Latham. I'm pleased to meet you, Mrs. Donnelly."

She accepted the handshake without hesitation. "And I'm glad to meet you at last, Elias. But please, call me Janet."

"Sorry," Sean said, apparently belatedly recalling his social duties. "And Elias, this is my father, Jim Donnelly."

Another pause, and then Sean's father stuck out his hand, too. "Hello, Elias." His smile looked strained around the eyes. He glanced at his son and the smile disappeared.

This is surreal. Janet didn't seem to know where to look. She stared down at her hands, twisting in her lap, then at Sean, with little darting glances at Elias. He had the impression she was bursting to talk, but his presence somehow made it impossible for her to begin.

"Sean," Elias said impulsively, "I'm going to step out for a few moments to . . . um, smoke a cigarette."

Sean raised an eyebrow at this patent lie but he merely nodded. "You really gotta give up those cigarettes, Elias," he said with a straight face. "They're gonna ruin your health."

Elias escaped out of the room, a bubble of something semi-hysterical welling up inside him. He walked quickly down the hall, past the nurses' station, and collapsed on the battered couch set by the elevators. There he sat, doubled over with laughter for a long time, until the laughter spent itself out, leaving behind only bitter residue that twisted itself into hiccuping sobs. Pulling off his glasses and covering his face with his hands, he fought to control himself, as tears and snot ran down his hands. People passed by, getting on and off the elevators, but no one stopped or paid the slightest attention to him. He found that obscurely comforting.

Finally, he lowered his hands, wiped them on his jeans, and slumped against the couch back, curled up in misery. Bleak light shone through the grimy window, making him blink. *His real name isn't even Sean.* He watched the dazzling motes of dust in the air for a long time and then finally closed his eyes against the glare, his head hurting, and tried to think.

He remembered a play he'd seen once—the main character had a speech about how each person was made up of layers, like an onion. And if you peeled away each layer, trying to find an essential core, all you ended up with in the end was nothingness. The idea had made him angry at the time. What was the name of that play again? Somebody Danish had written it—no, Norwegian. Ibsen, wasn't it? He'd remember the name of the play eventually.

A stark picture of Sean's wasting body and sunken eyes hovered in his mind. Well, Sean was certainly being peeled away, layer by layer of flesh now, he thought numbly. Stripped down to a shell, literally. Soon, very soon, he was going to find out whether anything was really beneath that shell.

"Elias?" a soft voice said beside him.

He opened his eyes. "Mrs.—uh, Janet." He straightened up self-consciously and put his glasses back on.

"Sean seems tired, and so Jim and I are about to leave for the hotel—here's the name and number if you need to reach us. We'll be back tomorrow." She handed him a slip of paper with the hotel information scribbled on it, hesitated, and then sat down beside him. She didn't ask for permission this time. "Rick told us how you've been caring for him, how much you've done for him. I just wanted to say . . . thank you." She smiled, but her mouth trembled. "Since we haven't been here to be much help. I'm sorry for that. It's not . . . It's just that we didn't know."

It surprised him greatly to be thanked. Embarrassed, he ducked his head awkwardly in acknowledgment. "Sean's been rather, um, closemouthed about his condition with you?"

She nodded. "About everything. He's been too angry at us, I suppose. Ever since he came out." She seemed to be looking at the dust motes, too.

Had it really started then? "How old was Sean when you married his father?" he asked curiously. Was that the trouble at the bottom of everything?

She gave him a startled look. "How old was— I don't exactly understand the question."

He opened his mouth and closed it again.

"I'm his mother."

He frowned, puzzled. "I guess I must be confused about something. Sean told me you were his father's second wife."

She nodded, understanding. "I am. Jim married briefly just out of high school. But I married him after his divorce, and we've been together for thirty-one years. It's Sean's little joke to call me his stepmother, you see," she said dryly. "Sort of part of the way he keeps me at arm's length."

"I don't quite see why," he said, bewildered. *My god. Yet another layer? Am I ever going to get down to the truth?*

"When he quit the seminary, he came home and told us it was

because he had discovered he was gay. Jim and I were so stunned, so hurt. I went out and read everything I could get my hands on about homosexuality, trying to"—she groped with her hands for an explanation—"to make sense of it all: Why had this happened to him? Why to us?" She sighed. "I read something that said homosexuality may be caused in the womb, by hormones or stress in the mother. I took it to heart; I told him I blamed myself. He said that"—a rueful smile played around her lips—"if I wanted to let myself off the hook, we could just pretend I was his evil stepmother instead of his real mother." Her smile faded. "I thought he was just trying to laugh it off, make me feel better. But I think it made him angry, too. He's kept up the joke ever since. Only it isn't really a joke anymore."

It suddenly occurred to Elias that if she thought Sean's being gay was her fault, maybe she would also blame herself now that he had AIDS. The idea appalled him.

She gave herself a little shake and stood, looking down the hall to where her husband had just emerged from Sean's room. "So . . . tomorrow then, Elias?"

He nodded, and she went over to push the elevator button. Sean's father walked toward them, holding out an arm toward her. "Good-bye, Elias," he said. "We'll talk with you then."

"Oh, and Elias," Janet said and stopped. She smiled uncertainly, seeming to search for something to say, or some gesture. "If you're sitting with . . . Sean anytime this week, and you want to get away for a little while to get a sandwich or something, just let us know. We'd be happy to stay with him until you get back. Don't forget to take care of yourself, too, okay?"

"Sure," Elias said, surprised again, and a little touched, too. "I appreciate it. Thanks."

When they got on the elevator together, Elias caught a glimpse of her, resting her head on her husband's shoulder before the doors closed all the way.

"*Peer Gynt*," he said aloud. He got up and walked back to Sean's room.

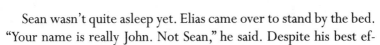

Sean wasn't quite asleep yet. Elias came over to stand by the bed. "Your name is really John. Not Sean," he said. Despite his best efforts, it came out sounding like an accusation.

Sean shook his head slowly. "It was John. Sean is just the Irish version of the same name. I did go to the trouble of having it legally changed when I came out." He smiled faintly. "I wanted a new identity."

Elias sighed, dragged the chair over, and sat down. That didn't work; the chair was too low. He got up, lowered the bed rail, and sat on the edge of the bed. Sean shifted over, painfully, to give him room. "Tell me the rest of it," Elias said.

"The rest of what?"

Elias frowned. "All the things you haven't gotten around to telling me yet. About yourself. So I *know.*" *So I know who I'm fighting for. And if worse comes to worst, so I'll know what I've lost.*

"Like what?"

Elias thought for a moment. "If you planted a garden, what would you put in it?" he tried at random.

"Mmm." Sean closed his eyes, considering. "Red roses. My grandmother had a rose garden, and I always loved it."

"I'd plant snapdragons. And tomatoes, I think. What was your favorite thing to do when you were a kid?"

"Building forts behind the couch with blankets."

"For me, it was soccer. What's your first memory?"

"The underside of the kitchen table, with the dog's nose poking through the tablecloth on the opposite side."

"I remember looking out the window overlooking our garden. Everyone else in the family was outside. My brother was jumping into the pile of leaves Father was raking; Mother was planting tulip bulbs, I suppose."

They went on like that, trading small pieces of each other back and forth, tucking them into the proper places like a mosaic. Surely, if they exchanged enough pieces, they would come close enough to each other that only the tiniest pieces would remain, and finally only points of light, until everything blended together like a shimmering pointillistic painting. As close as they could come to the truth.

But Sean grew drowsy, and his sentences came more and more slowly. Finally, Elias stopped asking him questions and let him slip into a light doze, content just to watch him breathe. Breathe in, breathe out. He might look like a starved bird, the skin of his face pulled back so that his nose looked like a bony beak, his arms, bent, like molting bird wings. But still Sean breathed. For now, that was enough to feed his heart's hunger.

A noise at the door made him look up, startled. A man stood there, in a dark suit with a clerical collar. He wasn't handsome; he had thinning hair, a long nose, and a rangy build, with arms and legs somehow out of proportion to the rest of his body. Although Elias had never seen him before, the expression in his eyes as he looked at Sean made Elias suspect all at once who he was.

Elias bent down to whisper in Sean's ear. "Sean. I think . . . I think it's Bill. Bill, from your seminary."

"Mmm?" Sean slowly opened his eyes and looked up, blinking. "Who?"

The man in the doorway smiled. "Me. Hello, ratface."

Chapter Nineteen

For I have heard the slander of many:
*   fear was on every side:*
while they took counsel together against me,
*   they devised to take away my life.*
But I trusted in thee, O Lord,
*   I said, Thou art my God.*
My times are in thy hand;
*   deliver me from the hand of mine enemies,*
*   and from them that persecute me!*
Make thy face to shine upon thy servant;
*   save me for thy mercies' sake.*
Let me not be ashamed, O Lord,
*   for I have called upon thee;*
let the wicked be ashamed,
*   let them be silent in the grave.*
Let the lying lips be put to silence
*   which speak grievous things proudly*
*   and contemptuously against the righteous.*

—PSALM 31:13–18

～Eliza had already left the bed again by the time Jonathan arose the next morning. The sweet tangy smell of cut apples greeted him when he clattered down the wooden stairs. Eliza and Goody Grafton were busy paring the first of the autumn crop, some to string up to dry and some to stew down into sauce. Goody Grafton pointed with the handle of her knife at a kettle set over carefully banked embers. "The mistress boiled up some oat porridge for you to break your fast."

"Your mistress is uncommonly good to me, thank you; I fear she shall think me an ungrateful dog to refuse it. But I must take a deposition this morning, and I have tarried too long nodding abed. Will she have patience with me and instead pack a bit of cheese and rye-an'-injun for me to eat as I ride?"

As Eliza looked up to smile at him from the stool where she sat paring, he thought suddenly that her eyes looked tired. But before he could ask whether she had slept poorly, the apple she was turning in her hand skipped out of her grasp like a surprised frog and went bumping across the floor. Jonathan hastened over to the corner to pick it up.

"Eh now, that's the third one you've dropped this morning," Goody Grafton observed, laughing.

Eliza blushed and ducked her head. Her hands and feet were newly swollen and clumsy from plucking and breaking the fresh nettles, despite the dock decoction she had slathered on them; she prayed that Jonathan would not notice the fresh blisters on her fingers.

"Sensible apples, they doubtless are wishful to avoid my pretty wife's kettle." Jonathan smiled. With a flourishing bow, he handed the half-pared apple to her, and in turn, she handed one to him from the pile at her elbow, her eyes dancing. He accepted it with a cordial nod of thanks, polishing it on his sleeve.

She rose and sliced off a hunk of cheese and another of bread for him, then tied them up in a cloth. He accepted the packet and brushed a kiss against her brow. She leaned against him, slipping her arms around his waist. "Tonight," he breathed in her ear, both a promise and a question, and she turned her face to kiss him lingeringly in return. He was whistling as he rode away into the crisp autumn morning.

Jonathan's route led him past the commons and to the outskirts of town. As he passed the cooper's shop, a man passing in the opposite direction raised a hand to hail him: "Mr. Latham, a moment, if you will."

Jonathan pulled his horse to a halt, squinting, and then tipped his hat in greeting. "Lieutenant Sewell, well met."

"Good morrow to you, sir," the other man replied. He pulled a sheaf of papers from the breast pocket of his coat and handed them to Jonathan. "I have the committee's report from Boston for you and Reverend Avery—oh, and Deacon Brownell instructed me to inquire of you, have you asked the Reverend the selectmen's question about his winter's quarter pay?"

"Nay, I fear I have not had the opportunity." Jonathan looked down at the papers in his hand, struck by an idea: he could go and speak with the minister now and leave the report for William to read at the same time, since his own business would probably prevent him from doing so for several days. After exchanging a few pleasantries with Lieutenant Sewell, Jonathan then rode on toward the parsonage.

There, William sat hunched over his desk, bleary-eyed from lack of sleep. He had passed a difficult night since returning from the churchyard, for although he had tried to pray, the turmoil of his thoughts chased away any semblance of serenity. Shortly after dawn, a servant brought him a plateful of Indian hasty pudding to break his fast. He ate quickly, barely tasting it, thinking only of how he could speak to Jonathan. The idea of going to the magistrate's house to meet with him there made William uneasy, for he did not like the risk that Eliza might overhear them. The safest thing to do, William decided, would be to send Jonathan a note, asking him to stop at the parsonage before the end of the day. He pulled his pen and inkwell toward him—and then glanced out the window just in time to see Jonathan dismounting from his horse. "Providence," William muttered, his heart lightening, and he hastened to the hallway to open the outer door.

Jonathan glanced over his shoulder as he drew the reins over his horse's head to tie them to the iron ring on the horse block. "Oh— good morrow, Reverend. I have the newest report from the council of safety for you. And a message from the selectmen: could you accept a cord of cut firewood in place of the two flitches of bacon as part of your pay this winter?"

"Perhaps, but that needs must wait. Magistrate Latham, there is a pressing matter I must discuss with you at once."

Jonathan raised an eyebrow, wondering a little at the gravity of the minister's expression. "Oh? And what is it, then?"

"I do not like to speak of it here in the street. Will you consult with me inside?"

Jonathan hesitated. "Can it not wait, Reverend? I go to Colonel Forster's to take his deposition today; the clerk was to meet me there."

William shook his head slowly. "I think you shall want to hear this. Nay, you needs must hear it. A matter touching upon your duties as magistrate, and . . . your own household."

"Indeed?" Jonathan cocked his head, frowning, and shrugged. "Very well, man. Inside, if you will but lead the way."

William did so, and when the door was closed and they had both seated themselves, he ran his fingers tiredly over the stubble on his chin and began. "I did not sleep well last night—"

"That much is clear to all, at least," interrupted Jonathan with a gleam of humor.

William held up a hand. "Have patience, and hear me speak. 'Tis no matter for jesting."

"Well then?"

William took a deep breath and plunged into an account of the previous night's events. He recounted his tale as dryly, as emotionlessly, as he could, watching Jonathan's face carefully all the while. As William described how he had seen Eliza in the middle of the night and followed her to the churchyard, the humor drained slowly from Jonathan's eyes. He pressed his lips together, eyes hooded, face like marble, as William spoke of the ghosts. William recognized that expression and quailed inwardly, but he continued telling the rest until he had nothing left to say.

Then he stopped. The silence stretched painfully between them.

"Those who bear false witness shall be damned, Reverend," Jonathan said. His voice sounded faint in his own ears. He felt light and weightless, scattered and chaotic, as if the shock had made him unable to command his own thoughts.

William felt a quick flare of anger, which he immediately suppressed. "With horror I speak it. Yet it is the truth, by my hope of Heaven."

"Heaven? Where is Heaven, if—" Jonathan stopped, squeezing his eyes shut tightly. He thought he felt the floor dissolving beneath him, as if his entire world were becoming unmoored.

"She is a witch, Jonathan."

"I do not believe it!" Jonathan cried, slamming a hand down on the desk; the crack made William start violently. Jonathan jumped to his feet, pacing to the wall and back, unable to contain the fierce nervous energy now boiling up inside of him. "No! She is good, she is pure, I would stake my life on it!"

"Would you stake your soul's salvation?" William replied coldly. "For that may be the price if you err. Evil may assume the guise of innocence, Jonathan, until the Devil has you entirely in his snare."

Jonathan stopped, choking. A vision came to him of Eliza handing him the apple, a warm glow in her eyes. . . . "Have you spoken of this to anyone?" he snapped, his coldness now matching William's.

"No."

"Good. As magistrate, I *order* you not to do so. Until . . ." He hesitated.

"Until when?"

Jonathan's jaw tightened. "Until you have more evidence."

William caught his gaze, held it, and nodded once, firmly. "If she be a witch, I shall obtain it."

They fell silent again for a moment, both breathing like fighters.

"Jonathan," William said finally, tentatively. "She plucked a whole sheaf of the nettles. Did you . . . Did you observe her hands this morning?"

Jonathan's breath caught in his throat. He remembered her clumsiness, the apple falling to the floor. "No. Not closely." He swallowed. "I would ask a favor of you, if I may."

"Only name it, my friend."

"Send a boy to Colonel Forster's, to tell him and the clerk I cannot attend to this day's business. Have him say . . . I am ill, and I have gone home."

"Do you think it wise—"

"I am going home, I tell you," Jonathan said sharply.

William searched Jonathan's face, worried. "I will do so. If . . . you will be very careful, Jonathan. Know that my prayers go with you."

Jonathan nodded stiffly and turned to go. He paused just inside the door frame and said huskily without looking back, "Remember, Reverend. Nary a word to a soul. Not until you have proof."

"I understand."

Jonathan swayed for a moment and shut his eyes against the dizziness. *Elizabeth. Elizabeth.* "Good day to you, Reverend," he said firmly and went out the door.

He rode home with his head down in a numb daze, ignoring greetings from the people he passed. A band of Indians could have come out of the woods and hailed him and he never would have noticed. All he could think of was his wife, sitting with her head demurely bent in prayer at the meetinghouse, or bending over a kettle tasting a stew, or looking up at him from her mending, with her head at the inquiring tilt that he loved, smiling. He remembered the first time he had seen her, trembling in the cave, all wild hair and enormous eyes. He could not understand how someone so frightened of *him* could have put herself in league with the Devil.

All too soon, he arrived home. He took his horse to the stable, and, refusing Jonas's help, he methodically set about unsaddling the animal and rubbing it down, as if they had been out for an entire day's hard ride. Then, out of excuses, he strode slowly into the house.

The apples still simmered over the hearth with Goody Grafton in attendance, but Eliza was nowhere in sight. Goody Grafton straightened up in surprise at the sight of him. "Mr. Latham! We did not expect you until nightfall, sir."

"I have ceased this day's business, for I fear I may be ill." He raised a hand to cut off her exclamation of sympathy. "Where is your mistress?"

"Why, Goody Pritcher came with Goody Carter, sir, for Goodman Taylor has called the women for his wife. They asked her to come sit with them to wait, and so I told her I would finish the apples. She took some things with her for Goody Taylor, too—apples and sugar and linen rags and such." Her words trailed off, for her master looked so strange. Goody Grafton frowned, and she wondered uneasily if he was displeased to come home and find his wife gone. "She never refuses anyone who asks for her help, sir," Goody Grafton offered in appeasement. "A good-hearted Christian woman she is, truly."

That, she saw with satisfaction, was apparently the right thing to say, for her master's face softened. "She is, then, do you think?"

"Aye, sir—but of course she will be that sorry she was not home for you."

Jonathan nodded. "I will be upstairs, resting. Please see I remain undisturbed—but send my wife to me when she returns home."

"Aye, sir."

Goody Grafton turned back to the kettles on the hearth, and Jonathan went upstairs. He turned toward his bedroom, wanting nothing more than to lie on his bed and stare at the ceiling, trying to bring order to his spinning thoughts. Instead, however, he stopped and stared down the hallway.

After a moment, he went down the corridor to the small room that he had set aside for her, reluctantly eased open the door, and went in. All looked unchanged. He looked around at the green hangings, the simple rush-bottomed chair, the chest underneath the window. He stood thus for a long time, soaking in the room's stillness, trying to let his fears dissipate. The floor was neatly swept, the candle on the stand in the corner half-burned down. The only sound was his own harsh breathing.

The chest—slowly, he walked over to it, squatted down, and unfastened the lid. But although his fingers tightened on the hasp until the metal's edge creased his fingers, he could not bring himself to raise the lid. A thousand possibilities raced through his mind, all seeming to lead into despair and darkness. "Father, help me," he rasped aloud through gritted teeth. "What must I do?" Sobs rose in his throat with a violence that astonished him. His fingers jerked away from the hasp as if burned, and he knelt, hands caressing the lid, and wept for a long time.

When the tears finally ceased, he rose, scrubbing his face with his fists like a tired schoolboy. He staggered out of the room and down the corridor to fall across his own bed fully dressed. With an arm thrown up over his eyes he soon escaped gladly into a black, soothing well of dreamless sleep.

When Eliza returned from Goody Taylor's that afternoon, Goody Grafton surprised her with the news that the master had come home early feeling poorly and now lay abed upstairs. Concerned, Eliza hastily brewed a balm and chamomile tea for him and carried it up with her. Tiptoeing into the room, she set the tankard down on the candle stand and sat by his side on the bed. He started awake as she gently stroked his shoulder.

"Uh . . . Oh, Elizabeth." Groggily, he struggled to sit up as she tenderly ran her hand over his cheek. She gestured to the tankard, and when he nodded, she picked it up and offered it to him.

But as she held the brim to his lips, Jonathan's memory came flooding back, and he jerked away from the proffered drink. He seized her hand with a grip that made her gasp, and she jumped in surprise, stifling an outcry of pain. They froze, staring at each other, and then Jonathan slowly took the tankard from her and set it on the floor. Wide-eyed, Eliza sat still and watched as he took her other hand and firmly turned them both over, examining them carefully, deliberately. At the sight of the swollen, blistering flesh, his face hardened into icy stillness, and in response she felt a tremor of fear, although she hardly understood why.

He released her hands again. "I . . . do not think I wish to drink what you have brought for me." His voice sounded cool; he fell back against the pillow, looking away from her. Eliza started to reach out to him, to touch his face again, but the sight of the blisters on her fingers made her check the motion, and she thrust her hands under her apron instead. Tears sprang to her eyes, and she stumbled to her feet. She wrapped her arms around herself, shivering, but he refused to look at her, and eventually, she stole away from the room.

She fled to the hall and tried to busy herself there in tasks over the hearth, but Goody Grafton's curious eyes eventually drove her outside. There, Eliza set a tub outside the washhouse, filled it with a kettle of hot water from the hearth, and busied herself sanding and scouring the pewter plates. She scrubbed until her poor abused hands cracked and bled in the wash water and her back and arms ached, but pain was what she wanted, something to distract her, to keep her from seeing again and again in her mind the chilling look in Jonathan's eyes. When she had rinsed and set aside the last plate, she looked up to see the sun just beginning to touch the horizon. Flinging her apron up over her face, Eliza burst into sobs.

Eventually, after calming herself down and wiping her face clean of all trace of tears, she crept back inside and helped Goody Grafton finish preparing the evening meal. Jonathan came downstairs looking pale and grave, and the household assembled to eat. He said little during the meal, and the servants, too, sensing something different, did not joke and chatter as they usually did.

When the meal was over and the plates cleared and washed, Jonathan brought his Bible to the fireplace in the hall and everyone gathered to kneel for the evening devotions. "I have decided," Jonathan said, "to read tonight from the Ninety-first Psalm." He turned to the correct page carefully as the servants exchanged covert, puzzled glances, for the daily reading had been following the New Testament for the past four months. Eliza kept her eyes downcast, her heart beating hard. "He who dwelleth in the secret place of the most High," Jonathan read, "shall abide in the shadow of the Almighty. I will say of the Lord, He is my refuge and my fortress: my God; in Him will I trust. Surely He shall deliver thee from the snare of the fowler, and from the noisome pestilence. He shall cover thee with His feathers, and under His wings shalt thou trust: His truth shall be thy shield and buckler. Thou shalt not be afraid for the terror by night; nor for the arrow that flieth by day; nor for the pestilence that walketh in darkness; nor for the destruction that wasteth at noonday."

His voice was growing tight with tension. He stopped to take a deep breath and then continued: "A thousand shall fall at thy side, and ten thousand at thy right hand; but it will not come nigh thee. Only with thine eyes shalt thou behold and see the reward of the wicked." His voice cracked on the last word. He looked up from the page and over at Eliza, wanting with all the frustrated longing of his soul to somehow reach her through her silence, and for her to understand, both the promise and the warning.

She felt the intensity of his gaze, so scorching that she did not dare look up to meet it. More keenly than ever, she, too, felt all the barriers the curse had placed between them, now on his side as well as her own. He was trying to convey something to her with the psalm, she knew—the urgency was clear in his reading. But she could not understand what he meant the message to be. Tears of frustration welled up in her eyes again, and she furtively wiped them away.

He cleared his throat and went on. "Because thou has made the Lord, which is thy refuge, even the most High, thy habitation; there shall no evil befall thee, neither shall any plague come nigh thy dwelling. For He will give his angels charge over thee, to keep thee in all thy ways. They shall bear thee up in their hands, lest thou dash thy foot against a stone. Thou shalt tread upon the lion and the adder: the young lion and the dragon shalt thou trample under feet."

He closed the Bible. No one spoke or even seemed to breathe. Finally, Jonathan rose stiffly. "I bid you all good night." He went up the stairs without a backward glance.

Methodically, Eliza went through the tasks of snuffing out the last candle and banking the fire so the embers would keep until morning. Then she went upstairs, where she found Jonathan already retired to bed. Slowly, she undressed and then slid underneath the covers beside him. They lay rigidly side by side for a while, and then timidly, she nestled in more closely, laying her cheek against his chest. He wrapped his arms around her as always, but he did not kiss her hair as he usually did. Still, she tried to take comfort from his touch and the slow, regular beat of his heart. She listened, and after a while it seemed to her that his breathing slowed into the rhythm of sleep. Experimentally, she stirred, and his arms around her immediately loosened. Carefully, she stole out from underneath the covers, wrapped a shawl that lay at the foot of the bed around her shoulders, and tiptoed from the room. She did not see the faint starlight from the window reflected in his eyes as they turned to watch her go.

Jonathan waited through the slow turn of the hours of the night, ears straining for sounds. He did not hear the door downstairs open to the outside yard, which reassured him a little, but still, hours passed before Eliza returned. He took care to close his eyes and slow his breathing again as she slipped into the bed next to him. He did not put his arms around her again.

Jonathan regained more command over himself the next day and resumed his duties. The casual observer could certainly have found nothing wrong with the magistrate's unfailingly courteous manner toward his new wife. In the days that followed, however, Eliza sensed a growing change in his manner toward her. It cut her to the soul, for although she felt it, she did not understand the reason. He grew watchful, distant and wary. The silence they shared in the evenings now felt strained and jagged with tension rather than companionable. More than once she turned to see him looking at her with an expression of such black anguish that she became frightened. She longed to reach out to him, to console him, but although he sometimes accepted and returned her embraces, at other times he stiffened and turned away from her touch.

Eliza tried to lose herself in the rhythm of daily tasks and hide the signs of tears as best she could. She took to wearing all the time under her chemise the feather charm she had fashioned. But it was the work she did weaving the coats for her brothers at night that gave her the most comfort. Working quickly, she finished coat after coat, extending her time at the task into the small hours of the morning. Soon, she thought hopefully, once the task was complete and she had found her brothers and broken the spell over them, she would then be free to end the silence between Jonathan and herself.

The weather grew colder, and one morning Goody Grafton looked out into the yard and remarked, "Eh, we must harvest the last of the cabbages today. Surely 'twill freeze hard over the garden in the next day or two."

Eliza thought with dismay of the dwindling pile of nettle flax stored in the chest upstairs. She had made good progress, for most of the coats were now complete, but there was not enough nettle flax left to finish them all. A hard frost would kill the last of the nettles in the churchyard, too. If she did not go there tonight, she would probably not be able to gather any more until the new nettles sprouted next spring.

The thought of following the lonely path in the dead of night and meeting the ghosts again terrified her. But her will was firm, for she thought of her enchanted brothers, facing the prospect of another unsheltered winter, perhaps harsher than any they had ever experienced before.

Once again, when the household had settled itself for the night, and she felt sure Jonathan slept, she eased herself out of bed as usual. She went to look out the window. The half-moon had begun to rise over the trees. She noticed that her hand on the windowsill was shaking; she wrapped her arms around her waist and prayed desperately for courage. Gradually, her shivering ceased again, and she reached for her petticoat, skirt, and bodice and began to dress.

Behind her, Jonathan instantly became alert at this, although he remained rigidly still. He watched her through lowered lashes as she pulled on her cloak and shoes and glided out of the room. At the sound of the outside door opening and then closing again, he rose, too, and dressed hastily to follow her, his heart hammering quickly.

He had to hurry to keep up with her, although he took pains to make his passage as quiet as possible. He was afraid she would look back and discover him, for the moonlight was bright enough to make every stone in the road gleam. But she never did. When she turned at the fork of the road leading to the churchyard, he stood behind a tree, watching with grim despair as she glided out of sight into the deeper shadows along that path. Then he crossed the road and hurried to pound on the minister's door.

A servant girl stumbled to answer the summons, her hand smothering a yawn, only to be rudely shouldered aside once the door was open. "Where is your master's room? He must come with me immediately."

She stared at him, blinking stupidly, and he impatiently snapped, "Don't stand there looking at me with your mouth agape! Go fetch him at once!"

"S-sir, pardon, sir." She bobbed a curtsey and backed away hastily, turning to do as she was bid.

But the knocking had roused William, too, and she met him coming out of his room, carrying a candle. "Well? Who is it, Dorcas?"

"Please, sir, it's Magistrate Latham, and he says——"

"Reverend? Is that you?" Jonathan hastened to his side and whispered urgently in his ear. "Your words are vindicated, William. I followed Elizabeth here—she is on her way to the churchyard."

William turned his head to look at him, startled, and a wave of shock flooded through his body, jolting him instantly awake and bringing with it a kind of silent, fierce exhilaration. "It will require but a minute for me to dress." He gripped Jonathan's forearm and squeezed it, and hastened back into his room. "Dorcas, bring my boots!" he flung over his shoulder before shutting the door.

A scant four minutes later, the two men left the house and were hurrying after Eliza. They approached the wicker gate leading to the churchyard, and William put a cautionary hand on Jonathan's elbow. "Softly, man. . . .We do not want her to see us."

"Aye." They slowed their steps, and with a quick gesture Jonathan indicated a tree close to the gate. They slipped behind it and peered cautiously around its sides. "Do you see her?" Jonathan breathed.

"Wait. . . ." William squinted, straining to see through the mists coiling in the hollow. After a moment, he pointed. "There," he whispered.

A tendril of mist danced away from his jabbing finger, hesitated, and then continued flowing away through the fence and oozing along the ground through the tombstones. It joined another patch of mist pooling around the hem of Eliza's cloak.

She stood rigidly still in the moonlight, shivering, staring into the mists just ahead of her. Perhaps it was the disturbance of air from her passage that made the wisps of night vapors roil and separate. Perhaps. . . .

"Blessed Father," Jonathan hissed. "What are *those?*"

"It is as I told you," William muttered in his ear. "See? She is conjuring them."

"No—Elizabeth!" Jonathan choked and took a step forward. William clamped a hand on his arm and pulled him back.

"Nay, are you mad?" he growled. "Be still, for pity's sake. Watch."

Eliza felt the first touch on her shoulder, soft and tentative. The touch slid down, heading for her waist. She wrenched away and hurried forward, feeling her way along.

Around the dim corner of one tombstone, one insubstantial figure crouched in front of another. The one floating above the ground moaned and Eliza caught in the shifting vapors a glimpse of something like a skull, grinning a rictus of a smile, with black gaps from missing teeth.

The touch of ghostly hands continued, gentle, reaching out to grope at her from all directions with the insistent desire of the dead for the living. The sensation made her shudder convulsively, and she brushed them all away like insubstantial wisps of fog, dispersed with the flick of a hand. Something like cold flesh pressed up against her, and wraiths swirled around her, whispering coarse, dimly heard suggestions in her ear with hoarse chuckles, only to disappear behind her as she pushed on.

Panting with fright, she stumbled through the long, yellowing grass to the nettle patch and plunged her hands in to yank the stalks up by the roots, as her lips moved in silent prayer. Grimly, she stripped the leaves from them and pulled up more, although the burning pain brought tears to her eyes, until the heap of bare nettle stems had piled to the height of her knee. She darted apprehensive glances behind her shoulder as she worked, but the ghosts had fallen back, watching her, once she stood among the nettles. When she lifted her gleanings and began to pick her way back, the ghosts parted before her, as if reluctantly, and dissolved into nothingness over the tombstones.

Jonathan and William crouched lower behind the tree as she fumbled the wicker gate open and passed through it. As she passed by them on the road, they carefully eased their way around the tree in the opposite direction, keeping it between her and themselves.

Jonathan collapsed against the trunk as Eliza's figure dwindled into the dark distance. "Elizabeth," he said, his tear-streaked face pressed against the bark. "I have lain with her, holding her in my arms. This very night her head rested on my breast—how could she . . . how *could* she . . . ?"

William winced, for the picture gave him almost as much pain as Jonathan. As compassionately as he could, he said, "The truth needs be faced now, Jonathan: your own eyes have seen the evidence you needed."

"Aye. They have, may God have pity on me."

William shivered at the expression on his face, but pressed on relentlessly, saying, "God will condemn the entire congregation unless we move now to root this pestilence out from among us. You and I should fetch help to lay her by the heels this very night."

"Must it be done? Nay, you are right," Jonathan added quickly. He passed a hand over his face, struggling to master himself in the face of such a terrible shock. "Alas, poor wretch! Then let it be done quickly." He stood up and started down the road, with William following in his wake, wondering if by *wretch* Jonathan meant his wife or himself.

Eliza was bone-weary and sore by the time she returned home. At the threshold, after removing her pattens, she wrapped the corner of her cloak around the nettle stems to muffle any possible noise and carried them up the stairs to the small room Jonathan had given her. There, she lowered them quietly to the floor in front of the chest and then gratefully collapsed beside them panting. It took her a few moments to regain her breath, and by the time she did, a leaden heaviness was already stealing over her limbs. She knew she had to return to her bed before Jonathan awoke and missed her. But perhaps, she thought sleepily, she could simply rest sitting here, for a moment . . . only a moment. Leaning against the chest, she drew from her chemise the charm she had made, turning it to see the silvery lines etched by moonlight along the edges of the feathers and wondering how her brothers were faring. She blinked wearily, and then her head drooped onto the lid of the chest, the feathers slipping from her slackened hand.

And that is how the men found her an hour later when they mounted the stairs and burst into the room. At the crash of the door against the wall Eliza came awake with a start and looked up, blinking with confusion at the strange, hard faces staring down at her in the crazily swaying lantern light. Jonathan entered the room last, his face the grimmest of all. Eliza's eyes widened.

William stepped forward. His gaze flickered down to the nettle stalks at their feet and then up to her face again. "Mistress Latham," he said, his voice quiet and calm.

There was a pause, and then Eliza scrambled to her feet and stood, swaying. The men in the room tensed.

"You are under arrest," William said evenly, "and ordered to stand trial for the capital charge of practicing the unholy art of witchcraft."

Horror made the blood drain from Eliza's face, and she thought that she might faint. Instead, she shook her head angrily, violently, making a vehement slashing gesture with her hand, and two of the men flinched in fear.

"Men, do your duty!" William snapped.

After a heartbeat of suspense, they seized her arms and backed her into the corner. She struggled for only a moment before stopping, but worse, words of fear, of protest, boiled up, hovering agonizingly at her lips until she thought she must shriek aloud or die. Terrified, for she had never come so close before to imperiling her brothers with her tongue, she bit her lip until she tasted blood.

William saw this and his eyes narrowed. He took a lantern from the man standing next to him and lifted it to scrutinize her face. Eliza's pupils constricted to pinpricks in the glare. The charm around her neck caught his attention and he warily took it in his hand, lifting it to examine it more closely. She gasped and held her breath. After a moment, he looked at her, lifted an eyebrow, and with one savage pull, tore it from her neck. She half fell to her knees, and the men holding her staggered.

William stepped back. "The chest. Open it."

The lid was dumped open; again, Eliza almost cried out. Almost. A perplexed silence fell.

Eyes glittering, William reached in and carefully lifted out the spindle, tossing it into the pile of nettles, and the frame loom holding a half-completed coat. He studied it for a moment, and then reached down, pulled out the completed tunics, and dumped them on the floor as if they were snakes. Eliza looked up and finally caught and held Jonathan's eye.

The message was as clear to him as if she had screamed it: *If ever I asked anything from you, please, please.* . . .

William raised a knee and with one swift motion cracked the loom over his thigh. He threw the tangle of wood, nettle thread, and cloth aside and gestured toward the coats on the floor. "Destroy the witch's work."

Eliza wrenched her arms as hard as she could and began fighting in earnest, a wordless, voiceless howl contorting her face. One man struck a blow to the side of her head, and another crashed to the floor with her in a tangle of limbs, but over the commotion, Jonathan's voice roared "Stop!"

The men froze. Eliza lay still, breathing in great gasps, face mashed to the floor, a splinter driven into her cheek.

"Why?" William demanded testily.

Jonathan shouldered his way forward. "Let her rise."

Clumsily, the man lying on top of Eliza clambered off her, and they hauled her unceremoniously to her feet. She stared at Jonathan, her eyes a vast universe of pleading that left him shaken. Then she closed them, and her tears mingled with the blood on her face.

He felt all his love for her welling up in him again like an aching pull, but he tried to tell himself it was only pity. Surely God would forgive him for that. "Do not destroy these . . . things she has fashioned. Let the coats be her covering in the gaol, and these"—he stirred the pile of nettle stalks with his foot—"they can be her pillow."

Eliza's eyes flew open, and she saw it all. He loved her, and he would give her this. But he believed her guilty, and he would not save her.

"Take her away," Jonathan said wearily.

She did not resist anymore as they led her out.

Chapter Twenty

Let us roll all our strength, and all
Our sweetness, up into one ball:
And tear our pleasures with rough strife,
Through the iron gates of life.
Thus, though we cannot make our sun
Stand still, yet we will make him run.

—ANDREW MARVELL, "TO HIS COY MISTRESS"

Bill!" Sean straightened up in his bed, looking almost awake again. "I can't believe it. How long has it been, man?"

"Too long." Bill stepped forward, smiling, and reached out unhesitatingly to shake Sean's hand. The smile transformed his face wonderfully.

"It's so *good* to see you again!" Sean exclaimed, pulling him in and reaching up to give him a hug. Bill returned it, and Elias winced, thinking of the newly installed chest catheter. But Bill seemed to be aware of it and carefully squeezed Sean only around the shoulders.

After pulling away, Bill looked over at Elias, who wondered whether it was time to declare the need for another smoking break. "Sean," Elias began, "maybe, um—"

"Bill," Sean interrupted, placing his hand on the small of Elias's back, "I want you to meet my partner, Elias Latham." It was the first time Elias could remember Sean introducing him as his partner. "Elias, this is Bill Addison—or, I should say, Father Bill—"

"No, it's Reverend Bill. I'm with the Metropolitan Community Church now." He extended his hand and Elias shook it.

"No kidding!" Sean said. "Here, grab the chair and sit down." He gestured vaguely, and Bill did so. Elias shifted over on the side of the bed so Bill could see both their faces without Sean having to crane his neck to look around Elias's shoulder.

"How'd you find me?" Sean asked.

"I'm on the chaplaincy staff here part-time. Your name came up on the new admissions list at this morning's weekly staff meeting."

"Ohh . . . so this is a professional visit."

"Professional and personal both, I suppose." Bill smiled again.

Sean looked down, and his hands began pleating and unpleating a fold in the sheet. "I suppose they go over each patient's diagnosis at that meeting."

Bill nodded slowly. "I know why you're here," he said, his eyes intent on Sean. *I understand everything* hung in the air, unspoken.

Sean nodded, too, pressing his lips together tightly.

"Tell me what's happened to you since I saw you last," Bill said gently.

Sean brightened, apparently glad for the change of subject. "Well, the first thing I tried after leaving seminary was law school." Bill raised an eyebrow, and Sean snorted. "I know. What a mistake. Thankfully, it didn't take long for me to come to my senses." Sean tried to turn over onto his side, and the movement made him gasp. Elias turned his head and saw Sean's face twist in surprised pain. "Ahh . . . I think the painkillers are wearing off a bit."

Elias got up off the bed. "Can I help somehow . . . ?"

"Where's that doohickey for raising and lowering the bed? Oh, here . . ." Sean pulled the bed control toward himself and pushed the red button. Nothing happened.

"I'm afraid the beds are often broken," Bill observed mildly. "Sorry. But look on the bright side: at least they finally fixed the shower in this room. I understand it's been busted for about four weeks."

"Here." Elias reached out to support Sean's head and shoulders and helped ease him down into a more recumbent position. Sean closed his eyes and sighed in relief. His shoulder blades felt painfully bony under Elias's hand.

"I think he's kind of worn out," Elias said apologetically.

"Well," Bill said, getting up. "I only meant to poke my head in for a quick hello today, anyway—I know you just got out of surgery."

"But I want to talk with you," Sean said fretfully. "It's been bloody ages since I've seen you, only I'm just so *tired*—"

"I'll be back tomorrow, and we can talk then." His big hand covered Sean's. "We'll have time. But now I think you need to sleep."

"Sounds good," Sean said faintly after a moment, eyes still closed.

Glancing up from Sean's face, Elias caught a fleeting glimpse in Bill's eyes as he looked at Sean of the same unguarded expression he'd seen earlier, a hint of something unspeakably sad. His eyes met Elias's and he smiled faintly. *Later,* he mouthed.

Sean was already asleep when Bill tiptoed out of the room.

Elias missed Sean's warmth in bed that night. He kept reaching out restlessly in his sleep, searching for a chest to curl his arm around, a flank to fit against his body, but he only embraced empty space. In dreams, he wandered barefoot in and out of vacant, echoing rooms, searching for something he never found. The sheets felt cold and damp, making his sleep restless. He awoke abruptly an hour before his usual rising time, shivering violently.

"Hell." Groggily, he wrapped the bed quilt around himself, staggered out into the living room, and started the coffeepot. Then he collapsed on the couch and sat there huddled up in a miserable ball for over an hour, watching the rain dripping slowly from the trees in the courtyard, making the bare twigs on the lowest branches tremble. Yellow leaves lay in circles around each trunk, plastered flat and slick against the pavement, as if the trees had undressed for the winter.

Finally, Elias uncurled himself painfully and shuffled over to the counter to pour himself some coffee. But as he lifted the mug experimentally to his lips, the hot, oily smell steaming up suddenly made his stomach heave, and he set the mug down hastily, jaw clenched tightly against nausea. Once the worst of the queasiness was past, he picked up the telephone and called the store.

"Van Hoosen Photography," said a clipped, nasal voice.

"Carl? It's Elias. I won't be coming in today."

"Again?" Carl answered. He sounded annoyed.

"I've got the flu."

"Yeah, yeah. I want you in here tomorrow."

"You don't want me to get everyone else sick, do you?"

A rather ominous pause followed. "No, and so you'd better be well by then, Elias. I'll be expecting you." He hung up.

Irritated, Elias went into the bathroom and took a shower, setting the water temperature as hot as he could stand it. That helped, some. But he felt cold again as soon as he got out, even after dressing in his warmest set of sweats. He wandered out into the living room, chose a cassette tape at random, and shoved it into the tape player. It was some of Sean's Irish music, and listening to the tune gave him such a wrench that he hurried over to shut off the tape just before the fiddle launched into its second time through the chorus. "Damn."

At that moment, the phone rang. "You're not at work," Patty's voice said accusingly when he picked it up. "You said you'd be at work."

"Did you call me there? Why?"

"To find out how the surgery went, stupid."

"Look, uh, I don't think you'd better call me at the shop about Sean."

"I thought you were out at work!"

"Well, I was. But there's this new manager, and so I'm trying to keep a kind of low profile for now——"

"Oh, and so you think you can just stuff that particular kitty back into the bag, huh?" Patty said, her voice dripping with scorn.

Elias shrugged, too weary to argue. "I don't know how long I'll be there anymore, anyway."

"Huh." Patty snorted, and then apparently decided to let the matter drop. "So anyway, how is he?"

"Fine, except he was totally wiped out when I left last night. But now that they've got him on the drug, maybe he'll be able to start eating more easily."

"Goody for him. Now, the next thing I want to know is, how come you're not punching the clock today? You don't sound good—or did you just take another day off to stay with Sean?"

Elias rolled his eyes. "What is this, the Spanish Inquisition?"

"Elias—"

"If you must know, I've got the flu."

" 'Zat so? And is that what your doctor told you?"

"Why should I see a doctor about something as ordinary as the flu?"

"*If* that's what it is. Are your lymph glands swollen?"

Reluctantly, Elias fingered his neck. "Of course they're swollen. That happens when you get the flu."

"Yeah, right. Go see your doctor, Elias. Better yet, go see Sean's internist—"

"What gives you the right—" Elias began hotly.

"Or I'll call Sean and tell him."

"You do that," Elias said tightly, "and you're no 'buddy' to either of us. And you'll only see Sean again over my dead body."

There was a long silence on the other end. "All right, I'm sorry," Patty said finally. She actually sounded contrite. "I'm sorry, Elias. That was way over the line."

Elias didn't say anything. He was afraid that if he did, he'd start crying and be unable to stop.

"Elias? You there?"

"Mmm-hmm," he managed.

"Okay. Okay, look, I may be an idiot, but I'm an idiot with my heart in the right place. Get yourself checked out, will ya?"

"I'll think about it," Elias said grudgingly. He cradled the phone against his shoulder with his cheek and pressed his fists against his eyes.

"And you'd better decide beforehand whether you're going to tell Sean," Patty said, her voice unexpectedly gentle, "if the news should turn out to be the worst."

"I don't know. I don't know." Tears were leaking out now, trickling down the curve of his nose. He grabbed a dish towel and wiped them away. "I can't be sick now. I just can't."

"Why not, Elias?"

"Sean needs me too much."

Patty sighed. "And so you think the universe is therefore gonna arrange itself for your convenience?"

"What should I do?" Elias asked. He felt small, vulnerable, very frightened.

"I told you. See a doctor."

"You're on your fourth AIDS patient now, and you tell me that? Doctors can't do anything against this."

"Maybe. Maybe not. Nobody can do anything unless you let them try. And if you've got AIDS, letting people help you is the only hope you've got."

Is it? Elias slumped down on the floor and curled his arms around himself, trying to stop his shivering.

"And one more thing: whatever time you have left—whether it's Sean's time or your own—just make the most of it, Elias."

He sat on the floor for a long time after hanging up the phone, leaning forward with his head on his knees. *Make the most of whatever time you have.* He thought of Sean, typing like a maniac to beat the deadline, and the wistful look on his face when he'd spoken of giving up on the idea of a world tour.

He reached for the phone and dialed another number.

"Hello?"

"Rick? It's Elias. Listen, I need your help with a special project. It's for Sean. . . ."

He called Sean later without mentioning he wasn't at work.

"I overheard a couple of residents talking about the drug I'm on," Sean told him. "This wonderful drug amphotericin they carved a hole into my chest so I could start taking. Apparently, it has a nickname: 'amphoterrible.' "

"Really?"

"Yeah, I asked the gastroenterologist about it and finally got him to admit they call it that because the side effects are so horrendous."

"Oh, great."

"I think he was headed from here to go chew out the residents for letting me overhear them. Apparently, he frowns on that sort of humor; it's rather hard on patient morale."

"How is your morale, by the way? Not to mention your appetite."

"Hmm. Maybe both would improve if I thought there was anything here worth eating." He laughed sourly. "My parents have been back already."

"And?"

"They're trying." Sean sighed. "They're staying through the weekend and then heading home. But I think they might come back next weekend, too."

"Did, uh, Bill come back to see you, too?"

"Oh, yeah—yeah, he did. We had a wonderful talk. Well, not exactly, actually: I mostly talked and he listened. I'd forgotten what a good listener he is."

Elias managed a politely interested, is-that-so sort of noise but the strength of his own feelings surprised him. Not jealousy, exactly—after all, he'd learned not to be jealous of Sean's tricks over the years.

But he knew that Sean's history with Bill had meant something different.

"Oh, and both my parents and Bill asked about you, too. They wanted to know what time you would be stopping by tonight."

"I . . . don't know if I can. I want to, Sean, but I think I'm coming down with the flu. The last thing you need is for me to give it to you."

"Oh, no, Elias. You going to be okay by yourself?"

"Of course I will." *At least he didn't ask if that was all it was, like Patty.* He wasn't sure if he felt relieved or disappointed.

"You sure?"

"Look, if it'll make you feel better, I promise I'll call somebody if I think I need help. Ruth or Leo or somebody."

"Well . . . okay, then." Sean sighed.

"I miss you," Elias whispered. "I hate not being with you."

"So, whatcha miss the most? My razor-sharp wit? My dazzling musical genius? The dramatic flair I have when throwing up in the bathroom?"

"Oh, all of them, I suppose."

"Admit it. You miss my cold feet in bed at night."

"I do! I slept terribly."

"So did I. Of course, having the nurses come in every few hours to clean the catheter didn't help, either. A vacation spa this ain't."

That night, Elias set his alarm to get up for work the next morning, but when it went off, he couldn't make himself get out of bed for over an hour. Finally, he dragged himself out into the living room and called the shop. A new employee, Luiz, answered the phone this time.

"Luiz, tell Carl I'm not coming in again today. Sick again."

"I'll tell him," Luiz said doubtfully. "But you better know, Elias, he was real pissed yesterday that you didn't show up. You gonna catch it in the neck if you don't come in today."

"What, I take a lousy vacation day and then get sick two more days and now my job's in trouble?"

Luiz lowered his voice. "Rick was right, man. They're looking for excuses to fire us. I'm hunting around for a new job already, are you?"

"Well, maybe they're not going to fire me. Maybe I'll quit first."

"Elias! I can't tell Carl—"

"No," Elias said, cutting him off. He felt utterly weary. "Don't tell him anything. I'll talk to him tomorrow."

Elias placed another call after that, setting an appointment with his doctor the next day. *That should keep Patty off my back for a little while at least.*

He made himself a couple of pieces of toast and ate them and went back to bed, but around noon he felt better, and so he decided to get dressed and go to the hospital.

As Elias approached Sean's room, he heard voices talking. He poked his head around the door and saw Bill sitting in the chair beside Sean's bed. Sean saw Elias and waved him in. He and Elias exchanged a kiss, and Elias took up his favorite leaning post against the window. "Hi," he said to Bill self-consciously.

"Elias," Bill said, nodding easily, with a hint of a smile.

"They don't come right out and say it, of course," Sean continued. "But I think it's confusing for them. Their big hang-up when I entered the seminary was that they'd never have grandkids, although they would have rather died than said it. But after they worked it all out and said, okay we'll support you, I left and said I wasn't going to take the final vows after all."

"So they couldn't say, 'my son, the priest,' " Bill observed, amused. "But they still wouldn't get the grandkids, either."

Sean laughed, but with a bitter edge. "A disappointment to them either way."

"Hmm." Bill considered for a moment and then smiled with a satirical glint in his eye. "You were kind of fooling yourself from the beginning, you know."

Sean snorted. "I know that. But I wised up. Why do you think I quit?"

Bill shook his head. "I'm not talking about kidding yourself you're heterosexual and then quitting once you found out you're gay. You quit because you discovered you had to pay a price. And you didn't like that at all."

Sean's eyebrows drew down in irritation. "What are you talking about?"

"Look, you told me you thought you were meant to be a priest because you weren't attracted to women, right?"

"Yeah. So?"

Bill shrugged. "How do you think *heterosexuals* become priests? They know that to be celibate, to make the commitment the church requires, they have to give something up. You thought you were getting off scot-free. And when you discovered you were wrong, that the fiddler did in fact have to be paid, you decided you didn't want any part of it."

Sean looked shocked and then angry.

"Well," Bill said, his voice gentle, "soon you may be called to give something up, my friend, like it or not."

"Give up what?"

"You already know. Don't you?"

The room was silent for a moment, and Elias held his breath.

"My life, I suppose," Sean said finally, his voice cracked and hoarse.

There. He had said it.

Bill nodded. "And if it comes to that, then maybe the time has come to decide where your true commitment lies."

Sean's face contorted for a moment. "Why did you quit, then? You said you were going to stay!"

"I did stay." Bill sighed. "I went all the way to the end of seminary and took the vows. And then two years after I started with my first parish, I was approached by a couple who asked me to bless their union." He raised an eyebrow. "Two men. I agreed to perform a commitment ceremony. The bishop got wind of it and ordered me not to do it." He shrugged, but Elias sensed his casualness was a hard-won facade. "I suppose it could have been worked out, if I hadn't said, uh, certain things. But in the end, it was a conflict of principles, and I decided I couldn't knuckle under. So I petitioned to be released from my vows."

"I'm sorry, Bill," Sean said. "That must have been hard."

"It was. But I still have a ministry, with MCC."

There was a clattering noise at the door. Bill looked over and frowned.

"What is it?" Sean asked.

Bill walked over to the door and came back carrying a dinner tray. He lifted the steel plate warmer, and Sean leaned forward warily and stared at the nondescript piece of . . . something underneath. Meatloaf, possibly—although Elias wouldn't have bet on it—along with cooked carrots and some discouraged-looking mashed potatoes. "Ick," said Sean dubiously.

"Did they do this at lunch, too?" Bill demanded.

"Do what?"

"Leave your meal on the floor just inside the door, instead of bringing it in and setting it up for you?" He put the meal down on Sean's bedside table. "How in blazes do they think you're supposed to go over and get it if you're tethered to an IV?"

Sean looked stunned. "I—don't know. I was asleep, and when I woke up, my dad was setting the lunch tray down in front of me."

Bill pressed his lips together. "Excuse me for a moment." He stalked out of the room without another word.

Sean looked down at his dinner, appalled. "Are they *afraid* to come in? Is that it?"

"I don't know," Elias said. He could hear Bill's voice, raised out in the hall, although he couldn't make out the words.

"My god." Sean pushed the plate away with a look of revulsion.

Elias pulled it back. "Well, don't let that stop you from eating it," he said gently. "You came here to gain weight, right? So eat." He reached for Sean's bread and buttered it for him. "Come on."

Reluctantly, Sean picked up his fork and took a bite. He paused in mid-chew, grimacing, and then, with the air of a man steeling himself for an ordeal, took a second bite. "So how did work go today?"

Elias hesitated, wondering how to answer without actually explaining that he didn't go in. "I don't like the new manager very much. And I don't think he likes me."

"Why?"

Elias shrugged. "Rick said . . . transitions can sometimes be tricky when chains buy stores and bring in new managers."

"I suppose so. I have a hard time believing you can't get along with anybody, though."

Elias didn't say anything for a moment, and Sean lowered his fork again, looking alarmed. "What is it?"

A number of answers flitted through his mind, most of them lies or evasions. "Sean," he said slowly, "when you started feeling you were getting sick, you didn't say anything to me about it."

"Do you think you might have AIDS?" Sean said, suddenly going white to the lips.

"I don't know! That's the truth, I swear it is." He watched Sean's face anxiously until he nodded.

"Okay. I believe you." Sean looked at his dinner plate with loathing and forced himself to take another bite. "Well, what is it, then?"

Would it be right to tell him? Aren't there silences that are kinder than the truth?

"Well, if I had some bad news to tell you . . . hypothetically speaking . . . or if I do get some bad news in the future, would you want me to tell you?"

To his credit, Sean thought about it for several minutes before answering. "I understand you don't want to upset me. That's the way I felt about telling you. Maybe I didn't trust you enough. But sharing hard things together—that's what partners do, isn't it?"

"I don't know," Elias said with a lump in his throat. *Is that what we are? Partners?*

"If you don't tell me something's bothering you, maybe it means you've given up on me already. You know—you've already written me off as someone who can't . . . can't be there to help you face something hard."

"I haven't given up on you, Sean." Elias leaned down and hugged him fiercely. "I'm never going to give up on you."

"Then tell me. I want you to. Or tell me at least as much as you can."

Elias took a deep breath. "I think I may lose my job soon."

"I see." Sean nodded slowly. "But you can find another one, can't you?"

How can I if I'm getting sick? But he couldn't say that. Not yet. He tried to smile reassuringly.

"Thank you for telling me, Elias." Sean reached out and squeezed Elias's hand with pitifully bony fingers.

Sean fell asleep soon afterward, still holding Elias's hand. It was strange how quickly he fell asleep now, as if the mere effort of holding a conversation were enough to wear him out. With infinite gentleness, Elias withdrew his fingers and brushed a tendril of Sean's hair out of his eyes. He'd have to see to it that Sean got a shampoo tomorrow. Maybe he could give him a haircut.

"Is he asleep?" a voice whispered. Elias looked up to see Bill standing in the doorway. He nodded and went out into the hallway to join him.

"I'll leave now then," Bill said, his voice low. "Tell Sean I, um, had some words with the staff. I hope you won't have any more nonsense about the way his meals are served." He glanced back into the room, and the same introspective expression flitted across his face.

"I think I know what you gave up to become a priest," Elias said impulsively.

Bill looked at him, raising an eyebrow, and Elias blushed. "It's that obvious, is it?" A crease appeared between his eyebrows. "It's not—I mean, I don't want you to think I'm any kind of threat—"

"I know that. I'm just sorry that you can't . . . Now that you're no longer a priest, I mean—"

"Oh, I am in my own way, I suppose. And I think Sean's in pretty good hands with you."

*   *   *

324

It took three more days for Carl to get around to firing him. It took three more weeks to get the project he had planned with Rick set up with all their friends.

It took five weeks for the doctor to confirm that Elias had AIDS.

The night he found out, Elias went up to Sean's room at the hospital, came directly over, and wrapped his arms around him.

"Hey . . . hey, Elias. What's happening?" Sean said, pulling back a little and smiling sleepily up at him.

Elias shrugged, struggled to find something to say past the obstruction in his throat. "I . . . just miss holding you."

"Here, lower the bed rail."

Elias did and then gingerly lay down next to Sean. Painfully, Sean shifted over to give him room. They lay together, their arms intertwined, for a long time, not saying anything.

"Elias?" Sean said finally as the room began growing dark.

"Hmm?"

"What would you think of . . . um, getting married, I suppose. Having some kind of partnering ceremony, for you and me?"

"What?" Surprised, Elias raised his head and peered to see Sean's face in the darkness.

"Ever since Bill mentioned performing one, I've been thinking about it. And about commitment." Sean sighed, shifting his head on the pillow. "This is going to sound corny, but you know, I realized I've studied a bunch of different things, had all sorts of careers. All kinds of friends, tricks, lovers. But I'd never really settled down to anything. Until I met you. I feel bound to you in a way I've never been to anyone else before. And there's a part of me that wants to let the world know that. While I still have time." He paused. "Do you understand?"

Elias twisted a fold of Sean's hospital gown between his fingers. "I do."

Sean cleared his throat. "And I've been thinking about my parents. Wondering what's going to happen to them after I die."

Elias made a movement of protest, and Sean held up his hand. "Wait a minute," he said. "Hear me out." He shifted again, with a soft noise of pain. "And then there's you, with no parents at all. What will happen if you get sick, too? Who's gonna look after you?"

Elias ducked his head, hoping Sean couldn't read the expression in his eyes. "I can think of a number of our friends who'd be pissed to hear you imply I couldn't count on them. You said being gay means we choose our own families."

"Right. That's what I'm asking you to do, to choose to make a family with me. That way, my parents would be your parents, too, and you can be a son to them when I'm gone."

He paused, giving Elias an opportunity to reply, but Elias didn't trust the reliability of his voice and remained silent.

Sean cleared his throat. "On the other hand, who knows? Maybe this drug'll work and they'll discover a cure for AIDS. We can go to Bloomingdale's and pick out matching towels together and live happily ever after."

"I don't want to wear a white dress."

"So you don't have to wear a white dress. Or even throw a bouquet. Will you at least consider it?" His voice became serious. "It would mean a lot to me."

"I think . . . it would mean a lot to me, too." Elias pondered. "We could get matching rings."

"Hey, we could." Sean's voice sounded pleased. "I know someone who makes rings, using Irish designs. Let me take care of getting those."

"All right, then." Elias tightened his arm around Sean, carefully. "I accept your proposal."

"Thanks, Elias."

"And we'll ask Bill to do the ceremony?"

"Naturally."

"I'm sure you understand this already," Bill said, "but I still have to say it. I can perform a ceremony, but it won't mean a rat's patootie in the eyes of the law."

"We know that," Elias said.

"Have you thought about seeing an attorney?" Bill asked. "You need to arrange your wills, and Sean, you might want to look at the question of whether you want to consider signing some kind of power of attorney, so Elias can act for you if need be."

Sean and Elias exchanged looks. "Okay, we'll do that," Sean said with a touch of impatience. "But we want to do a partnering ceremony for us, not the state."

"And your friends and family, too, of course. Do you plan on inviting them?"

Sean looked startled. "I . . . hadn't thought about it." He looked down at the tube erupting from his chest. "I'm a little . . . tied down, so to speak."

Bill shrugged. "The hospital has a chapel we can reserve, so your friends and family can come. If you like."

The first line from the tune "Chapel of Love" flitted absurdly through Elias's mind, and he had to bite down the urge to laugh.

Sean grinned. "Well, we'll see if anyone wants to come."

There were some doubters, when Sean and Elias announced their intentions and the date. Sean's parents "took it well," as Sean put it, although neither Sean nor Elias missed the swift look of dismay that crossed Janet's face when Sean broke the news.

"What is it?" Sean said, smiling dangerously at her.

Janet looked at her husband rather helplessly and then shrugged. "Nothing, it's just . . ." Her words trailed off.

"We never expected you'd do something like this," Jim offered.

"Something like what?" Sean asked with a note of challenge. Elias took his hand and pressed it warningly.

"Try to, er, get married," said Janet. "To a man."

"It bothers you?" Sean said, with a look that meant, *It had better not.*

Janet sighed. "Well, it does seem strange. We'll need to get used to the idea. But you know, when you first told us you were gay, I think one of the things that hurt us the most was the thought you'd never find someone to share your life, the way Jim and I have." She blinked, and Elias saw the tears in her eyes. "I'm just so glad that all our fears turned out to be for nothing."

She smiled, and then gave herself a little shake. "Well, my goodness, I suppose I must say, um . . . welcome to the family, Elias." She came over and gave him an awkward hug, which felt at once pleasant and dreadfully embarrassing to Elias. As he pulled away from Janet's embrace and solemnly shook Jim's outstretched hand, he caught a look of thoughtful surprise on Sean's face.

After Sean's parents had left and they were alone again, Sean admitted, "That went better than I thought it would."

"Hmm. Something your mom said gives me the impression they know they really blew it with you when you came out."

"I'd say they did," Sean muttered, his eyes kindling at certain memories.

"Just a guess, but I think they're glad they're getting a second chance."

Leo called the hospital when he got his invitation. Elias answered the phone because Sean was asleep. "Kiyoshi and me'll be there," Leo said.

"Good. Oh, and Sean said to tell you and any other musicians to bring instruments, so we can have music afterwards."

"Um, does that include Nick?" Leo asked cautiously.

"We sent an invitation to him and Amy," Elias said. "I don't know if they're coming or not."

"Amy can do what she wants," Leo said, "but I'll make sure Nick is there. Oh, and I have a picture for you. I caught my sister and gave her the mask just before she left for Florence on a buying trip, and she had it taken in front of Michelangelo's *David*."

Elias grinned. "That's perfect, Leo, thanks. Make sure you get it to me before Friday so I can add it to the collection."

Sean stirred and looked over, blinking. "Who's it?" he asked.

"Leo," Elias whispered to him. "He says he and Kiyoshi are coming."

"Ask about Philip."

"Leo, Philip won't be well enough to come, will he?"

"No, he's still hospitalized because he's taking an IV drug for the cryptococcosis—"

"Oh, I forgot; he's on amphotericin, too. It's a shame he isn't admitted here so he could just push his IV pole down the hall."

"He said to tell you," Leo added, "that he can't believe you and Sean are buying into heterosexist oppressive class structures by aping a marriage ceremony. And *then* he said, if you have pictures taken and he doesn't get to see them, he'll break your necks. I think you can count on him being there in spirit."

Elias laughed and repeated this to Sean.

"Ah, Philip," Sean said, smiling faintly. "Always the revolutionary."

The morning before the scheduled ceremony, Sean's fever spiked again. Concerned, the doctor ordered a series of blood tests and deduced from the serum creatinine levels that Sean could be showing signs of kidney damage. "You're getting anemic, too," he said. "Which might indicate bone marrow suppression; we'll have to monitor you for signs of neutropenia. It's the amphotericin, I'm afraid."

"So what do we do?" Elias wanted to know.

"Well, if the anemia gets much worse, we can try transfusion. As for the kidneys, we can cut back on the drug, but of course that will allow the candidiasis to rebound."

"Aren't there other drugs we can try?" Sean asked.

The doctor sighed. "I'm afraid we don't have very many choices in our arsenal."

"Okay." Sean nodded tensely. "Just tank me up on something that'll lower the fever for now."

The doctor looked doubtful, and Sean tried a grin. "Oh, c'mon. You can't let me miss my own wedding day."

They gathered the next day in the hospital chapel, with Sean's parents and about fifteen friends, for the simple ceremony they had planned with Bill. Sean managed to get dressed for the occasion and did his best to loop the catheter tubing out of sight under his coat, a mostly wasted effort, since he still needed the IV pole. Hunched in his wheelchair, he looked sallow-skinned and frail, but very happy.

They clasped hands before Bill and repeated after him the promises they had written together for each other. Then Bill took the rings from the small tray where they had been placed on the altar.

"Sean and Elias," Bill said, "have chosen to give each other claddagh rings, a traditional Irish design. Each ring shows a pair of hands, clasped around a crowned heart. The hands represent friendship, the crown loyalty, and the heart, of course, means love."

Elias took the larger ring and gently drew Sean's hand from the armrest of the wheelchair. Sean's palm was cold and sweaty. "Sean, I give you this ring as both sign and seal of my friendship, my loyalty, and my love."

Sean squeezed Elias's hand and then picked up Elias's ring in turn. "Elias, I give you this ring," he said, "as both sign and seal of my friendship, my loyalty, and my love." The cool metal slid on easily and then quickly warmed to blood heat.

Bill said some more things then, but Elias didn't really hear them; he and Sean were too busy looking into each other's eyes and grinning like fools. And then it was over, and the small crowd gathered around them, laughing and crying, as somebody pounded him on the back. Ruth and Minta leaned down to kiss Sean. Elias caught a glimpse of Janet and Jim, looking grave even as they tried to smile. "Let's have some music!" Sean cried out, and the group trooped out of the chapel, Elias pushing Sean's chair as Sean clung to the IV pole.

They reconvened in the small visitors' lounge, where a cake was set and the musicians unsnapped their instrument cases. "Play softly," Sean warned. "People are sleeping." But although they did keep the volume down, the patients wandering up and down the halls smiled at the music spilling from the lounge.

Elias sat in a chair next to Sean and looked at the ring on his finger. "D'ye like it?" Sean asked, grinning as he picked at his cake.

"Yes, I do." He looked across the room and caught Rick's eye. "I have a present for you, too," Elias said. At the signal, Rick came across the room to lay something in Sean's lap and then stepped back, grinning. Everyone looked up expectantly.

Sean looked down at the large photo album in surprise. His fingers traced the gold stamped letters on the cover in wonder as he read the words aloud. "Sean Donnelly's . . . World Tour?" He looked up at Elias, a crease between his eyebrows.

"Open it."

Sean stared at the first page and then turned it and looked at the next. His parents drifted over and craned their necks to see over his shoulder. "How . . . how did you do it?" he stammered.

"I did a blowup of your face, printed a bunch of copies, and mounted them on cardboard. Then Rick and I handed them out and explained the idea to people."

"Is that really the Arc de Triomphe in Paris?"

"That's you in front of the Arc de Triomphe."

"No, come on, who was it, really?"

"It was my dad," Patty said. "He was in Paris for an academic conference." The mask was set a little high, so you could see his beard underneath, but he was waving enthusiastically, and the view down the Champs-Élysées was stunning.

Page after page followed, each showing an ersatz Sean, smiling and waving in front of landmarks all over the world: a volcano in Hawaii, the Egyptian pyramids, Mount Fuji, the Wailing Wall in Jerusalem. There were also Irish pubs. Lots of Irish pubs. Occasionally, Sean held a guitar or some other instrument (inexplicably, he appeared to be playing a tuba in front of Mount Rushmore). Everyone drew in closer to watch Sean's face eagerly for his reaction as he turned the album leaves, his face lighting up again and again with delight.

"The Taj Mahal!"

"My cousin got that. He was taking an international semester—"

"Where's that?"

"That's in Bucharest—"

"—she really helped, she's a travel agent, and a lot of her clients sent pictures back—"

"I never thought I'd visit the Great Wall of China in a skirt!"

"—I told you those contacts in Ecuador would come in handy—"

"What a marvelous idea, Elias," Janet said. "How many people helped you?"

"Our friends spread the word fast. In the end, it was over fifty. I'm still expecting more photographs back, and I'll add them to the album."

Sean turned the last page, and Elias added, "But that will be the last one."

The last picture was in front of the penguin display at the Central Park Zoo. Rick had taken it, and Elias himself had posed with the Sean mask. He wore a parka and held a sign up that read "South Pole." White packing excelsior lay spread around his feet as artificial snow. A penguin diving in the underwater tank had turned, stretching its neck back to eye Elias dubiously through the glass just as Rick snapped the picture.

Sean looked up at Elias, speechless, tears in his eyes.

"Surprise!" Elias said.

Chapter Twenty-one

All witchcraft comes from carnal lust,
Which is in women insatiable.

——HENRICUS INSTITORIS, *MALLEUS MALEFICARUM*

The shocking news that Eliza had been arrested during the night raced throughout the town the next day. All morning people abandoned their work to cluster together in knots, whispering excitedly. Some heard the reports and were incredulous, but others declared they had known all along that there had been something most strange about the magistrate's new bride. Goody Holyoke recounted in hushed tones that once, on her way to the Sabbath-day meeting, she had seen Mistress Latham in the lane, followed closely by a black cat. And at the very instant Mistress Latham had crossed the threshold of the meetinghouse, Goody Holyoke remembered, the cat had screeched horribly, for no cause at all that she could see, as if someone had stepped on its tail. "And puffing all its fur about it, it was, with eyes a-burning like green lamps, all uncanny! It made me fair jump like a flea, I tell you; I said a prayer, for methought the Devil must surely be roaming abroad."

Other people also found themselves suddenly recalling similarly ominous bits and pieces. Everything under the magistrate's stew-

ardship had thrived this year—Captain Ingersoll had heard him remark only last week that this year's corn and cider crops were the
best he'd ever had. Some people now thought it strange that several
of his neighbors should have had such poor luck in comparison. The
magistrate's neighbor to the north, Goodman Wilkins, for example, had suffered the loss of three cows in one fortnight. And certainly the sickening of Goodman Peabody's son so soon after the
magistrate's wedding seemed suspicious. The fact that the lad had
shown himself to be stout and hale again within a day or two did
not cause nearly as much remark.

Men shook their heads, frowning seriously, and women clutched
their babes more closely to their breasts, shuddering at the thought
that the Devil had gained a foothold in the community. There was
no doubt in anyone's mind that such a dire menace must be dealt
with swiftly. Better that the eye that caused sin should be plucked
out and thrown away, everyone agreed, for all knew that God
would punish the whole community if the taint of evil were allowed
to spread. It was reassuring to many that at least the magistrate had
proven himself honest and God-fearing, willing to arrest his own
wife to prevent the danger. The fact that he had done so was also accepted as a sure sign of Eliza's guilt.

Everyone pitied Jonathan, but mixed with their sympathy for
him, people also felt a certain relief, even a measure of smug satisfaction. The Devil might have ensnared the soul of one person in
the town, and that was a grave and terrible matter. After all, however, she was a stranger. Deep down, many felt that making an example of her would be much easier than if she had truly been one
of them.

Patience did not hear any of the gossip until after most of her
neighbors. She had been called to a neighboring farm before dawn
to stay all day and into the following night by the bedside of a
woman whose labor pangs proved to be false. Returning wearily to
her home an hour after sunrise the next day, she found her neighbor Goody Griggs there, ostensibly to obtain some Solomon's seal

syrup. The garbled account of the previous day's sensation eagerly poured out by Goody Griggs astounded and horrified the midwife.

"God save me, I cannot believe it!" Patience cried passionately. "God forfend that such a wicked story be bruited about the town!"

Goody Griggs stared at her, wide-eyed. "What, say you so, Goody Carter?"

"She is no witch," Patience snapped. "Why, she has lived in my own house, and supped at my very table, and I know her to be a most right, proper, and God-fearing girl. Idle tongues may run on in the Devil's work, but——"

"The Devil's work!" Goody Griggs interrupted. "Aye, the minister and the magistrate themselves saw her conjure spirits. You dare not call *them* tattlemongers. And all the men who went together to lay her by the heels saw what lay inside that chest." As Patience glared at her, Goody Griggs added, "You are my gossip, and perhaps it is well you say this only to me. If the charges sworn out against her be proven, I would not think it wise to remind every Jack and Jill that she tarried long as a guest under your roof, consorting with you and your children." She placed a finger along the side of her nose with a significant look.

Patience's outrage seeped away, leaving a cold, sour residue of unease. "Bide but a moment, and I will fetch the syrup," she said gruffly, turning away.

As she measured out the medicine, her mind churned with fear and worry. Then she remembered something that made her breathe a sigh of relief. "They cannot do anything for many weeks," she remarked as she stoppered the flask and handed it to Goody Griggs. "Surely by now the court in Boston has finished its cases for the autumn season. They needs must wait until the court reconvenes."

Goody Griggs shook her head. " 'Tis said they do intend to try her here."

Patience's jaw dropped. "Try her . . . here?"

"Aye, in the local county court."

"But how can they do that?"

Goody Griggs shook her head. "I do not know."

Patience had reason to be surprised. For years, all cases of witchcraft had been tried in the great quarter court in Boston. But the changes in colonial government in the past year had literally swept away all the structures of the entire legal system, and the question of what court had jurisdiction to try a witch was no longer clear.

Whether a witch could even be tried at all until the Crown clarified the situation was a point that privately worried a few of the town selectmen. When the group met the next afternoon in the town tavern, argument waxed loud and hot. Some insisted that trial should take place immediately, and others warned that waiting until instructions should be forthcoming from England would be the wisest course to follow.

William, however, overbore this latter reasoning. To prevent the Devil from imperiling any more souls, he argued, the case should be tried locally, as swiftly as possible. One of the three judges for the panel had to be a magistrate, but the other two need only be associates.

"Reverend, the town confirmed you as an associate last year," Goodman Pitt suggested tentatively. "Could you not do it?"

William weighed the idea for a moment, tempted, but then regretfully shook his head. "I think it most right and proper that I serve instead as witness."

"Colonel Pynchon has volunteered to take a seat," someone offered.

William looked around; heads were nodding. "Very well, then. And for the second?"

Sunk into himself on a bench by the tavern's fireplace, Jonathan roused himself to speak for the first time. "Make it Captain Howell. He has proven himself to be astute in judgment as an associate on other cases."

William considered and then nodded. "A thoughtful, worthy man." He hesitated, licking his lips, and darted a look at Jonathan. "That leaves only the matter of the appointment of the magistrate."

Silence fell for a moment. Jonathan broke it finally, saying slowly, "Magistrate Quincy is frail. I believe he has lain ill abed much of the summer."

"He should step aside for another," one of the younger men grumbled.

Jonathan sighed. "Yet another matter that needs must wait for word from England." A line appeared between his eyebrows. "And Magistrate Cheever is not perhaps the best choice, either."

"Why say you so?" Lieutenant Sewell asked, frowning.

"He is a noted scholar of the law," Jonathan had to admit. "But . . ." His words trailed off reluctantly. In fact, Cheever had an exceedingly harsh view of the world and more than once had exhibited a hot, brittle temper in court. Heartsick, Jonathan pressed his lips together. He had believed in the sufficiency of justice all his life. But he wanted more than that for Eliza now; he wanted her to have the opportunity for repentance and redemption. Defendants who stood before Magistrate Cheever could expect to receive justice at his hands, true—but only the strictest kind possible, untempered by any hint of mercy.

As Jonathan considered, William watched his face carefully and came to a conclusion. The spouses of accused witches, the minister knew, faced the greatest danger of being charged themselves. That must not happen to Jonathan, William privately resolved, and it would not, if Jonathan could be shown to be utterly fearless in pursuing and rooting out evil, even in his own household. "Magistrate Latham," William said firmly, "I think you should be seated as the third judge."

The selectmen blinked in surprise. "Perhaps," Lieutenant Sewell said in a troubled manner, with a quick glance at Jonathan's face, "it would not be wise—"

William held up a hand. "Nay, not only wise, but appropriate, too. Has he not proven his courage and objectivity? Let no man doubt that Magistrate Latham puts his faith in the Lord before all, and that wisdom and prayer guide his actions. With his resolution serving as an example for us, will not the Devil flee immediately from our midst?"

Jonathan felt a faint hope stir. The scriptures, he reminded himself, said that an unbelieving wife may be sanctified by the husband. Perhaps he *was* the best hope she had. Not as a way to allow her to escape from justice, no—but he knew her better than any man in the town. It could be he had the fairest chance of persuading her to turn from evil so her soul could be reclaimed. The test to his own faith might be severe, but . . . He took a deep breath. "I am willing to do it."

Several other men still looked doubtful, but none voiced any further objections. William smiled, relieved. "Then shall we send riders for Howell and Pynchon?"

"Do as you will." Jonathan rubbed the stubble on his face wearily. "I pray they may come swiftly. I had liefer not let this business linger long."

He lapsed into a brooding silence again then, leaving it to William to give the order to send riders to find Captain Howell. When the discussion had wound down to uneasy mutters, William dismissed the other selectmen. Taking a tankard of cider and a plate of woodcock stew from the innkeeper and bringing them over to the fire, he nudged Jonathan's shoulder with the tankard. "Drink. Eat a little. Did you break your fast this morning?"

"No." Jonathan eyed the plate with reluctance, and then sighed and pulled it toward himself. He took a sip from the tankard and a few bites of the stew, forcibly swallowing them down with a grimace, and then looked up as a thought occurred to him. "What has she had to eat today?"

William shrugged. "She must pay the gaoler's fee, of course. Ten pounds. And then she will be fed if she can pay for her maintenance."

Jonathan's eyebrows drew together. "I had forgotten." He looked down at his spoon. "Tell the gaoler I will pay him twenty pounds for the fee and her maintenance. Let him see to it that she has all her meals." He spooned another mouthful of stew.

William felt a wave of irritation at this show of concern. He tried to keep his tone of voice mild, however, when he spoke. "You might have better use for your money than a witch's food and drink."

Jonathan's eyes flashed at him. "Do you think the Devil will keep her from starving? I intend to pay the fee, I tell you."

William lowered his eyes. "As you will."

A pause fell, punctuated by the peaceful crackling of the fire. "How does she?" Jonathan asked at last, his voice a thread. "Did the gaoler say?"

"She does not even pretend to hide her work now."

"Then she is still . . . ?"

William nodded. "Her hands never cease their labors." He got up to look out the window at the small, rough prison building across the town square. "Some say that in Hell the demons force the damned to work without rest." He mulled this over for a moment and then added with quiet, savage satisfaction, "She will feel quite at home there, no doubt, when her sentence is carried out."

Jonathan flinched, but said nothing.

The days grew shorter and the nights longer. Locked in the gaol and fettered hand and foot, Eliza suffered greatly from the increasing cold. Although the gaoler had received money to feed her, he feared her evil eye, and so her meals were all shoved through a slot in the door, leaving them sometimes out of her reach. Her single window was barred, and through it she could only catch a glimpse of the sky, never another person's face. She had no way to wash, and her cell quickly acquired a fetid stink.

And yet if she could have spoken, she would have called her prison heaven on earth, for now all her time could be devoted to working on the coats for her brothers. For the first few days after her arrest, she concentrated on spinning thread from the newly broken nettles. Since her spindle had been taken, she was forced to spin a coarse thread by rolling hanks of broken nettle fiber against her hip and thigh. She struggled with the puzzle of how to continue fashioning the coats without her hand loom. Then she found a few sticks in the straw on her cell floor, and after scraping off the bark and grinding points on two of them against a stone, she began knitting the tenth coat with raw, bleeding hands.

There was no doubt in her mind about the danger she faced; she had seen the execution of a convicted witch in England. Even more painful than suspense and fear was the searing memory of the expression on Jonathan's face the last night she had seen him. And so she did her best to consign her fear and her memories to God. Instead, to give herself courage, she tried to keep her thoughts fixed upon her brothers' desperate need, and her hope of freeing them. They, too, had been falsely accused, she reminded herself. She kept the coats heaped all about her, as if the men they were intended for were gathered around to comfort her. All her will, all her faith and devotion, made her fingers fly in their work, faster and faster, as if her labor were a prayer. Never had she worked so swiftly.

She had finished the front half of the new coat and was just about to begin one of the sleeves, when the sound of the bolts being drawn back on the door made her start. She scrambled to her feet and warily faced the man who stooped his head and entered her cell.

"The court summons you to the meetinghouse, for your trial begins this morning."

She put her work down carefully and shook her skirts out as best she could. After he unlocked her irons from the staple in the wall, she followed the man out of the cell into the pale sunlight, her heart beating quickly.

The trial, of course, was necessarily a one-sided affair. Every bench in the meetinghouse was full, and both the spectators and witnesses leaned forward eagerly to hear every word of the proceedings. The accused, however, could say nothing to defend herself.

Jonathan sat at the front of the meetinghouse, between the other two judges. When the guard brought Eliza in and guided her to her place opposite the judge's long table, Jonathan kept his face set and still only with iron self-control. He thought that the long hours of prayer and reflection had prepared him to see her again without any danger. He watched her carefully as she sat on the stool provided for her. A straggling tendril of her hair escaping from her cap caught a ray of sunlight, dazzling his eye with a tiny golden glint. His breath caught in his throat. He had always trusted himself, trusted his own discernment. Now, however, he felt a stab of doubt in his ability to act as her judge, guided only by cool detachment. He wondered suddenly whether he might be under her spell even still.

William came in and seated himself to one side as the guard withdrew. He leaned forward, frowning, to study Eliza. The movement caught Jonathan's eye, and he glanced over at him. William offered Jonathan a small smile and a nod, trying to convey all the reassurance he could. Jonathan returned the nod, without the smile, and then picked up one of the papers the clerk had placed before him and pretended to review it.

Eliza looked up and saw Jonathan sitting directly across from her. She realized with a shock that he was wearing his magisterial robes. Until that moment, she had never considered that he might be the one to decide her fate. She felt the threat of a rush of tears, and after that, she did not dare to look at him. Mostly, she kept her gaze fixed on the links of the chains resting in her lap. Her fingers occasionally twitched, as if with eagerness to return to their work.

Ceaseless silent prayer ran through her mind, so seemingly loud in her own imagination that she barely heard the clerk's instructions, the reading of the counts against her, the excited gabble of the listeners. Only when William stepped forward and recounted his story in a cold, clear voice did she raise her eyes in hurt bewilderment. She understood fully how badly the bare facts he told made her look. What she could not fathom was how God could allow His minister to act as her chief accuser. All her dedication to her task, her silent suffering for her beloved brothers, was held up before the congregation as something twisted and evil, deserving only condemnation. Her inner prayers faltered as his revulsion and contempt shocked and stung her. She stared at him with a small frown, wondering if everyone else in that assembled company could sense the spiteful malice oozing from him as clearly as she. He glowered back at her levelly, the corner of his mouth tugging up in a sardonic smile when she slowly shook her head.

A parade of witnesses followed with stories like the account of Goody Holyoke. Mistress Latham, they declared, had appeared in spirit form to threaten good people in their dreams. She had sent a storm that had threatened the crops; she had sent demons to harass and terrify children and animals. Like a miasma arising from a swamp at dusk to infect the community, she was the secret, silent cause of every possible setback, every accident, and every thwarting of God's will to reward the elect.

"What have you to say to these accusations?" they formally asked, in accordance with the ritualistic formula. "Will you not turn from this evil now and repent?" She almost laughed at the uselessness of the question. The fact that she could not answer was not in the least inconvenient to them. They had already made up their minds.

No hope of mercy would be found here.

The other two judges picked up their quill pens and wrote on pieces of paper before them; Jonathan merely toyed with his pen, the expressionlessness of his face masking the seething turmoil of his mind. The clerk stepped forward to retrieve the papers inscribed by Colonel Pynchon and Captain Howell and then bowed to Jonathan, who folded his paper, too, and shoved it forward with a quick, impatient gesture of despair.

A hush fell. The clerk unfolded the first paper. "Guilty."

The second paper was the same as the first. "Guilty."

No one moved. No one breathed.

The clerk slowly unfolded the third paper, blinked at it, and looked over his shoulder uncertainly. "Your Honors . . . the third paper is . . . empty?"

A muted roar broke out, and Captain Howell, frowning, thumped on the table with his fist. "Silence!"

Harsh cries seconded him, and the crowd hushed again. People craned their necks and leaned forward. "I cannot do it," Jonathan said softly, as if to himself. "I cannot condemn her."

"But . . . how can the verdict then be entered, sir?" the clerk asked, baffled. "The judges must speak unanimously."

Jonathan drew a deep breath. "The people must decide," he said harshly. He clenched his fingers around a fold of his robe, cursing himself inwardly for his cowardice.

A dead silence fell, broken finally by a mutter from somewhere in back; no one saw who spoke: "Guilty."

"Guilty," someone else repeated.

William rose to his feet. "Guilty," he said loudly.

Jonathan closed his eyes in despair as the approving mutters became cries, loud and insistent: "Guilty, guilty!" Eliza sat up very straight and still, torn between pity for him and terror for herself.

"Condemn the witch!"

"Aye, let her die."

"Innocent," called a voice firmly from the back.

Heads turned to identify the speaker. It was Patience. She stood. "She is innocent, I say."

'People nudged one another, shifting on their benches to look back at her, and a low buzz arose.

William leaned forward. "Your Honors," he said, sensing the undercurrent in the room hesitating, as if about to change direction, "the people have already condemned the witch. I urge the court to order the verdict entered."

"Does this court have the authority to enter that verdict?" Patience replied loudly, scornfully.

"Woman, by what right do you—" Colonel Pynchon began hotly, but Captain Howell's hand on his wrist interrupted him.

William gestured urgently, and when Jonathan looked over at him, eyebrows raised, he said, "A word in private, Magistrate Latham?"

Jonathan shook his head, indicating to William that he should take his seat again. The minister did so reluctantly. Patience waited, her arms crossed over her stomach, something like a smirk on her face as a buzz arose and several of the town selectmen shifted apprehensively in their seats.

Captain Howell bent his head to say in a low voice in Jonathan's ear, "It may be prudent to recess the court. If you are wishful to hear her speak, be ruled by me and hear her privately."

"I cannot like it," Jonathan said.

"She sees the weakness of our position," Colonel Pynchon muttered.

"Aye," Jonathan said, "and so she must be answered."

"But not publicly!" Captain Howell exclaimed, sotto voce.

"Indeed, publicly. If there be challenge to our authority, all must be satisfied with the reply." Jonathan turned and gave a low-voiced instruction to the clerk.

The clerk stepped forward. "Goody Carter, you are bid to approach the bench."

Patience, with a grunt, squeezed her way out of her row of benches and marched down the center aisle toward the front. Eliza looked up for a moment, gave her a fleeting smile, and then dropped her gaze back to her lap.

Jonathan studied the midwife as she came to a stop before his table, and she returned his gaze with a defiant lift to her chin. "You are not an attorney, Goody Carter," Jonathan remarked mildly. The room echoed with nervous laughter. "What argument are you wishful to make touching upon this court's authority?"

Patience licked her lips. "Your Honors, I know I am no lawyer. But my husband stood before the bench a time or two." She waited as the room rumbled with laughter again, for Josiah Carter, a great one for quarreling with his neighbors, had been constantly embroiled in legal suits, both as plaintiff and defendant. "I have learned a mite or two about courts over the years, I trow."

Jonathan considered her with hooded eyes, and the nervous chuckles died away. "Say on," he said abruptly.

"How, sir, can you presume to preside as judge in a case where the defendant is your own wife? Surely the law of England cannot allow such a thing!"

Jonathan said slowly, "I did not pronounce judgment against her."

Patience nodded. "Because you ask the people to vote for you. Do you not then slight your duty as magistrate?"

She waited, but Jonathan, flushing a little, dropped his gaze and did not reply. After a moment, she continued, saying, "Witchcraft is a capital crime. Why then is this case not being heard in Boston, where all felonies are to be tried?" Her eyes narrowed. "With no charter and no government since Andros has been ousted, can this case even be legally heard at all?"

Jonathan opened his mouth and closed it again, soundlessly. The other two judges exchanged frowning glances.

Patience shook her head in contempt. "You have no right to judge her. None of you do!"

Unable to contain himself any longer, William jumped to his feet again, furious. "You are pert, madam, you are saucy," he shouted over the rising mutters. "You push too far."

Patience rounded on him. "How, sir? By urging that the law be heeded?"

"Is it the law you heed? Or is it something else?"

Patience glared at him hard. "Come, unfold yourself, Reverend. What mean you?"

"You are very free and bold indeed, to defend a woman who has been seen to conjure spirits." He cocked his head, adding with heavy sarcasm, "Or did you forget my testimony?"

"Nay, I did not forget." Now it was Patience's turn to shuffle her feet uneasily.

"Oh, you did not forget." He came closer to her. "Perhaps you wish *us* to overlook it."

"I . . . simply do not know if I believe the tale."

"Do you not?" William sneered. "Do you not? You stand forth and proclaim her innocent. But yet you admit you do not *know.*"

He waited. Patience reddened but did not reply.

Eliza tightened her fingers around the fetters resting in her lap, and the shifting of the links clattered loudly in the breathless silence.

William came closer yet, and the click of his shoe heels sounded slow and deliberate. He lowered his voice. "Or perhaps you have . . . conflicting loyalties?"

Patience frowned. "Come, sir, what do you insinuate?" She tried to speak bravely, but her voice sounded small and breathless to her own ears.

William leaned forward and, his words pitched for her ears alone, said, "Have you signed the Devil's black book, Goody Carter?" As she stared at him, torn between wrath and dread, he added, raising a finger to rub the corner of his mouth leisurely, his gaze fastened on the mole at her upper lip, "Do you suckle a familiar? Hmm?"

She itched to slap the smug look from his face. And then her children's faces suddenly arose in her mind. The enormity of her danger made the hot replies crowding at the tip of her tongue congeal into dust. She felt a panic-stricken urge to flee, and her eyes darted toward Eliza. One misstep now, and the midwife knew she would soon be standing beside her, accused of the same crime.

William rocked back on his heels, smiling affably. "Well, then?"

She tried to wrap her dignity around her like a shawl. "I . . . I serve God only, the God who made the heavens and the earth." She waited, trembling and furious, for him to repeat his accusation for all to hear.

William studied her, seeing her fear and drinking it in. He rocked forward again, ready to open his mouth and deliver the blow—

"Reverend Avery," Jonathan said. At the sudden interruption, Patience jumped nervously. The minister glanced over, and Jonathan raised his eyebrows. "If you have aught to say to Goodwife Carter," he told William, "you must speak so that the clerk may record it and the court may hear it, too."

The minister wavered for a moment, tempted, and then he shrugged. "Well, then," he said heartily to Patience, "if you are God's servant, surely you know we are God's servants, too. Do you not?" He opened his hand, like a cat releasing a mouse it had been toying with.

"I know it, sir," Patience forced out between her teeth.

"We are here only to do God's will."

"Aye, sir."

"Then you do not dispute this court's authority now?" He lifted an eyebrow.

Patience's shoulders slumped, and burning with shame, she mumbled, "I didn't . . . I do not mean . . . God knows I do not dispute it." She shivered. "I cannot," she added bitterly.

William pointed to Eliza. "Is she innocent?" he asked, the menace in the question making the threat clear.

Patience wanted to turn, to meet Eliza's eyes and beg silently with her own, *Forgive me.* She did not dare. She merely stood, tongue-tied, hands twisting in her apron.

The corners of William's mouth twitched with triumph. "Have you not wasted enough of these learned men's time, Goody Carter?"

She turned and stumbled to her seat.

Eliza let out a long, shuddering breath. Jonathan stared bleakly into space as the room hummed with excited whispers, until a tug on his sleeve by Colonel Pynchon recalled his attention. The three judges huddled with their heads together, conferring in hushed voices. Finally, Captain Howell nodded, reached for a piece of paper and dipped his quill into the inkpot. The crowd hushed itself as he scratched a few words on the paper, blotted it, and handed it to the clerk.

The clerk scanned it and looked up. "Mistress Latham, arise."

Eliza did so, stiffly. The links of chain that had rested in her lap fell to the wooden floor with a loud thump.

The clerk held up the paper and cleared his throat. "This court finds the prisoner, Elizabeth Latham, guilty of the most grievous, heinous, and unnatural crime and sin of witchcraft and hereby sentences her to death. Elizabeth Latham, you are to be returned to the custody of the gaoler until an hour after dawn a fortnight hence. On the morning of the twenty-first day of December, in this year of Our Lord 1689, you will thence be conveyed by cart to the place of execution, there to be hanged from the neck until you are dead.

"And may God have mercy upon your soul."

When they thrust Eliza back into her cell, she reached out blindly for the coat she had been working on, longing to lose herself in the comfort of her task—only to discover that the knitting needles she had so laboriously fashioned were gone. Although the gaoler had not dared touch the coats or the thread she had already spun and wound into a ball, he had stolen the needles as soon as she left the cell. She scratched through the straw frantically but failed to find them, or any other stick that she could use to make new needles. Finally, she curled up in the filthy straw and wept in silent misery for a long time, until her eyes felt as if they had been scoured with sand. Then she slept.

The sound of a tray being shoved through the slot awoke Eliza again, and blearily, she sat up and brushed straw away from her clothes. Although she had no appetite, she pulled the wooden trencher of fish and boiled apples toward herself and resolutely began to eat. She had a fortnight left, she reminded herself, and the coats were not yet complete. Allowing herself to become sick or faint because she had refused her food would do her brothers no good at all. As she ate, she stared at the half-knitted coat lying beside her, wondering how she could possibly complete it now. First her frame loom had been destroyed, and then her knitting needles taken— Her teeth crunched on a fish bone, and she froze, her eyes widening as an idea blossomed.

Elated, she pulled the fish bone from her mouth and squinted at it in the dim light of the cell. That bone was small, but there were larger ones, too, still attached to the fish's spine. Delicately, she extracted one, carefully breaking it off so that part of the vertebra was still attached, forming a crude hook at the end.

Then she reached for her thread and slipped a loop around the hook to begin crocheting.

Ostensibly, life returned to normal rhythms when the trial was over. It was meat-curing season, and there were tools to be mended and meals to be cooked. Women still exchanged visits to trade spun wool for cloth, and men still gathered in the tavern to discuss politics. As always, each household assembled for devotions at dusk, and the Sabbath-day services were attended as usual.

And yet tension lingered below the surface, mounting every day as Eliza's execution date drew nearer. William had been satisfied by the trial's outcome, and yet in the days that followed, he had difficulty concentrating while trying to prepare his sermons. His concern for Jonathan distracted him, and so he spent as much of his time with his friend as he could. Although the minister had to admit the man seemed to be maintaining his dignity, he sometimes noticed a look in Jonathan's eye in unguarded moments that made him feel very uneasy. William took to inviting Jonathan to dine with him every night, an invitation that the magistrate usually accepted gratefully. It allowed Jonathan to avoid his own home in the evening. The memories of the quiet hours he had spent by the fireside with his wife were still too painfully raw.

Patience kept close to her house during this period. Eventually, however, it occurred to her that hiding from her neighbors might prompt dangerous talk, and that conversely, wagging tongues might best be stilled by going about her customary occupations as much as possible.

So she tried to show her usual interest in the health of babies, the lancing of boils, and the application of poultices. No one mentioned the magistrate's wife to her, or Patience's outburst in court. Yet whenever Patience walked by the town gaol, she cringed inwardly with shame, although she never looked at the building.

Sometimes, late in the still hours of the night while she kept watch over a sick patient, she wondered what more she might have done. No matter how much she turned it over in her mind, she could not see any way that she might have saved Eliza without endangering herself.

But this conclusion did not make her feel any better.

On the day before Eliza was to be hanged, William came to Jonathan's house in midafternoon in response to a summons from one of the magistrate's servants. He was admitted at once to the front room, where Jonathan sat at his desk looking out the diamond-paned window, turning a quill pen listlessly in his hand. He looked up with a tired smile as William removed his hat. "Good afternoon, Reverend. I am most grateful you could come."

"Good afternoon." Worriedly, William considered the lines of strain around Jonathan's eyes. "Tell me how I may be of service to you."

"I have sent for the midwife," Jonathan said, putting down the quill.

"The midwife?" William repeated, bewildered.

"I anticipate her arrival at any moment." Jonathan raised his eyes fleetingly and then looked at the floor. "So she may perform the examination."

"But why— Oh." William rubbed his chin uncomfortably. "Oh, aye, of course."

"I am the presiding judge and thus the responsibility to give the order is mine." He folded the piece of paper before him and pushed it forward. "You see the difficulty."

"I do. Shall she, er, be expecting the summons?"

"I do not know. Perhaps. Perhaps not. In any case, I expect some awkwardness. And I would be most grateful . . ."

Enlightenment dawned on William's face. "Would you like me to give her the instruction?"

Jonathan's eyebrows rose, and then he nodded, relieved. "I had not thought—but yes, that would be a great kindness, if you would. I shall be present, of course."

"Will she—" William began, but broke off at a knock on the door.

"Enter," Jonathan called, and Goody Grafton opened the door and bobbed a curtsey.

"Begging pardon, sir, but Goody Carter has come as bid."

Jonathan and William exchanged looks. "Show her in, please," Jonathan said.

Goody Grafton stepped aside, and Patience entered the room. Her eyes widened at the sight of William, and as Goody Grafton left the room again, shutting the door behind her, Patience flinched at the sound.

The three stared at one another for a long moment. "Thank you for being so good as to come," Jonathan said mildly at last.

Patience bit back her initial retort, which was to reply that the magistrate's servant had not given her much choice in the matter. "What will you be wanting from me, then?" she said, at once nervous and defiant.

Jonathan looked at William, who cleared his throat. "Goody Carter," William said in his deliberate way, "I am sure that you know that tomorrow is the date—"

"I know what tomorrow is."

"Yes. Well. Both custom and law require that when a female prisoner is to be executed, she be, uh, examined. We need to know that she will not be pleading her belly."

"Pleading her belly? Is that not why she was condemned, because she could not plead at all?" She snorted and muttered under her breath, "As the lamb before the shearers is dumb—"

"*What* did you say?" William snapped.

Patience stared at him hard and wisely decided not to answer that directly. Instead, she said, "She cannot speak a word to defend herself, Reverend. How then do you expect her to make her plea?"

William felt a wave of impatience at her obtuseness. "In order for the sentence to be carried out, there must be an affidavit sworn declaring that she is not now with child. You are the midwife. It is therefore required that you—"

"No!" Patience exclaimed with rising horror. "You cannot ask that of me!"

"Cannot?" William said frostily. Patience flushed deeply as he raised an eyebrow. "Do you wish to revisit our earlier discussion, Goody Carter, about what the court can and cannot do?"

Patience opened her mouth to reply hotly, but Jonathan looked up, meeting her eyes for the first time. "Please. Please, Goody Carter."

She wondered afterward whether he had meant then to signal to her that she should lie and declare Eliza pregnant, to delay the execution. But she was too angry to think of that at the time, so angry that she took the only revenge she could. "Oh, aye, indeed," she exclaimed, " 'twill be so much easier for you to sleep at night, knowing you did not murder your own unborn babe on the gallows. Only your beloved wife!"

"I do not murder her," Jonathan said, white to the lips.

"Yet you will not lift a finger to save her," Patience cried to Jonathan. She pressed a hand to her lips, and the tears spilled over onto her cheeks. "And yet how may I rebuke you for that? Am I not as great a palterly coward as you?"

A dreadful silence fell, and then Jonathan said gently, "I can do nothing, Goody Carter." The agony in his eyes made Patience's breath catch in her throat. "God help me, I love her still. That must be my punishment, for I fear my love will condemn me to eternal damnation.

"And yet I cannot save her."

Patience drew a shaky breath and dashed the tears from her face with an impatient hand. "I will do as you ask," she said gruffly. "Perhaps that is my punishment."

Jonathan dipped his quill in the inkwell, scratched a name on the square of paper before him, and handed it to Patience. "Take this to the gaoler and give it to him. He will take you in to see her."

Patience looked down at the paper in her hand. "If it must be done, it were best if done by a friend." Lifting her chin, she gave her eyes a last wipe with her apron and marched from the room, shutting the door firmly behind her.

After Patience had left, Jonathan blew out a breath and rubbed his hand over his eyes. "Do you remember the first thing I ever said to Elizabeth? When we found her in that cave?" Jonathan closed his eyes. The memory of his first sight of her came back to him, as she crouched in the dimness of the cave's recesses, hair tumbled wildly down her back, staring up at him with wary, huge eyes. "She was so afraid of us. And I said to her, 'We are not savages; we will not hurt you.'" He sighed. "Alas, that the first thing I would ever say to her would be a lie."

"Jonathan," William said, somewhat at a loss, "you forget where the fault truly lies."

"Do I?" Jonathan shook his head. "Goody Carter may be right. I rescued Elizabeth from the wilderness. But I have brought her to this place, where she shall die tomorrow. And you say I play no part in what is happening to her?"

"I am sorry. I do not know how to answer your pain." William eyed him worriedly. "Come sup with me tonight, Jonathan."

"Again?" The corner of Jonathan's mouth quirked ruefully. "I fear I have burdened you o'ermuch with my company as of late." He sighed. "I needs must face my own hearth alone some evening, Reverend."

"Yet must it be tonight?" William hesitated. "God has asked much of you, and I know that what is to come tomorrow shall be . . . very difficult."

"Difficult," Jonathan repeated, as if tasting the word and finding it wanting. He smiled without humor. "Yet remember, Reverend, those whom God loves, He chastises. Indeed, I must be His favorite child."

William tried to smile, although he found Jonathan's feeble attempt at levity chilling. "Do not persevere in this fond humor. You must not condemn yourself so heavily. Or let a friend bear you company, at least."

Jonathan heard the warm sympathy in the minister's voice. But the thought of Eliza, alone in her cell awaiting the dawn, made him want to recoil from William's compassion as something undeserved. "I think it were best if I keep vigil alone tonight."

"If there is aught else I might do to succor you . . ."

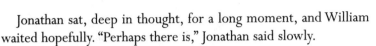
Jonathan sat, deep in thought, for a long moment, and William waited hopefully. "Perhaps there is," Jonathan said slowly.

"Only name it."

"There is one who needs comfort even more than myself. If you would, I ask that you go to the gaol to be with Elizabeth during her final hours."

"Me?" William replied in disbelief. "You want me to go?"

"Aye. I do not like to think of her being alone tonight." There was a moment's pause, and then he added in a low voice, "And if I were to go instead, I am not sure whether . . . whether I could trust myself."

Although he tried to hide it, William's reaction was utter dismay, for instantly he knew that the one thing that Jonathan asked of him was above all the one thing he did not wish to do. To cover his agitation, William rose and went over to the fire, ostensibly to warm his hands. "What you ask is unusual," he said crisply. "I believe witches are executed without benefit and comfort of the clergy."

"By custom, yes, but not by law."

"Does it mean that much to you?" William said, with his back still turned toward Jonathan.

"Reverend," Jonathan replied huskily, "if you would stay with her tonight, to tell her that God still waits to welcome home the soul that is lost, that would be the greatest comfort you could ever give to me."

"Very well, then," William said, turning around. He felt a touch of pride at how well controlled he kept his face and voice. "I will, of course, do as you ask."

William stopped at his home to pick up his Bible and then turned toward the gaol. Patience was just leaving as he approached it. He stopped in her path, blocking her way. "Well?" he said gruffly. "Is she with child?"

Patience pulled up her hood. "She is not."

William eyed her, noting carefully the rebellious set of her mouth. "Your examination must have been swift. It was also thorough, I trust?"

"There was no need," Patience replied, drawing on her mittens with quick, angry movements. "We were both spared that, at least. No, her courses are upon her. Once she understood what I wanted, she showed me her bloody clout; she had fashioned it from a bit of her petticoat."

She meant to embarrass him, and she had the satisfaction of seeing his face redden, but he merely asked again politely whether she was quite sure.

"You need not fret yourself, Reverend. Her womb has not quickened, and so there's naught to prevent her from dying tomorrow." She gave him a sharp look. "I am sure you will joy at this news."

He regarded her coldly. "I like not your manner, Goody Carter."

"Oh no, do you not?"

"A froward, mocking tongue does not suit a Christian woman."

She shrugged, and her anger held an edge of tiredness. "You have always hated her. I wonder why." She walked away as he stared at her openmouthed, unable to think of anything sufficiently cutting to say in reply.

After a moment, he forced himself to unclench his hands and turn back to the low building before him. He was here on an errand of mercy, he reminded himself, as a favor for a good friend. As he entered, the gaoler hurried forward, and after the exchange of a few words and the paper Jonathan had given William, the gaoler led William to the door of the chamber where Eliza lay.

At the rattle of the door latch, Eliza started in surprise and then scrambled to her feet to stand in the corner, hugging her work closely to herself. William was forced to stoop to enter. Though sunset had not yet come, he had to blink for a moment or two, waiting for his eyes to adjust to the room's dimness. The rank smell in the cell made his nose wrinkle.

He removed his hat, and the wild hope that had flared for a moment in Eliza, that Jonathan might have come to see her once more, died when she saw her visitor's face. He saw the eager light fade in her eyes and guessed what she must have been thinking.

As the gaoler shut the door again, William hesitated, once again at a loss for words. Greeting her with a *good evening* seemed absurd under the circumstances. He cleared his throat. "Magistrate Latham asked me to come."

She waited a moment and then lifted her chin and tilted her head a fraction, like a bird, meaning *Go on*.

William clutched his Bible tightly. "He was wishful that I stay the night with you," he said a trifle too loudly, "to offer God's comfort for what lies ahead." He stopped again. Speaking to her directly made him uneasy in a way he did not understand. It did not occur to him that he had avoided ever doing so until now.

Slowly, without taking her eyes from him, she stooped with a clatter of chains to pick up a handful of fibers with a blistered and bleeding hand. The juice and stinging nettle hairs had taken their toll where she spun the thread against her hip, and now a spot on her side, under her thin, worn clothing, was beginning to ulcerate.

He stared as she began rolling the next section of thread. "You do not repent? You continue with that Devil's work?"

Her eyes narrowed in anger, and he took a step back warily. But she did not move, and he straightened up again, ashamed of his own cowardice.

"You are a fool," he whispered hoarsely. "They are going to hang you tomorrow. Do you understand what that means?"

She looked away from him, continuing to twist the fibers against her side.

"They will wrap a rope around your neck and then push you from the scaffold. If you are unlucky, and your neck does not break at once, you will be left to dangle there, kicking, with your lungs burning and piss running down your legs until your heart finally stops. And when you are finally dead, they will cut your body down and consign it to the fire. *That* will be consumed, but the fire where your soul burns will never be quenched throughout all eternity. Do you not fear that?"

Eliza shook her head wearily.

"Death holds no terror for you? Not even everlasting damnation?" He could see the tension in the cords of her neck. He knew he was betraying the trust Jonathan had placed in him by speaking to her so. But the set stillness of her face goaded something inside him, igniting a hot spark that quickly fanned into a burning rage, pushing him past all caution, all memory of his own responsibility. "I only wish we burned witches alive here as they do in England," he hissed. "If you had to face the flames, I warrant you would find a tongue then to scream for mercy." Her face did not move, but he saw a change in her eyes.

Without knowing it, in probing for a way to hurt her, he had blundered through her wall of reserve and touched upon her deepest fear. She saw it all, suddenly, as he had described it to her: they would drag her up, to scaffold or stake, what difference did it make? And her blazing desire to live to live to live would burst from her heart and throat in desperately screamed words, despite all her efforts, despite her fear and her love, slaying her brothers, too, as her own life was ripped away.

Eliza dropped the thread and clapped both hands over her mouth as if to keep words from boiling forth. William's eyes widened as she half fell to her knees, a strangled noise in her throat.

"You do not dread death." He seized her arm, a fierce exultation rising inside him, for he sensed he had stumbled close to the heart of the mystery. "You fear something will force you to speak. Because you can speak, can't you?" He watched terror blossom in her eyes. "You can, I know you can! What keeps you silent?" He dropped his Bible and grabbed her other arm. "What is your game? What have you done to Jonathan?"

She tried pulling away from him, her terror changing to bewilderment, and he shook her until her chains rattled. "How did you entrap him in your toils? What foul spells did you use to seduce him?" The fetid stink from her clothing arose in his nostrils, underscored with the taint of blood. A picture arose unbidden in his mind, of Jonathan reaching out to cradle her body against his, greedily pressing hot kisses on her breasts to taste the salt of her sweat. She arched her back luxuriously as Jonathan's hands roved along her flanks, burying themselves in her hair, and then she lifted a leg over him to sit astride, smiling in triumph as he thrust eagerly inside her. Something within William cracked open in raw pain, and his rage utterly mastered him. "How did you make him love you? How did you make him love *you* instead of . . . instead of . . ."

His breath clotted in his throat, choking him, and they both froze, staring at each other, panting. And then he shoved her from him violently as if she were a viper. Jerked to a stop by her chain, she thumped to the floor, hitting her head heavily, and then raising it groggily to look at him in astonishment. William's fury drained away as if someone had unscrewed a stopper in his shoe heel, letting it all empty out into the straw.

How did you make him love you instead of me?

As he stood there stupidly, feeling his hands beginning to shake, she stood and raised her hand to kiss her wedding ring, her eyes flashing fiercely. She thumped that hand against her heart and then swept a finger up to point to the door. The meaning was plain: *Go now.*

William retrieved his Bible and hat and staggered to the door. He thumped on it until the gaoler came to draw back the latch. Then he stumbled out without looking back.

Eliza sank back into the straw, trembling. She plucked the coats out of the straw and pressed them to her, rocking back and forth. But the familiar comfort they had given her was gone, leaving her thoughts to whirl in painful confusion.

She had believed in her bright messenger, believed in her dream. Now, as she laid the coats in her lap and stroked the fabric, each one more hastily made and ragged than the last, Eliza felt the firmness of her faith crumbling beneath her, like a path dissolving at the very edge of an abyss. She marveled now at her own credulity, her reckless readiness to throw away her life because of something as ephemeral as a warning from a dream. She shook her head as if to clear it and raised her hands to stare at her oozing, blistered fingers. A sudden, cold thought made her heart sink: What *good* could it possibly do to labor making coats out of nettles? And *why* did she have to remain silent? Eliza's hands fell away from the coats. If all her toil failed to save her brothers, and she perished for nothing, what did her silence and suffering accomplish? What were they *for?*

And yet, if she were wrong, if she spoke and her brothers died for it . . . Her soul cried out in wordless desperation for surety, for a sign—and then she started violently at the whistling thump behind her.

Eliza's head snapped up, and in the last ruddy light of the setting sun, she saw a swan's wing beating against the barred window of her cell. *Benjamin!* The cry remained locked securely inside her, without even a thought of being spoken aloud, and in that moment she understood her prayer had been answered. She flew to the window, thrusting a shackled hand out to touch his feathers, and her heart sang within her even as she sobbed for joy. Hope still remained, even on the very last night she had to live. Her task was nearly complete, and her brothers had found her again.

Chapter Twenty-two

Suffering produces endurance, and endurance produces character, and character produces hope, and hope does not disappoint us.

—ROMANS 5:3–5

Even without a job, Elias's days were full, and frequently seemed to require more energy than he had available. Besides his time spent with Sean, he squandered hours on the phone each week wrangling with faceless, humorless bureaucrats about Sean's insurance coverage, an exhausting, frustrating process that made him feel as if he were trying to swim in gelatin. He continued researching the newest word on treatments and talking with Sean's doctors. He began consultations with Patty and GMHC about getting himself signed up with Medicaid. Friends called regularly to keep tabs on Sean's health and to pass the word along about other people's sicknesses. At Sean's insistence, he duly repeated this information when he came to the hospital each day, in a ritual Elias mentally dubbed "the roll call."

He didn't like doing it. Sean's strength was obviously dwindling, and Elias worried that each announcement about someone's new KS diagnosis or dropping T-cell count robbed Sean of a little more hope.

"I don't know why he's so adamant about pumping me for information," he complained to Rick. "You'd think he has enough on his mind without worrying about how everyone else's drug treatment is going."

Rick looked thoughtful. "I wonder. You know, I remember he loved playing poker in high school, and he was always real sharp about keeping track of other people's cards."

"So?"

"Maybe he wants to know because he thinks it'll give him a better idea of his own odds."

There might be something in that, Elias thought. Yet there was a reason Elias dreaded the roll call, and finally, he decided to talk with Bill about it.

"Did you really expect otherwise?" Bill asked when Elias explained. "He's a reporter. He's nosy. He's curious. Don't you think it's a good sign he's still interested in what's going on around him?"

"Yes, but why does it have to be this? Why does he want to know about other people dying?"

"I don't think he thinks of it that way. I think he wants to know about how other people are fighting against dying."

"Hmm."

"On the other hand," Bill added, "maybe he's probing because he doesn't want to come right out and ask you what he really wants to know."

"What are you talking about?"

"What do you think?"

Elias sat for a long moment, kneading his hands together. "Every time I tell him something I've heard about somebody," he said softly, "Sean'll ask me, 'Is there anybody else?' And I . . . just haven't figured out a way to tell him 'I've got AIDS, too.' "

Bill nodded. "I'm sorry, Elias."

"I've known for a while." Elias gave an embarrassed shrug. "I've got people to talk to and everything."

"Except Sean, right? Elias, when I finally told people I was gay, you know what the biggest surprise for me was? It was that so few people were surprised. People often know more than you think they do."

Elias thought back on the months before Sean had told him of his own diagnosis. "Yeah. I guess so."

"So what's keeping you silent? You're not going to make me sorry I did that union ceremony, are you? What do you think together in sickness and health means?"

He went to see Sean afterward. The phlebotomist had just finished drawing Sean's blood for the weekly complete blood count. She trundled the little cart of equipment out the door as Elias came into the room. He went over to the bed to kiss Sean gently on the forehead. Sean, drowsing, didn't look up.

Elias ran his fingers slowly from Sean's neck down to the tips of his fingers, trying to recapture the tactile memory of strong muscles under smooth skin. All gone now: instead, Sean's skin felt hot and slick with clammy sweat, fragile enough to split at the slightest pressure over the sharp edges of bone. A prickling rash covered his forearms, worsening into open lesions over his hands. An IV dripped into his arm, and a purple bruise showed above the edge of the dressing at his inner elbow. The sheet laid over the rest of his body did little to hide the wasting underneath. Sean's lips were cracked and bleeding, and the fungus in his mouth gave his breath a sour stench.

"Sean?"

"Mmm." Sean shifted wearily, his legs moving restlessly, as if trying to find a position free from pain.

"How did you . . . how did you find the nerve to tell me you had AIDS?"

"You told me to just blurt it out, so I did. That's what you'll have to do, too."

"Is that so?" Elias said, eyes stinging.

"Mmm-hmm." Sean looked up at him with dim, sunken eyes. "Come on, now. Blurt."

Elias swallowed. "I have AIDS."

Sean nodded. Tears trickled slowly down his face. "I'm sorry, Elias. So sorry I won't be there to help you when you go through this yourself." He batted at the moisture on his cheeks, as if too weak to wipe it away. "But I'm glad you've told me."

Elias got a tissue and mopped him up, and Sean dozed off soon afterward. Elias stumbled over to the chair and gratefully surrendered to oblivion.

When he awoke again, the doctor was conducting an internal exam. Sean's sheet had been pulled back, and the doctor was bent over the bed, percussing Sean's withered body with light taps, his face serene and intent. *Thoom, thoom,* came the sound from under the swift, strong fingers over Sean's lungs, *thoom, thoom.* Elias watched, rapt, to see his lover's body manipulated like a great, bony xylophone being played by a virtuoso. The sound changed over the abdomen to *thunk, thunk,* and then *tup, tup.*

Sean grimaced. "My intestines keep going out of tune. How come there's never a pitch pipe available when you need it?"

The doctor didn't laugh. He put the stethoscope to Sean's skin, over the jutting ridge formed by his ribs, and listened. Elias tried to guess whether he liked what he heard. It was hard to tell; the doctor had a good poker face.

Finally, he pulled the earpieces out of his ears and raised the sheet over Sean's chest again. "How is the eating? Better?"

Sean shrugged, apparently not quite willing to lie out loud.

The doctor sighed. "We'll wait for the results of the blood count. Then we'll talk further." Slowly, he pulled the stethoscope off his neck, coiled it up, and put it into the pocket of his coat. "Meanwhile, I must ask you to make a decision." He pointed to a piece of paper lying on the table, which had been pushed to the side during the exam. "New York law stipulates that, unless a patient signs this form—it's called the 'Do Not Resuscitate form'—every in-house cardiopulmonary arrest must be immediately treated with a full-scale resuscitation attempt."

"Meaning CPR?"

"Mmm-hmm. CPR and more. Regardless of the chances of success."

Elias felt queasy. They both knew what that meant. Sean's last roommate, another AIDS patient, had suffered a code blue the previous week, and the frenetic, violent flurry of people and equipment around the bed had terrified them both. Elias could still vividly remember the sickening *crunch* as the man's breastbone and ribs broke under the force of the physician's assistant pounding on his chest. His eyes had bugged out, body jerking violently from the pressure of the pushes, as vomit oozed out from underneath the edges of the bag mask the nurse used to pump oxygen into his lungs. Eventually, they had moved him down to the ICU, still barely alive as far as Elias knew. He wasn't sure if it was a life worth living.

Sean stared at the piece of paper on the table as if it were a snake that somehow had wriggled onto his dinner tray. "So we're at that decision point already?"

The doctor hesitated. "A good doctor tries to prepare for all eventualities."

Sean made a face. "Especially the most probable ones. So does the good little patient, I suppose." The sarcasm in his voice stung.

"Do you want to sign the form?" the doctor prodded gently. "Or do you want everything possible done to keep you alive?"

Sean looked at Elias. "I'm *tired*, Elias," he said, his voice cracking.

Elias did not misunderstand him. *Tired of the pain. Tired of dying.* "I know," he replied as soothingly as he could. "You've done the best you possibly can. I . . . want you to do whatever seems right for you to do. I'll support whatever you decide."

Without hesitation, Sean picked up the pen and weakly scribbled his name to the form. The doctor had to hold the paper steady for him. When Sean was done, the pen dropped from his fingers as if he were too weary to hold it upright anymore. Looking relieved, the doctor picked up the paper and tucked it under the clip on his clipboard. *He thinks Sean did the right thing.*

"I wonder," Sean said in a small voice as the doctor left, "how much time I really have left."

Elias tried to smile. "The same that all of us have. You've got the rest of your life."

"Ah. Then I'd better make it count." He shifted again, painfully. "Smuggle up some Guinness the next time you come, okay?"

But the next time Elias came, obediently bearing Guinness, Sean was in no condition to drink it. He was unconscious, breathing in fitful jerks. A newly erupted red rash with a white, ashy coating covered his yellowing skin.

"That's the candida, the same fungus that's causing the thrush infection in his mouth," the doctor said. "The main problem is the neutropenia, as I feared. But his kidneys are shutting down, too. And there are other infections that we don't entirely understand. The antibiotics aren't—"

"How long do we have?" Elias asked numbly.

"I can't say exactly."

"Of course not." Elias closed his eyes, hearing the sarcasm in his own voice, but he couldn't bring himself to care in the least.

But if the doctor noticed, he didn't seem to take offense. "A few days, I think. A week at the most."

Elias nodded. "All right." He went to call Patty and Sean's parents.

Time began flowing strangely. Janet and Jim came from Boston to wait with him. Patty was suddenly there beside him, pressing a mug of stew into his hand and making him eat it. He shoveled it into his mouth absently without tasting it, only vaguely aware that the heat of it had burned his tongue. Leo, Nick, Kiyoshi, Frankie— a parade of friends shifted in and out of his peripheral vision like the flickering images of a kaleidoscope. He thought he heard Irish music once; had someone brought a tape recorder? The room darkened, lightened, and darkened again. People came and went, and he forgot that they were ever there, for all he saw was Sean, dimly, through a shifting scrim of tears. And Sean couldn't see him at all.

This couldn't be the end, he thought over and over again. If only they had more time! Time enough for a new treatment, a cure . . . and worse, he hadn't even had the chance to say anywhere near all the things he now desperately wanted to say. How could you pack a lifetime's worth of words to the person you loved the most in all the world into just two or three days? Impossible: the very thought choked him, and so he said nothing at all as he sat, holding Sean's hand, hour after weary hour.

Gradually, the sound of crying penetrated his consciousness, a thin, animal wail of pain. He recognized it, for something inside him was making the same sound. Blearily, he tore his gaze away from Sean's face and looked up. Janet stood at the foot of the bed, clutching a rosary, her weeping muffled on Bill's shoulder. He bent his head, whispering something in her ear. Jim sat perched awkwardly balanced on the windowsill, his eyes bleak as the barren winter landscape outside as he stared at his dying son.

Janet raised her head, tears streaming down her face. "But how?" she choked out. "Why? I've held on to God, believed in him all my life. How could God do this to him? What has he done to deserve this?"

Bill shook his head. "No, Janet, don't. That's the trap Job's friends fell into, thinking that suffering comes only as punishment for the guilty." He gripped her shoulder, gave it a little shake. "This is AIDS. It's a disease, not a punishment. It takes down the innocent and the guilty both." His red-rimmed eyes glistened as he looked down at Sean, lying on the bed. "And even the guilty could never deserve a death as ugly as this. It's our failures and our fears that have spread it. Not God's vindictiveness."

She shook her head, a trembling hand wiping away her tears.

Sean's voice came suddenly then, a ghost of a whisper that startled them all. "Rafe."

"What?" Janet pulled away from Bill and leaned forward. "What did he say?"

Sean's head lolled on the pillow. His eyes were open now, but didn't seem to see them. "Jerry."

Elias leaned forward, too. "Jerry's not here, Sean."

If that penetrated, Sean gave no sign. "Ian."

"Who is Ian?" Jim whispered hoarsely, coming over to stand by the bed. "Does he . . . does he want us to call him, or something? Bring him here?"

"We can't," Elias said. "Ian died of AIDS."

"Harry. G-Gordy."

Realization came slowly. "They're all people he knows who've died of AIDS."

Sean mumbled something, another name perhaps; Elias didn't catch it. His eyes shifted to a point above Elias's shoulder.

Janet stared at Sean, wide-eyed. "Can he . . . can he *see* them? Is that what's going on?"

"I don't know," Elias breathed. His skin prickled with awe. He had no trouble believing it though, the gathering of unseen friends around the bed, come to help ease the soul's journey from the body.

I've fought so hard for you, Sean. I never understood until now that the hardest thing of all to do would be to let you go.

Sean breathed more slowly and fitfully now, releasing each lungful of air with a low moan, like a woman laboring to bring forth a child. Dying looked like hard work, Elias thought, but then Sean had never been afraid of hard work. He hoped Sean wasn't afraid now. He lifted Sean's hand and kissed it with infinite tenderness, savoring the warmth that ebbed from his thin flesh, like the last flicker of a dying ember.

"Philip."

Elias raised his head. "I didn't even know Philip was dead yet," he said numbly, his tears falling on Sean's fingers.

"Last rites," Janet said suddenly. "Can we get someone to come here to do the last rites?"

"Do you think he would want them?" Jim said.

Janet looked at him with surprise.

"I mean because of the problems he had with the church, maybe he would prefer not to . . . ?" His words trailed off uncertainly. Janet looked stricken.

"I don't know," Bill said slowly. "We hadn't talked the decision through yet. I thought we would have more time."

Elias thought Janet was going to protest, but then to his utter surprise, she turned to him instead. "Elias? Would it be all right with you?"

"You're asking me? I'm not even Catholic."

"You're his partner. I think . . . if he can't tell us, he'd want you to be the one to decide."

"I . . . Bill, could you do it?"

Bill hesitated. "Not the official sacrament, no. I don't have the book or the oils, and I'm no longer a . . ." His mouth trembled, and he said quickly, "But we can all lay hands on him, and I'll say a prayer for him, commending him to God."

Elias nodded numbly. "I think Sean would like that."

They all gathered around the bed to place their hands on Sean. Elias gently clasped Sean's hand in his.

"Go forth, Sean, from this world in the name of God the almighty Father, who created you, in the name of Jesus Christ, Son of the living God, who suffered for you, in the name of the Holy Spirit, who was poured out upon you, go forth, Sean. May you live in peace this day, may your home be with God in Zion. . . ." Bill spoke evenly, deliberately, his voice soothing, as if lulling a child to sleep. It was only when Elias raised a hand to wipe his own eyes that he saw the tears on Bill's cheeks as well.

When Bill had finished speaking, they all raised their heads and opened their eyes. Sean was quiet now, his breaths much more shallow and far apart. His feet were blue and stiffly arched down. Elias picked up the Kleenex box on the bedside tray and offered it to the others.

Bill took one and Jim did, too, blowing his nose with a honk, but Janet didn't notice, for her eyes were still fixed on Sean. She tugged at her husband's arm. "There isn't much time," she said tensely.

Then she looked up at Bill. "Could you . . . I'm sorry, but isn't there a way to have a real priest come, so that he can be absolved?"

Bill looked at her for a long moment, saying nothing. Elias felt his own throat tighten in pain and outrage. *Sean would have wanted no one but Bill!* But then Bill managed a flicker of a smile. "No, of course. Let me call Father Tom for you at once."

The hospital chaplain came quickly in answer to the summons, bringing his stole and the consecrated oil. Through his tears, Elias watched Sean take his last short breath just as the priest began the same prayer that Bill had used. Gradually Sean's open mouth turned into a faint smile. Then he lay still and silent, an empty husk discarded on the bed. His parents, absorbed in their private prayers, did not notice.

Elias reached over and touched Sean's claddagh ring. *Go in peace, with all my love.*

But oh, I will miss you so.

"I want to thank . . ." Elias paused and took a deep breath to keep control of his voice. "I want to thank you all for coming." He looked down at Sean's rose-covered coffin, lying before the altar. "Sean always liked a good crowd at his concerts. I think he would have appreciated a turnout like this one today."

There was a slow rumble of laughter from the pews, even as people wiped away their tears. Janet lowered her head and pressed a tissue over her mouth.

"I've looked for the right words to say to honor Sean, but . . ." Elias faltered again, "it's very hard. Sean was the writer. I'm a photographer; I tried to think of a picture to tell you about, to show you how I feel about him. The problem is, there isn't just one picture; there are so many, because Sean Donnelly was everything to me. He was my friend, my teacher, my lover, and in the end, he was my life's companion.

"Sean and I met a little over three years ago. Not many of you know I was living on the streets when he found me. He took me in, helped me find a job, gave me a home. By sharing his own life with

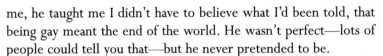

me, he taught me I didn't have to believe what I'd been told, that being gay meant the end of the world. He wasn't perfect—lots of people could tell you that—but he never pretended to be.

"There are people who are totally convinced that AIDS has come as a punishment from God. If I had never met Sean, I might have believed that." His eyes met Sean's parents'. "And there are others who maybe aren't convinced that AIDS is a punishment, but deep down, they still wonder why.

"Well, I don't have to stand up here and tell you that Sean didn't deserve this. Nobody deserves this. It's not our business to pass judgment on Sean or anyone else with AIDS. I think instead that it's our job to judge ourselves, on whether we supported him or failed him when he needed us. Maybe that's why AIDS has come: it's our opportunity to show how we love one another.

"Evaluating his life is now a matter between Sean and his God. I don't know what his God will think of him—they've had their differences in the past. But I hope . . ." He felt his throat closing. "I hope that Sean's God will look as kindly on him as Sean always looked on me."

There was a pause, and then he painstakingly loosened his grip on the lectern and stepped down stiffly. Nick, sitting in a chair to the right, picked up his harp and began to play, softly, his wet face bending close to the strings. It was a lament by O'Carolan, written upon the death of his best friend. Sean had always loved it.

Elias walked to the altar and picked up the white rose lying there. Its scent was cool and soft and sweet. He went to place it on top of the red roses resting on Sean's coffin.

Chapter Twenty-three

The latest sun is sinking fast, my race is nearly won
My strongest trials now are past, my triumph is begun
O come Angel Band, come and around me stand
O bear me away on your snowy-white wings to my immortal home.

I know I'm near the holy ranks of friends and kindred dear
I've brushed the dew on Jordan's banks, the crossing must be near
O come Angel Band, come and around me stand
O bear me away on your snowy-white wings to my immortal home.

I've almost gained my heavenly home, my spirit loudly sings
The Holy ones, behold they come, I hear the sound of wings
O come Angel Band, come and around me stand
O bear me away on your snowy-white wings to my immortal home.

——J. HASCALL AND W. BRADBURY, "ANGEL BAND"

When William stumbled out of Eliza's cell shortly before sunset, the gaoler took one look at his face, suffused with horror, and cried out, "In God's name, Reverend, what has the witch done to you?" William shook his head, unable even to attempt an answer, and fled the gaol. His steps turned instinctively toward the empty meetinghouse, where he had always chosen to go whenever he needed comfort.

But a long night spent pacing and praying in the dim, cold building with only a single lit candle to keep him company only deepened his anguish. For the first hour, his thoughts were a mixture of sheer fury and icy panic. When he had entered his accusation against Eliza, he had believed her to be a powerful witch, and he had braced himself for the danger of challenging the Devil. But never in his worst nightmares could he have dreamed that Hell would counterattack in such a way. Even in the midst of his wrath, a part of him marveled at the foul, vicious *cunning* of the strike against him. Somehow, the forces of evil had possessed him—him, a minister of God!—with the foul lusts of a Sodomite toward an honest man, the man who had been his dearest friend. . . . William paced, almost flying from one side of the wall to the other, raking his fingernails at the tears running down his face, longing desperately for a way to reach inside himself and tear out the poisonous evil from where it had rooted in his heart.

For as if a veil had been dropped from his eyes, he saw the depth of his own lust, unimagined until now: he wanted Jonathan, oh yes, he did. He burned to put his hands on Jonathan's body and press his mouth to Jonathan's mouth. He ached to have Jonathan return his kisses with urgent, answering desire, as Jonathan's strong hands seized his own body, and . . . William groaned in heartfelt despair, wondering how any witch could have imagined such a damnable spell to cast over him.

Then he frowned, perplexed, and his pacing slowed. He tried to regather his scattered wits and think back over his extensive studies, straining to remember whether he had ever heard of any case of a witch creating such a spell. Sitting on a bench, he began methodically sorting out his memories.

All ministers were familiar with many kinds of *maleficium,* the supernatural harm performed by witches: children and animals could be made to sicken and die; people could be bewitched into strange behavior, or cursed with losses of memory or periods of confusion. William knew that witches visited the afflicted in spectral form to bite and pinch and smother. Witches could also perform other mischief, such as ruining the brewing of beer or the spinning of wool. But something like this . . . William frowned again. Witches themselves were reported to be lecherous, craving fornication with the Devil. But he had never heard of a witch attacking anyone by implanting the lust of a Sodomite into an innocent heart.

The cold of the empty meetinghouse seemed to sink into his bones, chilling him to the marrow. Desperately, he tried to remember when he had first felt his suspicions about her. He had objected when Jonathan proposed bringing her back to the town. He had tried to block their marriage, too. Now he wondered whether she had sensed from the beginning that he was her enemy, and had made him her very first victim.

And then another layer inside him cracked open, and the unexpected and terrible truth shone forth with a clarity that stopped his breath. It flooded the secret recesses of his soul, illuminating an ugliness he had harbored within, never dreaming it was there. No, this was a taint that had been inside him long before they had found her in the woods. It had always been there, buried deep within his sinews and flesh, waiting only for the first sight of Jonathan to awaken it. Jonathan was not to blame, he was sure. Jonathan had never acted in any improper way or shown the slightest sign of awareness of William's feelings—not any more than William had guessed himself. But somehow William knew that, had Jonathan ever realized the truth coiled deep in William's soul, he would have turned his face away in revulsion.

And if so, William realized in growing horror, perhaps she could not be blamed, either. He would have been jealous of anyone who had come between him and Jonathan. Her arrival had simply forced the issue. His reluctance to allow Jonathan to marry, his eagerness to level the accusation of witchcraft, the motives of protectiveness he had prided himself upon: all simple covetous envy, nothing more.

A part of him protested feebly at the thought. He had seen Mistress Latham conjure ghosts, he reminded himself. Surely she was truly a witch. But a cold suspicion remained inside him that, even if she were, he should not have been the man to make the accusation. He had relied his whole life long on an inner certainty that he was one of the blessed elect, that the Lord had written his name in the Book of Life since before creation began. A new certainty now gripped him: he would not stand with the elect at Judgment Day, for he was instead one of the eternally damned.

He raised his eyes up to the dark ceiling and wept. How strange, he thought, to know himself damned and yet still long with every fiber of his being for Heaven. How painful to think himself incapable of love, and then, when he had finally found it, to discover that love has brought only destruction.

William felt light and hollow, like an empty eggshell. He wiped away the last of his tears and glanced toward the window. The first signs of lessening darkness were just beginning to show in the east.

Slowly, he rose and went over to the candle and stared into the flame. The words spoken before the congregation when a soul was excommunicated came back to him: *Whatever is bound on earth shall be bound in Heaven, and whatever is loosed on earth shall be loosed in Heaven. . . . Depart now into the darkness, cut off from the church and cursed forever, into the eternal fire prepared for the Devil and his angels. . . .*

William blew the candle out.

Benjamin had stayed with Eliza until after the sun had set and so was forced to return through the woods on foot to find the rest of the brothers and bring them back with him. As the coming dawn slowly warmed the darkness with a misty grayness, they gathered in the yard in front of Jonathan's house and beat upon the door with their fists. Goody Grafton came awake with a start at the tremendous noise. Hastily wrapping a shawl over her nightgown with trembling hands, she hurried down the stairs and fumbled to unbolt the latch.

The sight when she opened the door rendered her speechless. A crowd of men, dressed as fantastically as princes, turned their faces to her earnestly. "Is this the house of the magistrate?" James demanded.

She blinked. "Aye, it is," she replied warily. "And who might you be, asking after him?"

James and Henry exchanged nervous looks, and James took a deep breath. "Go tell him the sons of the Earl of Exeter require immediate speech with him."

"The sons of— Are you mad?" she exclaimed, clutching her shawl to her throat more tightly. "What idle tale is this? Nay, by my life, I cannot wake him now. Why, 'tis not even dawn yet! You must come again later—"

"We have traveled all the night to find this house; dawn will be too late! We must speak with him this moment!"

"Go and rouse him at once."

She stared at the pale, eager circle of faces. "This is a house in grievous trouble, and my master is sick at heart and has barely slumbered this night. He shall not be disturbed at *my* doing."

Charles elbowed his way toward the door. "But we *must* have words with him! We have come to see him about the young woman kept in the gaol—"

Goody Grafton's eyes narrowed. "What business have you with the magistrate's wife?"

Charles's jaw dropped as the others gasped. "His wife!" Charles exclaimed. "Is she his *wife?*"

"Aye." A spasm crossed Goody Grafton's face. "His wife they are to hang this morning for being a witch."

"*What!?*"

"No!"

"In God's name, woman—" Frederick began desperately, but as they all started forward, she took fright at the ferocious light in their eyes, slammed the door shut, and bolted it.

Instantly, they began beating on the door again, shouting for admittance. Trembling, Goody Grafton retreated a step on the other side and then, covering her ears, fled to rouse the manservant Jonas.

After a few minutes, during which time the brothers continued to batter the door, Jonas came, slid back the bolt, and opened the door to look out into the yard, frowning. Goody Grafton peered over his shoulder. "What's all thi—?" Jonas began and then stopped, his eyes widening.

"We *must* speak with your master at once."

Jonas stared. "Now then, what fleering impudence! The magistrate, look you, cannot be pulled out of bed for every japing Tom, Dick, and—"

" 'Tis near dawn," Stephen cried urgently, looking over his shoulder. *"Please."*

"Open the door to us!"

"Nay, I'll not—"

"Damn your eyes, man!" Henry exclaimed in exasperation.

"I don't hold with that kind of talk. You go back to where you came from and wait—"

"Stand aside or we'll cut your throat!"

With an oath, Jonas slammed the door shut. But the brothers fell on it from the other side, and the door jerked under the servants' fingers as they struggled to shove the bolt closed again. Goody Grafton yelped in fright.

Behind them, Jonathan clattered down the stairs in his nightshirt, drawn by the noise. "Jonas," he said blankly, holding a candle high, "what in the name of Almighty Heaven is causing that fearsome racket?"

" 'Tis a most villainous group of strangers, master," Jonas said over his shoulder as he continued struggling with the bolt. "They curse us, demanding that you speak with them."

Jonathan lifted his head to listen, a crease between his brows. Thumps and cries of "Open up! Open up!" came, muffled through the door.

"Stand aside, Jonas," Jonathan said, striding forward.

Jonas hesitated, but Jonathan reached out and slid back the bolt under his reluctant fingers, even as the cries on the other side of the door changed into incoherent, panicked shouts.

As Jonas stepped back, Goody Grafton quavered, "Oh, have a care, master." Jonathan gave her a frowning look and threw back the door.

And ducked, stunned, at the wild flapping of powerful wings in his face. A flock of swans rose from the yard in panicky haste, circled the house once, and flew off toward the east. Jonathan slowly rose from his crouch and took a step over his threshold, openmouthed in astonishment, squinting after them as they disappeared into the pale yellow light of the rising sun.

When they came for her, Eliza was ready. She had already donned the coarse garment of sackcloth they had given her. Terrified that her coats would be taken from her even now, she kept the ten completed and one unfinished coat clutched tightly in her arms, and the last pitiful remnants of spun nettle flax wadded up in her hand. The gaoler edged back warily as she stepped out of the cell, but as she turned away from him, he suddenly darted forward and snatched the fish-bone hook she held in her fingers. She almost shrieked aloud in rage and frustration. She and the gaoler glared at each other, and then the guards raised their flintlock pistols menacingly. Eliza backed away, hugging the coats even more tightly. No one moved, but no one attempted to take the coats from her either.

One of the guards licked his lips. "Yonder is the cart," he said, gesturing out the door. After a long pause, she turned in the indicated direction and stepped barefoot out into the snow.

The morning had dawned pale and clear, and a white hoarfrost still clung to the trees, outlining each twig with a delicate edging of crystalline lace. Eliza shivered, and her breath puffed out and lingered visibly in the air. Before her, an old horse stood in front of the gaol, harnessed to a cart piled high with straw. The horse looked over its shoulder at her and blew out a snorting breath, its sides shuddering.

"Get in," said one of the guards behind her.

She stood for a long moment, swaying, feeling the blood drain from her cheeks, and horror made her sight dim. But they prodded her firmly in the small of the back with a pistol, and with a shudder, she forced herself to scramble into the back of the cart. Quickly, she piled the ten completed coats around herself, laid the eleventh in her lap, and began knotting and looping the flax on the uncompleted sleeve by hand, her lips moving in silent prayer. With a violent lurch, the cart began to roll.

People began to stream out of houses as the cart passed, craning their necks to stare at Eliza, their faces variously curious, somber, and hostile. One of the onlookers was Patience, and she dropped her eyes, ashamed, as the cart passed her, but Eliza did not look up. At first all were silent, but as the cart drew nearer to the place of execution and the crowd followed it, murmurs started and gradually grew louder.

"The witch . . ."

"See, there the witch goes. . . ."

"Look how she mutters."

"She prays to the Devil to rescue her."

"She has no hymnbook in her hand."

The crowd grew thicker, and the people following the cart jostled one another. As Eliza's fingers flew deftly, looping and winding the flax, some dared to walk closer to the cart and shove the rails to make it rock. Eliza cast one despairing look toward the sky and then bent to her work again, warily tucking corners of the coats under her knees to keep them close to her.

Jonathan and William stood waiting near the foot of the gallows. William had been there since dawn. When Jonathan had walked up and taken his place beside him, the two men said nothing to each other. But as the cart turned the corner of the path and came into sight, Jonathan's fists clenched convulsively. "She made no sign of repentance to you while you were with her, Reverend?" he said, prodded by the last feeble stirrings of hope. "Perhaps, even now . . . if a confession could be prepared . . . if she would set her mark to it . . ."

"I am sorry," William said, gently but inexorably. "But no. She never ceased in her work while I was with her." He swallowed, unable to meet Jonathan's eyes, and his face grew hot. "She made it clear she was not wishful for me to stay."

"Then it is all over," Jonathan said to himself numbly. "For the last hope is gone."

William heard him and closed his eyes, as if the words had rendered a mortal blow. His own torment was not finished, he realized bleakly; it would never be finished for him, not until the day he died. Even when the witch was hanged and her body burned, things would never be the same again between him and Jonathan. He knew better than that now. "Indeed," he said hollowly, stone-faced. "Soon this shall all be over."

The mutters of the crowd grew louder and more menacing as the cart came closer.

"Still she works at her foul sorcery."

"Destroy the witch's work."

"Aye! Tear it from her hands!"

Fingers began reaching through the rails of the cart, grasping at the coats. Eliza made a strangled noise in her throat and threw herself over them—and then looked up at the cries of amazement from the crowd. What she saw sent her spirit soaring in glad astonishment.

For the eleven swans had swooped down and alighted on the cart. Hissing, arching their necks and flapping their wings over their heads, they clouted at the few unlucky enough to still be near. The buffets from their wings were like blows from a cudgel, and the people scrambled back in alarm. "What does it mean?" they exclaimed to one another, terrified.

Jonathan and William each fell back a step, too, their mouths open in amazement. Patience stared at the swans, her heart beginning to hammer, and with a glad cry, she began pushing her way forward through the press of people. "Innocent!" she cried. " 'Tis as I told you! She is innocent! See, God sends His own angels to protect her."

Her shouts penetrated William's shock, and his fists clenched. Innocent—could she truly be? If *she* were innocent, could even he . . . And then he remembered the ghosts in the graveyard, and he shook off his paralysis. "Executioner," he shouted with a sweeping gesture, hardly knowing whether he was reaching for salvation or putting the final seal on his own damnation, "the gallows await. Take hold of the witch at once and do what you have been charged to do."

"Wait, wait!" Jonathan cried, even as the executioner stepped forward, reaching into the cart to grasp Eliza's hand and drag her forth. Before he could touch her, she scrambled out of his reach, snatched up one of the finished coats and jammed it over the head of the nearest swan. A flash of brilliant light flared, making people scream, and Hugh's head burst from the neck of the garment. As his arms transformed back, thrusting through the sleeves, his fist shot out, connecting with the executioner's jaw in a meaty, satisfying crack. The man dropped into the dirty snow as if poleaxed. "Get back!" Hugh roared.

Eliza threw a coat over another swan's head, and with another flash, Charles appeared. He sprang up to guard the other side as the rest of the swans hopped down from the cart railing into the straw, their heads bobbing up and down in excitement. The people screamed and the horse reared in panic as Eliza seized coat after coat, transforming her brothers back, one after another. For a flurried minute, all was screaming and flailing wings and flashes of light and confusion. William backed up, trembling, until he felt a post supporting the gallows at his back. Jonathan remained rooted to the spot, frozen in astonishment.

Eliza threw the last coat over the last swan. The spell's dissolution revealed him to be Benjamin, but the coat had not been finished, and he had a swan's wing instead of an arm. She leaped to her feet then, her eyes wild.

"Now I may speak!" she cried in a cracked, hoarse voice. "Hear me speak!"

The crowd hushed in awe.

"I am innocent! I am . . ." Her eyes rolled back into her head, and she sank into Michael and Geoffrey's arms, overcome at last by suspense, anguish, and pain.

"Elizabeth," Jonathan whispered in the shocked silence. "Elizabeth!"

"Aye, she is innocent," James said, standing up. He went to the rail of the cart and raised his voice to address the crowd. "By the most solemn oath, by the blood of the blessed Christ Himself, I swear to you that she is not a witch!" he cried raggedly. "We are the sons of the Earl of Exeter, and she is our beloved and faithful sister. We were placed under a spell by our mother-in-law and have been doomed for the past eight years to assume by day the form you have seen. All our sister's labor has been to undo the terrible evil done to us, and free us of the magic's curse. She is not a witch; she has been undoing the work of a witch! We have resumed our true forms only because of her perseverance, in the face of all who tried to prevent her from finishing her task."

The crowd wavered, breathless, torn by doubt, not knowing what to believe. "But the ghosts," William whispered in bewilderment. "Why then did the ghosts . . . ?"

Jonathan felt the blood drain from his face. "She did not conjure them," he breathed. "They came instead to frighten her, to stop her!" Remorse, grief, and rage at himself shook him. "Just as *I* tried to stop her!"

And then a woman's voice cried out, high and thin, "Look you! Look!"

William felt something at his back, glanced behind himself to see, and scuttled back a step, openmouthed. The faggots piled high for the burning had taken root in the snow and burst forth with climbing vines. Branches were thrown out, and more vines hurried up, as if leaping out of the ground. Soon the pile of wood and the timbers of the gallows were entirely covered with buds, which quickly opened up into hundreds and hundreds of red roses, nodding above the snow. A sweet fantastic fragrance filled the air.

"A miracle," someone breathed.

One deep crimson blossom nodded just above William's shoulder. He reached with a trembling fingertip toward the velvety petal edge—but then drew back and turned his face away, ashamed, nails cutting into the palms of his hands.

On the top of the pile, one bud opened into a perfect white rose, shining like a star. Moving as if in a dream, Jonathan reached up and plucked it and then came to the cart, where Eliza's brothers knelt bent over her, chafing her cheeks and bleeding hands. They looked up at Jonathan and sat back as he climbed into the back of the cart.

"Is she . . . Does she live?" he said fearfully.

"I do not know," Benjamin said, blinking back the tears in his eyes.

"Elizabeth," Jonathan whispered, clutching the rose tightly and looking down at her.

James looked up at him solemnly. "Her name is Eliza."

"Eliza?" Jonathan knelt down beside her in wonder and took her hand. He laid the white rose upon her breast, and its scent was cool and soft and sweet. "Eliza." Tears sprang to his eyes. He could hardly believe it; he had thought she had betrayed his love, but now he understood that instead he had betrayed hers. "She cannot be dead!" he cried, his voice cracking, unable to bear it. "I must not lose her now, before I can make my confession to her!"

"Nay, look you, she breathes."

"Eliza?"

Slowly, her eyes fluttered open and he held his breath. A tear trickled down her cheek, and she smiled up at him. "Eliza," he said brokenly, "oh, Eliza, I have wronged thee so. Oh, how my pride and cowardice must have hurt thee! Thou wert true and faithful always, even when I . . ." His own tears nearly blinding him, he pushed a tendril of her hair from her eyes. "Canst thou ever find it in thy heart to— Nay, I cannot even dare to ask it. I do not deserve it." He squeezed his eyes shut, bending over her, his tears raining down. "God forgive me for being such a fool!"

She raised her hand and placed it against his cheek. "Jonathan . . . Jonathan, I love thee," she whispered.

Astonished, he opened his eyes and looked down at her. At the look in her eyes, he captured her palm and pressed a kiss against it, hardly daring to believe in the grace that allowed her to forgive him. "And I love thee, Eliza."

He reached for her hesitantly, almost afraid, but she raised his hand to her lips and drew his other arm around her. He helped raise her shoulders so that she could sit, and she laughed as her brothers embraced her. They all turned their faces to the sun to watch the birds that came from every direction, swooping and diving over the profusion of roses, singing as if in the garden of Paradise.

Epilogue

June 25, 1988

The cab pulled up to the curb on Fifth Avenue, and Elias fumbled at the door handle with stiff and swollen hands for a moment or two before managing to open it. His GMHC buddy Tim came around to the other side to help him get out. Elias straightened up slowly and turned to look out over Central Park as Tim turned back to the cab and paid the fare.

I'm glad I lived long enough to see this day.

"You got your balance?" Tim asked as the cab pulled away.

Elias took a tentative shuffle forward and nodded. "Yeah. I think so."

"Do you think you can make it down the path here? There's a little slope."

"Yeah, I can make it. I think. If we stop to rest a few times."

Slowly, with Elias leaning heavily on Tim's arm, they picked their way along the path heading for the Great Lawn. Walking hurt. He had so little flesh left now that his feet felt like bony sticks, making balancing difficult, and he could feel the fissures between his toes and on the soles of his feet starting to crack and bleed again.

It had not rained for many days. The grass was all dead, baked to straw, and the air hot and dry. *Everything is desiccated, ready to blow away on the wind. Just like me.* The dust swirling around them made him double over, racked with hoarse, hacking coughs, and they had to halt several times to allow him to get his breath back. People streamed past them, all heading in the same direction. When the two of them finally came out of the shelter of the trees, Elias paused and gasped, squeezing Tim's arm tightly.

"Oh, man," Tim breathed.

The Quilt lay spread out majestically before them on the Great Lawn, arranged in blocks surrounded by a white plastic walkway. It was spectacularly varied in style and materials, bewildering the eye with a hodgepodge of colors and textures. At the same time, it was a formal unity, pulled together by the repeating pattern of the squares of fabric and bound by the walkway, like a white frame. People gathered around it on all sides, clustered along the edges. The scale of the Quilt made them look tiny in comparison. Some of the squares were still empty; the unfolding ceremony was still going on.

"It's so huge!" Elias whispered. He was not prepared for that. He had seen many of the panels already while working on Sean's at the Lesbian and Gay Community Services Center, but knowing how many there were still did not ready him for the visual impact of the Quilt being displayed, lying under the scorching sky. And the panels here today represented only a small portion of the Quilt as a whole.

"Everyone's so quiet," Tim said, his voice hushed, too.

The unfolding teams, groups of people dressed in white, continued to work their way down the Great Lawn toward the southern end of the Quilt. Slowly, reverently, each team circled a square bundle of fabric placed on the ground. They stopped and stood still for a moment, holding hands around their bundle. Then, they stooped and pulled back the folds from the center and laid them on the grass, making a larger square. They stepped to the side and pulled back the second set of folds from the center, stepped to the side again and pulled back the third set of folds. Then they lifted the Quilt block high like an offering to the heavens, and the cloth billowed up as if inhaling. They paced a few steps around to the left in a circle to align the Quilt block with the others and gently placed it on the ground, completing another portion of the pattern.

All in utter silence.

Elias felt tears in his eyes. "It's so beautiful."

After a moment, Tim stirred. "Didn't you say Sean's parents were coming to this? Are you planning on meeting them somewhere?"

Elias nodded. "Down by Sean's panel, in half an hour." They had offered him the chance to go on ahead, to allow him some time alone with his memories before they joined him. It was an example of their sensitivity, another reason why he had grown to love them so.

He had tried several more times to contact his own parents and his brother, but all his overtures had been rebuffed. They had hung up on him whenever he called, and returned his letters unopened. It had hurt like hell, but Janet and Jim had stepped into the void, moving to New York to care for him as he weakened. They were his parents in truth now, just as Sean had wished. *He would have been so pleased.*

"How do we figure out where the panel is?" Tim asked.

"We need to ask one of the volunteers. They're the ones in the pink T-shirts."

A volunteer checked the list and directed them to a block about a third of the way from the northern end, along the edge. They started walking again, but soon their steps slowed as one panel after another caught their attention. The colors and shapes and textures that had seemed so jumbled together at a distance now resolved themselves into discrete stories, portraits of individual lives. *Michael Pappas . . . Blossom . . . Luis . . . Rocky Saterwhite . . . Bill "Leggs" Bohle . . . Julianna . . . Freddie . . . Dick Ammons . . . Ben Connors . . .* Glitter, teddy bears, neckties, baby shoes, photographs, university pennants, military medals, feather boas . . . *Alex Vallauri . . . Dion Sexton . . . New York Rebel . . . Robert . . . Stephen R. Gibson, M.D. If a picture is worth a thousand words, how many words have been cut off here unsaid?* Interspersed with the names, birth dates, and death dates were broken hearts, cut from velvet, and embroidered tears, the familiar signs of fear, suffering, agony, and desperate love cheated by death. "There are too *many* of them!" *And how many more panels must be made and added to the Quilt before this cursed disease is broken?*

As they walked farther, Elias realized that the onlookers were part of the Quilt, too. A man sat on the ground to run his finger along the satin edge of a panel, and then buried his face in his knees, sobbing. Another man bending over him to whisper in his ear had KS lesions entirely covering his arms and face. Two women, perhaps a mother and a daughter, stood with arms around each other's waist, staring down at a panel of navy blue, embroidered with stars and a unicorn, their faces etched with devastation. A little girl about four years old sat cuddled in her father's arms, sucking her thumb as he dabbed at tears with a tissue. A white-haired woman leaned down to place a bouquet of flowers on a panel, smiling a tender, private smile. *Jim Hurley . . . Rebel Owen . . . Ken Jackson . . . For the One Who Left Unknown . . . El Lampi . . .*

"Here we are," Tim whispered. "Look, they're just opening it now."

Elias watched, his heart beating hard, as the unfolding team lifted the fabric. It strained against their grip as if trying to float away. But they held on to it firmly, turning in a circle like a wheeling flock of great white birds holding a net, and then bent to return it again to the earth. The air that had filled the material dissipated like a slow, sighing exhalation.

There it was: Sean Donnelly. 1955–1984.

They stood for a long time, looking at it in silence. Finally, Tim said, "It's wonderful, Elias."

"Yes," Elias replied, quietly pleased. "It is, isn't it?"

Sean's panel was simple and elegant, with a few hidden surprises. Elias had chosen a cream-colored background because it reminded him of the Irish sweaters Sean had loved to wear. With Ruth and Minta's help, he had painstakingly stenciled an intricate Celtic border around the edge using dark green paint. Janet and Jim had painted his name and Bill had painted the dates. A graceful Irish harp made of felt adorned the corner.

"Those look like real harp strings," Tim said.

"They are. I had Nick and Amy cut them from Sean's own harp"— Elias's throat constricted—"so no one could ever play it again."

Tim bent down to look more closely. "What's that in the upper corner, peeking out of the scrollwork?"

Elias smiled. "A penguin. Ruth embroidered it." After a moment, his smile faltered and his face twisted.

Tim saw, and his hand tightened on Elias's shoulder. "Maybe you'd like to be alone with him for a few moments?"

Elias nodded gratefully. "Thanks, Tim."

"Okay. I'll go check with a volunteer to find out—what were some of the other panels you want to see?"

"There are a bunch of them. Kiyoshi Uno, Jerry Simms, and Patty . . . I don't think her panel has a last name. Let's start with those."

Tim walked away and disappeared into the crowd. Elias looked down at Sean's panel again and at last let the tears fall freely down his ravaged cheeks.

It won't be much longer now, Sean. I know you'll be waiting for me. He sighed and stared out across the Quilt, feeling the crushing weight of his own grief and imagining it multiplied a thousandfold by all the panels he had seen this day. One panel for each person. Each panel a gift of love, made in agonizing pain. All the people who had lived and loved as he had, and who, like him, had simply run out of time.

All this pain. . . .

His tears dried quickly in the ovenlike heat, making his face itch. Elias wiped at the salty tracks, and as he turned his head to look for Tim, a striking panel in the next block caught his eye. He went over to look at it more closely and caught his breath.

The background had been fashioned in bands of watered silk ribbon, arranged in subtly shifting gradations of colors. Quilted into the panel were snow-white swans, wings raised in exquisitely graceful flight, the outline of their feathers stitched in delicate, painstaking detail. "Ohhh . . ." Elias breathed.

"It's beautiful, isn't it?" a voice beside him said quietly. "My sister made it."

Elias looked up. A man and a woman stood to one side, looking down at the panel, too. The man might have been anywhere from seventeen to twenty-five, but the lines on his face, etched by pain and wasting, made it difficult to tell. He had a constrictive bandage over his elbow, immobilized by a white sling.

"It's extraordinary," Elias said. He blinked and looked more closely at the woman. Was she the sister? Tall, wide-mouthed, with long and wavy reddish blond hair stirring lightly in the hot breeze . . . something seemed strangely familiar about her. . . .

"They were our brothers," the man said simply.

Elias looked down at the panel again, his eyes widening. *How many brothers?* One . . . two . . . three . . . He glanced up again, and the significance of the man's swollen joints suddenly became clear. The elbow must have been immobilized by a bleed. He'd seen others similarly marked in his AIDS support group. "Hemophilia?"

The man nodded. "We were all born with it. I'm the only one left." He looked down at the panel, his face still. "It's female sex-linked, you know. There's only a fifty percent chance of inheriting the gene, but we had bad luck, I suppose. Our mother always said she had cursed us."

Elias swallowed hard. "I'm so sorry," he said gently. His gaze turned curiously toward the woman again. Where *had* he seen her before? "It's . . . it's a breathtaking memorial. You must have taken a long time to make it."

She looked at him for a long moment without answering, her green eyes wide, brimming with grief so deep, so intense and aching that she seemed to shimmer with a strange serenity, far beyond the reach of tears.

I know, he realized in wonder. *She's the woman that Sean took me to meet, who he said could tell me the future.*

She turned her face away from him and gazed into the distance over the Quilt.

"I'm sorry," her brother said softly in an undertone. "Since our last brother died, well . . ." he adjusted his sling wearily, "she doesn't talk much anymore."

All this pain is for us. . . . Impulsively, Elias reached out to touch her arm. She looked down at his hand, and he jerked his fingers back self-consciously, for his hands were covered with oozing herpes sores.

But she surprised him. When she saw the sores, she didn't recoil but instead gave a little gasp of sympathy. She brought his hands up and gently pressed them against her lips. Her tears fell upon his skin, and it seemed to Elias that where her tears fell, the pain in his hands ceased.

He dreamed of her that night.

In his dream, she sat dressed in black on the bench in Central Park, watching the swans quietly swim in languid circles. It was November, and the sky overhead was a featureless gray. She turned her eyes from the swans to him, and he felt a tug of something, wordless and urgent, stretching over the infinite gulf between them, echoing through the centuries.

Sean's voice came to him then, as if from a great distance: *Ask her a question.*

He took a step toward her. "If I can't save them, and I die for nothing, what did all the silence and suffering accomplish? What was it all *for?*"

Her lips parted, and for a moment he thought she was about to answer. But the swans stopped swimming in their slow circles, spread their wings, and extended their necks. She turned toward them again, rising from the bench and walking toward the water's edge, her face alight. As if this were a signal, the swans wheeled and suddenly began swimming away, their feet churning the water into surging foam as their wings beat the air, splashing silver drops from the water's surface, faster and faster.

"No," he whispered sadly. "Come back." But the swans became airborne, tucking up their feet, their necks stretched out full length.

He came to stand beside her to watch as the swans flew away, dwindling until they disappeared into the west.

Author's Note

———

I start to write whenever something haunts me, and this book is no exception.

Sometime in the autumn of 1993, I had a dream set in a deserted city park on a gray day. There, I saw a woman dressed in black sitting on a park bench, watching swans swim in the pond before her. She didn't say anything to me. I knew, with that strange certainty sometimes felt in dreams, that she didn't consider herself to be beautiful, although I thought she was. She had an untamed mane of hair and an angular face that made you look at it twice. But the most striking thing about her was the mute grief in her eyes. I knew she had something heartbreaking to tell me, if she would only speak. Yet I knew she never would.

At the time, I was trying to decide what my next book should be. I had already decided I wanted to try retelling a fairy tale. But which one? The swans in my dream, and the woman's sadness and silence made me think of a favorite from my childhood, Hans Christian Andersen's "The Wild Swans."

My first thought was to set the story in Puritan New England. I began doing research, enough to convince me that the story could work if told that way. But I couldn't seem to start writing because one thing still bothered me: that park bench. The woman in my dream obviously wasn't living in the seventeenth century. Could I find a way to set the story in the contemporary world instead?

One day on my way to work, I saw a bus lumber by with an AIDS awareness billboard on its side that read: "Silence = Death." And I thought, *Huh*. Strange connections began to form in my mind, and I started to study the early history of the AIDS epidemic. The more I read, the more parallels I saw with Eliza's story.

But which approach should I use? I just couldn't decide, and thrashed around in misery for a while until I explained my dilemma to fellow Minneapolis writer Pamela Dean. She didn't bat an eye. "You'll simply have to write both of them."

And so I did.

Some people claim that fairy tales have nothing to tell us anymore, that stories full of heroes battling evil may be amusing but they're mostly a waste of time for all but the very young. I don't agree, because in the course of writing this book I've discovered that real heroes and heroines still exist in this world, racing against time while combatting betrayal and bigotry, just as Eliza did—and their actions have meant the difference between life and death for millions.

Their story is not complete, for we haven't yet found the way to break the curse.

I would like to thank the many people who have encouraged me in the writing of this book. In no particular order they are Hans Christian Andersen and Loreena McKennitt, who provided a seed; Jenna Felice, who watered it and gave it permission to grow; and Pamela Dean, Pat Wrede, and David Cummer, who offered preliminary guidance.

Reading and commenting on the manuscript in various stages were Pat Wrede, Lois McMaster Bujold, Elise Matthesen, Carolyn Ives Gilman, Mark Tiedemann, Joel Rosenberg, Bruce Bethke, David Cummer, Denise Coon, Robert Ihinger, Kij Johnson, Ashley Grayson and the staff of the Ashley Grayson Literary Agency, Jaime Levine, Richard Willett, and, of course, my editor, Betsy Mitchell.

For computer support: thanks to Bruce Schneier, who provided the first computer; and Zelle & Larson LLP, which provided the second—and in the nick of time, too. (Kij Johnson, however, has not now, nor has she ever, provided any technical computer support.)

In the course of doing my research, I drew upon the expertise of many. For books and insight about gay culture and community, I turned to Elise Matthesen, David Cummer, and Kurt Chandler; for information on home wine-making, Terry Garey; for fiber and fabric craft, Lynn Litterer; for photography and commercial photo developing, Mark Tiedemann; for medical information, Drs. Lisa Freitag and David Bucher; for information on Manhattan past, Chet Kerr and Heather Thomas; for information concerning New York law, Mary Cayley; for Irish and folk music, Sherry Ladig of the group Dunquin, and Barbara Jensen; for the big picture on folklore, Professor Ellen Stekert; for information about seventeenth-century English and colonial history and dialect, Karen Cooper, Tim Powers, and Lisa Lewis. Joel Rosenberg was absolutely thrilled to have me ask him about guns. Special thanks also to Pat Morgan, who provided historical information about the 1988 Central Park Names Project Quilt display; to Eugene McDougle of Les Ballets Trockadero de Monte Carlo, who graciously provided a videotape and a program from the early 1980s; to Pastor Dave Beety of Hope Lutheran Church; to Father Leo Tibesar of Spiritual Health Services of the Fairview-University Hospital; and to Father George Wertin and Tom Smith-Myott of St. Joan of Arc Church.

Thanks to my agent, Ashley Grayson; to Rob Ihinger, who kept the home fires burning; to David Lenander, Webmaster extraordinaire; to Jon Lewis, who assured me that he really wants to read it; to Pat Brooks; and finally, thanks to Garth Danielson and the other loving and imaginative friends of Karen Trego.

If there are any I have missed naming here, please know I have thanked you with my heart, if not my head. All mistakes contained herein, of course, are solely the author's own.

Minneapolis, Minnesota
August 30, 1998